A MAN'S WORLD

GRACE NEWMAN

ISBN: 979-8-9906008-9-8

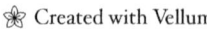 Created with Vellum

To all of the women who have been denied opportunities simply because of their gender – this one's for you.

Chapter One

GRIN IT AND BEAR IT

Georgia

While being the sister of racing star Henri Dubois had its benefits – I had a built-in, lifelong supporter and best friend who constantly challenged me – it also had its downside: the constant comparison by the media. Even though we were twins, we couldn't have been more different from birth. Henri was incredibly outgoing, and everyone who met him immediately fell in love with his gorgeous smile, generous laugh, and charming disposition. I, on the other hand, was more reserved, straightforward, and, as the media often complained, 'boring'. I didn't hype up the crowd at public gatherings or, more importantly, woo the sponsors at private Valkyrie F1 Team events that I was forced to attend.

My close friends and family saw the real me – the constant prankster and jokester of the family, as Hugo, my eldest brother, would like to say – but the rest of the world saw the dull, quiet, and somber young woman whose reserved nature was uninteresting and unacceptable in comparison to my brother's.

As a young girl from Monaco, I dreamed of racing in F1 – it was the premier racing league, and only 22 drivers got the privilege to compete. Henri was offered to join the prestigious Hermes F1

1

racing academy at sixteen, but when that dream didn't come true for me, I decided to take an Indy Car seat in America – trying my hand at something new and exciting. The thrill of Indy Car was real, and the fans, much to my surprise, welcomed me as a female driver more than I expected. There were plenty of bitter, misogynist comments thrown my way – saying that I slept around to get my wins and didn't deserve my trophies, but for the most part, the community had welcomed me and set me up for success – leading to my first Indy Car championship.

When Italian racing legend Isabelle Bianchi, CEO and Team Principal of the newly created Valkyrie F1 Racing Team, approached me and told me she was building a predominantly female F1 team with two female drivers, I was shocked – shocked that Isabelle had gotten enough funding to build something so new and risky, but mostly shocked that she wanted me as the team's number one driver. The decision to join was a no-brainer – driving in Formula 1 with my brother had been our dream since we were two five-year-olds racing in go-karts. And while I knew the challenge would be difficult, the cars were much faster than Indy Car, I knew the challenge would be worth it. I wanted to show young girls that they, too, could make it to Formula 1. I wanted to prove to the world that women belonged in motorsport, that we could be champions, and this was my best chance.

My fellow driving partner, Lily, was the partner every driver hoped for. At just nineteen years old, she had won the W-series championship, and at twenty, she was now the youngest Formula 1 driver on the grid and the youngest woman to compete. Lily was everything a Formula 1 team wanted. She was the definition of beautiful inside and out, and the press ate her up. It didn't matter how many ridiculous questions they threw her, Lily answered them with finesse and ease that movie stars would envy.

Still, even if our personalities were different on track and in the paddock, our friendship had started to blossom. Lily managed to navigate my introverted personality and made me feel incredibly comfortable. In return, as the older, more experienced driver, I gave her driving tips and helped her get mentally prepared before races. *In Formula 1, you were in for a miserable season if you didn't like your teammate.*

While the media had tried – and failed – to paint us as two bickering women, the reality couldn't have been farther from the truth. Lily and I had a shared mission: show the opposition that a couple of 5'4 female racers, who had been written off by every other team, could, in fact, win Formula 1 races.

The 2021 season started with an unexpected bang. Testing in Bahrain was one of a kind – an absolute dream come true, and the car miraculously had the speed and pace of the other top teams. The fan base was building quickly, and sponsors began to show genuine interest in the team. Much to Valkyrie's excitement, having female drivers opened opportunities for new sponsors such as make-up companies and handbag designers, companies that didn't typically approach the male drivers.

By the end of pre-season testing, the F1 press had declared Valkyrie as the team to beat and had marked me as F1's most unexpected rookie. But by the season's third race, one thing was becoming apparent: I was quickly becoming the press' public enemy number one. Comments about my "ambition" and "pushy" nature on the track had already made headlines after race two. By the third race, the press was branding me this season's viper after an 'incident' with Noah had forced their beloved, reigning champion off the track. While male drivers like 3x World Champion Noah Hendriks could get away with short, snippy remarks in the media pen while glaring at the camera, it was clear that the press had no intention to let a female driver get away with similar behavior.

When Isabelle approached me with this opportunity, every bone in my body knew this wouldn't be easy. I knew there would be bitter comments about any success I had, but what I wasn't expecting was for the media to ask me questions like, *"Georgia, how does your boyfriend feel with all your traveling?"* and *"Georgia, how do you deal with your menstrual cycle during races?"*.

Apparently, my snarky reply of *"The same way you deal with your period, Bill,*" didn't get the chuckle I had expected. No one likes a woman talking about their cycle on national TV, it so happens.

The media also didn't seem to like my *lack* of a boyfriend. Rumors had already circulated about my brother's close friend and fellow race car driver, Éliott Simon, and me a couple of years ago when I had come to visit Henri at some races in previous seasons, but now the rumor mill was rampant, and the obsession with my dating life was fascinating to everyone – except me. On the one hand, the media scrutinized the fact that any boyfriend I could possibly have would be so heartbroken with my constant traveling, so I couldn't possibly have a boyfriend, and on the other hand, I was dating every man under the sun.

At the start of the season, the media had dubbed me "Sissy Dubois," a somewhat rude but at least boring nickname referencing the fact that I was the sister of Henri Dubois, the Hermes F1 Team's precious number one driver. By race three, I was "Sassy Dubois" – something my team principal deemed much worse, especially with big sponsorship names hovering around, discussing deals. Even though our car had parts backed by huge automobile giants, our funding was minimal. We had to sustain enough funds to prove ourselves, just like any other team. With a majority female engineering team and paddock crew, a lot was at stake here.

Still, I knew I couldn't let it bother me. Within my first three races, I had secured two podiums and had come 5th in the third race. I was second in the drivers championship, with the rest of the season to play for.

I was a lion living in a man's world, and no one would stop me.

The first win of the season had been magical. After just four races, I managed to not only get on the podium but stand on the tallest step. As I looked to my left, I saw my brother splashing me with champagne while attempting to give me the world's most enormous bear hug. The look of pride in his eyes gave me a warm feeling, a reminder of my family's support for the last twenty-four years. Even though I had passed Henri on track in what I'm sure the media would deem a *"tense battle between siblings,"* I could see the look of love and happiness for me in his eyes.

"Congrats, Peaches, I'm so proud of you," I heard him whisper as we left the podium celebration. As kids, we visited America often. Our aunt and uncle had moved there when we were younger, so we visited their beautiful house in Georgia every couple of years. It's there that Henri had started to call me Peaches after a round of peach picking at a local farm – and after that, the name had stuck.

Drenched in champagne and smelling of sweat, I smiled back at Henri, giving him one last hug before running down the paddock and back to my team, who were waiting for me with open arms.

Valkyrie's race strategist, Fiona Schmidt, wife of Felix Schmidt, the Rennen F1 Team Principal, was first to greet me. I'll never know how Valkyrie F1 managed to steal her from the Rennen F1 Team, but over the last several years, she had become my confidant and mentor. Being a Formula 1 test driver, she knew the pressure I was facing and the challenging work it took to be a driver. In Formula 1, it felt like everything was made *by* men and *for* men.

"Congrats, Georgie. P1! Well deserved." Fiona gave me a huge hug and a big smile, followed by a pat on the back.

"You know what I think this win deserves?" I chuckled, a little hint of mischief playing on my face, which I could tell Fiona noticed by the slight uptick of her brow.

"You still have to do media duties; don't even ask."

The smile on my face immediately dropped. I knew that would be the case, but I had let myself hope for one millisecond that maybe the joy of the team's first race win would allow me some reprieve, which was ridiculous even to hope. A race winner was expected to do media, and if Valkyrie F1 were to keep gaining sponsors, I needed to get my face in front of a camera and smile and chat about how happy I was.

I looked to Isabelle, the Valkyrie team principal, who smiled and waved at me. I think in all my time of knowing her, Isabelle had smiled maybe three times, so I was honored that my race win was one of them.

Isabelle Bianchi was an incredible woman. Her success in the W-series and Formula E was well-regarded. She was a brilliant strategist, and while you could only describe her as having a formidable personality, she had the finesse to manage the media like a genius. Isabelle had faced her own challenges with the press, and while she had mastered them with great talent, her reputation was known across the paddock. Before coming to Valkyrie, she did a stint as the Hermes F1's Communication Director, where the press learned that messing with Isabelle was more trouble than it was worth.

Unlike me, her demanding nature and direct comments were revered by the press and the F1 community alike. She could command a room full of men in this male-dominated sport and get precisely what she wanted. Her hard exterior was always on display at races, but I knew there was someone soft and gentle underneath. She fiercely cared about the people who worked for her and put her name and reputation on the line to start a woman-owned Formula 1 team because she believed in us – believed that women could be as successful as men in motorsport if given the chance.

I gave Isabelle a quick nod and wave and headed to my driver's room to freshen up before the post-race media conference started. As I exited the driver's room, I was met by Lizzie, my poor Media Manager, who had been saddled with what could only be her most challenging assignment to date. Still, even if I was likely a nightmare to manage at press events, she wore her assignment with the world's bravest smile and most uplifting nature. I was sure the paddock could be on fire, and Lizzie would still announce, '*At least we have free lighting!*'

"Georgie!" Lizzie gave me a massive hug, practically strangling the upper part of my body. Lizzie was an impressive 6'0, so she always towered over me compared to my petite stature.

"Hi Liz, thanks! What a marvelous race at the end, fighting with Henri and Noah like that, just incredible." I paused, seeing the tension in Lizzie's eyes form as she started to open her mouth in response. "But now I assume it's time to feed the vultures?" I asked with the best drawl I could muster, my voice dropping with the question.

"Yes, yes, time to go show the media that you are the star we all know you to be." Lizzie gave me a big wink and shoulder squeeze, all while gently pushing me towards the garage entrance, like she wasn't convinced that I would show up to the press conference without a little push.

When we arrived at the media center, I stared directly at the center chair. For the first time in my career, it was mine, a feeling so thrilling I didn't even notice my brother walk in.

Henri reached out and gave my shoulder a squeeze, whispering, "Just grin it and bear it, Peaches. We'll soon be out drinking to celebrate." I smirked back and settled into my chair, nodding to Noah, who smiled at me from the third-place seat, whispering another congrats before the conference started.

I never understood why my body reacted this way, but no matter what the circumstance was, the moment I sat down in a press chair and the lights turned on, I immediately began to feel this rush of intense anxiety, and dizziness started to overcome my body. Here I was with a phenomenal, well-deserved win, but all I could focus on was the feeling of my profusely sweaty hands and blurring vision. To make matters worse, the words that tumbled out of my mouth never seemed to be quite what I wanted to say – or what the media wanted to hear.

"So Georgia, congrats on your first win with the new Valkyrie F1 Team. It must feel thrilling to be the second woman to win a Formula 1 race and the first in the last three decades. How do you feel?"

"Phenomenal, it's truly a dream come true," I replied, giving the journalist the biggest smile I could muster, hoping my response didn't sound too curt. A few uncomfortable seconds passed, and I could sense that the journalist clearly expected me to say more. I let my eyes shift to Lizzie, who was standing in the back of the conference, her expression willing me to continue, but before I could muster another word, the journalist had already moved on.

"So Henri, I saw you and Georgia had quite the battle around lap forty. How did it feel to be beat out by your sister?"

"It was a great battle! My sister is an incredible driver, and that Valkyrie F1 car is fast as lightning. Disappointed I couldn't keep up, but it's hard to fight with that kind of talent. Plus, I knew if she beat me, she would have to buy the drinks tonight, not me, so it's not all a loss." With that, he turned and winked at me, getting several chuckles out of the crowd.

I rolled my eyes, leaning over to shove Henri's shoulder. These press events were always more manageable when Henri was there. He was undoubtedly my biggest fan, and his light-heartedness always made me feel more at ease.

As the press conference continued, most of the questions were targeted at Noah and Henri, leaving me with few questions to answer. While I should have been more offended that the media spent most of their time asking the 2nd and 3rd place drivers the majority of the questions, in truth, I felt relieved. Fewer questions asked meant fewer chances to screw this up for myself.

As the hour started to come to an end, I was feeling more confident. I had answered a few more questions with a little more 'of my sunny disposition,' as Lizzie would say, and felt like I was beginning to improve on my media relations – albeit as much as you could after an hour.

"So Georgia, now that you're a race winner, I bet you're beginning to see the World Driver's Championship in your view. Do you think it's time to see more women in racing?"

Ah, there it was, the stupid question every male journalist loved to ask all the drivers, especially me. They always asked this question as if they were trying to find me in a lie and get me to admit, "*Actually, I think women should get back to the kitchen where they belong.*" Unfortunately, before I could stop myself, I let out the most exasperated sigh, matched only by my rather noticeable eye-roll.

"I think we all know the answer to that question because you have all managed to ask it at every press event I've ever attended. What are you looking for me to say... No?"

I could see Lizzie waving in the background, her finger crossing her throat, signaling for me to quit before I said something I couldn't take back.

But it was too late.

'Sassy Dubois' had been released, and the silence was deafening. I looked to Henri for help, but his face told me I should have listened to his earlier advice – *'Just grin it and bear it, Peaches.'* But I hadn't listened, so I opted for 'door number two,' an option not quite as grand as the first.

"Obviously, I want more women in the sport. If we had more women, maybe you would all stop focusing on 'my love life' or 'my menstrual cycle' or 'what racing bra do I wear' because Lily and I wouldn't be the shiny, new toys to harass." As soon as the words left my mouth, I knew it had been the wrong thing to say.

After a few more awkward moments, the F1 Media and Communications head came on the stage and thanked all the journalists for attending. Before Henri could say anything, I quickly jumped out of my seat and sprinted towards the exit, hoping to quickly escape before fans and journalists bombarded me.

Lizzie took off after me, her long legs allowing her to catch up quickly. As we walked back into the Valkyrie F1 hospitality suite, I could see the look of displeasure on Isabelle's face. The smile on her face just an hour earlier was replaced with a disappointed frown. She pointed her finger at me, signaling for me to 'come hither' to her office.

"Look, before you say anything, I know. I should have dropped it and answered the usual answer, *'Yes, of course, I want more women in motorsport, blah blah blah.'* But I couldn't do it this time. It's becoming morose, repetitive, and quite frankly rude," I started to argue as I entered Isabelle's office.

"Georgia, I appreciate that the press are morons," Isabelle retorted, taking a seat at her desk, her piercing green eyes slicing me open, as if she was reading a book she had already read before but needed to re-read in case she had missed something important. "But unfortunately, the F1 journalist community isn't going to change overnight, so it's our job to help guide them to that change. It'll be slow – you *know* this – and yelling at a reporter will only make you look like a hot head, something the press want to *see* and *definitely* want to write about for some God-forsaken reason."

I knew Isabelle was right. Change in a male-dominated sport would be slow, and we had to be careful. Generations of racing women depended on our every move, and the fight wouldn't be won after four successful races – it wouldn't even be won after a successful season. Having the media hate me wouldn't encourage the other teams to hire female drivers, lest they end up with their own 'Sassy Dubois' nightmare.

"I know, I'm sorry. I'll work on it for the next race and get some answers prepped with Lizzie."

Isabelle nodded, knowing there was no reason to further the conversation. She might be annoyed, but she didn't want to dampen my day. I was now a Formula 1 winner, and the fight for the World Driver's Championship was on.

After leaving her office, I saw the Head of Strategy, Fiona, and my Media Manager, Lizzie, slide into Isabelle's office and shut the door. My gut told me I would hear about their discussion at the next race, but I didn't care – tonight was for celebrating.

Chapter Two

A COLD DAY IN HELL

Georgia

The night of my race win in Barcelona was indescribable. Spain was a beautiful country, and the weather was not as cold as it typically was in early spring. Not too long after I arrived at my hotel room, Henri was banging on my door, a champagne bottle in one hand and a slice of my favorite chocolate cake in the other.

"So, did you bring this cake all the way from Monaco in case I won?" I asked, aggressively lunging towards the cake.

"No, I brought it in case I won," he replied snarkily, winking at me as he lifted the cake in the air to a height I couldn't reach. "But since you won, I figured we could share." I chuckled at his poor attempt at a joke and nodded for him to sit on the bed, offering him a spoon.

"So..." Henri began, and I knew exactly what he wanted to discuss. We didn't need to be twins for me to know he wanted to address the press outburst.

"... so I shouldn't have yelled at the reporter. Yes, I know," I groaned as I shoveled another large bite of cake into my mouth.

"What did Isabelle have to say about it?"

"She was displeased, obviously. We have this huge Maison de

Klotho sponsorship deal in the works, and I know she's worried it will fall through. It's a huge brand, one of the largest fashion houses, and the brand will be exclusive to Valkyrie F1. I just... I wish sponsors cared about my racing potential and wins instead of my ability to bat my eyelashes at the press."

Even as I said the words, I knew in my heart that this wasn't the case with any athlete. Even Noah Hendriks, the current holder of the last three World Driver's Championships, had to woo sponsors and show up at events with a smile. Being talented was one thing – being talented and able to manage a crowd was another. I just wasn't so good at the second one.

"Just raw talent doesn't get you sponsors, Peaches. In fact, it seems to mean less these days. I mean, look at Oliver. He's struggling in this year's Wilmington F1 car but still holding onto all his sponsors." I gave Henri a slight nod before shoveling another bite of cake into my mouth. I knew Henri was right, and we often discussed Oliver's situation.

As much as Henri wanted to understand what I was going through, he didn't get it. He had always been the one to shine in front of the camera; even at a young age, he loved getting interviewed and discussing his racing, the car – anything. On the other hand, I had mastered running to the bathroom any time a camera got within ten feet of me. Before joining Indy Car, my social media probably had fewer than twenty posts. I was a private person, and I hated being put in front of people I didn't know, only to be asked questions to which everyone already knew the answer. I felt like a monkey at the circus, on display for everyone to see.

"You had to deal with this in America," Henri mused.

"I did, but it was more behind closed doors. Oddly enough, the American public might have been interested in how one deals with their menstrual cycle while racing, but no one was bold enough to ask me on national TV. Bit of a squeamish group of people – Americans," I said, earning a chuckle from my brother.

My first year in Indy Car had been tough, but after my first win, things settled down. I was impressed at how much respect I began to receive once the public started to see the real me, and most importantly, my team and the media loved the number of female fans I was bringing to the sport. If there was one thing Americans were good at, it was making money off of sports teams, and no one was looking to piss off a new segment of fans who were buying up merchandise and subscribing to the journalist's streaming channels. *Money talks in America*, as my manager liked to say.

After munching on the cake and drinking the rest of the bottle of champagne, Henri left for his hotel room so we could both get ready. I had agreed to push all my negative thoughts out of my head and instead focus on enjoying my race win, something easier said than done. As I reviewed the afternoon's press footage, I kept debating how bad my outburst had actually been. I knew it wasn't great since I was too much of a coward to check Twitter or read the comments on the team's most recent social post.

When my alarm went off at 9 p.m., I grabbed my jacket and purse and headed towards the elevator, fumbling with my wallet along the way as I frantically looked for my keycard. As I approached the elevator doors, I felt my body crash into something hard. Before I could fall backward, a large hand grabbed onto my waist, pulling me forward. Without thinking, I put my hands up to steady myself, making contact with a chest that my romance books would describe as *'built from solid muscle'* – or perhaps built by Apollo himself. The next thing I noticed was the smell – cologne that smelled like a mixture of lilacs and pine. I saw his Cheshire Cat grin as I looked up to see who had just saved me from falling on my ass.

Luca *fucking* Rossi. Playboy of the year and bane of my existence. How my brother dealt with Luca Rossi as his racing teammate at Hermes each week was beyond me.

"You know, Cara, if you wanted to be close to me, you only had to ask. I'm always here for support," Luca said with a wink and a voice much too sultry for my liking. He made a show of letting his eyes rake up and down my body, and I suddenly felt naked in front of him. I chose to ignore how my body went a little warm at the attention, and I quickly straightened my dress, forcibly removing his hands from my waist.

"Luca, flattering yourself as always, I see."

The elevator doors opened, and Luca motioned for me to go in first. I obliged, standing on the opposite side of the elevator as Luca followed me in, smirking at my visible discomfort. Fortunately, we continued the elevator ride down in total silence. I could feel his eyes look down at me occasionally, but I refused to face him out of fear that I would make eye contact with the Italian.

It didn't matter that Luca was undoubtedly the most handsome driver on the grid; he was definitely the most insufferable. He knew he was handsome, and girls threw themselves at him everywhere he went. Last year, he had been caught 'borrowing' a yacht off the coast of Majorca, a total embarrassment to his family, who were racing legends in Europe. The amount of messes his public relations team has had to clean up should have that company advertising as a janitorial service, not a PR firm.

The elevator dinged as we hit the ground floor, and when the doors opened, I quickly bolted out of the elevator, practically running to where I could see Henri, Éliott, and Oliver waiting for me. As soon as he saw me, Oliver greeted me with a huge hug – picking me up and swinging me around.

"Congrats little Dubois!" Oliver announced, putting me down with a thump.

"What a nice surprise, Oliver! Sorry to hear about P12, but better luck next race. I think Miami will be your race. I think Miami will be your race. I think you strike me as a Miami kind of guy," I said with a wink. Oliver chuckled as he thanked me, still grasping me in his warm embrace.

"Yeah, a bit of a rough one. The Wilmington F1 car isn't what we had hoped, but I am excited to celebrate the first female winner in over thirty years. I could have come last, and I still wouldn't have missed celebrating with you."

When asked to describe Wilmington F1 driver Oliver Williams, I think of the scene where the Grinch's heart grows three times its original size. Oliver's heart was three times the size of a normal person's, and he was nothing but love and laughter. I always enjoyed hanging out with him. When my seat at Valkyrie F1 was announced, he had been one of the most supportive drivers, constantly texting me congrats and asking if I had any questions. His mentorship was endearing and greatly welcomed. He was having a hard season at Wilmington, and I could see that he was grappling with the fact that at thirty-two, he had fewer F1 days in front of him than he did behind him.

"Well, well, well, the Dubois family now has two Formula 1 race winners. How exciting." I turned around to face whoever had congratulated me and saw Éliott Simon, another racer and close friend of my brother's, standing there with a massive smile as he gave me a pat on the back and a quick hug.

"Congrats Georgie," he whispered. "By the way, the parents said to tell you that they are so incredibly proud of you." Éliott's parents had been there through every step of my journey. They had even traveled with my mother to see me race Indy Car during my winning season. The Simons were close family friends, and it meant a lot to me that they were at this race, cheering me on.

"Tell them thanks, and I hope we will all have dinner together in Miami."

"I'm sure they would like that," Éliott nodded.

Turning around, I heard my brother's voice, "Hey Luca, thanks for joining us. It'll be good to have another Spanish speaker around. Lord knows Peaches didn't pay attention during school." I immediately stopped, making a pointed glare at my brother with severe satisfaction.

"First off, I'm not the one who was caught snoring so loud during Languages class that the school called our parents because they didn't believe we were sleeping at home." Henri laughed at that, remembering the occasion all too well. Our parents had been furious – and very embarrassed.

"Second, surely Luca has better plans tonight, no?" I asked, probably a little too quickly, causing Éliott to chuckle at the urgency in my voice. Before Henri could respond, I heard a slight scoff behind me.

"Don't be silly. I can't think of anything better than celebrating our race winner," Luca crooned, giving me his signature Cheshire cat grin. I internally cringed but kept my smile plastered on my face. For some reason, I couldn't mask my feelings in press conferences, but with Luca, I had no problem hiding my frustration. I knew letting Luca see how he got under my skin would mean he had won, and I couldn't have that – both on and off the track.

And with that brief exchange, Éliott cleared his throat, announcing to the group that we were setting off for the evening. We arrived at the club a short time later, all of us piling into the VIP section reserved for the drivers. Off in the distance, I waved at Edward, the other Wilmington F1 driver, and his girlfriend Lauren, who had managed to arrive just in time to see Edward race. While Lauren and I had only met this year, she had started to become a close friend of mine, and I always appreciated her company in the paddock. Sometimes, I needed another female companion to talk to besides Lily, and in a paddock full of men, there weren't too many women outside of the Valkyrie garage.

"Well, if it isn't Sassy Dubois," laughed Edward as he waltzed over to our booth, his posh British accent smoothly rolling off the tongue. "I have to say, I thoroughly enjoyed the ending to that press conference. Although next time, I think you should switch it up and tell them '*no, this is, in fact, a man's sport*,' give the vultures something *actually* interesting to write about." Edward winked at me, knowing all too well that he was getting under my skin. I couldn't help but smirk at Edward's comment, even though I knew this journalist situation was no laughing matter.

"Very funny, but if you're looking to give the journalists something fun to write about, maybe you should tell them about how you once got to the paddock without your driving shoes and had to embarrassingly call your mum to bring them to you." Edward huffed a sigh of annoyance, but I could see a twinkle of amusement in his eyes as he remembered that hilarious day.

"No, I should tell them about the time you dressed up as a Wilmington F1 mechanic and snuck into my driver's room to scare the living daylights out of me." I couldn't help but laugh at that one; that was one of the best pranks I had ever played in the paddock.

Edward and I had been pranking each other for over a decade, but recently the prank wars between us had started getting out of hand, to the point where Arthur Johnson, CEO and Team Principal of the Wilmington F1 Team, had banned me from the Wilmington garage last year, lest he end up with another hamster running around his office.

"I think my image in the media is tough enough, don't need the media hating me because I scared Britain's favorite darling boy, Edward Davis," I grinned, wrapping my arm around his neck, scratching the top of his head affectionately.

"You should have seen the look on Isabelle's face," Lily interjected as she waltzed over to the group. "It's a good thing Georgie won that race, or I think she might have broken the TV when the journalist asked that stupid question."

"I can only imagine the look on Isabelle's face. Scary probably doesn't even describe it!" Edward quipped back, shuddering as he undoubtedly pictured Isabelle's intense and unimpressed stare, something Edward had seen often.

The rest of the night continued smoothly, with drinks being poured and consumed to great lengths. I danced on the light-up, checkered dance floor with various drivers, their girlfriends, and some of the trainers that had attended later in the evening. As the night began to close, I saw Luca off in the corner by the bar, his hand around the waist of what could only be some model that had thrown herself at him.

Classic Luca, no wonder his sponsors are starting to back out, I mused to myself. I recently overheard Isabelle and our Director of Sponsorships conversation discussing the Hermes F1 Team's attempt to get Luca to reel in his playboy tendencies.

Good luck to them.

As I turned around, I waved to Edward, who was signaling for me to join him in our booth.

"So, tell me, love, why do you hate Luca so much?" Edward mused, staring at me with those beautiful, big hazel eyes.

"I don't hate him," I insisted, trying to hide the disdain in my voice. Edward just quirked an eyebrow at me, as if to say he didn't believe a single word from my lying mouth.

"Fine. He's just so cocky and self-absorbed. Girls throw themselves at him everywhere we go, and you know he thinks incredibly highly of himself. He shows up each week with a different model on his arm, just like the playboy everyone thinks he is. I mean, the man commandeered a yacht, and all he got was a wrist slap," I scoffed, but as the words tumbled from my mouth, I knew how petty I sounded.

Why did I even care? Luca was my brother's teammate, nothing more. And now that I had my own F1 team, I barely had to see him during race weekends. It's not like I was allowed in the Hermes F1 garage anymore – lest I steal some of Hermes' strategies, as Francesco, the team principal, liked to joke. Truthfully, I was pretty sure it was because Francesco didn't want me distracting Henri, Hermes F1's darling number-one driver, which was fair. I had once spiked Henri's coffee with chili flakes, only to find out later that it was Francesco's coffee that he had left in Henri's driver's room. *Not one of my finer pranks.*

"I think someone sounds a little jealous," Edward teased.

"Not a chance. It'll be a cold day in hell before I ever date Luca Rossi," I gritted out.

Edward gave me a pointed look but let it slide, the conversation ending with Oliver and Lily coming over to announce an after-party full of pizza in Oliver's hotel room, a very enticing offer. I let Lily help me up as she linked arms with me, softly humming the bar's closing music to herself.

As we left the bar, I saw Luca climbing into a cab, a beautiful woman in tow. We made eye contact, and he winked at me before getting into the back of the cab. I internally reprimanded myself, annoyed that Luca had caught me looking.

Chapter Three

IT'S IN MY NATURE

Georgia

We arrived in Miami the Monday before the Miami Grand Prix. The non-European races always required more time zone adjustments from the European-based drivers, so we often arrived 4-5 days early to prepare for the time zone shift. As I walked off of the plane and onto the jet bridge, I was hit with what could only be described as unbearable heat and humidity.

Awful – just awful, as Lily put it.

I watched Lily pull her hair into a ponytail, her face scrunched up, clearly in discomfort from the heat. Lily was always so put together, so prim and proper; this sweat-drenched look was new for the British-born driver. We had been here for fifteen minutes, and we were both soaked to the bone. Surprisingly, this was only Lily's second time in the United States, with the only other time being when she raced Formula W at the Circuit of the Americas.

After we settled into the hotel, Lily and I headed downstairs to grab a drink and a quick bite with Henri and Hugo, my eldest brother, who had also gotten into Miami early. We all had to be up early tomorrow for race meetings, and I wanted to get myself as accustomed to the time change as quickly as possible.

"So, I'll see you tomorrow morning, Peaches," Hugo said as he got up from his seat, wiping off the last of the crumbs from his mouth.

"Oh yeah, you coming to help me with media training?" I teased, although I wouldn't have been surprised if Hugo *was* invited. My eldest brother was incredibly well-spoken, and like Henri, he was a master at speaking to the media. He and Isabelle had spent much time in the paddock together, having long chats about my future as a racing driver, and they had become quite close.

"Something like that. See you tomorrow."

I frowned, unsure what Hugo meant by that, but let it go. Hugo had been my racing manager until I moved to America, and then even he admitted that I needed a professional manager to help guide me through Indy Car. Hugo was always full of cryptic one-liners, and I knew I would eventually figure out what he meant.

The following day, I woke up in a sweat, regretting not cranking up the A/C even higher in my hotel room. I quickly showered and threw on my Valkyrie team clothing, a lovely royal blue polo and white jeans. As I entered the valet area, I saw the beautiful Bugatti Chiron waiting for me. When I started at Valkyrie, the team gifted me a Volkswagen Beetle, which I knew Isabelle thought to be hilarious. Other teams gifted supercars to their drivers, but at Valkyrie, much to my dismay, we had to "earn" our supercars, so Isabelle had given us what she called "sensible automobiles" from one of our sponsors.

Cheap bastards, but classic Isabelle.

But now that we were out and about in Miami, the team felt Lily and I needed something more suitable for F1 drivers, which earned no complaints from either of us. While I secretly was starting to love my little bug, I wasn't going to turn down one of the fastest street-legal cars ever built. Lily hated driving in America, so we both piled into my Chiron, with me at the wheel and took off towards the temporary Valkyrie F1 offices.

As we walked into the paddock, Isabelle motioned for me to join her in the conference room.

"I'll see you in a few, Lily!" I yelled back to my teammate, but she had already abandoned me for my athletic trainer, Chris, who, by the looks of his face, had some major gossip to share.

What I encountered as I entered the conference room was far from what I had expected. In fact, I would have bet my entire F1 salary that I never would have seen the sight that was seated in front of me. Sitting at the Valkyrie F1 conference table were my brothers, Henri and Hugo, followed by Francesco, the Hermes F1 Team Principal, Hilda, the Hermes Communications Director, and the one and only Luca Rossi – my brother's teammate and absolute nuisance of a man.

I gave Henri a quizzical look, but he just looked away, pretending to look outside of the makeshift window. I could tell he was doing his best not to make eye contact with me, and truthfully, that should have been my first sign that something dreadful was about to happen. Henri's biggest tell that he had a secret was his lack of eye contact. It was the one time his naturally charming nature didn't work in his favor. Hermes' golden boy, Henri, *always* made eye contact, except when he was guilty of something.

As I sat down, Fiona and Lizzie came into the room and sat on either side of me, like an army flanking their general – or a prison warden guarding their prisoner. Lizzie plopped a latte in front of me, smiling slightly, but I could see some concern on her face – as if she was preemptively waiting for me to splash the coffee she had just gotten me in her face.

"So... will anyone tell us why we're at the enemy's headquarters?" Luca chuckled, trying to lighten what was starting to feel like a tense situation.

I turned to Isabelle, who just frowned at Luca as she closed the door.

"Before I begin," Isabelle announced, standing in front of the room, "I want everyone here to know that this was not an easy decision, but after chatting with Francesco and our Sponsorship team, we think it is the best course of action for both teams. I know neither of you will be pleased with this, but we truly believe this will help boost both of your images with the media and, more importantly, your sponsors."

I looked around, curious about who Isabelle was talking about. *Was she referring to me and Henri? That couldn't be right because then why would Luca be here?*

"Well, there's no reason to belabor this – Georgia and Luca, after much discussion, we've decided the best thing for the two of you is for you to start dating."

Before I could help myself, I started to laugh, albeit a bit uncontrollably, like a jack-in-the-box that had just been let out of his box. This seemed so outrageous that I figured it had to be a joke. I started to stand up, moving towards the door.

"Hilarious, Isabelle. Did Henri set you up to this? Is this revenge for that prank I did last week?" I spit out between laughs.

Before I could get close to the door, Fiona grabbed my arm slightly and motioned for me to sit down. "This isn't a joke, Georgia," Fiona said slowly, and as I began to sit back down, panic started to fill me.

"The F1 journalist community loves Luca. He's good at working the camera and answering questions, which you need serious work on. A relationship with Luca will allow him to join you in some media press conferences, helping smooth the way when we have hiccups. He has a large swath of social media fans, almost ten million, and his account can help boost you in the media's eyes."

Luca went to open his mouth, but before he could say anything, Francesco pointedly interrupted him, "And Luca, your playboy image is putting several of our Sponsorship deals at risk, most notably the Helios Sunglasses deal. They are the world's largest sunglasses supplier, and they are looking to up our exclusive deal this year, but with all your partying and yacht commandeering, they aren't sure you are the best person to represent the brand. Dating

Georgia will give you the legitimacy you need and credibility that you are a serious driver and not just in it for the social perks." Luca scoffed – *loudly* – but said nothing to defend himself, likely as stunned as I was.

"No one is going to believe this!" I yelled, frantically gesturing between me and Luca.

"That's where Henri comes in," chimed Lizzie. "People will believe that Henri introduced you two last year and that you have been casually hanging out since. He'll help sell the story."

"But what about the other drivers, who also happen to be my friends – like Éliott and Oliver – they'll never believe this."

Before I could continue, Hilda cut in, "Which is why we hope you will explain to them the severity of this needing to work. Like it or not, the funding for both your seats is at risk. We've spoken to Arthur Johnson, who has agreed to chat with Oliver and Edward over at the Wilmington F1 Team. Hugo has offered to chat with Éliott about this since you are such close family friends. As for the rest of the drivers, we'll gauge their reactions as this comes out and then decide on how to react."

I couldn't believe what I was hearing. There was no way the other drivers would suddenly believe this – or go along with it. I wasn't sure what I hated more – having them think that I had settled for someone like Luca or convincing them to lie for me because I was too stupid to talk to journalists. I looked over at Henri, who was twiddling his thumbs awkwardly, still looking at anything in the room but me.

"You're fine to go along with this terrible idea?" I asked Henri coldly, a look of betrayal on my face. He finally turned to me and sighed.

"I'm sorry, Peaches, but they're right. I finally got you in Formula 1. We're living our dream together, and I don't want to lose you because Maison de Klotho or anyone else can't see that you're as amazing as I know you are." I scoffed and pointedly rolled my eyes at my brother—a perfectly crafted statement from Henri, as per usual. Hugo, going along with this, I could understand. He was my older brother and my former manager, but Henri knew how this would affect me. He knew how much I would loathe this agreement, and the lack of heads-up felt like a betrayal.

"This is fucking ridiculous!" I yelled, stomping my foot on the ground like a toddler throwing a tantrum. "I won't stand for this, and I won't do it. And if I have to give up my Formula 1 seat, then fine, I don't want it. I'm one of the best damn drivers out there, and it's ludicrous that this is what I have to do to keep sponsors happy. When did we stop caring about driving talent?"

Before I could stop myself and register what I was doing, my feet had moved me to the door, and I was sprinting down the hallway toward my driver's room, tears pouring down my face. I slammed the door and leaned against it, falling to the ground as I cradled my legs.

This can't be happening, this can't be happening, I repeated over and over as tears streamed down my face. I obviously didn't mean those final words. The truth was, I would do just about anything, even start a fake relationship, to keep my Formula 1 seat. *But why did this sham have to be with the one driver I couldn't stand?*

I heard a knock on my driver's room door, immediately knowing the group had sent Hugo. He didn't have to announce himself for me to know who was standing at the other side of the door. Henri wasn't stupid enough to think I would want to talk to him, and Hugo had always been my sounding board for big decisions.

"Go away, Hugo!" I yelled.

"Georgie Pie, come on, let's talk," he said, his voice low and soft. Against my better judgment, I got up, opened the door, and motioned for him to come inside.

"Feel free *not* to make yourself at home," I said spitefully, the pathetic words sounding even worse when they left my mouth. Hugo chuckled a bit and sat on the couch across from my massage table.

"Look, I know this situation isn't ideal. Hell, I know it just fucking sucks. I don't know what it's like to be in your shoes. You've had to go through so much more than Henri. I have watched you work twice as hard to get to where you are today.

But Georgia, this is *why* this is a good idea. You know I am your biggest supporter through and through. If you genuinely don't want to do this, then I'll tell the team, but the truth is, I'm worried for you. Isabelle has let me in on some of the sponsorship conversations, and while it's unfair, they *expect* you to be more like Lily. I know it's wrong, we all do, but this is a short-term solution that could help bring you more than a decade's worth of races in Formula 1. You have a chance to be the first female World Driver's Champion. I don't want to see you lose that dream, even if it means dating someone as frustrating as Luca." Hugo finished and moved towards my massage table, plopping down next to me. He laced his arms around my shoulders and gently hugged me.

I let a few minutes of silence pass, truly contemplating what he had said. Deep down, I knew Hugo was right.

Bastard is always right, I internally grumbled, drying the tears from my eyes.

"But why Luca? Was Éliott not free?" I said, a small chuckle leaving my lips.

"While I am sure Éliott would do it just to help you, the team chose Luca because he also needs the good press. You both have something big to lose." And there was the truth. We both did have something valuable to lose, and that motivation would help sell the whole fiasco.

"Fine. I'll do it. But the moment my sponsorship prospects start to turn around, we're ending this."

"Agreed." Hugo held out his hand as if we were about to shake on a business deal. I let out a small laugh and took it, shaking it as if we had just reached the agreement of a century.

Well, someone alert the Devil, I thought. *A cold day in hell has finally arrived.*

After the talk with Hugo, I slinked back into the hallway and moved towards Isabelle's office. It's as if she had read my mind because before I could even knock, she yelled, "Come on in, Georgia." I felt like a pig being led towards the slaughterhouse. There was no turning back now.

As I entered the office, I saw Fiona and Lizzie sitting on the sofa across from Isabelle's desk. Lizzie smiled at me, a smile so warm that I couldn't help but give her a small – *very small* – smile in return. I walked towards the chair next to Isabelle's desk and plopped down. Several silent seconds went by, not one of us uttering a word. After a few more moments, I sighed and decided to break the ice.

"Do you three truly believe this is my best option?" I asked, more level-headed than I expected to be.

"Yes," Isabelle replied simply. "If I could have found something better than having to endure Luca Rossi visiting our garage for the next several months, I would have found it." While she didn't smile as she said it, there was a pleasant nature to her voice.

"So what is the plan then?" I supposed I didn't need to tell them that I would obviously accept the deal. My seat was too important, and they knew that.

"We'll take it slow," Lizzie piped up, getting up from the sofa. "This week in Miami, we'll do some small stuff like have you and Luca head to dinner together tomorrow and then get drinks with Henri and Edward on Thursday – nice and easy. Hermes F1 has agreed to let you pop by Luca's garage a couple of times this weekend, and they'll 'accidentally' catch you on their social media, which will create some speculation with fans."

"I'm not kissing Luca if I get onto the podium." The idea of kissing a man I barely knew was bad enough, but kissing Luca in a fake burst of joy was enough to ruin my podium celebration, and I wasn't having that.

"No one's asking you to do that." While Lizzie didn't say *for now*, I knew it was implied. The moment any driver made it on the podium, the media immediately looked for their significant other – every photographer trying to capture that winning kiss.

"This weekend is about sowing the seeds of the relationship, getting the fans to speculate on what is going on. The good news is, with the other Hermes F1 driver being your brother, the fans will love the idea of your brother's teammate dating his sister. It should be an easy sell."

I sighed in agreement because I knew Lizzie wasn't wrong. It's what fairytale romances were made of. I had no doubt the fans would eat up our relationship – Hermes F1's golden boy Henri Dubois's sister dating their incredibly handsome number two driver – what was not to love if you were a fan?

"I have the details of this week all put into your Miami outline so you know when and where you are expected." Lizzie grinned at me as if she was proud of all this nonsense. I took the pink Lisa Frank folder with dolphins on it, no doubt to represent Miami, and opened it. To be fair to Lizzie, she had done an excellent job organizing the week, down to the thirty-minute intervals and small visits to Luca's garage. I nodded in agreement as I flipped through the pages, opting not to look at her directly since she seemed a little too pleased with herself. I knew I should have felt more guilt. My screw-up with the media wasn't just affecting me. It had now given Lizzie an extra job as my personal assistant and relationship manager, something I knew she hadn't signed up for.

"Thanks, Liz. Do Lily and Chris know?"

"We'll tell them in a few. We're about to meet with Lily on race strategy. Why don't you head to your gym and start your workout?"

And with that, it was decided. Starting tomorrow, I would be in a relationship with someone who could only be described as the most insufferable and arrogant driver on the grid. I nodded to Lizzie and skulked to my driver's room to nurse my wounded ego.

"Knock, knock, can I come in?" I heard the voice of my athletic trainer, Chris, at the door. Chris had been my athletic trainer since my first year in Indy Car, and we were inseparable during race weekends.

When I moved to the U.S., I knew no one in Indy Car, and getting Chris as my trainer was like being thrown a lifejacket in a pool where I was drowning. He was kind, thoughtful, funny, and probably the sassiest person I had ever met. His journey as a gay man working in the racing industry inspired me, and we quickly became close friends.

"If I said no, does that mean I can skip today's workout?" I turned around to see a stupid grin on Chris' face, followed by an apologetic smile that told me, *'You could be married to the Devil, and I would still make you do your workouts.'* I scoffed at his grinning face. Clearly, Isabelle had already told him about the outrageous plan the team had concocted.

"I know you and Luca don't have a close... friendship, but hey, if you're going to fake a relationship with anyone on the grid, at least they picked the most attractive, and dare I say sexiest, driver. There's no denying it, Georgie, that man is sex on wheels – *literally*." Chris wiggled his shoulders as he laughed at his terrible pun.

"Plus, his dad is probably one of the nicest people on the planet. Maybe you'll get to visit their vacation house in Majorca. Now that would be worth the hassle!"

Chris was nothing if not an optimist. It's probably why he and Lizzie got along so well. I often saw them in the back of the garage, giggling away while looking at ridiculous social media videos. They were the two chattiest people on the planet, and when they were together, nothing could stop them. I let out a long, exasperated sigh as I leaned back and finished my hydration packet.

"The whole thing is ridiculous. No one is going to believe this."

"You might be surprised. Luca is, if anything, a good actor. He's probably one of the better choices."

I gave Chris a pointed look to remind him *who* he was talking about. I couldn't believe what I was hearing. It was as if Chris actually thought this was a good idea. As I was going to say something I would probably regret, I heard another knock at the door.

"Good grief, am I going to see the whole paddock today?" The exasperation came out ruder than I had intended, but before I could immediately apologize for my statement, in walked Lily – a huge smirk plastered across her face that made me instantly forget my apology.

"Morning Georgie. Thought I'd come in, see how things are going," she said in a voice that sounded like it was dripping in sweet caramel. I stared at her blankly. My teammate knew exactly how things were going.

"Just dandy, Lily. I suppose you've heard the fun news: I managed to win myself that boyfriend the press are always so worried about." Lily giggled at that and patted me on the back.

"Keep your head up, Georgie. Who knows, maybe under that rugged, dark, handsome exterior, you might find something you like about Luca Rossi." Before she could utter another word, I picked up my pillow and threw it at her, causing her and Chris to snicker at my unfortunate position.

"The only thing I imagine I'll learn about Luca Rossi is that he is exactly as insufferable as I imagine him to be." Lily gave me a look that told me she was not entirely convinced by my charade.

"Well, if I knew that we'd be given handsome boyfriends if we sucked at media, maybe I would have taken a page out of your book." She stuck her tongue out at me and then turned around, heading towards my driver's room door.

"I'm happy to swap if you would like," I yelled back after her. Lily picked up my pillow and threw it back at me before leaving the room, still chuckling to herself.

The rest of Tuesday went smoothly – or at least as smoothly as it could go, considering I had been told my life was about to be turned upside down. As I hopped into bed that evening, I stared at the ceiling for an eternity. Henri had popped by my hotel room earlier, trying to make amends, and while I knew it was wrong to be this mad at him, I couldn't help it. I had asked him to leave me alone, and to my surprise, he had decided to listen. I was frustrated and angry, and if I was honest with myself, I was *jealous*. Jealous that Henri was the *'better Dubois'* that everyone loved. Jealous that

Hermes' golden boy could talk to the press like they had been best friends for a lifetime.

The truth was – I was mad and petty, and for one day in my life, I just wanted to be mad and petty.

Luca

When I left the Valkyrie F1 headquarters that Tuesday morning, I was fuming. This had my dad's stink all over it. My old man had been pressuring me to "get my act together," as he ever so kindly put it, since the season began. But after the yacht incident in Majorca, he had made it very clear that I had precisely four races to get my shit together before he got involved. I guess he was serious because here we were at race number five, and this charade had his meddling written all over it.

I entered the Hermes F1 offices in a huff, heading straight to the hospitality suite for families, where I saw both my father and mother enjoying an elegant cup of Italian coffee. I took a quick peak, ensuring the Dubois family wasn't present, before slamming my hands down on the table.

"A little heads up would have been nice," I said, staring straight into my father's eyes.

"If I had done that, then I doubt you would have attended today's meeting at Valkyrie?" I was annoyed by my dad's tone, but I knew he was right.

"And pray tell me, why Georgia Dubois? She's the most boring woman on the planet. I don't think she's even capable of having a conversation that isn't centered around racing."

"Good, maybe she'll teach you some things about racing, so you'll be better suited to answer *actual* questions about the car," my dad retorted.

I couldn't help but roll my eyes at his response. I knew plenty about the car, and my dad knew that. What he meant to say was,

'*Good, maybe you'll become more focused on racing and less focused on partying,*' but I let it slide. I had survived being the insufferable Noah Hendriks's teammate during my rookie year in F1. I could survive pretending to be boring, 'know-it-all' Georgia Dubois' boyfriend for a season. The only thing she had going for her was that she was undoubtedly one of the most beautiful women in the paddock. It was a shame her good looks were overshadowed by her dull personality and propensity to dress like a grandmother.

"Now, Flash, don't be rude. She's doing you a favor, and I think you'll find that there's a lot more to her than meets the eye, my love." I scoffed at the insinuation that Georgia was doing *me* a favor; she needed this as much as I did, but my mother could never say a single bad word about anyone. I loved her for it, but it was also her most infuriating quality.

As soon as my childhood nickname left my mother's mouth, I felt my anger simmer. My mother knew I could never stay mad at her. I stared at both parents blankly for a moment longer, but I knew I had lost this battle. The fact was, there was no going around my father. He was a legend in the racing world, and if he and Francesco Bianchi, my team principal, had agreed on this, then it would happen, whether I liked it or not.

"Now that you are done throwing a hissy fit, why don't you head to Matteo's office and get your schedule for the week? You have a hectic week, both on and off the track, and I expect you to adhere to the schedule that Hermes and Matteo have created for you."

I grabbed a cookie from the table and turned in the other direction, not daring to look back. Matteo was my dear cousin and manager, but I learned today that he was definitely my manager first and cousin second.

When I arrived at his office, I knocked lightly and walked in without waiting for a response, knowing he was expecting me.

"Ahh Luca, lovely for you to join me this morning. Come, sit. I'm sure you have many questions." I nodded and sat on the sofa, taking the cup of coffee he had just poured me.

"So, in this folder is your itinerary for the weekend. Tomorrow, you and Georgia will go on a lovely date we have booked for you at a tiny restaurant by the ocean. Very romantic," he said with a wink. I just shuddered in response and gave him a look that told him to continue, but with fewer adjectives.

"From there, you have drinks with Henri and Edward, a walk around the track, and a little 'accidental' meeting in your garage. It's all explained in this folder, but of course, I'm here for questions."

I took the folder from him, holding it like a bomb about to explode at any minute. At least I would see more of Edward, my former racing partner from when I raced for Wilmington F1. Edward had turned into one of my closest friends, and it was a relief that he would be helping me with this fiasco.

Matteo chuckled, "I know this seems unfair to you, but trust me, this is good for us. Once we have secured the deals, we'll end this little nightmare for you." I nodded, putting the folder into my bag.

"Right, well, best you get going to your workout. Miami is a big one."

Georgia

The following day, I woke up with a massive headache, likely from the heat and lack of water, but I decided to blame my situation on Luca. Today was Wednesday, which meant it was date night and the official start of this dating sham. Reaching for my phone, I saw several missed calls from Henri and a text asking if I wanted to get breakfast.

Not really, I thought to myself, but I knew I couldn't avoid my twin brother forever. I texted him that I would meet him downstairs in an hour and proceeded to prepare for the day. As part of our clothing collection, Valkyrie brought us some cute blue sundresses, which matched the car's color, for all of the media events this weekend. I wasn't typically a dress person, but these were nicely made, and the fit was perfect – plus, it was boiling, so the dress was welcome. A benefit of having a women-run team with female drivers was that we had quite a few fashion brands itching to give us clothing. We undoubtedly had better clothes than all of our male counterparts.

As I walked out of my hotel room, I turned to see none other than Luca Rossi, dressed head to toe in Hermes F1 gear. He looked up, eyes meeting mine. For the first time since I had known him, his face was genuinely unreadable. The usual Cheshire cat grin was replaced with a blank stare. I nodded in his direction, but he didn't move, staring blankly at me as if I were a mirage that was slowly disappearing. As the elevator doors opened, we both hopped inside, making sure to stand as far away from each other as possible.

"So, I, uh, guess I'll see you tonight?" I wanted to continue ignoring Luca, but as the oppressive silence became unbearable, I had to do something to break the awkwardness. Luca, still not looking at me, just nodded, a slight tilt of his head in my direction.

Great, he's gone from flirting with me to being mute. Real cute, I thought to myself.

As soon as the elevator doors opened, I zoomed out of the elevator so fast someone would have assumed a zombie was chasing me. Truth be told, it felt like I was being chased by a zombie – the lifeless zombie of Luca Rossi.

As I entered the hotel's restaurant, Henri spotted me and waved me down.

"Nice dress, you look beautiful," my brother announced as he got up from our table, kissing me on each cheek.

Kiss ass.

"Thanks, you don't look too bad yourself. New girlfriend dress you?" I said with a chuckle.

He nodded, a look of annoyance on his face. He was well aware of how I felt about his new girlfriend. Henri had recently begun dating Christine, an influencer who seemed less interested in my brother's racing and more interested in the VIP suite. But while Christine and I had very little in common, I had to admit, Henri had started dressing considerably better over the last several months.

"So, about yester-"

"Look, I know-" We both said simultaneously. I let out a small laugh and gestured for him to go first.

"I'm sorry you felt ambushed when you went into that meeting," Henri began. "They had just finished telling me right before you got there. Otherwise, you know I would have said something to you earlier."

I nodded, knowing full well that Isabelle and Fiona weren't stupid enough to tell Henri too much in advance. We were practically joined at the hip now, and Henri had never been known for being able to keep a secret.

"I know. I'm sorry I was so angry. It's just a tough predicament to be in." My brother nodded, his hand snaking across the table to hold mine.

"Look, Luca seems like an ass, but once you get to know him, he's not so bad. He's actually quite funny and surprisingly a great golfer. I think you two will have more in common than you think."

"I severely doubt that," I scoffed. Henri might have been trying to make me feel better, but this wasn't a battle I planned on letting him win. Henri rolled his eyes, but he knew when to quit.

"Regardless, I'll be there for drinks tomorrow, as will Edward. It'll be fun. We haven't hung the three of us in a while."

"Except it won't be *just* the three of us. Luca will be there," I said pointedly.

"Well then, it's a good thing Luca and Edward get along so well, then, isn't it?" Henri retorted, his face telling me that I wasn't going to win *this* small argument.

Instead of continuing with the argument, we opted to discuss the various silly events that our teams had ready for us. Both Hermes and Valkyrie had little challenges, photoshoots, and meet and greets scheduled throughout the day. Sometimes, I wondered if the press days before the race were more challenging than the race itself.

At 4 p.m., I looked at my watch, letting out an exasperated sigh that caught the attention of Lizzie, who only gave me a sympathetic look in response. Maybe it was because I was dreading the date night I was about to have with Luca, or perhaps I was beginning to get used to these silly media days, but today had gone by much quicker than I had hoped. It was probably the first, but I secretly hoped it was the second.

When I walked into my hotel room, I first noticed a beautiful purple dress splayed out perfectly on my bed.

"Of course, it is Hermes purple," I grumbled.

I rolled my eyes, picking up the dress to examine the style. It was bad enough that I had to date a Hermes driver; now they expected me to wear their color.

The plan was to have Luca out front of the hotel at 7 p.m. We had a reservation at a little Cuban restaurant on the waterfront, and Luca was to drive us to the spot in his car, a bright yellow Lamborghini. The Hermes F1 team got their engines from Lamborghini, so the automobile manufacturer gave their drivers a Lamborghini Aventador as a gift. *Must be nice.*

By the time the clock read 7:10, I had finished getting ready, knowing I would be slightly late for Luca downstairs.

Good, Luca could wait a bit, I thought to myself. I grabbed my purse and jacket and descended the stairs. *The slower, the better.*

As I approached the hotel's main doors, I could see Luca leaning against the passenger door of his Lamborghini, scanning through his phone mindlessly. I cleared my throat, and he looked up at me, immediately letting his eyes scan my dress – and my body. I could tell by the look on his face he was not expecting me to show up wearing a purple dress. His eyes quickly flickered up and down my figure, and if I hadn't been acutely aware of him at that moment, I might have missed the expression of shock and awe on his face. Almost as quickly as it appeared, his expression was gone, and Luca was back to the stern, neutral Luca Rossi I had gotten to know earlier that morning in the elevator.

"Georgia, good of you to show," he said dryly. Before I could respond, he had opened the vehicle's passenger door, signaling for me to get in. Part of me wanted to protest, throw a little fit, and lecture him on feminism and how I could open a door myself, but now didn't seem like the time or place. Plus, it seemed a bit petty, and I had promised myself in the stairwell that I would work on the pettiness.

"Can't put a time on beautification, Luca," I retorted back, climbing into the passenger seat of his car.

Luca hopped in on the driver's side and started the car, not uttering another word to me. The car ride was short and quiet, which was for the best, as I didn't exactly know what to say to him. Before I left, Lizzie had given me a set of questions that I was meant to ask Luca, a catch-all of things two people in a relationship were meant to know about each other if they were to convince an entire community that they were dating. I palmed the question cards in my hand, not having the courage to pull them out during the tense drive.

When we arrived at the restaurant, Luca parked the car in front of the valet and quickly approached my passenger side door. He stuck his hand out, which I gladly accepted, if only because getting out of a car that low to the ground with heels was next to impossible. I mumbled a pathetic string of thanks and walked up to the hostess stand with Luca trailing behind me. Before I registered what he was doing, Luca gently put his hand on the small of my back and let it rest there as the hostess began to guide us toward our table.

As we walked through the restaurant, I could see the eyes of various people looking us up and down. Did they recognize us? It was likely – our faces had been all over billboards for the last several weeks in Miami. You would have to live under a rock not to know that a Formula 1 Grand Prix was happening this weekend. When we sat down at our table, I saw a couple a few tables down from us pull out their phones and pretend to text, but I knew they were taking a photo of us.

Well, cats out of the bag. No turning back now.

If Luca noticed this, he didn't say anything. Instead, he went straight to the menu, clearly starving from a day full of training. Truth be told, if I weren't so nervous, I would have been equally as ravenous. Within minutes, a waiter approached and asked us for our drink order.

"Sparkling water," I responded quickly. Luca looked at me as if I had just ordered poison.

"We'll take a bottle of the Duckhorn Vineyard Merlot," he said. The waiter nodded, and after explaining the specials to us, he left us to choose our main courses.

"I don't drink on race weeks, well, not until after the race," I said finally once the waiter had disappeared from earshot. Luca quirked his eyebrow at me as if I had said something so ludicrous he couldn't possibly understand it.

"If we're to get through this, you might want to change that habit," he bit out.

Ever the gentleman is Luca, I thought sarcastically.

I wanted to further my response but decided against it. It would be a long season if we didn't learn to be civil.

"So, Lizzie and Matteo have created some questions for us. They're worried we won't know enough about each other when the media comes along asking questions." Before he could respond with something that I was sure would be plenty rude, I pulled out the small stack of cards and read the first question.

"Besides racing, what is your favorite thing to do?" I wanted to groan internally at that question – *how morose* – but kept myself composed. I needed to know these things if we were going to sell this stunt. And I needed to sell this stunt if I was going to keep my seat.

"I golf." I motioned for Luca to continue, but the waiter was back with my water and the wine. Before I could protest, the waiter had already poured out two glasses.

Fuck it, I thought to myself, *maybe Luca is right. A little wine might salvage this evening.*

I took a sip, and to my annoyance, the glass of wine was probably some of the best I had ever tasted. I was no wine snob, but Luca had chosen an excellent bottle. *Because, of course, the spoiled brat was also a wine snob.*

Luca smirked as he dutifully watched me drink the wine. The bastard knew I would like it and reveled in the fact that he had convinced me to break my pre-race ritual.

"I like to paint," I said casually, taking a second sip of the wine. "Your turn." I passed the cards over to Luca. He frowned but opted to read out the next question.

"What is your favorite color?" He asked, scoffing ever so slightly.

"Gold. Yours?"

"Purple."

I looked at him, my mouth slightly agape. Of course it was purple, Hermes prick. Truth be told, I had wanted to say blue, but I thought I would sound *stupid* admitting that my favorite color was the color of my F1 team car. After hearing Luca say purple, it turned out I was right – it *did* sound stupid. I smirked internally at that and patted myself on the proverbial back.

Good one, Georgia.

Before I could continue to pat myself on my back for my internal snarky monologue, Luca passed the questions back to me.

"Favorite movie?" I asked.

"Who wrote these stupid questions?" Luca groaned, snatching the cards back from me. "No one is going to ask us what each other's favorite movie is or which type of pasta we like." I ignored his comment and answered my question.

"My favorite movie is Atonement."

"Never seen it." Now, that didn't surprise me. Luca didn't strike me as someone who watched romantic movies about two people whose love was doomed from the start. He struck me as a Terminator, Transformers, Michael Bay sort of guy.

Lots of action, pretty girls, little plot.

"Here's something I *do* want to know," Luca said suddenly. "Every time Henri talks about *you*, he goes on and on about how funny and darling you are." He said the darling with air quotes, but I chose to ignore them. "Why can't you be like that in front of the media?"

All at once, I had a million things cross my mind, a million things that I wanted to say, but I knew the truth would make me look weak, and like hell was I going to look weak in front of Luca Rossi. What I should have said was that when I got in front of the media, it felt like the wind was being kicked out of me. Or when I approached the media pen, my palms got so sweaty that I struggled to focus on anything but the drops of sweat dripping down my face and hands. How my quick remarks weren't meant to be snippy – all I wanted was for the interview to be over as fast as possible so I could retreat to the ease of my garage.

But I couldn't let Luca know any of that. *Show the enemy no weakness*, I reminded myself.

"The same way you can't stop yourself from making bad choices when you're out partying, Luca. It's just in my nature," I said with a sneaky grin. I knew that the snide remark wouldn't be lost on him.

Georgia: 1 Luca: 0

After that, the waiter came back and took our order. The rest of the dinner was relatively quiet. Before exiting the restaurant, we went through a few more questions, but nothing exciting. As we left, the manager approached us, asking for a photo. He apparently was a big Hermes F1 fan – *typical* – and had the nerve to ask if *I* could take a picture of him and Luca. I agreed, much to my chagrin. I would definitely be hearing about that from Henri later.

Still, date 1 was complete. I had survived dinner, and now I just had to endure drinks on Thursday and a couple of visits to the Hermes garage. I could do this – *what could possibly go wrong?*

Chapter Four

HEAT? I EAT PEPPERS RAW

Georgia

Thursday morning arrived, and much like Tuesday and Wednesday, it was full of more publicity stunts and small media stories. We visited the local children's hospital in the morning, which I truly enjoyed. Visiting the children's hospital and speaking to the young girls truly brightened my day. I was on cloud nine – until we got to the paddock, and Lizzie reminded me that I had a track walk with Luca scheduled after the mandatory drivers meeting.

For the first time in the history of my driving career, I wanted this FIA drivers' meeting to last forever, but to my dismay, this one ended up being incredibly short. Before I left for the Hermes garage, Lizzie slid another index card into my hand with even more questions.

Because the other ones had gone so well last night, I mused to myself. I thanked her and headed off with my Valkyrie F1 hat and Helios sunglasses. I figured wearing sunglasses made by Luca's number one sponsor might remind Luca what was at stake, and if it got under his skin, then even better.

When I arrived at the garage, I smiled sweetly at Francesco, waving at the Hermes F1 team principal, who also happened to be Isabelle's husband.

"You here to see Henri?" Francesco asked, a friendly little twinkle in his eye. It took everything within me not to roll my eyes at him in exasperation. The bastard knew I was here to see Luca, but he wanted me to say it.

"No, actually Luca promised me a little walk around the track," I said with as much sweetness as I could muster, "plus I figured it would be a good time to get all the details on this weekend's Hermes F1 strategy," I added with a wink. Francesco's face told me he didn't think the last part of my sentence was amusing, but I didn't care − Fiona, our Valkyrie F1 strategist, would get a good laugh out of it.

Francesco nodded and gestured for me to follow him. The Hermes garage was beautiful and well-designed. I was impressed, but I guess that's what decades of Formula 1 races got you − a well-oiled machine. As we approached Luca's driver's room, I knocked on the door gently.

"Come in," Luca yelled from the other side of the door. I'm unsure what I expected from Luca's room, but it definitely wasn't this. I suppose I was expecting whatever I saw when I walked into Henri's room − an absolute mess. But instead, I was greeted with what could only be described as serial killer cleanliness. His room was in immaculate shape. Luca must have noticed the shock on my face because he let out a dry chuckle.

"Not all men are slobs like your brother." I wanted to retort something sassy back to him, but honestly, it was a slight relief to know that some men could pick up after themselves.

"Shall we go?" I responded.

Luca nodded, and we exited the garage quickly, heading towards the track. The Miami track was brand new to F1, so several of the teams were out, walking around the track and analyzing everything from the curbs to the width of the straight. As we continued to walk down the track, I saw a bright green shirt ahead of us.

"Oliver!" I called out, causing the green shirt to turn around.

Luca groaned, clearly not interested in chatting with Oliver, but I made a point to ignore him and continued to wave Oliver over.

"If it isn't Little Ms. Sassy Dubois," Oliver announced, running up and giving me a big hug, lifting me ever so slightly off the ground. He nodded to Luca, who nodded back, doing his best to put his eyes anywhere but Oliver's face.

"Miami treating you well?" I knew Oliver lived in Los Angeles, and he visited Miami often, but there was still no hiding his excitement every time he visited the city.

"It's marvelous as always. How about you, Luca, enjoying the deeply rooted Cuban culture and cuisine?" Oliver knew the answer. There wasn't a cultured bone in Luca's body as far as either of us was concerned, but it was still fun to watch Luca squirm. Luca only nodded, clearly looking around the track, searching for a way out of this conversation.

Where was his friend Edward when he needed him? I internally giggled to myself.

"So Edward says you're all going to drinks this evening. That sounds fun." I knew Oliver was itching for an invite, but we needed to sell this an intimate evening between a couple and their two closest friends.

"Don't worry, we'll save the good drinks for Sunday once we celebrate my win," I said, winking at him. He grabbed my shoulder playfully, giving me his big Oliver laugh.

"Well, if we're going to get to drinks this evening, we better finish this track walk," Luca bit out, clearly done with this conversation. I reluctantly nodded in agreement. There was still a lot to do before tomorrow's Free Practice sessions.

Luca and I finished the rest of our track walk in complete silence. As we passed Éliott on the way out of the track and back to the pit lane, he waved at me, giving me a little squeeze on my arm and a wink as he walked by. I gave him a look that said, *"Please, God, save me,"* but Éliott was gone before I could force him to talk to me. As soon as we made it back to the garages, I dropped Luca back off at Hermes and headed back to the

Valkyrie garage without saying anything else to the Hermes group.

"Have a nice track walk?" Fiona asked, raising her head from her computer screen as I walked into her office. I gave her a look that, in my opinion, said it all. She just chuckled and handed me a tablet.

"Here, go finish reviewing the track analysis. We'll talk more tomorrow."

I spent the next several hours reviewing the track analysis that Fiona had put together and discussing various race strategies with the team. It wasn't until I saw Lizzie pop into my driver's room that I lifted my head, checking the time on the clock. I set the tablet down and turned to see Lizzie, all smiles and bubbles as usual.

"Alright, Georgie, ready to go conquer the world?" Lizzie asked, a sparkle much too bright in her eyes for my liking.

"You mean ready to go feed the media dragon?" I replied sarcastically, raising one eyebrow at her.

"Same thing," she quipped back. I had to laugh. Never a dull moment with Lizzie.

We made our way to the media center, where all the other drivers were waiting. Truth be told, these media days were some of the better ones because at least I had four other drivers in the conference room with me. They always split us up between four groups, five to six drivers per session, so you were never with your teammate. If a couple of drivers had a crash in the last race, the FIA would make sure to put them together. In the FIA's eyes, the more drama, the better, especially if the BBC was filming that press conference for Full Throttle, their Formula 1 documentary show that had been airing for the last several years.

Typically, the FIA put Henri and I together. They enjoyed the sibling banter back and forth, although they learned their lesson when they added Edward to our session. I don't think the media got any of their questions answered, and Edward spent half the interview in literal fits of laughter.

I walked into my segment, and of course, sitting next to my seat was Luca.

Oh, FIA, how you never let me down.

Undoubtedly, there had been some whispers in the paddock after our track walk and dinner last night. While it hadn't blown up on social media, the team was expecting this press conference and tonight's drinks to give us the push forward that everyone wanted – everyone except Luca and I.

I nodded at Luca, who got up and gave me a mini hug.

"Twice in one day, Cara, lucky me," Luca said quietly, but not quiet enough so that the front row of journalists couldn't hear. I just smirked at him and sat down, thankful that Eric, a 6x World Champion and one of my driving mentors, was to my right. He gave me a fist bump and a knowing look. *Nothing* got past him. From my understanding, Hugo had filled Eric and Otto, another one of the older drivers, in on the drama because they were the ones most likely to say something to me about it, and they were always the first two drivers to defend me during negative press interactions.

The conference started with the usual questions on the track, possible strategies other teams would take, and managing under volatile weather. Miami in May was known for rain, and tomorrow's weather report was inconclusive. It would either be blistering heat or pouring rain. No in-between.

"So Georgia, how does it feel to be back in America, racing Formula 1 cars?"

This was a simple, straightforward question. I could answer this nice and easy. But as I opened my mouth to answer, I could feel my hands start to clam up. I immediately swallowed, trying to alleviate a dry spot that had formed in my throat. I looked to my right and saw Eric, who was smiling brightly at the camera; I could see his eyes shift ever so slightly towards me. He wiggled his finger at me as if to say, "*You got this kid.*"

"Yeah, it's, uh, it's nice to be back." The journalist nodded slightly, clearly expecting a bit more.

"Since you've raced in the South before, do you think you'll be ready for the heat tomorrow? I heard several of the drivers dropped a few pounds today due to the heat." It was true, the heat was dreadful, and I had left the car considerably lighter than when I had gone in. I wanted to roll my eyes a bit. The journalist had neglected to ask any of the male drivers if they could stand the heat in the car, but I decided not to let it bother me.

Still, I guess my internal conflict was taking too long because before I could answer, I heard Luca say, "Please, I can't think of anyone more prepared to fight the heat – last night at dinner I saw Georgia swallow a jalapeño pepper whole," Luca joked, turning to me and winking.

It took me a moment to register the sultry nature of his voice and the light smirk that was now crossing his face, but when I did, I turned to give Luca a *'what is wrong with you look*,' my face a little shocked. I could feel myself blushing, a slight heat rushing to my face. To my right, I heard Eric choke out a laugh, clearly trying to hide his amusement, as did the two other drivers in the press conference. Eric just winked at me, clearly getting Luca's innuendo.

Luca was known in the paddock for loving spicy foods, so much so that he would do spicy food challenges on the Hermes F1's social media pages. It had become a crowd favorite watching Luca challenge my poor brother, Henri, to spicy eating contests. His team loved to joke that he basically was a jalapeño pepper because he rarely ate foods that didn't have jalapeños in them. I once watched him chop up a jalapeño and put it in his pasta dish, which was decisively one of the most disgusting things I had ever seen.

Truthfully, it was an incredibly lame joke and a perverse stretch from Luca, and I hated that he had gotten a few giggles out of the immature drivers on either side of me.

If the journalist also got the joke, he didn't say anything, although he did let out a laugh.

"Fair enough," I heard the journalist respond, clearly not sure what to make of that interaction.

The rest of the conference went reasonably well. Fortunately, the journalists let me off with just a few more easy questions, which, after Luca's slightly embarrassing response, felt reasonably easy to answer.

I guess Fiona is right; the bastard is at least good at media.

Lizzie met me inside of my driver's room once the press conference was over. Typically, she would walk me back to the garage after the conference, but a meeting with Matteo, Luca's manager, had distracted her.

"Right, Georgie, time to head back to the hotel and get ready for drinks tonight," Lizzie said, popping her head into my driver's room. Chris, my athletic trainer, just wiggled his eyebrows at me and helped me off the massage table, a slight grin on his face.

"Ah yes, another date with the infamous but devilishly handsome Luca Rossi," he chimed in. I tried to ignore his comment, but I knew Lizzie was secretly loving this. Chris, on the other hand, was *openly* loving this far too much.

In a desperate attempt to ignore them, I grabbed my bag from the table and headed to my parked Bugatti. As I hopped into the driver's seat, I saw Edward pass by, waving his hands at me. I rolled down my window, and he gave me the world's biggest high five.

"Not the hands, Edward. Gotta save those for driving tomorrow," I quipped.

"I don't know, Georgia. As far as I see it, if I remove you from the grid, I'll get to move up a spot," he joked.

I simply waved my hands at him and yelled, "See you tonight, loser."

Drinks tonight were to be at a bar reasonably close to our hotel. Again, Luca was to pick me up and drive us to the bar in his Lamborghini. This time, I had grumbled about why we had to take his Lamborghini again, especially since I knew how to *actually* drive in America, but I was told to shove it and move on. Apparently, no one in my all-female team wanted to hear about the sexism of a woman constantly being told she couldn't drive to dates – they had bigger fish to fry. Isabelle gave me a look that told me to quit while I was head, so I did.

You win some, you lose some.

I decided not to be late to meet Luca this time. Truth be told, I was excited to see Henri and Edward and figured the quicker I got there, the quicker I could start ignoring Luca's presence. I put on a cute top with some new jeans that Lauren, Edward's girlfriend, had given me. I met Luca again at the front of the hotel. He was wearing a nice, dark gold button-down shirt.

Of course, he's decided to wear my 'favorite color' – guess someone was listening during last night's 'question time,' I mused to myself.

As much as I hated to admit it, Luca looked really good in the gold button-down and Lucky branded jeans. Gold was a tricky color to wear, but I suspected Luca looked good in just about anything he wore. As I approached the car, he looked up at me and smirked, obviously noticing me staring at him. *Cocky bastard.*

Georgia: 1 Luca: 1.

When we arrived at the bar, I immediately ran up to Henri and gave him a big hug. My anger from Tuesday had simmered down, and we had managed to sneak in a few more conversations throughout the last two days. Edward greeted us by giving Luca a big hug, which surprised me. I knew the two were close friends after being teammates for two years at Wilmington, but I didn't realize they were *hugging* friends. Figured they were more *'friends because we had to be'*. To be fair, Edward was friends with everyone. You could give him a rock, and he would manage to make it his best friend.

"Luca, Georgia, good to see you both," Edward said, wiggling his eyebrows suggestively at the two of us. He quickly stopped when he saw both of our faces. I have no idea what expression Luca had on his face, but I imagined it looked like mine – unimpressed and disinterested in Edward's antics. Henri laughed awkwardly, ever the peacekeeper of the group. As teammate to Luca and my twin brother, I didn't doubt that he wanted to play the situation very delicately. The four of us took a seat at the table, Luca and I sitting together with Edward and Henri across from us.

"So, how is the car feeling for tomorrow, Edward?" I asked.

"Breaks are going to be rough with the heat, but we're hoping for some kind of breakthrough," he replied, a tint of sadness in his voice. Edward loved racing for Wilmington. It was the team that had given him his F1 start, but the car they had built this year just wasn't good enough to win races – at least not yet, as he would say.

"It's going to be willfully hot this weekend, not looking forward to it. Whoever thought racing in Miami in May was a good idea should be fired." Edward and Henri chuckled, but Luca looked disinterested in my comment. I supposed Luca was more used to the heat, having grown up in the warmth of Italy. At least, he never seemed concerned about it.

As we chatted some more, a group of guys approached our table and asked for a photo. Here it was, our big moment as a small group. Needless to say, these kinds of photos always made it across social media. By tomorrow, everyone who was interested would have seen this photo of the four of us.

We scrunched together, and before I could protest, Luca put his hand on my waist, pulling me ever so slightly closer, which forced me to lean into him for the photo. Before I had time to react, I smiled at the camera, remembering where we were and why we were doing this. I felt flustered all of a sudden, and I hated it.

On the one hand, Luca Rossi had intimately touched me, and I was annoyed, but on the other hand, Luca Rossi's soft grip around my waist had felt nice, comforting almost – likely a testament to how touch-starved I was feeling recently. It's not like I could date while I was in the middle of this charade.

As the group thanked us, I noticed several other people sneaking photos of our group. After the commotion of the first photo, people were starting to notice us. Luca let his hand slip from my waist but kept it on my back, rubbing up and down ever so slightly. Not enough to where it was overtly noticeable, but just enough so that someone would unexpectedly capture the moment.

As much as I hated to admit it, I could see why the team had paired me with Luca. Without even saying a word, Luca was a master at manipulating both the fans and the media. While those closest to us, like Edward, Henri, and Oliver, knew this was a farce, to the rest of the world, we were this tight group of friends – with some of us becoming closer than others.

"Peaches? Earth to Georgia?" I was all of a sudden snapped away from my thoughts by Henri, who was looking at me with a questioning look.

"Want another beer?"

"No, thanks, I'm good. I already broke my no alcohol rule twice this week; no need to push it before Free Practice tomorrow."

"Always focused on racing, do you ever relax?" Luca scoffed.

"Yes, after I win." Luca scrunched his eyebrows in annoyance at my comment but let it go.

The boys each got one more beer before closing the tab. We continued to chat a bit more about our cars and the track, keeping it light and easy. Edward, Henri, and Luca discussed a bit of golfing that they had done earlier in the week.

Once the beers were drunk, we made our way back to the parking lot. I hugged Edward and Henri goodbye and wished them both good luck, as it would be unlikely I would see either of them before the Free Practice sessions. The ride back to the hotel was quiet, and it took everything inside me not to ask, *'Cat got your tongue?'* but I instead opted for another one of Lizzie's questions.

"Here's an interesting question," I said, finally breaking the silence as I pulled out a card that Lizzie had given me earlier in the day.

"Who is the most important person in your life?" For several moments after I had asked the question, there was an awkward silence floating around the car. Perhaps I had asked a question too personal, but Luca didn't strike me as someone who cared much about that kind of stuff.

"My father," he said suddenly. I motioned for him to continue, but he didn't, so I just nodded because, on some level, I understood that. I came from a very close family, one that supported each other through everything.

"Besides my mother, who does her best to stay neutral, it's my brothers. My family is the best thing to happen to me." Luca, for a moment, looked as if he was thinking about my answer.

"Surprised you didn't just say Henri. You two are always joined at the hip," he sneered. And just like that, what could have been a nice moment about our families had ended, so I just scoffed in response.

"I love both my brothers *equally*," I snipped back. *Asshole*.

"Of course you do," I heard him whisper under his breath. As much as I wanted to say something, I thought against it and let us continue the rest of the ride in miserable silence.

The weather on Friday wasn't quite so brutal, *quite* being the operative word here. The weather was rough and still terribly hot, but the clouds had given us some shelter. When I arrived at the track, the paddock was buzzing with excitement. There were photographers, fans, and media everywhere. When I arrived, I waved to a few of the cameras but made a beeline to my garage as quickly as I could.

As I entered the garage, I stepped into my driver's room, only to see Lily, Chris, and Lizzie all circled around Lizzie's phone.

"And to what do I owe this honor?" I asked, earning myself a squeal from Lily, who was clearly eager to tell me what was going on.

"Your little stunt worked! *Look* at these photos of you and Luca!"

I hobbled over to the desk where they were all huddled and took a look. There we were – Luca and I at the restaurant – both drinking our wine and staring into each other's eyes.

I knew that pesky couple next to us were taking photos of our date, I grumbled to myself.

As I scrolled down the Instagram feed, I saw countless photos of the two of us – both at the restaurant and then at the bar from last night, including pictures of his arm around my waist and on my back. Such little touches that meant so much to everyone, and Luca had known that.

"Looks like your little plan is working," Chris chimed in. "The fans seem to *love* the two of you."

Of course, they did. As far as they were concerned, it was a match made in heaven.

"Oh, look at this one! The dinner date looks so romantic," Lily sighed, as if she was *actually* jealous of this ridiculous conspiracy I was now a part of. "It even says you've been dating for weeks. Now that speaks to your chemistry." She winked at me, clearly aware of how much she was getting under my skin.

 **F1INSIDER**

Liked by F1GossipGirls and 50k others

F1INSIDER NEW COUPLE ALERT! Are Luca Rossi Jr. and Georgia Dubois an item? Sources tell us they've been seeing each other for several weeks now. Click our link to find out what the brothers think of Luca dating their sister! #LucaRossi #GeorgiaDubois

"Did you happen to ask him any of the questions I wrote for you?" Lizzie asked, eager to see if her plan for us to get to know each other was working. I just nodded, attempting to make it clear that I had no more interest in discussing this.

"Annndddddd...?" Chris looked at me with exasperation in his eyes. I knew he was dying to learn more about this new, mysterious boyfriend that had been thrust upon me.

"I learned he likes the color purple," I responded simply.

"Good thing I put you in that purple dress then," Lizzie said, shaking her shoulders with unhinged giddiness. With that, she, Lily, and Chris burst out laughing.

"He must have thought he had died and gone to heaven!"

"I doubt it," I said solemnly, although none of them seemed to believe me. "Now, if you don't mind-" I began, but before I could continue, Chris pulled up a new Instagram post.

"Now look at this one!" As much as I wanted them all to leave, I let my curiosity get the better of me and motioned for Chris to read it for me, even if I had seen enough social media for one morning.

"It says, *'Rumor has it Georgia Dubois has moved on with a new driver in the paddock – Luca Rossi Jr., son of famous F1 champion Luca Rossi Sr. Sources tell us that rumored ex-boyfriend and fellow racer Éliott Simon is fuming at the match.'*"

At that, I let out the biggest groan I had ever heard myself utter. Apparently, I had better luck getting fake boyfriends than I did real ones. According to the press, I had managed to snag two fake ones in just a couple of days.

"I am sure Éliott will love that," I said sarcastically. For years, the media and fans had speculated that Éliott and I were dating. Sure, he was flirty, and our relationship was quite touchy-felly, and we were close enough to where it might look less than platonic, but the truth was, Éliott was my brother's best friend – and Henri had made it very clear we were both off-limits to each other, something Éliott and I had decided to – *somewhat* – respect.

"Well, I am glad your little publicity stunt is working, but I must be off to get ready for Free Practice," Lily announced, getting up from her seat and giving me a small hug.

"Good luck out there!" I yelled back, but my attention was still on Chris' phone as I re-read the social media post over and over again.

Free Practice sessions 1 and 2 ended up going better than I had expected, considering the weather. I came P3 in both, which, considering the heat and issue with my front wing in the second practice session, was not a bad result. I was annoyed that both Noah and Henri had beaten me, but at least I had beaten Luca, who had come in P4 and P6, respectively. After the sessions were over and I had adequately reviewed the data with my race engineer and Fiona, I caught the eye of Lizzie, who was motioning for me to come over. I knew what she wanted. It was time to stir the rumor mill and give the fans a little something extra. Time for the dreaded garage visit – Garage visit #1 of the weekend. If I didn't die during this visit, I was to be sequestered to a second visit tomorrow.

Just lovely.

Lizzie met me in the garage as I popped out of my car.

"Alright, time to go!" she shrilled, swaying her hips a tad as if she thought that was going to get me more excited.

"Ok, so when we get to the garage, you need to be all cheeky and ask Francesco if Luca is there."

"Why wouldn't Luca be there? He's a Hermes F1 driver..." I cut in, giving Lizzie a pointed look, which she aptly ignored, continuing on.

"And then Luca will come out and give you a hug, ask you how Free Practice went, blah blah." I loved how she added '*blah blah*' at the end. The only thing Luca and I had in common was that we raced cars – discussing Free Practice seemed like the obvious and only choice for the two of us.

When we arrived at the Hermes garage, Lizzie fixed my helmet hair, and I put on the biggest fake smile I could muster. As I approached, Francesco caught my eye. Clearly, he had been prepped for this.

"Hi Francesco, is Luca around? We were just walking past the garage, and I thought I would see how his session went?" I asked casually.

Francesco nodded, and before he could even call out his driver's name, Luca came swaying out, his racing suit tied around his hips. Like me, he was drenched in sweat from the Miami heat, and his fireproof clothing was sticking so close to his skin that you could see the ridges of his abs and chest underneath his fireproof spandex. I did my best not to stare – I didn't need Luca getting even more of an ego boost.

"Oh, look who popped by? How did free practice go, Cara? Heard you got P3, nice one." I internally winced at the nickname. Since when did I say it was okay for him to call me romantic pet names? Before I knew it, Luca had his arms wrapped around my waist, and we were joined together in a large hug. My head was placed flat against his muscly chest, and he gave a big squeeze, which I might have secretly enjoyed if he wasn't completely drenched in sweat. Luca was incredibly attractive and in great shape; there was no denying that.

"Yeah, the car felt good, but the heat was draining. Hoping we get some rain tomorrow before qualifying, would make it cooler."

Luca and I awkwardly chitchatted for a bit more, and out of the corner of my eye, I could see a Hermes F1 social coordinator '*accidentally*' filming our conversation. After a few more minutes, Luca put his hand on my back and led me further inside, pretending to give me a tour of the garage, as if my twin brother didn't also race there. I had experienced this tour a million times, and I tried not to roll my eyes at Luca's presumptuousness. *How was anyone going to believe this stupidity of a charade?*

Another ten minutes passed, and I could see Matteo and Lizzie both nod their heads as if to say, "*Good job faking it, guys.*" Lizzie approached me and made up some story about us needing to get back to the garage, and then we set off. Awkward garage visit one complete. I was sure once this particular social media story was out, I would be hearing about this embarrassing visit from Oliver and Éliott, something I wasn't sure my frail ego could handle.

Chapter Five

NO POLE, NO PROBLEM

Georgia

By the time Free Practice 3 was complete Saturday morning, I was feeling ready for qualifying. It had rained a tad in the morning, which did lower the temperature, but that only meant the humidity had increased, which was going to be rough on my engine – and my body. After a rough couple of laps due to being blocked by a Rennen F1 car, I easily passed through Q1. Q2 was a different story, but I managed to get P9, which at least got me into the final stage of qualifying.

"All you need is top ten," I heard Mel, my race engineer, say into my radio, a poor attempt at trying to cheer me up. I was a championship contender, and I didn't want to settle for P9 in Q2. Fortunately, Lily had also made it through, which was great for the team. We were coming into our cars, and the new wing upgrades were phenomenal.

As Q3 started, I heard a loud sound from my car on the out lap.

"Shit, what is that?" I gritted out into the radio.

"Box, box," was all I heard back from Mel. After a quick look at the car, the mechanics found some debris stuck in my flooring.

Great, just great. Not what I need right now, I lambasted quietly to myself. The team quickly got the car back onto the track, but the best I could pull was a starting position of P8. Lily, however, managed to squeak out a P5.

As I returned to the garage, I tried to hide my fury, but the look on Mel and Fiona's faces told me they knew how I was feeling. I hopped out of the cockpit and went straight to my driver's room, throwing down my helmet onto my sofa.

"Fuck!"

Every race counted towards the championship, and now I had my teammate in front of me, which would make it even harder to pass tomorrow. I threw off my racing gear and hopped into the shower, opting to get it as cold as possible. As I came out of the shower, I heard a knock on the door.

"Georgie, it's me, Oliver. Can I come in?" I quickly threw on some clothes and opened the door to see Oliver standing in front of me with a bottle of wine and two solo cups.

"Figured you could use a drink." The Wilmington driver came in and plopped himself down on my massage table, making himself at home. I nodded, happily taking the cup from Oliver's hand.

"So... how are things with Luca?" He asked gently. I couldn't help but notice the slight twinkle in his eye – clearly he, *too,* was also enjoying my misery.

"As good as can be when I'm *fake* dating a *real* buffoon," I bit back. Oliver laughed at that, raising his drink and colliding it with mine.

"Yeah, when Arthur informed Edward and me about the plan, I have to say we were both quite shocked. That said, Edward has a bet that by the end of the season, you'll be *actually* dating."

"Well, Edward is *actually* an idiot," I deadpanned back.

"True... but he thinks Luca likes you, you know."

"Doubt it. The only thing Luca Rossi likes about me is his ability to get under my skin."

"So, how long do you think this will have to go on?" I could see in Oliver's eyes that he hadn't meant to antagonize me, and I appreciated his attempt to quickly steer the conversation in a different direction.

"Until the sponsors decide we're worthy of their money, I suppose." Oliver got up from the massage table and moved to give me a little hug and squeeze.

"Keep your head up, love. Who knows, you might find something you like about Luca?"

I didn't have it in me to ask why everyone kept saying that, and instead, I gave Oliver a big smile as he left my room. *What was Luca, an enigma that the entire paddock except me had figured out?*

After Oliver left, I packed my bag for the hotel. The likelihood of tonight being a long, sleepless night was strong. But, on the plus side, the best part of not getting pole? *I didn't have to face the media today.*

"And we have a blistering 100 degrees Fahrenheit here on this beautiful Miami Sunday," I heard the radio announce. I quickly turned it off, mourning the loss of the clouds that we had seen during yesterday's qualifying session. Saturday had been brutal, as seen by my embarrassing eighth place grid start. Even Lily had managed to qualify better than me, not that I was begrudging her for the excellent fifth place qualification, but I had never qualified lower than fifth place in the last four races, and as the team's number one driver, it hurt when my teammate out-qualified me even if she was the sweetest person on the planet.

With a 12:30 p.m. race start, I was expected at the paddock early in the morning – especially if I was to casually drop by Luca's garage again. Except this time, it was going to be more than a little 'pop in,' Matteo and Lizzie had decided. Since things were going so well on social media, an Italian coffee date was clearly in order.

My love of coffee was known all across the track. Fans even made me little coffee canisters and gave me mugs as gifts when they popped by for signings. I had done a couple of joint Instagram posts supporting local coffee brands in the countries our team had visited over the last few months.

I made it clear to Henri last night that he was to make sure he was available at 9:30 this morning, less I have to face Luca alone again for another awkward *"OMG, can't believe I found you here... at the Hermes garage.... where you're supposed to be"* moment with Luca.

I arrived at the paddock by 9 a.m. with Chris, my athletic trainer, in tow. Chris knew I liked to typically arrive at race day events by myself, a ritual I had started at Indy Car. I enjoyed being alone in the morning before a race – just me, my thoughts, and a carefully crafted playlist and cup of coffee, but with everything going on these days, Chris offered to hop into the car with me, and I couldn't bring myself to say no. I appreciated the company.

"Good morning," Lizzie announced as Chris and I walked into the garage together. She was wearing a bright yellow bandana that made her look as though she was emulating the very sun that was providing the blistering Miami heat. I told her as much, and she smiled a smile that could only be described as 'ear to ear.'

"Thought I would try and bring the sunshine in case Miami brought rain, but now I fear it worked too well," she giggled. I dropped my stuff off in my room and grabbed my phone.

"So, should we get this little coffee date over with so I can go back to focusing on my race?" I suggested.

"Yes, yes, off we go," Lizzie sang.

As we walked through the paddock, I saw a few familiar faces, notably Éliott and his parents, who waved at me as I entered the Hermes hospitality entrance, a smug grin on Éliott's face. Clearly, Henri had told him about this morning's activity.

We arrived at the Hermes entrance, and the guard let us in without even questioning us. I supposed he had been told a small group from Valkyrie would be arriving this morning. As I walked into the hospitality suite, I saw Luca and Henri waiting for me, Luca holding two cups of coffee.

Smart man – if he had some already brewed, we could cut down the interaction by... 2 minutes? I mused to myself. If there was one thing we could agree on, it was that every minute we didn't have to spend together was a win.

"Oh, look who it is, Henri, it's the Valkyrie F1 team here to steal our race strategy," Luca laughed while shoving the coffee cup into my hands, albeit a little too forcefully, causing it to spill slightly onto the floor.

"Don't be silly, we don't steal losing strategies over at Valkyrie," I quipped back. Luca huffed out a laugh, one that almost seemed genuine, but Henri didn't seem quite so amused. He was very touchy about Hermes F1 strategy – or lack of one, as he often bemoaned.

"Nice of you to visit us over at lonely old Hermes," Henri proclaimed, giving me a small hug and an '*I'm sorry you have to do this*' smile.

"Well, when Luca boasted that Hermes F1 had the best coffee in the paddock, you know I had to come try it out. That's a bold claim. You know how I feel about Italian coffee," I said, winking at the both of them. I felt a little stupid saying that – Italians were known for incredible coffee, and last year, I had done a coffee trip through Italy with my brothers.

Luca gave me a quick, bemused glance, likely because he had seen me drink a good amount of Italian espresso over the last week, but he said nothing and motioned for the three of us to sit down at a table, pulling out a seat next to him, leaving Henri to sit across from us.

"So, you feeling ready for today? Must feel real good to have pole position?" I asked Henri, trying to sound excited for my brother. He deserved pole position; he had driven exceptionally well all weekend.

"I'm sorry I didn't bring any cake from Monaco with me in case you win," I added with a wink.

"It's fine. I'll just have to settle for forcing you to go out with me tonight to celebrate my win." I rolled my eyes, secretly praying that I could turn my eighth place into first so that I didn't have to go out with Henri and Luca, a 'cherry on top' reward that I knew I likely wouldn't be getting.

We continued with a little more chit-chat between the three of us for another ten minutes before Lizzie motioned for me to leave. I knew she had ensured that the Hermes F1 social coordinator had gotten all the footage they needed of the three of us. I gave Henri one last hug, and as I went to turn around, I felt Henri push me slightly into Luca, giving me a pointed look that said, '*Hug him.*'

Perhaps a little too awkwardly, I wrapped my hands around Luca's waist and gave him the weirdest side hug I had ever experienced. Luca chuckled, wrapping his arms around me as he pulled me flush against his body, causing my own to heat up from his touch. He was incredibly warm, and he was wearing that cologne again – the one he had worn the night I ran into him while waiting for the elevator in Spain – the one that smelled of lilacs and pine trees. I closed my eyes for just a moment and drank it in before opening them quickly, backing off from Luca.

"Right, better get back. First place won't be easy, so need to go prepare." I gave my brother a little smirk and then headed off in the direction of my motor home.

"See, Georgie, that wasn't so bad!" Lizzie announced as we left the Hermes hospitality suite. She was right, it had been manageable, but I wasn't going to let her know that.

"Yes, it was good to see my brother," I let out softly. Lizzie just smirked at that. She knew I would never admit that the coffee date wasn't *that* bad, but I knew she would accept her wins where she could.

The next several hours revolved around me prepping for the race. There were training sessions with Chris, reaction time exercises, and race strategy reviews with Fiona and Isabelle. I knew I was going to need a bit of a miracle if I was going to get on the podium, but I was prepared to put the work in. All I needed was for a few of the cars in front of me to drop out of the race – and the Blaue Flügel F1 Team, even the Hermes F1 team, were getting good at those.

"Alright, time to get in, Georgie," I heard my race engineer Mel yell from across the garage. I nodded, crawling into the car and attaching my radio.

"Is it always this hot in here?" I muttered to myself. I felt around for my water and then pressed the radio button.

"Umm, there seems to be an issue. The water is basically empty," I called out.

"No issue, Georgie, we needed to lighten the car. Every ounce matters," Mel casually responded.

Did my racing team not know it was 100 degrees outside? I grumbled into the radio but said nothing else. Mel had been with me since last year. She was a brilliant race engineer, one of the best, and when I signed for Valkyrie F1, I knew I had to take her with me. She had the strongest southern drawl I had ever heard, but her mathematics were on par with the best over at the Rennen F1 Team, a team that had previously won seven of the Team Constructor Championships in the last decade.

"Fine, but let's not make a habit of it." I knew part of this was my fault. I had gotten eighth place on the grid, and we needed to make up time. The championship was at stake, and I could survive a ninety-minute race with just a little less water.

After a few more moments, I was out of the pits, completing my formation lap.

"How are things, GG?" GG was the name Mel called me over the radio – she had been doing it ever since Indy Car after she proclaimed, "*Georgia is much too long!*" during our first race together – so GG stuck.

"Feeling ok, wish me luck."

"You never need it."

I got to the eighth-place spot and waited. The wait for the lights to go out was always the worst part of the race. The anticipation was on par with a group of people who were at the very top of a rollercoaster's drop. I loved starting the car off the grid. There were no words to describe the magic and wonder of driving a Formula 1 car. Every day I got into that car, I lived my dream.

The fifth light went out, and I started the car as if I were a person who hadn't eaten in a week and food had just been offered to me. I was hungry for this win – or to at least get on the podium. Within three seconds, I had already jumped two places. Two other team cars had gotten bad starts, and I certainly wasn't going to let this opportunity pass. *A good driver takes any opening they can get.*

As I started lap twenty-five, I saw the lights of a Blaue Flügel F1 car blink in front of me. Before I knew it, I was passing the driver, and in my wing mirror, I could see his car die on the side of the track.

"Yellow flag, GG, that's P5 now." *Great, only two more places to go.*

"Order is Henri, Luca, Lily, Noah. Noah has something wrong with his front wing, slowing him down. Box Box."

"Roger." So Lily had managed to pass Noah – *nice one, Lil.* I went into the pits, got a fresh set of tires, and then continued on my way.

"Yellow flag will be lifted this lap. Let's push."

Within another ten laps, I had gained DRS on Noah and had quickly overtaken his car. I was now sitting P4 in the race, albeit with Noah close behind.

"It's real hot in here, Mel. Everything okay?" I mumbled into the radio. She agreed to check and quickly came back to confirm that the car was fine and that I was to keep pushing. And push I did because as I reached lap forty, I was on the back of Lily.

"Tell Lily I have the pace; she needs to get out of the way. She's driving too slow." I demanded on the radio. Not one of my finer moments, typically team orders came from engineers to drivers and not the other way around, but I knew I could pass my less experienced teammate. Noah was close behind, and I knew if we didn't pick up the pace, I would use the rest of my tires defending my P4 position.

"Hold," was all Mel responded.

"No, tell Fiona that either Lily gives me the position or I'll take it from her.

Isabelle had made it clear when I joined that we were a team of drivers, and while I was the number one driver who had the best hope of winning the World Drivers Championship, Isabelle wasn't about to take podiums away from the other driver if we could help it. Demanding Lily give me her place wasn't going to make Fiona or Isabelle happy, but I knew I could get on this podium. *I had to get on this podium.*

"Lily has been instructed to give you the position on the straight. Go quick." I didn't respond, and as we reached the straight, I sailed on by her.

"Thanks," I mumbled, a little embarrassed by my outburst earlier, but now I was P3, and Luca was only five seconds ahead of me. I could do this.

"And that's fastest lap, GG."

I'm not entirely sure what changed, but as I reached lap forty-two, I began to feel my heartbeat slowing down, but I knew it had to be beating fast at this kind of racing speed. As I settled into the race pace chasing Luca, I became acutely aware that I was incredibly hot – and my head felt like someone had just whacked it with a baseball bat. I sucked on my straw, but I knew I was out of water. I had been out since lap thirty. My lips and mouth were completely parched, and yet salty sweat was dripping down my face so quickly that I felt like I was constantly tearing off my visor. I hadn't felt this nauseous since the very last race of Indy Car when I knew that if I won, I was taking home the championship trophy.

I went to press the radio button, but nothing came out of my mouth. I wasn't sure what I was going to say anyway. There were only fifteen laps left now, and I could survive another fifteen laps. I put my head down and focused on the road in front. I could see Luca's car up front, and I just needed to close the 2.5-second gap.

"GG, you slowed down last lap more than expected. All ok?" I wanted to respond by telling Mel how I was feeling, but I didn't have the energy to utter the words, so I just kept driving and uttered an "*uh huh*" on the radio.

Lap fifty. Seven more to go.

"Gap is now three seconds, GG." I knew Mel was trying to encourage me to push. We had lost time on Luca. She sounded slightly frustrated, but in that smooth voice that engineers used when they were annoyed with their drivers but didn't want to distract them. How could I tell her I was just trying to focus on just not passing out? The heat index had to be almost 115 degrees outside.

Lap fifty-six rolled around, and my radio went silent. It had become clear that they had accepted I was going to get P3.

"Last lap, GG, let's push for the fastest lap. Henri currently holds it."

I took a deep breath. Fastest lap would give me an extra point, and every point counted at this moment in time. I lifted my visor and put it back down again, enjoying the two seconds of air that swept onto my face.

"Fuck it, Georgia, let's push," I mumbled to myself. It was as if time had stopped, and I was the only one on the track. I was flying in what was probably the best lap of a Grand Prix I had ever done. I might have been blinded by the heat, but I would be damned if I was going to let my brother take this one tiny victory from me.

"That's P8 to P3, GG, very good and fastest lap. Congrats! Unfortunately, Lily DNF'd at Lap fifty-three. Issue with the battery forced her to come in and retire. Race order was Henri, Luca, you." I silently groaned to myself. Well, at least I didn't have to feel guilty about passing Lily.

It wasn't the race win I had hoped for, but I was still fairly proud of myself. I pressed the radio button and went to say something to the team, but as I opened my mouth, a wave of intense nausea hit me   the adrenaline of the race had run out, and I all of a sudden realized how intensely ill I felt.

"Yeah... uh... thank... the team..." I gritted out, just barely. I supposed the team thought I was upset about the race, as no one said anything back to me. Truth be told, I was surprised I could utter anything at all. As I made the last cool-down lap around the track, I entered the pit lane where the third place sign was waiting for me and parked my car.

As I arrived at the parking spot, I could see Henri in the background, celebrating his win on top of his car. I smiled just a little bit.

Bastard did it after all; good for him. I went to pull myself up out of the car so I could go congratulate my brother, but my body didn't move an inch. I pulled again on the halo, but nothing happened.

Maybe I just needed a quick moment to regroup, I thought to myself. I made sure I was unhooked from the car and tried again.

Shit.

As my vision started to fade black, I felt someone begin to lift me out of the car. Strong arms lifted me out of the cockpit, wrapping my arms around their shoulders.

"I got you," I heard a soft voice whisper. Henri? No, it couldn't be; the person was taller than him and slightly stockier than my brother. Whoever it was quickly took my helmet off and put a straw in my mouth, still holding me up in my cockpit.

"Drink slower," he reprimanded as I began to quickly suck the hydration liquid out of the water bottle. I inhaled a large breath and smelled something familiar.

Lilacs and pine trees.

The realization hit me – it was Luca holding me.

As I began to come to, I opened my eyes and looked straight into his brown eyes. They were soft, full of concern, and staring right back into mine. As I observed his face, I noticed he had the smallest freckle on the side of his right eye. Our faces were mere inches apart, and his breathing was steady. He really was a beautiful man.

What is wrong with you? I internally reprimanded myself. *You almost passed out in your car, and here you are ogling the enemy. Must be the heat exhaustion.*

"Keep drinking," Luca commanded, and I listened, grabbing onto his shoulder tighter as he pulled me from the cockpit. Out of the corner of my eye, I could see my brother running towards me, panic written all over his face. Luca set me on the ground but held onto me firmly, letting me put my weight on him. My feet were unsteady, but as I began to feel the breeze against my face, I was feeling a bit stronger.

Henri reached out to grab me from Luca, but Luca blocked his way. "I got her. Don't crowd her," he told my brother. Henri wasn't one to listen to anyone, but I could tell he was panicked enough to back off just a tad, giving me some room. By now, a few of the other drivers had come over, Noah and Eric included.

"Let's take her to the medical tent," I heard someone suggest.

Before I knew what was happening, Luca had picked me up in his arms bridal style, and he and my brother were moving me toward the medical tent. I could hear Mel and Fiona behind, calling out to Luca and Henri, asking after me.

"Probably just heat exhaustion," the doctor declared as we entered the medical tent. He had seen the footage and was already prepping IV packets. As Luca set me down on the medical bed, I was beginning to feel myself again, the waves of intense nausea had settled down.

"I'm fine. Just give me a minute, and then I can go weigh myself." Henri scoffed at my insistence to get up and put his hand on my chest, pushing me back down.

"Peaches, you need to lie down for a bit." But before anyone could stop me, I threw myself off of the makeshift medical bed – a little unsteadily – but caught myself and launched myself upwards. My brother had just won his second F1 race of the season, and I had fought long and hard to be on that podium with him – nothing was going to stop me.

"How about this," the doctor suggested, "you can head to the podium celebration, but I expect to see you back here for more fluids after it is finished. Take this water and hydration package with you." Before I could protest, the doctor dumped water and hydration mixture into the Hermes F1 water bottle I was still holding – which I then realized was Luca's water bottle.

Henri helped me from the tent, and we set foot towards the cool-down room, where I proceeded to rip off my race suit and tie it around my waste. My fireproof shirt was completely soaked through and sticking to me. Not the classiest look, but if the Fı cameras weren't in the room, I definitely would have taken my shirt off.

Not that the Fı TV cameras had stopped Luca. As I turned around, I saw a shirtless Luca sitting on one of the chairs, rubbing his soaking wet hair with his shirt. I stared for what was probably a little too long and then sat down next to Henri, who was forcing the water bottle back into my mouth,

"Drink, Peaches," he demanded, a serious look in his eyes. I knew he was annoyed that I had come to the cool-down room, but I had been insistent.

As Henri turned to his left, he saw the shirtless Luca, who was watching the race replay on the screen. I heard him mumble something to Luca, who only scoffed something dryly back to Henri. Henri turned back to me and smirked a little. I had been caught staring. So sue me, Luca was attractive. No one had accused me of being blind, just of being bad at media. It was clear that Luca had been told to put his shirt back on because he rolled his eyes but slapped his sweaty shirt back anyway.

Show is over, ladies, I chuckled to myself. I knew there would be hundreds of GIFs of shirtless Luca all over the internet by tomorrow.

Soon, the three of us were ushered onto the podium, wearing our winners' podium hats, as we sprayed champagne all over Henri. If someone had asked me for one of my favorite memories, I would happily say it was any of the times I stood on the podium with my brother. It didn't matter who had the higher step – being with Henri on that podium was a dream come true.

Once the anthems were done and the champagne spraying was finished, we walked back down to the cool-down room. Paula, Valkyrie's team doctor, met me at the bottom of the steps and ushered me back towards the medical tent. After some more fluids and Tylenol, I was beginning to feel like a new person. While I hated getting the fluids, I figured it was better than attending the press conference.

"How do you feel?" I heard a voice call from behind me. Isabelle had arrived just a few minutes ago to check on me.

"Much better, thank you."

"That was an excellent race today. You showed great pace. We'll get them next week." I nodded in agreement but eyed her warily. I suspected Isabelle wanted to address my outburst on the team radio, but when she said nothing, I let out a small sigh of relief. It seemed as though Isabelle would give me some reprieve today.

"Well, since you're feeling better, Georgia, I guess you had better get prepared for the winner's conference. Starts in thirty. They pushed it back in hopes that you would feel better." If I had known better, I could have sworn that I saw a slight smile on Isabelle's face.

Well, shit, so much for that dream of missing media duties.

Had Isabelle asked the race organizers to push back the conference as punishment for my outburst on the radio? Most definitely. Isabelle knew how to push my buttons. The fact that if I hadn't pushed so aggressively to make it to the podium, I wouldn't have had to do media duties was not lost on me.

When I entered the press conference, I walked over to Luca and handed him his water bottle.

"Thank you... for today," I said softly. He took the water bottle and shook it a bit.

"You should finish what's in here." I raised my eyebrow and gave Luca a questioning look. Why did he care so much? I mean, he had had to care somewhat; he needed this arrangement, too, but even I had to admit he was being awfully nice for us having 'just started' our relationship. I simply nodded at him and took a seat on the other side of Henri, who was enjoying being in the middle seat this time.

Henri leaned over and whispered, "Hermes water bottle looks good in your hand, ya know."

"Oh yeah, you going to give me your seat next year?" I whispered back, earning me a chuckle from Luca.

Before Henri could get another word in, the press conference had started. The journalists started with their usual questions they had for the winner – a discussion on the tires and new track. As the discussion turned to the temperatures, one of the journalists turned to me.

"So Georgia, how are you feeling after that? You looked pretty worse for wear out there at the end of the race." I nodded, picking up the microphone to respond.

"Yeah, as you know, we've been dealing with weight issues, and the team felt it necessary to limit my water. It was a bit of a tough call because we needed to better balance the car due to my starting eighth, but still, I don't think it's a call we can make again." I winced at the last part, probably not what Isabelle wanted me to say, but it was the truth. I couldn't do that again.

"Well, we're glad you are ok. But I have to ask since there's a big push to get more women in the sport, do you think your heat sensitivity had anything to do with the fact you're a woman?" As the journalist asked the question, I just stared at the guy blankly; dumbfounded was the only way I could express how I felt. I could feel Henri tense up next to me, but before either of us could say anything, I heard a thick Italian accent in the microphone next to me.

"Did you not just hear her? She said the lack of water in the car was the reason. What does that have to do with being a woman?" The voice was rough and laced with frustration. I turned to the right and saw Luca now standing, getting closer to the journalist, clearly expecting an answer. The journalist looked shocked, his mouth agape as he stared directly into Luca's eyes.

"You know, we all struggle with water consumption in the cars. With the weight restrictions, we often have to face minimizing water with our setups, depending on the track temps and our place in qualifying," Henri spoke up, trying to clear the tension in the air and de-escalate the situation. We knew the press didn't like me, but we couldn't risk them starting to turn on Luca as well. Henri stood up and tapped Luca on the shoulder. Fortunately, Luca had already started retreating to his seat, a look of fury still in his eyes.

"Right, yes, sure," was all the journalist could think to respond, still shocked from Luca's outburst. I turned to look at Luca, who was making a point to glare at the journalist.

"Judging by the fact that Lily was able to complete 98% of the race without passing out, I would say no, it has nothing to do with me being a woman and everything to do with my setup and lack of water," I said, starting to gain confidence in myself.

"We drive 300kph in temperatures well above 100 degrees. We learned a lot about the car this weekend, and we learned about our limits, and that's what matters. But what I can say is that I'll be back next race, stronger than ever. I mean, someone has to show Luca how to get on his home race's podium."

I gave Luca a sly smile, and as I turned back to the journalist, I heard laughter coming from my right. I'm not sure if it was shock, but Luca was head back, eyes closed, *hand clutching his chest* laughing. Henri also had a smile on his lips.

"We'll see about that, Cara, we'll see," Luca chuckled, a slight smile on his lips.

Chapter Six

A LOSING DECK OF CARDS, PLEASE

Georgia

After Miami, Lily and I were requested at the factory so we could hop into the simulator, a machine we used to practice our races virtually. The team had further upgrades on the cars, which they wanted to bring to Monza, an exciting prospect for the two of us. The Miami upgrades had been incredible, and I knew that the Monza upgrades would further increase our race pace.

But the best part? After a few days in the factory, I had a solid five days at home in Monaco, just me, Henri, and Lily, who had decided to visit before our trip to Italy.

No Luca, no demands, and most importantly – no journalists.

On my last day at the factory, I was called in for a 'social media meeting.' While Lizzie made it sound like we were having a general meeting about both Lily and I's engagements over the next week, based on the guest list, I knew what we would *actually* be discussing. I was going to get the low down on the Monza "fake dating" plan.

When I walked into the brightly lit Valkyrie F1 board room, the first thing I saw was a huge projector reflecting a photo of me and Luca at the Miami Grand Prix. It was a picture of us in the cool-down room. Luca was shirtless, and I had the biggest smirk on my face that I had personally ever witnessed.

Good fucking grief, I thought to myself, *please, for the love of God, tell me this is photoshopped.*

Before I could react to the photo on the screen, I heard a burst of laughter from behind me. Lily and Chris had walked into the conference room, and both of them were giggling like school girls as they stared at the boardroom's TV, which conveniently still displayed the photo of me staring at a shirtless Luca, a sultry smirk on my face.

Mortified didn't even come close to describing how I felt.

"Please take a seat, and we'll get started," Lizzie said, motioning for me to take a seat next to her. As much as I wanted to take a seat, all I could do was stand and stare at the photo, my face no doubt showing a look of absolute shock.

I felt frozen.

"Georgia would sit, but she can't stop staring at Luca with those puppy dog eyes," Chris chuckled. I immediately flicked him off and stuck my tongue out, a childish move, but I had just been caught staring at Luca like a teenage girl who had just been asked to prom by the varsity quarterback, so I was feeling childish.

I sat in the closest seat next to me, still staring at the photo on the screen. It soon switched to an Instagram post, which featured the shirtless Luca photo.

"Oh good, now I know everyone is talking about the *look*," I grumbled to myself. "Lucky me." Lizzie chuckled a bit but cleared her throat, signaling for everyone to quiet down.

"Right, well, needless to say, things are going great in the social media department. We've been monitoring different posts, and the fans are loving the two of you. Speculation is high. After the race, Luca and Georgia were trending on Twitter." Lizzie clapped her hands together, the loud boom making me jump slightly in my seat. She was a little too proud of herself, in my opinion.

"The helping you out of the car, absolutely priceless. Defending you to the journalist? The cherry on top. Couldn't have asked for a better media interaction."

I scoffed at that. There I was, dying of 100+ degree heat, but all the social media team could think of was the gold mine that was discovered. Sure, Luca had fiercely defended me in front of the media circus, something that had taken me by surprise, but I had also stood up for myself. Not that anyone mentioned that in any of those post-race debrief articles.

"So since the fans have bought into this so nicely, and since this upcoming race is Luca's home race, Matteo and I have decided to move up the timeline a tad." With that statement, I lifted my eyebrows warily.

"How much is a tad?" I knew the somber tone of my voice would not be missed.

"Next week, you and Luca should be more public in the paddock..." Lizzie drifted off, clearly a little worried about what she was going to say next. I motioned for her to continue, unconsciously sitting on the edge of my seat.

"We're going to have you hold hands throughout the paddock and attend a couple of events together," she said very quickly, probably hoping I wouldn't hear it all. I pictured her at the paddock directing me around, saying, "*Well, I told you back at the office,*" in hopes that she could insinuate that I wasn't listening during the social media meeting.

Her plan certainly wouldn't work on me. I was on high alert anytime Luca's name was being thrown around. I let out a big sigh because I knew it was only a matter of time before we were going to have to escalate the relationship. In a fan's mind, a couple that had been friends for years and dated for about a month held hands.

After a brief pause, I finally nodded, knowing there was no point in arguing my case.

"Fine, I guess that makes sense." I could see Lizzie's face lighten up. Clearly, she was expecting me to fight this, but the relief that washed over her face gave me a little bit of happiness.

At least I can make Lizzie happy today. She clapped her hands and headed over to give me a big hug as she dropped the newest itinerary in front of me, a folder with Italian flags all over it.

"Excellent! Here's the rest of your itinerary. Oh, and just one more thing – we booked two rooms next to each other. It's Luca's home race, and fans will expect you guys to be all *lovely dovey* – didn't make sense to have you in separate hotels."

"Separate rooms, right?" I asked cautiously. Like hell was I going to share a room with Luca Rossi.

It didn't matter if he was the most handsome driver on the grid... or if he smelled incredible... or if he had been acutely aware enough to pull me out of the car before I passed out from heat exhaustion... A shared room is an absolute no.

My thoughts were cut off by Lizzie, who shrilled, "Of course! I know how much your sleep is important to you before a race, which is the story you and Luca will share if anyone questions why you have separate rooms, got it?" I nodded my agreement. It seemed easy enough.

The rest of the meeting concluded with Lizzie going through a few more Instagram posts that people had posted of us. One was from the Hermes F1 social media team, who had done a cute post on my visit to the Hermes garage for the orchestrated, '*accidental*' tour Luca had given me. To be fair to them, it did look cute. Luca looked like a kid in a candy store, showing me all of the coolest new items that had just arrived.

I enquired to see if any sponsors had seen the posts and if there were any changes to the deals. Lizzie denied it, which made sense. We were going to have to put in a lot more effort if we were going to turn this sponsorship situation around.

Luca

Miami was undoubtedly my best race of the season to date. I had managed to get onto the podium, and I was starting to feel real confidence in the car. The sooner I got my driving life together and my personal life more private, the sooner I could be rid of Little Ms. Sassy Dubois. However, after my help with getting her out of the car, the media and fans had gone wild. I was being hailed as "Georgia's Hero" – which felt ridiculous. All I did was help a driver out of her car. I was a decent human being, and I didn't appreciate everyone making hoopla about me doing the basics – did no one expect me to help her?

The moment she pulled up, I knew something was wrong. Georgia had a signature jump out of the car she did when she made it to the podium of a race. It was, to be fair, pretty cute, and when she didn't jump out this time, I knew something was wrong. I figured she would be pissed that she had lost to her brother, but no way would she neglect to get out of the car to celebrate with Henri.

When I pulled her out of the car, the look of panic on her face was real. I felt like, for the first time, I was seeing a glimpse of the real Georgia. She wasn't her usual straight-laced, composed self. She seemed human, and it was a breath of fresh air to see Little Ms. Perfect have a normal reaction to the environment. And when she looked into my eyes, it sparked something inside of me that felt difficult to ignore.

On the last day of the visit to the Hermes F1 factory, Henri and I had been summoned to a communications meeting – which I knew instantly was going to be about Georgia and I's relationship at Monza. As I walked into the room, Bella, my communications manager, patted me on the back.

"Good stuff, Luca, pulling Georgia out of the car like that, absolute gold. And then defending her at the press conference? Just great," she congratulated. I brushed her off, trying not to look too annoyed at the lack of congratulations for getting P2, my *actual* achievement from last weekend.

"I'm not going to leave any driver in their car. What her team did to her was stupid and dangerous – plus that journalist was an asshole. I've been wanting to put him in his place for a while," was all I could mutter back as a reply.

"Well, regardless, the audience seems to be loving this relationship. Henri, that little live story you did at the bar was gold. Speculation is running high that Henri has set you two up, which is going to lead us into a perfect weekend where we can make the relationship public at your home race," Matteo chimed in.

Of course, they were going to take advantage of my home race. I finally had a chance to win at Monza, and my communications team was more worried about how Georgia and I were going to interact as a couple. The team explained the plan for us to walk through the paddock hand in hand. There would be the usual garage visit, probably a track walk, and then an event if the schedule allowed it.

"And who knows, maybe if you get on the podium, she'll give you a little congratulations kiss," Matteo said with a chuckle. At that comment, Henri cleared his throat, clearly unamused by my cousins' antics.

"Let's not get ahead of ourselves," Henri said dryly.

"Don't worry, mate, no one wants to kiss your sister less than I do," I quipped, giving Henri a dramatic pat on the shoulder. I thought he might have appreciated the joke, but instead, he turned to me and actually looked offended. He didn't want me to kiss his sister – but he clearly wanted me to *want* to kiss his sister.

Noted.

"You'll have rooms next to each other this race, so we can easily get footage of you two coming and going from the paddock. We'll rotate this race; Georgia will drive some, and you'll drive some."

Clearly, my horrified face said it all because before I could say anything, Matteo butted in, "Luca, you have to share. You being the only one driving makes it look like a one-sided relationship, and the fans are going to start commenting that you don't let her drive anywhere. We're getting ahead of that." I knew he was right, but still, getting in a Bugatti felt like an offense to all human nature.

"Fine, as long as I don't have to share a room with her, I'll do it."

Henri's eyes widened, as if he had just thought of the possibility that one day, they would probably shove me and his *beloved* sister into the same hotel room. I chuckled at that.

Oh, Henri, Hermes' naïve, little golden boy.

Georgia

We arrived in Monza fairly early, and our shuttle from the private plane took us straight to the hotel Lily and I were staying at. The hotel was a lovely old building in the center of the historic downtown. As I opened the door to my room, I saw what was probably the largest, most lovely suite I had ever laid my eyes on. Within the room were two bedrooms and a vast living room.

Finally, a decent-sized room.

I texted Henri that I had arrived and asked if he wanted to meet up for dinner tonight. Fortunately, I had been spared dinner with Luca this evening since he had an important dinner with potential sponsors and VIPs. Apparently, no one thought we were that ready to be put together at a sponsorship dinner. *Fine by me.*

> Georgia: Dinner tonight?

> Henri: Yeah, I'll text Éliott and Oliver.

> Georgia: Sounds good.

I unpacked my clothing for the race weekend. Again, Valkyrie F1 had set us up with some pretty fun items for the week: more sun dresses, blue jeans that matched the car, and various tops for the weekend. Several designers had reached out to the team and asked if they could design better polos than the classic men's version the rest of the paddock wore, to which Isabelle said, *"Of course."* Isabelle wasn't just here to sell our driving abilities; she would happily sell anything that made the team money. I was convinced she would auction off picnic dates with Lily and me each weekend to make money if she could get away with it. But I didn't mind hawking the team's clothes – if I was going to walk around the paddock holding hands with the devil, at least I was going to do it in style.

I decided to take a shower before I got dressed for the day. We had an afternoon meeting with some VIPs at the hospitality lounge, and going drenched in sweat and smelling like an airplane just didn't seem appropriate for someone trying to convince wealthy brand ambassadors to become sponsors.

As I was finishing up my shower, I heard a banging noise from the main room, and panic began to fill me. Had someone broken in? There were some crazy fans in F1, and not everyone was thrilled that the sport was 'letting women in.' Lily and I had received a lot of harassing messages on social media, although they had all fortunately turned out to be hot air.

Must be Lizzie here to fill me in on some extras for the weekend, I convinced myself. Still, usually, she knocked first.

But as I walked out of the shower, wrapped in only a towel, ready to chastise Lizzie for not knocking before entering my room, I saw something much worse – *Luca Rossi.* As soon as he saw me standing in just a towel, his eyes gleefully raked over my body, and he smirked at the sight in front of him.

"Well, hello to you too. I guess after Miami, it's only fair I *also* get to see you *shirtless*, although you definitely need to buy me dinner first," he said with a wink.

"What the actual fuck are you doing here?" I screamed, running back into the bathroom. I poked my head out of the door and looked at him, still demanding an answer.

"Well, according to the front desk, this is my room. So, I think the question is, why are you here, showering in my shower?"

"This is my room, you idiot."

"Well, looks like we're sharing a room then, 'cause clearly my key card works," he retorted, motioning towards the door with his key like a buffoon.

"Absolutely not. No way. Not happening. Now, turn around so I can run back to my room. And don't get comfortable. I am sure Lizzie will get this sorted."

Luca chuckled but turned around. The moment he did, I dashed to my room, cell phone in hand. I frantically dialed Lizzie's number as if she were a radio host, and I was a hopeful fan who was going to be lucky caller number nine.

"Lizzie, thank god you picked up. There's been a mistake. Luca is in my room, claiming we're sharing a room! I thought you said these rooms were next to each other."

"Wha-what do you mean he's in your room?" I could tell from her voice that she was as equally confused as I was. "Let me call the hotel and get this sorted out."

I hung up and threw my Valkyrie team clothes on. On the other side of the wall, I could hear Luca's muffled voice, clearly complaining to Matteo on his end. After I got dressed, I walked out of my room and heard the tail end of their conversation.

"... this is not acceptable. You need to fix this," I heard Luca hiss. "It's bad enough that I have to spend my downtime in the paddock with her. I need my space in my hotel room!" Luca turned to see me, a stern look on his face as he observed the fact that I was still there.

"Good to see you found some clothes." Before I could retort something back to him, Lizzie was returning my frantic call.

"Please tell me you have some good news," I spit out, giving Luca an annoyed glare.

"Unfortunately, Georgia, when the Hermes F1 coordinator called to get the rooms next to each other – the hotel heard two rooms side by side, they booked you a suite with two rooms in it, and with the grand prix this weekend, the hotel is completely booked..." She trailed off at the end, but the truth was I had stopped listening after the word "unfortunately."

Luca could tell from my face that the news was bad because as I turned to him, he slammed his bag down on the sofa and sat down, letting out an enraged sigh. Before I could say anything, he was opening his suitcase and unpacking his toiletries.

I was seething. I had one request, and it was broken. Luca looked at his phone, and his face said it all. He had been told the same thing by Matteo.

"Just stay out of my way," I bit out, rushing back into my room and slamming the door.

As soon as I was ready to head to my VIP experience, I rushed out of my room, not giving Luca another thought.

The VIP experience had been beautiful and informative, and it was clear from the guests' reactions that we had made some good progress with a couple of potential sponsors, fashion house Maison de Klotho being one of them. The majority of sponsors asked me questions about the car, but one sponsor in particular had asked me about Luca – well, more like congratulated me. I did my best not to roll my eyes and pretend to barf as Lily stood behind the sponsor, staring at the interaction, all while giggling like a small child. Lily was getting far too much enjoyment out of this.

I made sure to complain to Isabelle about the hotel room situation, but she made it clear I would not be switched to a different hotel than the rest of the team.

"At least this means you and Luca will be on time to the paddock," she said with what I thought was too much of an attitude, considering I was the one who had to endure Luca Rossi in *my* hotel room, not hers.

After the strategy meeting, I returned to the hotel to get ready for dinner. Truth be told, I was incredibly excited to have dinner with Henri, Éliott, and Oliver. It had been so long since the four of us had hung out, and I had a lot to fill them in on. Plus, I had sent Edward a box of Krispy Kreme donuts, which I had conveniently loaded full of peaches, so I was eager to hear about his utter disappointment when opening the box. Edward had gotten a sponsorship from the donut brand because of his absolute love of donuts. When we were kids, he would easily knock back half a dozen in a sitting and then go back for more.

When I arrived at the front door of my – *our* – hotel room, I took a big breath.

You can do this, Georgia; you can survive this weekend, I said to myself. As I walked into the living room of our suite, I heard the shower running.

Perfect, I can make a quick getaway. I immediately ran to the safety of my suite room and quickly changed into a lovely blush pink dress. Matched with my light tan heels and my Cartier bracelet, I, for the first time in a while, felt relaxed and beautiful. I was going to have dinner with my brother and best friends, and for once, all felt right in the world.

Before I could truly reminisce in my moment of relaxation and clarity, I walked out of my room and was, once again, hit with the reality of my situation – a shirtless reality of my situation.

There, standing in front of me, was none other than Luca Rossi, fresh out of the shower, steam still pouring out of the bathroom. His towel was wrapped around his waist, hung rather too low around his hips, and it looked as though it could fall to the floor any moment.

God, I almost wish it would, I immediately thought, before internally chastising myself, pushing that comment deep down to a hidden place.

What is wrong with you, Georgia? This is Luca Rossi – the playboy both your teams have saddled you with because he can't keep it in his pants. Unfortunately for me, before I could finish my internal conversation with myself, Luca had already turned to face me, and I had been caught staring – again.

"Enjoying the view?" Luca asked with a wink. I immediately snapped out of my thoughts and turned away, pointedly giving him my shoulder with a huff.

"Any chance you can put some clothes on? This is a shared area, in case you forgot," I responded snarkily.

"And deny you the opportunity to get a second peak of your

favorite racer? What kind of man do you think I am?" He teased as I grimaced because now I knew that he had seen that post-Miami photo that had caught me staring at him shirtless in the cool-down room.

"A man that has probably never been told to put his shirt back on by a woman, but there's a first time for everything, Luca, so put it on," I hissed back. He chuckled in response to my defiance. Out of the corner of my eye, I could see his form in the mirror in front of me. He was directly behind me and starting to inch closer. He kept moving towards me, and before I could react and move towards the door, I felt Luca's breath on my neck, which caused a slight chill to go down my spine.

"If you play your cards right, Amore, you might be able to see more of me," he whispered softly into my ear. It was as if my body had forgotten who he was because I could feel warmth start to build inside of me, my legs becoming a tad more shaky than I cared to admit. Having Luca this close to me, his warm breath on my neck, it felt like my nerves were being set on fire. I tried to respond to him, come up with something witty, but at that moment, all I could think about was how close his lips were to my neck, how good his breath felt on my skin.

So, instead, before I embarrassed myself any further, I turned around and headed toward the door, but before I could stop myself, I yelled back into the room, "Well, hopefully, I have a losing deck of cards, because what I really want is to see less of you, so if you could turn that into making yourself disappear – I'd be delighted!"

As I slammed the door, I knew the bastard had a smirk on his face. Not my finest comeback, but it would have to do in a pinch – a real pinch.

Chapter Seven

BOYS, AM I RIGHT?

Georgia

I huffed it straight to the elevator, grumbling to myself along the way, not paying attention to any of my surroundings. Unfortunately for me, I was too unaware to notice that I had just stepped into the elevator with not one but three BBC journalists and Michael Clifton, one of F1 TV's presenters, dressed impeccably for whatever dinner they had scheduled that evening. The whole damn media pen was standing there, clearly amused and staring at me as I muttered some inconsiderate thoughts about Luca *out loud*.

After I heard a slight clearing of a throat, I looked up and came face to face with Michael. He gave me a small smile and quirked his eyebrows – clearly, he had heard my muttering.

Great, Georgia, just great, I cursed to myself. *You have managed to ruin the entire thing before it began – absolute moron.*

I knew I had to save face and fast, so before I could properly think of a reasonable thing to say, I blurted out, "Boys... am I right?" I winked at Michael and gave him a small, devilish smile as if to imply Luca had simply gotten up my sleeve about something and not to worry world, we were still real – *fake* – dating.

Michael just quietly chuckled to himself, nodding at me in

agreement. Fortunately, the female journalist behind me let out a louder chuckle, making me feel a little less on edge.

"You have your hands full with that one, Georgia." She had no idea.

"Hermes must have a requirement that their drivers be devilishly handsome but ridiculously obtuse," I grinned in response, earning a genuine laugh from all four journalists.

Nice one, Georgia.

Georgia: 1 Journalists: 356,876

The elevator doors opened soon after that, and I nodded to the group before quickly running to the front of the hotel, trying to get as far away from the elevator as possible. At the front of the hotel was Henri, waiting for me in his Lamborghini. In my personal opinion, I felt like I had been getting into too many Lamborghinis recently, but the idea of parking in Monza gave me more anxiety than being in an elevator full of journalists – well, *almost*.

"About time, Peaches," Henri remarked as I hopped into the passenger seat.

"Sorry, there was a bit of a mishap back at the hotel, so getting ready took longer than expected." Henri put on a small, sympathetic smile. He had clearly been told of my predicament.

"So I heard. I'm very annoyed with them. They shouldn't have done that to you – or Luca."

"Or Luca? Forget Luca, he's enjoying it," I blurted out. I didn't want to tell my brother about the incident between Luca and me back in the hotel room – how I had been caught staring at his half-naked teammate. It was much too embarrassing, but I also was annoyed that Henri seemed to feel bad for Luca, who, I would say, seemed to be enjoying this – or was at least making the most of it.

"I'm sure that's not true, Peaches. I mean, back at HQ, Luca made a big stink about not wanting to share a room. He's much more of a private person than you might expect."

"If he is such a *private* person, why does he need all of this 'good' media attention to overwrite all of his *public* blunders?" I bit back.

Private person my ass. Henri just chuckled.

"Fine, fine, so Luca needs a little help. All I am trying to say is don't judge a book by its cover, all right. You might find you like the story after all."

Henri was good at giving these little 'pump you up' speeches. He had been giving them to me since I was a little girl. He was a lot cheesier than people realized, and I loved him for it – most of the time. I grumbled lightly in response, signaling that this wasn't a conversation I intended to continue.

"I mean, it's not like you have to kiss him or anything. Plus, you have separate rooms, right?" Henri kept his eyes on the road, but I could tell from his demeanor he was trying to balance the line of protective brother and teammate to Luca.

"We might have to share a bathroom, but I at least get my own bed and a room to hide from the ghost of Luca," I grinned back to Henri, who let out a chuckle.

The rest of the car ride was fairly uneventful. It was obvious that Henri wanted to keep discussing the Luca piece of the conversation, but he was at least able to take a hint this time. We discussed the track and my upcoming visit to the Hermes garage on qualifying day. Luca and I were to arrive each day together, hand in hand, at the track starting Thursday. Fortunately, the next time I would directly interact with him would be at a small press dinner on Friday evening that the drivers had all been invited to. Just a small reception from the Monza committee. Luca was expected to say a few words, and I was expected to sit next to him and smile like a pretty little flower that the sponsors could prune and then sell.

As Henri and I pulled up to the restaurant, I spotted Oliver already at the host desk. He was no doubt wearing some newly launched designer, and he looked delightful, as always. I hopped out of the car and ran over to my longtime friend and mentor, giving him a hug fit for a king.

"Well, if it isn't Edward's new archenemy," Oliver chuckled.

"Who..? Moi...?" I said casually, although the grin on my face gave me away. "I have no idea why Edward Davis would harbor any resentment towards me."

Oliver just snickered and pulled out his phone, showing me what was probably one of the best photos I had ever seen. It was a picture of Edward, a huge frown on his face, his brows furrowed, holding a Krispy Kreme donut box, which was inconveniently filled with just peaches, not a donut in sight. I knew they occasionally sent him boxes of donuts during race weekends to share with the team. He was always posting about them on his live stories.

"Of course, the muppet didn't even think to look at the contents inside the box before sharing the box on his social media feed, so needless to say, he was flabbergasted when he opened the box to show his fans, and all he saw was fruit – peaches, no less." At this point, Henri had parked the car and rejoined the group, peering over Oliver's shoulder to look at the photo of an annoyed Edward.

"You better watch out, Peaches; he's going to get you back for that one," Henri chuckled, and I just grinned in response. I had no doubt that Edward would wreak havoc on me at some point over the next few race weekends, but this prank felt pretty glorious, and I intended to bask in my success.

Georgia: 3 Edward: 2

Truthfully, it was Georgia: 4, but we decided not to count the hamster incident in Arthur's office.

"Well, whoever sent those to Edward has great taste in fruit," I replied simply, patting Oliver on the back as he let out another booming laugh.

"No doubt, I hear Peaches are all the rage these days," I heard a voice from behind me declare. I turned around and saw Éliott smiling at me, as dashing as ever. He was wearing a delightful blue button-down and some new designer pants. I gave my friend a warm smile, and he came over and gave me an equally warm hug. I could smell his cologne – cinnamon and strawberries. Éliott always smelled like home.

"Nice of you to join us, Éliott," I said sarcastically, motioning to my watch.

"A Frenchman is always a little late; you know this, Georgie," he grinned.

The hostess motioned for the group of us to follow her. We had a gorgeous table in the back of the restaurant, which would be a little more private and away from prying eyes, a relieving notion after being front and center of the media circus recently. I hadn't been able to truly talk to the guys in person since the charade with Luca had started, so I was excited to just relax and have an honest conversation without there being some media spin on it.

The four of us sat down, and Éliott ordered a nice bottle of red wine for us to share. It seemed as though my tradition of not driving before races had been thrown out the door the moment I started 'dating' Luca. *So be it; I wasn't a very good teetotaler anyway.*

"So, Georgie, how are things with Luca?" Éliott started; his eyes were full of mischief, but his voice had genuine care in his question. Éliott, over the years, had become as much of a close friend and confident as Henri had. After my brothers, he was always the person I would call with updates and questions.

"They are what they are," I responded dryly.

"Lizzie says things are going well. Fans, media, and sponsors love the two of you," Henri interjected quickly, nodding at me to continue.

"Yes, so I've heard," I said bluntly, earning a chuckle from Oliver. "Fortunately, we've barely had to spend time together. Just the occasional marketing stunt. But this weekend will be different; it's the first weekend we have to actively pretend to be a couple, hold hands... nonsense like that." The three of them immediately let out a laugh, and I knew it was at my last comment.

"Oh Georgie, you're the only girl in the world that would call handholding with her boyfriend *nonsense*." Éliott was very amused by how annoyed I was with the entire situation.

"Well, if he was a *real* boyfriend, I'm sure I'd feel less annoyed by it. Walking around, holding hands with the Devil doesn't exactly bring me joy," I hissed back.

Éliott had always been good at getting under my skin. It's why I found him to be quite annoying when we first met. He always seemed to be picking on me, teasing me when I was younger, but as I got older and gained the courage to give it back to him, our friendship quickly blossomed. And then, for a *very* short period, it blossomed into something more.

For years, the media had speculated about me and Éliott, and for what was a fun couple of months for two eighteen-year-olds, they would have been correct. I had spent so much time longing after Éliott when I was in high school that I had built up the type of relationship we would have in my head far beyond any realistic expectations. I was young and fancied myself in love.

Turns out our personalities were opposites, and not in the opposites-attract kind of way. We drove each other up the wall for all of six weeks and then quickly realized we were much better friends than lovers. As much as I had wanted to keep up the friends-with-benefits stint we had going, I knew in my heart I wasn't that kind of person. I also knew that if Henri had found out, he would have been furious with Éliott, and I didn't want to come between their friendship. Still, Éliott was my first love – *even if it was young love*. He was the first guy I had ever slept with, so he had a special place in my heart. His opinion meant something to me.

"Oh, Georgie..." Éliott just smiled back at me and shook his head, clearly a little amused by my answer.

"Why do you have so much beef with Luca anyway?" Oliver asked.

"I don't think there's enough time in the world to tell this story," Éliott said snidely. He was the only one who knew why Luca irked me; even Henri just believed it was because Luca was a pompous ass. That was certainly part of it, but the rest of the reason? It didn't seem like a good time to share with the group. We might be secluded in a restaurant, but there were eyes and ears everywhere. Plus, Luca's relationship with Henri was important. They were teammates, and they needed to be a united front. I didn't need to come in with my drama and add fuel to the fire.

"Oh, I don't know, his constant flirting with the W-series drivers, lack of respect for his fans, playboy lifestyle..." I raised my hand and started to count the reasons on my fingers in a dramatic display to Oliver. It was, to be fair, a little petty, but when it came to Luca Rossi, I couldn't stop myself.

If Luca was Luca 'Playboy' Rossi, I was Georgia 'Petty' Dubois.

"He did defend you at the press conference," Henri pointed out, to which I gave him a pointed look that screamed, *"Why are you defending Luca so much?"* I wondered if Henri spent this much time defending me to his teammate. I had just been stuck in a room with a man that I could only describe as insufferable, a man who had decided to use the entire suite like his private room, and all Henri had done the last few days was insist that I see Luca's side.

"True, and he pulled you out of the car. How did he even know you weren't feeling well?" Oliver asked, sneaking a glance at Henri, whose face was covered in guilt. I knew my brother felt guilty that he was too busy celebrating to see that I was on the verge of passing out. I told him that it wasn't his fault; he didn't have a responsibility to check on me after each race. I might be his sister, but at these races, I was simply another driver, and I wanted to be treated as such.

"I have no idea," I replied truthfully. "I never asked."

Éliott furrowed his brow at me, clearly a little unimpressed that I hadn't bothered to ask. Truth is, I didn't want to know. It scared me that Luca read my body language well enough to know that I was suffering in Miami. I knew deep down that I was too much of a coward to face the possibility that another Luca was hiding under the monster I had created, one that was perhaps observant, kind, and caring. *Because if there was another Luca, then this whole stunt was going to be a lot harder than expected.*

There was an awkward silence among the four of us, and no one knew what to say after that. Fortunately, the waiter arrived and took our order, and the food followed shortly after. The rest of the evening went by smoothly, full of Luca-less conversations. We sat and chatted for a while before Henri motioned to me that it was late, and we should go.

As we hopped into Henri's Lamborghini, I called out to Éliott and Oliver, "Good luck this weekend; I'll be sure to wave when I lap you!" They both gave me their middle fingers and laughed, I'm sure cursing me under their breath.

Henri walked me back up to my room, giving me a big squeeze before heading over to his room. When I opened the hotel room door, I crept in silently, truly hoping that it would be empty. I had probably drunk a little bit more than I should have, and I didn't want Luca to witness how much a couple of glasses of wine had affected me. Éliott had ordered a second bottle of red, and it tasted more like grape juice instead of wine, and I was not one to turn down delicious red wine. If kryptonite was Superman's weakness, a good bottle of red wine was definitely mine.

Fortunately for me, there was no sign of Luca anywhere.

Must have been held up at the sponsorship event Hermes F1 had asked him to attend, I mused, kicking off my heels, not particularly caring where they landed. I moved towards the plush couch, grabbing a bottle of water from the fridge on the way. I picked up my phone and scrolled through Instagram for a while, doing the one thing I should never do before a race – read the comments on the Valkyrie F1 social media page. I was, however, pleasantly surprised at the number of F1 Fan accounts speculating over our relationship, all of it positive.

"Why do they love me and Luca so much?" I grumbled, continuing to scroll until I could feel my eyes close. I knew I should probably get up, take my makeup off, and go to bed, but the couch was so inviting. I'm not sure how long I had dosed off, but I woke up to Luca coming into our shared living room. He was kicking off his shoes and staring at me, a big, stupid grin on his face. As I was sleeping, my dress had ridden its way up my body, and I realized my lacy black thong was on show for him.

"Why hide such sexy underwear from me, Cara?" he asked, and I tried to pull my dress down quickly. I could feel my cheeks heating up as his eyes drank up my embarrassment. The top of my dress had come down, and my bra was on display for the world to see. Luca started to move towards me, his eyes transfixed on mine as I sat still on the couch, slowly pulling my dress back into place. I knew I should get up and move, but my body felt frozen. Maybe it was the several glasses of wine, but part of me wanted to see what Luca would do if he approached me.

"Did you have a good dinner?" he asked casually. Here was Luca stalking towards me, pupils blown, the body language of a lion, and he wanted to have some casual chit-chat.

"I'm sure better than your sponsorship evening," I quipped. Luca was now standing in front of me, and his hand reached out and softly touched my cheek. Before I could react, Luca had moved to a seated position on the sofa, and he had pulled me onto his lap. I was now straddling his deliciously thick thighs as his strong hands held onto my waist while I sat on top of him, dress once again hiked up, all care in the world lost forever.

I knew I should be alarmed. I should get up off this sofa and go straight to bed before I did something I would regret — or *enjoy* a little too much. But I couldn't find it in myself to move. Luca's hands on my body felt delightful, and truth be told, I hadn't had a man grab me like this in years – not since my last boyfriend I had while living in America, and he wasn't a master of anything, especially not the art of making a woman climax.

Luca, on the other hand – it didn't take a genius to see that he knew exactly how to please a woman in bed. I knew there was a reason all of those women kept throwing themselves at him; it wasn't just his good looks and money. The entire paddock gossiped about how Luca knew his way around a woman's body.

"Would have been better if you were there to keep me company," he whispered gently into my ear. "Especially if I had known you had this lovely little lace set on."

I blushed, not entirely sure what to say to that. I knew I needed to get off of him and go to bed, but a small part of me wanted to find out what it was like to have Luca's hands all over me – and inside me.

Why shouldn't I reap the rewards of this fake relationship? I contemplated. It's not like I could go and date someone else while I was *fake dating* Luca, so my ability to get laid during this season was incredibly low. I dipped my head down, letting my lips rest mere inches from his plump, red lips.

"Well, maybe if you weren't too busy trying to annoy me, I'd have let you in on my secret. Play your cards right, and maybe I'll tell you what kind of underwear I actually plan to wear under my racing suit on Saturday."

With that, Luca raised one of his eyebrows, clearly interested in what I had to say, his face silently begging me to say more, and I tried to hide my smirk. I obviously was only going to wear my fire-proof underwear, but if I knew anything about Luca Rossi, I knew that he would spend the entire Sunday thinking about me breaking the rules and wearing a sexy purple lingerie set under my suit.

"You really are all talk and no play," he whispered. "I bet you haven't broken a single FIA rule in your life."

I rolled my eyes, but he had called my bluff on that one. I couldn't think of a rule I had broken. *I was a goody-two-shoes, and I was damn proud of it – most of the time.*

Luca took advantage of my inability to respond and pulled me in for a slow, passionate kiss, which I greedily returned. He slowly let his hands work their way up and down my body until one of his hands began to fiddle with the waistband of my lacy black thong. He looked at me, silently asking permission to let his fingers play with their target – like a cat playing with its food before dinner. I slowly nodded, letting myself give in to Luca. His fingers slid into my waistband and started to slowly stroke where I desperately wanted him most. As soon as he felt how wet I was, he slowly let one finger tease its way into my wetness, just barely sliding into me. I let out a loud moan, trying to push my hips down further on his finger, but his other arm was wrapped around my waist, stopping my movements.

"Ah ah ah, not so fast," he smirked. I loudly groaned, letting my frustration be known, but Luca just kept smirking, loving my frus-tration. Still, he allowed me some reprieve when he sunk his entire finger into me and started pumping in and out. Even if it was slow and excruciating, it felt incredible. Fortunately for me, my moans had earned me a second finger, which Luca started to pump a little faster. His face was now mere inches from mine, and I could feel his breath on my lips. His eyes were staring directly into mine as he watched my every expression as he finger fucked me with better precision than any other man I had slept with. Truth be told, the only man that had made me cum from his fingers was Éliott, but we were practically kids, freshly eighteen, so neither of us had any experience with what we truly liked. With Luca, however, you could tell this man had experience and knew exactly what he was doing as he curled his fingers in just the right spot. I could feel myself getting closer, and I started moaning louder.

"Oh, Luca... more... please..." I began to beg, a little embarrassed at how quickly I had fallen apart for him. He smirked at me and slipped a third finger inside of me, causing the lewdest moan I think I had ever heard to fall from my lips.

"Fuck, you're doing so good for me," he purred into my ear. I'm not sure if it was his soft praises in my ear or the fact that he had picked up the pace, but I was now hurdling toward what could only be described as a mind-numbing orgasm. As I reached my high, I screamed his name and tumbled quickly into my intense pleasure, holding onto Luca's shoulder as he fucked me through my entire orgasm.

All of a sudden, everything stopped.

It felt as though my body had been thrust from a heavenly dream, and instead of being on top of Luca's lap in the living room of our hotel suite, having just received an incredible orgasm from the Italian, Luca Rossi was standing in front of me, quirking his eyebrow up at me with a silent question – a cocky smirk on his lips.

Shit, shit, shit. Had I just dreamt that? I knew at that moment that I had failed to hide the panicked look on my face.

"Everything alright, Cara?" Luca asked in a low, deep voice. The simple question came from a voice that sounded more like a lion that had just trapped its prey and had decided to play with it versus someone who was *actually* concerned. Luca sounded like he had just won the lottery, and my embarrassment and confusion were his prize.

"Um... yeah... of-of course, why wouldn't it be?" I responded, albeit a little more flustered than I would have liked. "Just fell asleep on the couch, a bit of a pre-race tradition," I awkwardly lied to him.

Why would I say that? Who has a tradition like that? I scolded myself. *Moron.*

"Of course, sorry I woke you. You were just calling out to... someone, and I wasn't sure if you were having a nightmare." If Luca had truly thought I was having a nightmare, he wouldn't have said that last sentence with a grin so devilish it could have given the devil a run for its money.

"Nope." I said, popping the 'p' at the end. "Was just dreaming about getting onto the podium this weekend."

"Oh, well, that makes sense as to why you were calling out *my* name then," he grinned. "Assuming you were congratulating me on getting the top spot on the podium?"

I don't think, in the history of my twenty-four years, my cheeks had never gone that red. I, for the first time, had absolutely no idea what to say to Luca. My face blanched, and I could feel my palms become incredibly sweaty. I had been caught. The likelihood that Luca actually believed my little lie seemed as likely as the last-place team winning the constructors championship this year. It just wasn't happening.

Still, I wouldn't be myself if I didn't make sure to get the last word in, so I got up off of the couch with as much gusto as I could manage and looked Luca right in the eye as I replied, "Don't be silly, Luca, I was simply calling your name because I needed some help carrying back my champagne and trophy to the garage. Isn't that what boyfriends are for, even if they are fake?" I said cheekily.

Before he could respond, I headed straight for my room and closed the door loudly. Forget taking my make-up off; I wasn't coming out of this room until I had to tomorrow.

Chapter Eight

TRACK FIGHTS LEAD TO LATE NIGHTS

Georgia

As soon as the morning rolled around, I sprinted out of my room to the bathroom, showered and changed as quickly as I could, and then hurried back into my room, lest I see Luca in the flesh – *or towel* – again. I wasn't sure what was more horrifying to me, the fact that I had a sex dream about Luca Rossi or that Luca Rossi had caught me having a sex dream about him.

The latter, it was definitely the latter.

God, this isn't going to do anything to help his inflated ego, I thought to myself.

How was I supposed to face Luca this morning or any other time of day, for that matter? I looked down at my watch to see the time – 8:00 a.m.

Great, just one hour before Luca and I have to meet downstairs to hop in my car.

Today was the official start of the hoax. Luca and I were to arrive at the track together, hand in hand, like a newly in love couple. Because he had so many fans waiting for him, Hermes had asked that we come earlier than usual, which meant I was also going to be dragged around the paddock early each day.

Once I was done changing, I crept out of my room and turned my head to Luca's room, only to notice that his door was open, as was the bathroom door.

Oh, thank god, he must be downstairs having breakfast, I sighed to myself, relieved because it meant I could sneak down to breakfast without disturbing Luca. I grabbed my Valkyrie bag, which was a beautifully designed Ted Baker shoulder bag, packed it full of my things for the day, and headed to the elevator.

Please be empty, please be empty, I silently prayed to whatever God was listening. As I heard the ding on the elevator, I looked up at the open elevator doors and realized one thing – I had definitely wronged someone in a past life.

There, standing in front of me, was Luca Rossi's parents. *Is the elevator where fun goes to die?*

His mom saw me and put her hand over the elevator doors to stop them from closing as his father waved for me to come in.

"Georgie Pie!" his mom exclaimed. I felt slightly taken aback by how comfortable she felt using my nickname, but I did my best to hide my shock. "How lovely to see you. You look dashing in this Valkyrie outfit. They really do know how to dress you and Lily." As annoyed as I wanted to be at this situation, Luca's mother's smile was warm and incredibly inviting.

"Morning," I responded casually, hopping into the elevator. Luca's father gave me a warm smile as he patted me on the back.

"Oh good, Luca wasn't sure if you'd be joining us for breakfast. Said you were feeling a bit poorly last night. Hope you are feeling better," he said with a sympathetic smile.

In truth, I had no idea what to say to that, and I did my best to stop my cheeks from turning red, but I knew they were showing a bit of a red tint as Luca's mom tilted her head, looking at me with those gorgeous brown eyes. I *definitely* didn't want Luca's parents to know that I had a sex dream about their son last night.

"Um... yes, all good, just needed a solid night's sleep."

How can I get out of breakfast with the Rossi's? How can I get out of breakfast with the Rossi's? I questioned over and over again. I ran through various scenarios, trying to think of an excuse believable enough that wouldn't insult their intelligence. Unfortunately for me, before I could think of any excuse worthy of Luca's incredibly endearing parents, the elevator doors opened, and his mom linked her arms to mine, gracefully dragging me out of the elevator.

"Luca has a table for us downstairs," she exclaimed. Her cheeriness was starting to get on my nerves, but I nodded in response. As we entered the restaurant, I could see a look of surprise on Luca's face as he sat at a table for three people, not four.

"Luca, look who we ran into in the elevator. Get the hostess to pull up an extra chair," Luca Sr. called out to his son. For a moment, it looked like Luca was going to deny his father's request, but after a few moments of staring at me in disbelief, he trotted over to the host stand and asked for a fourth chair to be placed at the table. His mother shuffled me into a chair and grabbed my bag, placing it under the table.

"I am just so excited for this weekend, " she exclaimed. "It's just lovely to be back in Italy. Flash has been looking forward to this weekend ever since we had the PR photo event at the Monza track a few months ago."

I wasn't entirely sure how to respond to that, but I understood where she was coming from; I was equally excited for Monaco's Grand Prix. A racer's home grand prix was truly the crown jewel of the season for that racer, and winning it? That was a dream every driver had, a dream to win their home race in front of their closest friends and family.

The hostess pulled up the fourth chair next to me, and Luca awkwardly sat in it, clearly trying to regain his composure. There was a lot of pressure on him this weekend, and I could tell he wasn't prepared to have breakfast with his pretend girlfriend quite yet. I gave him a small smile, an apology of sorts.

I immediately regretted it when he winked back at me, a sultry smile forming on his lips as he whispered, "Hope you were able to get some proper rest last night. Wouldn't want you to be distracted this weekend." The twinkle in his eye was unmistakable – Luca Rossi was not going to let this go anytime soon.

I frowned at him, "Don't be silly; nothing can distract me from beating you this weekend." While I thought I had said that in a voice low enough that his parents couldn't hear, clearly I had missed the mark because his father let out a big laugh.

"Oh, Flash, you have some real competition this weekend, I see. Good! I look forward to an exciting race. That Valkyrie F1 car has incredible speed, and your girlfriend clearly knows how to drive her car." I blushed slightly at his father's reference to me being Luca's girlfriend. I knew people would be calling me his girlfriend pretty consistently by the end of the day, but hearing it for the first time, out of his father's mouth, no less, left me with a weird feeling that was a mixture of butterflies and dread.

Today was going to be different; I knew that. I had never arrived at a track as someone's girlfriend, only ever as a driver, and while I shouldn't feel any different about walking into the paddock, I couldn't help but immediately think of the media circus that focused on the driver's girlfriends. Lauren, Edward's girlfriend, often complained about it. It was a constant assessment of what they wore and how they acted around their boyfriends – a constant evaluation from the media and public of '*is this girlfriend good enough for this driver that none of us actually knows*.'

As I considered the pressures of being both a driver and a driver's girlfriend, my hunger started to simmer. I knew I should eat something, but the thought of putting food in my body when I had this huge wave of anxiety made me want to throw up. I'm not sure if Luca noticed my shift in demeanor, but I suddenly felt a hand on my leg.

The hand squeezed my leg lightly, and I heard Luca whisper, "You should have a little more breakfast; it's going to be a warm one today, and greeting all of *my* fans will be more exhausting than you know." He gave me a small smirk, clearly trying to make light of the situation, which a small part of me appreciated. Much to my – *brief*

– disappointment, his hand quickly removed itself from my thigh, and Luca went back to his breakfast.

I gave him a pointed glare, trying not to let his parents see, but I picked up another spoonful of oatmeal and did my best to finish the bowl. Luca was right; our lunch in the Hermes paddock wasn't scheduled until late afternoon, so I had to survive a lot of media until then. The four of us sat in silence a few moments longer before I finally found my voice.

"So I know that you have all been calling him Flash since he was a little boy, but I am curious, where did the nickname come from?"

"Ahh, a good question," his father pondered, taking one more bite of his eggs before setting down his fork. "I wish I could say it had a long, riveting story, but it's quite simple, actually. You see, as a child, Luca was obsessed with racing his go-kart, but his mother was always worried about him racing – even karts can be dangerous. So, in order to smooth his mother's worries, he would tell his mother before every race, *'Don't worry, Mama, I'll be back in a flash.'* An American slogan he had heard on TV, but it had stuck with him. Before long, it had become the slogan the family had adopted, and before we knew it, we just started calling him Flash at races. It was the fans that had adopted the lightning bolt logo once he got into Formula 1, and it stuck from there." Luca looked a little embarrassed at his father's retelling of the story – but he continued eating as if nothing was wrong, although his slightly red cheeks told another story.

"I can only imagine what a cute momma's boy little Luca was." I gave Luca a quick smile at my attempted jab, but his mother just looked at him with the most loving expression, and he smiled back at her; for a moment, my heart warmed at their interaction.

So Luca "Playboy" Rossi was also Luca "Momma's Boy" Rossi – interesting.

As 9 a.m. rolled around, Luca signaled to me that it was time to go by tapping on his watch. We said our goodbyes to his parents, who said they couldn't wait to see us for lunch and then headed to the front of the hotel where my beautiful blue Veyron was waiting for me. Isabelle had wanted to put us in a Volkswagen Beetle, but Hermes said absolutely not. I was torn because the look on Luca's face when he realized that we were getting into a Beetle would have been hilarious, but on the other end, I never turned down the opportunity to drive the new Veyron. As we hopped into the car, Luca slowly slid into the passenger seat, clearly annoyed that we weren't in his black Lamborghini.

"Don't worry, Luca, you won't catch a disease from the car," I chuckled at his hesitancy. He smirked and rolled his eyes, buckling his seat belt in the process.

"So, I was told we, uh, needed to go through some more questions since we'll be so public this weekend," Luca said, his voice a little uneasy. I was shocked at his change in demeanor. Luca had always been so cocky, so *Mr. Confident*, it was odd to hear his voice wavering with uncertainty.

"Sure, fire away."

"When did you know you wanted to be a Formula 1 driver?" he asked.

"When I was five, our father took us to the Monaco Grand Prix. It is still, to this day, one of the best weekends of my life. I remember it like it was yesterday. The cars were shiny and beautiful, the weather was incredibly sunny, and my father held me for most of the race, pointing out the different cars and explaining the racetrack to me. I knew in that moment that I wanted to be a race car driver, wanted to make him proud." There was a comfortable silence in the air as if Luca was considering what I had said.

"I guess I always just knew I was going to be a professional driver since my dad was one," he said simply, shrugging his shoulders. I didn't quite know what to say to that, but I supposed it made sense, all things considered. I wondered what Luca would have been if his dad hadn't been an F1 champion, but I decided not to ask. Luca pulled out another sheet of paper from his pocket and read the question.

"What is your favorite pasta?" As he said it, I couldn't help but let out a snort.

"They really want us to know this one, don't they?" I teased, trying to lighten the mood. "Mine is spaghetti, a total classic. Henri makes an incredible spaghetti bolognese. Whenever we have a family dinner night at his, he makes it for us with the most delicious Texas toast, a recipe he learned when we visited our family in America."

"Henri a cook? Now that I wouldn't have guessed," Luca huffed out, a little shocked at my revelation. "I like macaroni; it's simple, classic, and easy to make, no matter the sauce."

How practical of him, I thought to myself. Luca didn't strike me as a mac and cheese kind of guy, but now all I could picture was Luca shoveling mac and cheese into his face like a five-year-old – with jalapeños on top, of course. I let out a small laugh at the image.

"Is my pasta funny?" he scoffed, apparently a little offended.

"No, no, I'm sure grown men eat mac and cheese all the time," I teased. He rolled his eyes and went to say something but decided to keep his mouth shut as we arrived at the paddock. As we entered the parking lot, I could see fans everywhere – waiting for a driver to arrive.

"Here we go," I heard Luca whisper to himself; his voice was almost inaudible, and I could see the weight of the situation in his eyes. The fans adored him, and that pressure was a monster that was hard to describe.

I took a deep breath, put on the biggest smile that I could muster, and stepped out of the car. I looked at the crowd that was starting to form around the cars and barricades.

Italy really does bring out a crowd, I thought to myself, once again stealing a glance at Luca, who was staring at the endless sea of fans. After a few more moments, Luca stepped out of my passenger side door and waved, sending the crowd into a frenzy. All of a sudden, there was screaming and cheering from all directions, cheering on Luca, asking for signatures and photos. Luca walked to the trunk and took out my bag and his, carefully handing me my bag. I put the strap over my shoulders and then looked at him, a small smile on my face.

Luca knew what that meant – it was time to give the people

what they wanted. He looked down at our hands and grabbed mine, interlocking our fingers with one another. He looked back up into my eyes and smiled that huge Cheshire cat grin.

"Ready to walk down?" he asked. I just nodded in response and let Luca lead us toward the paddock gates, the both of us signing merchandise and taking selfies with as many fans as we could.

"Georgia! Georgia! Are you and Luca dating?" I looked down at the voice to see a young girl brightly smiling up at me, a Valkyrie cap in her hands. Before I could answer, Luca bent down and gave her a big smile.

"Snagged me the best racer on the grid, don't you think?" he grinned at the little girl, and she chuckled as she asked for a selfie with the two of us, which we happily obliged.

The second best part of being a racing driver was interacting with my young female fans. Watching their eyes glow up when I spoke to them reminded me why I was doing this. Change had to happen in this sport, and I was proud of myself for leading the way with Lily. *Women were no longer grid girls – we were drivers, engineers, and Team Principals.*

Luca and I made our way through the barricade of fans and to the security entrance of the paddock walkway, still hand in hand. As Luca and I walked through, Wilmington F1 Team driver Edward, in his ridiculous bright green-colored hoodie, came bounding over to us, like a golden retriever who had just seen his newest play toy.

"Well, well, well, if it isn't F1's hottest new couple!" Edward called out to us, a large smile on his face as he wiggled his eyebrows at the two of us. "I don't know why Henri gets the credit for this. I feel like I should have the honors," he announced proudly. Luca poked him in the stomach, reminding him not to be too loud. We didn't need Edward Davis spoiling this for us. I was already doing a good job of that myself.

"Why are you here so early? Team principal trying to keep a short leash on you?" I teased.

"Just getting some extra debriefing on the breaks this morning, figured I might as well come in early and see the Luca Rossi madness unfold." Luca scoffed at that, batting Edward over the head.

"I hear the three of us will all be in the same press conference this morning; wonder how that could have happened," Edward smirked. The FIA was known for trying to stir the pot, especially if it meant more people would watch the pre-race media coverage.

"Never a dull moment with the FIA," I groaned. "Well, as lovely as it's been chatting with you, Luca and I have media duties to attend to," I said pointedly, pulling Luca away with me.

"I'll see you at the press conference," Luca yelled back in his thick Italian accent. Edward waved at us, chuckling away as he watched me pull Luca to the Valkyrie paddock entrance. As we rounded the corner and stepped inside the garage, I dropped his hand in a show of both frustration and pleasure that this first charade was over – for now.

"Pick you up at 11!" Luca yelled back at me as I huffed it towards my driver's room.

I spent the next ninety minutes being debriefed by the team on various activities for the weekend. After the press conference, I was to come back to the garage, get more strategy debriefs, and then get lunch at the Hermes hospitality center with Henri and Luca – another publicity stunt to show just how excited my brother was for this budding relationship. Of course, this one was Henri's idea, which was truly frustrating to me. He knew I had to spend all this time in a room with Luca; now, I had to give him my lunch break, too. Henri said that he was just trying to use the situation to see me more, which sounded sweet at the time but was also frustrating as hell.

Eleven o'clock rolled around, and Luca, as promised, was standing outside of the Valkyrie garage waiting for me. The press conference was to start at 11:15, and Lizzie and Matteo wanted us to arrive on time as a unified front, hand in hand, like a sappy couple in love. As we high-tailed it to the press conference, Lizzie walked beside Luca, happily chatting away with him as if they had been best friends for years. If Luca was annoyed by her constant chatter, he didn't show it, instead responding to her in fuller sentences than I think I had ever gotten out of him.

I walked into the press conference room, and of course, in addition to Edward, sat Éliott, a large smile on his face when he saw Luca and I walk into the room. They had strategically sat in the two leftmost seats, while Oscar Parker, another British driver who drove for the Rennen F1 Team, sat in the rightmost seat, leaving the two seats in the middle for Luca and me. I looked straight at Edward, shooting death glares in his direction, but he just kept chatting to Éliott, pretending not to notice me.

Looks like Edward has joined the list of people enjoying this a little too much.

As I went to take the middle seat, Michael Clifton, F1 TV's lead presenter, came up to me with a large grin on his face and whispered, "Glad you and Luca worked it out." He gave me a subtle wink as I smiled at him, doing my best to hide my gritted teeth.

Great, so Michael had heard me muttering away in the elevator. I just nodded and gave him a small smile, truly unsure of what to say but feeling a bit of relief that I had gotten away with that earlier blunder.

I sat in the middle seat, nicely tucked between Edward and Luca, and waited for the press conference to begin. Lizzie was in the back, waving her hands at my face, indicating that I needed to smile. Before I had left the paddock, Isabelle had reminded me, *"People in happy relationships smile, Georgia,"* to which I just flicked her off – my team principal – probably not the brightest move for my career.

Michael called the press conference into order and started the conversation with a talk on porpoising, something that had truthfully been affecting all of the drivers. Oscar, of course, had plenty to say on the matter, although I probably would too if I was driving a Rennen F1 car. The conversations continued to flow, with the presenter finally stopping at me.

"So, Georgia, we hear you are feeling better this week. How are things?"

"Good," I responded slowly, letting my eyes dart to Lizzie for reassurance. She nodded, motioning for me to go on. "I'm 100% recovered and looking forward to getting into the car tomorrow. We have some new upgrades which I think are going to truly bring something interesting to the race."

"Going to make sure you have enough water this time?" the commentator joked, clearly trying to poke fun at my expense from the last race. I just frowned.

Was this what we were calling journalism these days? I could feel Luca about to say something, but I put my hand out, signaling that I had this.

"Now, now, Jeremy, you know I can't give away Valkyrie race secrets," I said playfully, batting my eyes just a bit at the journalist, who awkwardly chuckled in response, clearly expecting to get a rise out of me. He looked a bit disappointed. *Good.*

Out of the corner of my eye, I could see Luca's eyes narrow at the journalist, a small grin forming on his lips. I'm not sure what it was, but something about having Luca there gave me the encouragement and confidence I needed to engage with the media. Seeing Luca about to butt in on my behalf might be the push I needed to engage with the journalists. Instead of sulking away or yelling, I dared to quip back at them, a little hint that they should leave me alone, without actually saying it.

Maybe Isabelle was right; having Luca Rossi teach me how to do media might be a good thing.

After the press conference, I trudged my way back to the Valkyrie paddock with Lizzie trailing behind me. Once the lunch at Hermes was complete, I would be free of Luca until this evening. Luca had a gig tonight with one of the big F1 podcasts. They were doing a live evening show with Luca, something they tried to do with all the racers at their home race, sort of a home race live series where fans were invited and got to submit questions beforehand. They had already organized one with me and Henri next week in Monaco.

Something else to look forward to, I thought sarcastically.

No one at Hermes F1 had thought to inform Lizzie before today, and as much as I didn't want to go to Luca's podcast session, Lizzie was right: I had to show up to Luca's live podcast. Fortunately, I had been let off from the after party, with an excuse that I had an incredibly early sponsorship meeting with VIPs. A small "*I'm sorry*" that Isabelle had gifted me with after she told me my evening would be spent among a group of fans, with me *pretending* to fawn over Luca while everyone around me *was actually* fawning over Luca.

At least Henri and Éliott had offered to go, so all wasn't lost.

Luca had arrived early to prep for the podcast, so Henri, Éliott, and I were ushered into a VIP room with some champagne, something I decided to definitely take advantage of. If I was going to listen to Luca drone on about Hermes for an hour, I might as well be tipsy for it.

The show hosts were nice enough. I figured they were overanalyzing Luca and me, trying to spot any inconsistencies in our behavior. Fortunately for Luca, he was a pro at winning over the media, and after a few awkward exchanges, things started to feel a bit more normal. About five minutes before the show started, the coordinator moved the three of us into our seats at the front. As we walked in, the crowd cheered, and the three of us took a few selfies along the way.

The hosts opened up with a nice bio about Luca, his history of karting, and his entry into Formula 1. They discussed his father and his life growing up as an Italian driver, plus his undying love for AC Milan. At about the forty-five-minute mark, I started to feel some relief; maybe the podcast hosts weren't planning on mentioning our relationship. I knew that was a bunch of wishful thinking because, as if on queue, the podcast host cleared his throat, indicating we were about to change the subject.

"So Luca, rumor has it that F1's most eligible bachelor is no longer single," the podcast presenter said slyly, wiggling his eyebrows at Luca, making the audience laugh. I grimaced a bit, but Henri poked my side, reminding me that we were in public.

"Ooh, you heard that rumor too," Luca chucked, winking at me from the stage. I could hear a couple of girls behind me whisper about how lucky I was.

"I mean, can you blame me? With a smile that gorgeous and talent that enormous, it was pretty easy to see that Georgia was someone special." The audience 'ooh'd and awed' at Luca's comment, completely enamored by the Italian on stage. I did my best not to roll my eyes, hoping there weren't cameras pointed at me.

Bunch of crap, I thought to myself.

"I'm sure it wasn't easy getting her brother's approval, even if he is your teammate?' the presented joke, gesturing to Henri in the audience, who was giving Luca a sly smirk.

Oh, Henri, I thought to myself, *always ready to play the part of Hermes' golden boy.*

"Well, I was basically her biggest fan from the day she started. I did my best to drop hints to Henri over pre-season, but by Imola, I finally had to tell him – well, *beg* him – to let me have a chance. Henri, of course, told me the usual, you know, if I hurt his sister, he would make sure to ram his car into the back of mine. I told him not to worry; I'm sure his sister would beat him to it... I mean, she is the faster Dubois driver, after all." Luca chuckled at his comment, and Henri waved him off, much to the audience's amusement.

Have they practiced this already? I thought to myself. I could just picture Francesco, dressed in his Hermes F1 gear, ignoring the clipboard he was holding full of racing strategy, instead educating Luca and Henri on what they were supposed to say during these media exchanges.

"You know, I gotta say, we were all kind of shocked when we saw you guys walk hand in hand into the paddock today. Not to be rude, but we didn't think you could pull such a lovely lady like Georgia," the presented laughed.

I wanted to throw something at the presenter. Why didn't he

just say what he actually wanted to say: *How did Georgia Dubois manage to bag dashing, attractive playboy Luca Rossi? How did she manage to tame F1's heartthrob? Why had Luca Rossi settled for Little Ms. Sassy Dubois?*

If only he knew the truth.

"What, you saying she's out of my league?" Luca quipped back, causing the audience to erupt into laughter. "You know, I was as shocked as you were. You see, the rest of the world sees Georgie as this quiet, boring racing driver who only has eyes for winning, everything else be damned. But the Georgie I know, it couldn't be further from the truth." I closed my eyes, unable to bear the thought of where Luca was going with this one.

"Oh?" The presented asked, motioning for Luca to continue.

"I think what really won me over is her ability to always have a witty remark handy... and her pranks. I have never met someone as quick-witted as Georgie. And her pranks on Edward? The stuff of legends. You should ask him about them when you have him on before Silverstone. Absolutely hilarious.

As for Georgie, you'll have to ask her in Monaco why she's dating me 'cause I certainly have no idea; she must be blind!" Luca shrugged his shoulders at the audience as they playfully booed his last remark.

I could feel my cheeks heating up, and a blush was taking over my face. I guess I shouldn't have been surprised that Luca knew about my pranks on Edward; he was Edward's teammate for years at Wilmington, and I had played some great pranks on Edward, hence my 'semi-enforced' ban at the Wilmington F1 garage.

"Georgie Dubois a prankster? Now that is definitely something we'll have to discuss next race, Henri," the presented announced, wagging his finger toward my brother.

Henri just laughed and nodded, yelling back at the podcaster, "Oh, do I have some stories to tell!" I slapped Henri on the shoulder and gave him a dirty look, much to Éliott's amusement.

"Now, let's talk about Miami. When Georgia pulled up into the P3 spot, it was as if you already knew she wasn't feeling well. Fans have speculated that the teams put a radio for you to chat inside the cars – any truth to that?"

Now, I really wanted to roll my eyes. As if Valkyrie would allow me the extra weight so I could chat to my boyfriend. Who did he think this team was run by, middle school girls? I heard Éliott very lightly chuckle next to me, clearly enjoying the ridiculousness of the F1 podcaster. We barely got water; the engineers weren't about to add in 'relationship radios.'

Luca did his best to chuckle through that one. At first, I thought his hesitancy to answer the question was because he was set aback by the ridiculous fan theory, but his answer was even more surprising.

"No, no, believe me, I don't need anyone hearing me chatter to myself throughout the race; I think I'd be called certifiably insane," he laughed, his face slowly turning more serious. "Georgie, after each race where she gets a podium, does this cute jump out of the car; she puts both her hands on the bars and hops out of the car with what you can only tell is a huge smile on her face. Both of her arms go flying into the air, and she does this silly 'window washing' dance. It's really quite adorable. When she didn't immediately hop out of the car, I just knew something was wrong. If there's something I know about the Dubois twins, it's that they're the first to congratulate each other. It doesn't matter who has won."

As the audience around me started to ooh and awe, I felt completely frozen, shocked by the admission from Luca. Had he really noticed that about me? I could feel Henri harden next to me, his back straightening up as he contemplated Luca's words, likely hating himself for not noticing this at the Miami race. Henri still wasn't over the fact that Luca had come to my rescue first. Whether I was independent or not, Henri was always going to be protective of me. Even Éliott fiddled with his hands, unsure of what to say.

"So, did you know this was the reason?" Éliott whispered into my ear. I just shook my head lightly, trying to keep the smile Isabelle had told me to wear plastered to my face.

Truthfully, at that moment, I was feeling incredibly confused.

When did Luca start caring enough to notice this? What else had Luca noticed about me? That was the real question I wanted answered, but I knew I was going to have to wait patiently for that one.

"What a true gentleman, Luca," the presented preened, slapping him on the back. "We're glad Georgia is alright, and we're definitely looking forward to seeing the two of you fight it out on the race-track. This is our last question of the night, and then we'll let you go. Do you think your fights on track will affect your relationship at all? You're both title contenders this year. Has any animosity on the track spilled over to off-track drama?" I did my best to hide my scoff as Henri elbowed me in the side.

"Not at all, we're both fierce competitors on the track, that's true, but the fact is, every moment I spend with Georgie makes me a better race car driver, I mean hell, even a better person," he said softly. Luca was now looking directly at me, his lovely brown eyes felt like they were looking deep into my soul. I felt frozen as I stared back, silently daring Luca to end this with something sarcastic or witty. Anything to make these butterflies go away – anything to remind myself why Luca Rossi was the enemy.

"For example, our battles on the track make me better at driving defensively. When we spend our dinners chatting about the engineering makeup of a car, I learn something new about how to better manage a Formula 1 car. And when we spend an evening snuggling and watching Atonement, her favorite movie, I get this incredible peacefulness that transcends into race weekends."

Luca paused for a quick second, as if he was contemplating what his last comment would be. Slowly, a smirk crept up onto his lips as he added, "Plus, the more fighting we do on the track, the more making up we get to do off the track."

I could feel my cheeks go bright red, and I impulsively put my hands over my face, trying to hide my redness as much as possible. The crowd burst into applause and fits of laughter, with much of the audience jumping from their seats in a standing ovation for Luca as the announcer got up from the desk and shook Luca's hand, still laughing loudly from Luca's final joke.

I was pissed. Pissed that while Luca had ended it with something sarcastic and witty, just as I had hoped, the butterflies I had felt a few moments ago hadn't left; in fact, they had gotten stronger.

Despising the womanizing, egocentric Luca was easy, but this Luca? This was going to be harder than I thought.

Chapter Nine

NEVER UNDERESTIMATE GEORGIA DUBOIS

Georgia

After the podcast event last night, Éliott and Henri had stopped by my room for a nightcap. There had been considerable amounts of teasing from the Frenchman, most of which I tried to ignore. Still, even as I woke up with a fresh head this morning, there was one comment I couldn't ignore from Éliott: *"Either Luca is the best actor on the grid, or I would say someone has a crush on you."*

I knew Éliott had meant it teasingly, but that comment stuck to me like glue. *Why had Luca said so many nice things?* We were still new in our relationship; he could have just made a few hints and played it off. Instead, the Italian driver doubled down and dedicated the end of the segment to our relationship.

I picked up my phone from the charger and opened Instagram, trying to take my mind off of the man who was starting to consume my thoughts this morning. I had no idea why I thought social media would be an escape from my relationship. As soon as I opened Instagram, my search page was flooded with photos of Luca and me – F1 page after F1 page full of comments about the podcast.

"Since when did the entire world decide to start listening to podcasts?" I grumbled to myself.

I couldn't help but roll my eyes as I came across a photo of us holding hands – well, what seemed like hundreds of pictures of us holding hands. I guess Lizzie was right; the media and fans were going to eat this up.

Not the worst thing, I thought to myself. We wanted to sell this, and my, oh, my, the fans were buying what we were selling. I stopped at a particular post; it was about the podcast from last night.

LightsOutPodcast

Liked by Valkyrie F1 Team and 30k others

LightsOutPodcast Last night Luca Rossi stopped by to tell us about his racing dreams and aspirations... and most importantly, his spicy relationship with Georgia Dubois, both on and off the track!

Filtering through the Instagram comments, I was pleasantly surprised that fans were receptive to Luca's comments about me. After last night's talk, I was worried that the hate towards me would just increase; jealous fans were always a problem, but to my surprise, the comments were focused on how Luca was good for me and how he had already made me a more likable person.

Well, that is the whole fucking point of this, I thought to myself, trying not to take too much offense. A part of me *was* pleased that this stunt was working; the sooner it worked, the sooner I could be rid of him. I heard some noise from the living room and turned to my alarm clock. 7:00 a.m. on the dot. I could still get another hour of sleep since Luca and I weren't planning on leaving until 9:00 a.m.

Why on earth is Luca up and awake? I hadn't heard him come in last night, so I assumed that he had come back reasonably late.

I jumped out of bed and headed to the door of my room, incredibly curious to see why the world's worst morning person was awake. I opened it slightly, only to see Luca Rossi sitting on the sofa, his head in his hands, mumbling quietly to himself. He was rocking back and forth, a look of stress on what little parts of his face I could see. I shut the door slightly, not entirely sure what to do. It seemed like a private moment, and as much as Luca annoyed me, I didn't feel as though it was right to invade his personal moment.

About a minute later, I heard the bathroom door close. I took that as my queue and tip-toed out into the living room, making my way to the little kitchen. I filled my pour-over kettle with water and began to grind the coffee beans. This week's coffee beans were from a little roaster in Denver, Colorado, that I had adored, a gift from Oliver Williams, who had recently visited some friends up in the mountains. As I was pouring the water over my coffee beans, I saw Luca leave the bathroom, his shirt now in his hands. I couldn't help but wonder if Luca walked around shirtless just to annoy me.

I opened my mouth to make a rude comment about this being a public living room where clothes were necessary, but as his face turned around, I could see that his eyes were red and puffy, slightly sunken in. Not the usual bright, determined eyes that I was used to from the Italian. I couldn't remember a time when I had seen Luca cry, not even after his first win last year. I quickly shut my mouth as Luca simply nodded to me, turning back towards his bedroom.

I'm not sure what prompted me to call out to him; maybe it was because I had experienced the look he had on his face more times than I could count. Anxiety was natural in the racing community, and I couldn't imagine what this home race meant to him, the pressure that he was under. He had never won before at Monza; he had barely even finished a race here, constant DNF after DNF in recent years. Now, he had a first-class car and a real opportunity to win.

"Want some coffee? There's enough for two here," I called out to him. Truth was, the way I drank coffee, there was barely enough for one, but I figured the gesture was probably more important than my coffee addiction.

I could see Luca contemplating my offer, his eyes flickering up and down from the kitchen to his toes. Much to my surprise, he nodded, taking a seat on the sofa – still shirtless. I tried not to stare at him; he was clearly not feeling well, and he certainly didn't need me ogling him. Although something told me that would, in fact, make him feel better.

As soon as the coffee was ready, I handed him a cup and sat down next to him, letting the silence sift across the room. I didn't know what to say and considered that maybe I didn't need to say anything at all. Sometimes, the act of having someone near you was enough.

After a few more minutes of sipping our coffee in silence, Luca finally spoke up. "I'm surprised you take your coffee black."

"I would never insult a coffee roaster by putting cream and sugar into my coffee," I gasped, pretending to sound offended, although I was slightly offended on behalf of coffee everywhere.

"A woman of much mystery," Luca chuckled.

I let a few more moments go by, and then I gathered as much courage as I could to ask about the elephant in the room. "You feeling ok today?"

Luca diverted his beautiful brown eyes from mine, letting out a deep breath. It was as if he had wanted me to ask – like he was too scared to volunteer what he was keeping to himself without my permission.

"Just a lot on my mind, you know, being the home race and all. I have never wanted to win so badly. There are so many expectations for me today – expectations from family, friends, the team, and even the country. An Italian driver hasn't won at home in well over a decade." It's as if the words just kept spilling out of him – like Luca was realizing as every word left his mouth, the load on his mind was a little easier. I just sat and listened, internally processing everything he said. I could feel his words in my heart because I had the same feelings about Monaco.

"Sometimes I feel like it's all too much, like it would just be easier if my car crashed, and then I wouldn't have to face the possibility of completing the race, the possibility of not even making it to the podium." His last comment shocked me a bit, although part of me understood. I had never seen Luca this vulnerable before, so I took in what he said and thought carefully about my next statement.

"The only person that you can let down is yourself," I said finally. "You don't owe anyone anything. You drive for you. You're many things, Luca, but you aren't a coward. You're going to drive this weekend with the same amount of passion you have for your country, and I think it'll transpire into something you'll be proud of."

Luca finally looked up; his gaze felt like it was starting to burn a hole into my mind. For a moment, his eyes drifted to my lips, and I could feel butterflies once again forming in my stomach as Luca licked his lips, his face starting to soften and his eyes just ever so slightly darkening. As the silence continued to sit comfortably over us, I could see Luca begin to slowly lean in, his eyes burning into mine with his teeth slightly biting on his bottom lip.

Is Luca Rossi going to kiss me? I panicked for a bit and then considered why I hadn't leaned away, why I was still staring at him. *Did I want him to kiss me?*

Before either of us could process what was about to happen, a loud banging sound came from our doorway. Luca and I both jumped, and Luca pulled back from me, his cheeks a little red now, as if he was slightly embarrassed by the intense moment we had just shared.

"Georgie, any chance you're up?" I heard Lily on the other end of the door.

I quickly scrambled from my spot on the sofa. Lily and I were close, but it was unusual to hear her knocking on my door at 7:30 in the morning. I opened the door for her, and there stood in front of me was a slightly ruffled Lily.

"You alright, Lil?" I asked, looking her up and down, checking for any visible signs of injury. She nodded shyly, clearly a little embarrassed that she had come to my room so early while I was still in my pajamas. I opened the door and motioned for her to come in.

I had forgotten that Luca was sitting on the sofa – *shirtless* – wearing some skimpy soft Puma shorts as pajamas, which became evident at the reddening on Lily's face.

"Oh, sorry if I am interrupting something!" Lily chuckled, a slight smirk forming on her face. I gave her a look that told her not to even think about it, and she took a seat in the armchair across from the couch. I went back to the kitchen and began making a second round of coffee.

"I was, uh... just on a run and thought I would stop by. I listened to the podcast last night; really funny, Luca," she giggled. I could see Lily's eyes give him one more once over as she blushed a bit. Luca grinned, clearly pleased that Lily wasn't quite as good as I was at hiding her ogling. As I watched their interaction, I felt a slight twinge of jealousy form in the pit of my stomach. Luca might be a fake boyfriend, but Lily could at least not silently flirt with him in front of me. I couldn't blame her, though. Luca was incredibly attractive and a shirtless Luca? Well, he was just hot.

"The podcast was a good time," Luca agreed, finishing his cup of coffee. Once the first round of coffee was finished, I poured everyone a second cup and sat back down on the couch, this time slightly closer to Luca than before, as if to remind Lily who he was actually fake dating.

The internal battle within me had lost – jealousy had won.

"I mean, I appreciate you dropping by, Lil, but 7:30 is a little early, even for you." Lily was a notorious early riser. She had a weird thing about watching sunrises before race weekends; she claimed it gave her peace and serenity before she entered the race car.

"I know, I'm sorry. I just feel like the last few weeks haven't gone well in the car, and I'm just so nervous for today. I mean, the upgrades are going to be great, but I just can't seem to get ahold of the car. Feel like I'm working against the car." I nodded, understanding where she was coming from. Lily was a great driver, but getting ahold of a Formula 1 car was difficult, and she was so young.

"I know you know this, but I'll say it again. It's your first year, Lil. It takes time to get used to a car of that quality. I have a lot more years than you, and while this isn't Indy Car, the cars are very similar to Formula 1. There's a lot of learning that comes with age. Isabelle picked you for a reason. All you need to do this weekend is put your head down and drive like the incredible driver the team believes you are."

I could see a smile form on Lily's lips, her eyes perking up a bit. If my job as a driver didn't succeed, there was potential in a job as a therapist.

"Wisdom comes with age, as my father always says," Luca added. "I have no doubt you'll have some championships ahead of you, Lily – probably more than this one will get," he added, ruffling my hair as he gave me his favorite, Cheshire cat grin.

"And *definitely* more than Luca will get," I retorted as Luca showed me his middle finger.

Lily stayed for another twenty minutes, finishing her cup of coffee, before returning back to her room to get ready for the day. As soon as she left, I heard a ding on my phone, a text from Lily lighting up the screen.

> Lily: Why have you not had some angry hate sex with this fine man yet? Or was that what I was interrupting this morning?

> Georgia: A classy lady never tells.

I couldn't help but slightly laugh at her text. Lily had interrupted something, but I had no idea what *it* was, and I wasn't sure I was ready to find out.

Luca and I spent the rest of the morning in silence, and as soon as nine a.m. rolled around, we left the room – together this time – and headed towards the valet to pick up his Lamborghini.

The drive to the paddock was quiet. Luca and I exchanged a few comments on the weather but nothing further on the morning's earlier conversation. Once we arrived, we did the same routine as yesterday. Luca handed me my bag, took my hand in his, and we walked through the paddock as a united front.

As soon as I walked into the Valkyrie garage, I was dragged by Lizzie into what felt like the world's biggest hug.

"Georgie, incredibly good to see you. How was the podcast taping last night?" she asked cheerfully, and I gave her a look that said, '*As you if you didn't listen to it and spend all night checking social media?*' Before Lizzie could answer, Isabelle called us both into her office. There was no smile on her face, but I could tell that she was pleased.

"Good morning. Georgia, looks like you had a productive evening last night. I just got off the phone with Maison de Klotho, and they have asked for us to meet them the week of Monaco." As soon as the words left Isabelle's mouth, I felt a huge sigh of relief ripple through me.

"Oh! My! God!" Lizzie screamed. "This is amazing!"

"It's just a meeting, but still, it's a step in the right direction for us. Keep it up, and we should have a sponsorship deal scored before the summer break." Isabelle turned directly to me and squinted her eyes a bit. "That means no Sassy Dubois to the cameras, got it, Georgia?" I wanted to give her a piece of my mind about the toddler treatment, but I knew it wouldn't be fruitful, so I opted for a sweeter approach.

"Yes, yes, I'll do my best to quell the beast inside of me."

"Good to hear. Now, remember, we have the Italian Drivers Association event tonight. You will be attending with Luca, and you and Luca will be seated at a table with me and Francesco, Henri, and Lily. A car will pick you up at 7 p.m. Do *not* be late. I took the liberty of having a dress sent to your room."

"I'll be there with bells on," I whistled back. "Now, if you don't mind, I have a free practice to top!" And with that, I trotted out of Isabelle's office, feeling quite undeservedly pleased with myself.

Free Practice 1 and 2 had gone great for the team. I had topped the first Free Practice, but Henri and Eric had beaten me in the second. I knew Luca wouldn't be happy that he hadn't managed to top the tables in either of those sessions.

As soon as the day ended, I headed back to Luca's car and plopped down into the passenger seat. I could see the look of disappointment on Luca's face. The calm and teasing nature that he usually had was now replaced by anxiety and discomfort. As we drove back to the hotel, I considered approaching him about the issue again, but the coward within me won.

When I opened the door to our suite, I saw the dress Isabelle had sent me lying across my bed. As I opened the dress bag, I was slightly horrified to see what lay waiting for me. There, inside the bag, was what I could only describe as the sexiest black dress I had ever laid my eyes on. I immediately knew this had Lizzie all over it, and I opened my phone to give her a piece of my mind. It was as if Lizzie knew I would be calling because she answered the phone after just one ringtone.

"Ummm, care to explain the dress Isabelle sent to my room?"

"Isn't it just so gorgeous? You are going to look stunning." Lizzie had her sickly sweet voice on, the one that told me she was loving this far too much.

"No way I can wear this."

"What better way to secure a Maison de Klotho sponsorship than you making headlines with that sexy black dress designed by them?" I grumbled in response, but before I could give her a piece of my mind, the line went dead, and I knew that was the end of the conversation. The dress was a statement piece and was sure to turn heads – and photographers' cameras.

After completing my hair and makeup, I went back into my

room and changed into the dress. Lizzie was right – I did look stunning, which was confirmed as soon as I walked into the living room. As I walked into the room, I heard a loud whistle from Luca, who was seated on the couch. His eyes looked tired – *and slightly red* – but his features were relaxed, and he had a smirk on his lips.

"What did I do to deserve this honor?" Part of me wanted to punch the cheeky smile off his face. I could see his eyes rake over me, going slowly from the top of my frame to the bottom, paying careful attention to my leg that stuck out of the dress' slit.

"Don't kid yourself, Luca, this is for a woman called Klotho. You might have heard of her, you know, the goddess of fashion." Luca raised his eyebrow a bit, not entirely sure if I was telling the truth – his face told me a part of him thought I had *possibly* worn this for him, which irked me to no end.

"Ready to go?" I asked, grabbing my purse.

"Almost, I have a small gift for you first." Luca pulled out a small box from his bag, and my interest was definitely piqued. He set the box down on the coffee table and motioned for me to take it.

I cautiously took the box in my hands, opening it slowly as if it were a bomb about to explode. There, inside the Aphrodite's Jewelry box, was a small necklace with a lightning bolt insignia dangling from a silver chain. As I stared at the necklace, I could feel the internal battle start to range inside of me. Aphrodite's Jewelry was one of the most famous jewelry stores in the world, with some of the most beautiful designs I had ever seen.

To my surprise, the necklace was very tasteful, as tasteful as you could have with a lightning bolt hanging from it, but the idea of wearing my competitor's symbol around my neck definitely annoyed me. I looked up at Luca, letting my eyes meet his beautiful brown ones.

"Really? A lightning bolt?" Luca ignored the sarcasm dripping from my voice as he continued to smile at me.

"Designed it myself, Tesoro. Don't want the other drivers getting any ideas when they see you in this black dress. I've seen how Éliott looks at you." Luca's voice was cocky, but I could hear a hint of jealousy in it when he mentioned Éliott.

"Well, be quick and put it on then," I mumbled, conceding to Luca's silent request to have me wear this ridiculous necklace. His day had been tough, and the least I could do was throw him a bone. Luca took the necklace from my hands, motioning for me to turn around. As Luca's hands slid over my bare shoulders, adjusting the necklace into place, I could feel goosebumps form on my arms and chest. I silently prayed that Luca hadn't noticed how much his touch had affected me, but I knew he had noticed because his hands went even slower, buckling the necklace with such a gentle touch.

"Bellissima," he whispered in my ear as he pulled away from my back. A blush immediately crept onto my face, one that I knew I couldn't hide.

Luca grabbed my bag and handed it to me, and as we exited our room, he placed his hand on the small of my back as he guided us toward the elevator. Luca and I stepped inside once the elevator door opened, and I breathed a sigh of relief when I saw it was empty. The elevator started to descend, but unfortunately for me, it stopped just a few floors down, opening up to reveal none other than Éliott Simon.

"Wow, Georgie, you look incredible," Éliott gasped, giving me a hug and a kiss on the cheek as he entered the elevator. He nodded in Luca's direction, and the two shook hands, a begrudging look on Luca's face as he pulled me slightly closer to him. His fingers started to trace circles on my waist, ever so casually, as he side-eyed Éliott, like he was trying to provoke an angry bear that didn't need disturbing.

Éliott, to his credit, just continued to ignore Luca, chatting away as the elevator continued its descent, although I could see a twinkle in Éliott's eye, some silent laughter dancing in his blue eyes, as if he was continuing to blab at me just to annoy Luca even further.

As soon as the elevator opened to the lobby floor, Luca grabbed my hand and dragged me away from the elevator – or, more likely, Éliott. As promised, Isabelle and Francesco were waiting outside in the car. As soon as Isabelle saw us, she waved, her eyes dropping to the necklace around my neck. She raised her left eyebrow, silently asking me a question that I didn't particularly have an answer for myself. I just shrugged and hopped into the car, taking the open seat next to Luca. Henri and Lily were already inside the car, chatting away about the silly video the Wilmington F1 Team had released early today of Oliver and Edward. Both of their eyes also flicked to my chest, the necklace getting Henri's attention. I gave them both a dead stare, daring him or Lily to comment on it.

We arrived at the Divers Association dinner and took our seats at one of the front tables. Luca's parents were at the table next to ours, and his mother gave me a huge hug as we passed.

"Oh, Georgia, that necklace is so beautiful. Luca did a great job designing that," she purred. I put on my biggest smile and nodded, thanking her for the compliment.

As Luca and I took our seats at the table, I looked down at Luca's hand, noticing the small tremors rippling through his fingers. Every so often, he would rub his hands against his napkin, and I could tell that he was wiping away the sweat from his hands.

I reached out and took his hand in mine, smiling at him as I leaned over and whispered, "Your speech is going to be great, Luca."

Luca nodded at me, but he released my hand from his grip, instead wiping his sweaty hands on his pants. It was odd seeing Luca like this. A very different demeanor from Luca's usual happy-go-lucky, cocky self, and it almost pained me to see him full of worry and anxiety. While I was starting to dislike Luca a little less since we had started this arrangement, I knew for sure that I didn't like *this* Luca in front of me.

I made an effort to turn back to Henri, attempting to rejoin the earlier conversation we were having with Isabelle, but as I watched the two of them converse, I couldn't find the mental capacity to care about the new specs the FIA was going to release on next year's car – my only concern at that moment was Luca.

I gently reached back out to Luca, letting my hand rest on Luca's thigh. As if instinctual, I felt my hand rubbing little circles on his leg, squeezing gently. I let my fingertips gently caress him, and I saw Luca shift slightly in his seat, unsure of what I was doing. Luca turned and looked at me, raising his eyebrow ever so slightly, a silent question on his face. I just smiled at him and turned back to Henri and Isabelle, answering a question that was thrown my way while I kept up my ministrations, continuing to gently caress him under the table.

I could feel Luca start to relax a bit, with his form starting to droop a bit as he started to regain his composure.

I'm not sure why I thought it was my responsibility to help Luca get over his anxiety about the speech. My head knew it was in part because if Luca fucked up the speech, it would be a setback in how the media viewed him, and right now, I couldn't see this Luca getting a single word out.

But there was something more to that, more than just selfishness of wanting everything to look outwardly perfect. I knew what intense media pressure felt like. I knew the anxiety he was feeling, and not even I could watch Luca experience this.

As I internally battled on what to do, a mortifying idea hit me.

Fuck it, I can't believe I'm going to do this.

I quickly stood up and excused myself, walking towards the restroom, purse in hand. When I entered the stall, I quickly slid my purple lacy thong off, putting it in my purse. I took a moment to stare at it, wondering what on earth had gotten into me. Luca was going through an incredibly valid, emotional moment, and here I was, sliding my panties off like they were going to be his saving grace.

I sauntered back to the table, waving at a few of the other drivers on the way back. As soon as I sat down, I put my lacy thong in my hand and discretely slid it into Luca's jacket pocket, shaking him a bit to get his attention. Luca felt the movement of his jacket and looked at me, his brows furrowed with annoyance.

I gave him a quick wink before whispering, "At least now you can picture one person in the audience naked – I hear that's good for pre-speech nerves." Luca gave me an incredibly confused look, but I just smirked at him and turned back to my conversation with Lily about qualifying tomorrow.

While Lily was responding, I let my eyes slightly wander to Luca, who had his hands in his jacket pocket. I knew the moment he realized what I had slid into his pocket because a huge grin immediately slid over his face, and his eyes started to dance as if he could see the game I was playing with him, and he was welcoming the invitation. Luca removed his hand from his jacket pocket and put it on my thigh, mimicking the movements I was doing earlier, a sly smile still dancing on his lips. Luca turned back into the conversation and joined us for the next ten minutes before his name was called to the stage.

As Luca walked onto the stage, I saw him put his hands in the jacket pocket that I had snuck my thong into, another smile gracing his lips. I could see him visibly relax, and he began his speech, which, to my surprise, was one of the most funny and endearing speeches I had heard this season. He spoke about his time karting as a little boy on the Monza track and gave the Hermes F1 Team a heartwarming thank you for allowing him to compete for a win tomorrow. As he ended the speech, the crowd erupted into cheers for Luca.

Well done, Georgia, I congratulated myself, which was a bit ridiculous since all I had done was slide my panties off like a girl gone wild.

The rest of the evening went off without a hitch, with Luca settling into his normal behaviors now that the speech was complete. As the evening started to die down, Luca stood up, signaling that it was time to go. We said our goodbyes, and Luca hailed us a cab, opening the door for me.

The ride back to the hotel was quiet, neither of us wanting to discuss the fact that I was no longer wearing any underwear, although the grin on Luca's face told me enough. Luca quickly ushered us out of the cab and got us into the elevator. As soon as the doors opened to our floor, Luca grabbed my hand and dragged us into our suite at the same speed as our Formula 1 cars.

"Luc-" I began, about to chide him for dragging me through the hotel like a misbehaving toddler, but before I could even finish my sentence, Luca's lips were on mine, his hands on my waist and neck as he pushed me against the wall. As if instinctual, I pulled Luca closer to me, letting my hands rest on his back. The kiss was deep and passionate, even better than I had imagined in my dream. As Luca broke away, he rested his forehead on mine, his eyes staring at me as we both caught our breath, neither of us saying a word for what felt like a lifetime.

"What was that for?" My voice was all but a whisper as I attempted to regain some composure.

"I think you know what that was for," Luca grinned.

"Any chance I can get my underwear back?"

Luca pulled the thong out of his jacket pocket and studied it for a moment. "And give away my good luck charm?" I didn't appreciate his sly grin or the fact that he was holding it out of reach. "You want it back; you'll have to earn it," he added in sneakily.

"Oh?" I questioned, attempting to reach for the thong. Luca put the thong back into his jacket pocket and moved towards the couch, taking a seat in the center and patting his lap. I knew that Luca was messing with me, seeing if I would call his bluff.

But I wasn't in the mood to let Luca win, and after all of that champagne, I was suddenly feeling bold and sexy, especially as I watched Luca's eyes rake up and down my body. Maybe Lily was right – maybe I should have sex with Luca, get it out of my system.

I stalked towards where he was sitting on the couch, and surprising both Luca and myself, I straddled his lap, letting my dress start to hike up my body. I reached for Luca's belt, and he raised an eyebrow, clearly curious to see my next move. I began to unbuckle his belt, letting a grin cross my lips as he let a soft moan fall from his lips. As I pulled down his zipper, I let my hand slip into his waistband, raising my eyebrow in silent question to see if he wanted me to continue. While his expression was one of shock, I could see something else in his eyes – desire. He nodded, albeit a bit wearily, and I slid my hand into his waist hand, palming his already hard and aching cock.

I grabbed the edges of his pants and boxers and instructed him to lift, letting his cock spring free as his pants slid down. I'm not sure exactly what I had expected of Luca, but *wow* was all that came to mind. His cock was thick, with pre-cum already glistening at the tip. I licked my lips and slid down to the floor on my knees, letting my tongue run up from the base of his shaft all the way up to the tip. Luca let out a loud moan as he put a hand on my head, slightly gripping my hair. I took him deep into my mouth, letting him hit the back of my throat.

"Oh fuck," Luca gritted out. "That feels-"

Before he could finish his sentiment, I went down on him again, slowly bobbing up and down on his length with gentle touches. In response to my teasing, he grabbed my hair even harder.

"Stop teasing, Amore," he demanded, letting a large sigh fall from his lips. I continued to work him, letting my hands gently massage his balls as I kept a steady rhythm. I could tell Luca was starting to get closer because his moans were getting louder, and both of his hands were in my hair, grabbing it as I continued to work him. It didn't take long before Luca was a moaning mess above me.

"I'm going to-" Luca didn't need to finish his sentence – I knew he was about to come. I doubled down on my efforts as he came in my mouth, sucking up everything he gave me as Luca came down from his high.

Once I was finished, I wiped my mouth and looked up at him, a large smirk on my face. At that moment, I truly saw a Luca I had never seen before – a speechless one. Clearly, he was not expecting me to call his bluff, not that he was complaining. I stood up and put my hand in his jacket pocket, grabbing my thong.

"I'd say I earned this back, wouldn't you agree?" Before Luca could answer, I sauntered back to my room, letting my hips sway just a little bit more than usual, awfully proud of myself. I didn't even look back, but I knew Luca still had a look of shock on his face.

Never underestimate Georgia Dubois, I thought to myself.

Luca

After the incredible evening at the Italian Driver's Association on Friday, Saturday was undoubtedly a little awkward between Georgia and me. We both went out of our way to avoid each other; it was clear neither of us knew what to say to the other. Georgia had looked amazing at the dinner on Friday, but she had looked even better on her knees, sucking my cock after the dinner.

The truth was, I was starting to feel a bit enamored by her. She had single-handedly managed to calm me down and given me the confidence I needed to surge through the weekend. The little stunt she pulled with the underwear was so shocking, especially from Little. Ms. Prim And Proper, but it left me feeling more impressed with her than I cared to admit.

I did know that, of all the emotions I was feeling, I was a little irked that Georgia had just sauntered off after I had finished Friday evening. I wanted to repay the favor, and most importantly, I didn't want to let her have the upper hand, which I now felt like she had. She had made me feel incredible, and I hadn't repaid the debt.

I hated being in debt to other people, but I despised being in debt to Georgia.

The fates had left me feeling so good on Saturday that I was able to get some revenge on her during qualifying. Her choices Friday night had made me feel so relaxed that I had actually taken pole on Saturday – my first ever pole, and at my home race, no less.

Maybe I should rile up Georgia more often – it seemed to really work well for me, I laughed to myself.

Now it was Sunday afternoon, and I was sitting in first position on the grid, anxiously waiting for the race to start. Georgia had gotten P3 in qualifying, with Oscar Parker sitting in P2. Henri fortunately had to take a new engine, so he was starting at the back of the grid, which meant I had one less person to worry about.

As soon as the lights went out, I launched off the starting line like my life depended on it. The car felt incredible, but I knew better than to get my hopes up because, recently, they seemed to be constantly dashed by the team's strategy.

As soon as lap twenty hit, I could see Georgia really gaining on the Rennen car behind me. I silently prayed that she wouldn't pass him. I could keep Oscar back in the Rennen, but a Valkyrie behind me would be a different story. Georgia drove like she had a rocket ship underneath her. It was no surprise to me that after two more laps, Georgia had passed Oscar, and she was gunning for me next. Within another five laps, I could see her right on my rear, well within DRS range.

Neither of us had pitted, and I knew she wasn't going to until I had, both teams trying to hold for as long as we could. By lap twenty-seven, Georgia had caught me on the straight, and she sailed on by. I swear, for just a second, I saw her wave to me.

Had I imagined that? My blood boiled just a bit, but I put my head down.

I could hear my race engineer come into my ear. "Georgia is going to pit. Box box." Just as he said, I saw Georgia heading into the pits; moments later, both of us came out as positions P3 and P4. By lap forty, we had both regained positions P1 and P2.

As we approached lap forty, I saw Georgia's car in front of me do a 360. Her car was still on the track and facing forward, but for a moment, her entire car had lost control, and I felt my heart stop.

How close was the Rennen behind me? What if he didn't see her?

As quickly as Georgia had spun, she had started back up again. I could see her car in my mirrors, regaining speed, and Oscar Parker was quickly back behind her again.

I quickly hit the radio button. "All okay with Georgia?" I asked.

"Yup," my engineer replied, probably a little confused as to why I was asking. "Head down, Luca, only thirteen laps to go."

While I knew Georgia would be furious with her mistake, this had given me the opportunity I needed to get out in front. This was my time, and it was my race to lose. As Georgia had said earlier this weekend, I only owed this race win to myself. It was up to me to win it – and earn it.

As lap fifty came, I could see Georgia gaining on me again, with Oscar Parker quickly behind, a DRS train forming. I held on, defending every move Georgia put on me. As soon as I entered the final lap, I knew Georgia was about half a second behind me, trying to get around me. I held on tightly. Within a minute, I could see the checkered flag up above, and as a few more seconds passed, I had crossed the line, my car just barely in front of Georgia's.

In that moment, it was as if the entire world had gone silent. Only a second later did my brain register the screaming in my ear.

"You did it!" I heard Francesco come on the line. "What a race!"

"Grazie to the team," I called back out, and I could feel tears start to slowly trickle down my face. I had done it. I had managed to stave off Georgia and win my home Grand Prix.

I parked my car in spot one and looked to my right. There was Georgia in the P2 spot, on top of her car, doing her window washing dance as her engineers looked on, laughing with her. I knew she would be disappointed because that was her win that she lost purely on driver error, but still, P2 was an excellent result, one all the other drivers on the grid wished they had for themselves – all except for me.

I hopped out of the car and ran towards my family, who were waiting for me. I gave my father a particularly big hug, and he hugged me back with such force I could barely breathe. I ripped my racing helmet off and hugged and kissed my mother, noticing the tears in her eyes. As I turned toward the interview area, I felt a tap on my shoulder. Georgia was behind me, a huge smile on her face. Her eyes were glistening, and for once, her smile looked completely genuine.

Georgia hopped up into my arms, her arms wrapped around my neck. I could feel her warm breath on my neck as she leaned in and whispered, "Congratulations, Flash, a race well won." I went to thank her, but she added, "Don't get used to it; I'll be back next week." Georgia winked at me, a smirk on her lips. I went to put her down, but then I felt it — her lips against mine.

The kiss was nothing like yesterday. It was slow, messy, and passionate, probably too passionate for the cameras around me, but I didn't care. I held onto her tighter as I kissed her back, forgetting for a moment that we were in public. Next to me, I heard Oliver whistle loudly as he and Edward came up to greet us.

I finally set Georgia down on the ground and whispered, "Until next time, Cara." Georgia just chuckled as she walked towards the interview area; my eyes following her form as she walked on.

Chapter Ten

REVENGE IS A DISH BEST SERVED COLD

Georgia

After the kiss with Luca, I marched myself over to the cool-down room, not ready to face what I had just done – or why I had done it. I mean, Lizzie told me I had to sell this, and what girlfriend wouldn't kiss their boyfriend if they had just won their home race? *That was the reason I kissed Luca.*

It definitely wasn't because, at that moment, Luca had the most kissable face I had ever seen. Or, because I felt so much joy for him at that moment, I just couldn't help myself. Or because I was so pissed at myself for that mistake that a kiss from Luca was all I could think about to relieve my anger at myself.

Nope, not a single one of those reasons made any sense, I concluded.

Oscar Parker, the Rennen F1 driver who had taken P3, walked into the cool-down room shortly after and gave me a big hug. "What a race there, Georgie! I thought I might have had you at the end, but that defensive move in the second half of the last lap was brilliant."

I chuckled at his comment and hugged him back. Oscar might be the most British driver I had ever met, but he was also one of the sweetest. We continued to chat quietly as we watched the replay on the TV screen. After another couple of minutes passed, and Luca finally came sauntering in, a huge smile on his face. Oscar and I both clapped for him while bowing at the same time, as if Luca were royalty and we were merely his servants. Although in Italy, Luca might as well have been royalty at that moment. The crowd's cheers were louder than what I think the Italian royal family had once received.

Luca just walked in and gave me a smug grin, slapping me on the shoulder, as if to congratulate me for the kiss we had both just partaken in. I was a little annoyed at that. I was supposed to have the upper hand here. The cocky bastard was still cocky even when he didn't have a right to be.

After the cool-down room and podium ceremony, Luca, Oscar, and I were shuffled into the press conference room – or, as I liked to call it, *the lion's den*. I walked in first and took my spot at the end. Oscar walked in next, and as soon as he saw me, he gave me another high five, a huge grin on his face. It was no secret that the Rennen F1 Team had some issues this year, but Oscar was driving the car phenomenally. He no doubt had a long future at Rennen, and he was clearly buzzing after this podium.

Only a few seconds later, Luca walked in, his clothing still drenched in champagne. We were supposed to clean up before these post-race press conferences, but it was clear the Hermes team had kept on partying. Luca walked in and gave me a huge grin, winking at me in the process. There was no other way to describe it: Luca looked like the cat that had got the cream.

Oh God, am I going to have to drive his Lamborghini back to the hotel? I contemplated Luca's drunkenness and immediately knew my answer. I wasn't sure what was worse, losing the race or having to drive a Lamborghini home, but I accepted it as my punishment for losing. *If I had won the race, I wouldn't have had to drive home at all; I'd be the one sloshed at the press conference.*

I heard Oscar giggle as Luca walked in and gave him a huge high-five. As soon as Luca took his seat, the presenter's voice came on over the loudspeaker, and the press conference began. I sucked in a deep breath. I knew I was going to have to discuss the terrible spin that had ultimately lost me the race. I could feel my hands start to get clammy, anxiety slowly starting to take over my body – like a python circling its prey. I hated discussing my racing errors. What did they want me to say? *I knew I had fucked up. The media knew it. The team knew it. The fans knew it.*

"Let's start with Luca. Luca, congrats on a well-deserved win here at home for you. How does it feel?"

"Incredible, just incredible. This has been a dream of mine since I was a child, to win at Monza in a Formula 1 car, and now here I am." I felt some warmth go through me at Luca's response. I knew how important winning at home was.

"So Luca, when you saw Georgia spin behind you, what were you thinking? Were you slightly relieved, knowing that your main race competitor was going to lose some time on her lap?" I didn't think the journalist meant it to sound quite so rude, but Luca didn't look amused by the question.

"No, my first thought was, '*Is my girlfriend okay.*' You never want to win a race because another racer puts themselves in potential danger. We're competitive, but ultimately, there are only twenty-two of us in the world. I know many of you find this hard to believe, but we're also friends. Once I knew Georgia was okay, I put my head down and focused on *my* race."

I looked over to Luca and smiled. His eyes were still facing the journalist, but I could see them slightly shift to the right as if he were observing me while he gave his answer.

So much for having the upper hand, I thought to myself.

"The next one is for Georgia. Georgia, you almost had Luca at the end. Tell us, what happened in the car today?"

"Unfortunately, I made an error in the car, which caused it to spin. I was fortunate that the spin was minor, and I was able to recover quickly in order to grab P2. We were close at the end, but I am pleased to end with P2, keeping me in the championship lead with some solid points." I applauded myself for the casual response, and I felt confident in my answer.

"Sure, you're in the lead now, but aren't you worried mistakes like this will keep you from winning the championship? All these small mistakes add up to something." The journalist looked at me with a sturdy face, clearly unhappy that I had mentioned my championship lead. The second he asked the question, my blood started to boil. The frustrated part of me wanted to stand up and throw my water at the journalist, but since Sassy Dubois was meant to be left at home, I opted for a deep breath. I had a Maison de Klotho sponsorship to worry about it.

"That applies to all the drivers. Yes, small mistakes happen, but champions don't make them every race. If I am to win this championship, I can't worry about what will happen in the next race. I just have to focus on winning. A mistake happened this race. I'm not worried about the next race until I'm in the car again." I knew it was a good answer because I saw Lizzie in the back give me a thumbs up, a rarity at my press conferences.

"Sure, champions don't make these mistakes every race; that's evident by Eric Spencer and Noah Hendriks's past wins. But, so far, you've made three mistakes in the last six races. How do you account for that and still think you'll win the championship? You're only a few points ahead of Henri and Noah. That's just a couple of third-place finishes, and then they take the lead."

Before I could stop myself, I felt my legs start to move. I was now standing, my fists clenched, and my face scrunched up. The entire world was red.

"What the fuck is wrong with you people?" I yelled, looking straight into the eyes of the sports reporter who was now standing in front of me. He looked, to be fair, a little taken aback. He had clearly wanted to antagonize me, but I don't think he was expecting this kind of outburst.

"What do you want me to say? No, I plan on making a small mistake every weekend. Can't wait to lose the championship!" I threw my hands up in the air, my frustration growing with each word. "I have a car that is 15x more reliable than Henri's Hermes F1 car and 20x more reliable than Noah's Blaue Flügel F1 team car. At least I'm on the podium every race, mistakes or not." I felt a hand on my shoulder. Luca was standing behind me. His face was soft, his eyes deep with concern. He laced his hand in mine and smiled at me, that huge, beautiful smile.

Before Luca could say anything, Oscar piped up. "Want to know why Georgie is going to win the championship this year? It's because you guys have spent the last six races pissing her off; nothing motivates an athlete more than proving the media wrong. Plus, she's got the only car that doesn't look like a whale coming up for air," he added with a laugh.

I turned to Oscar and smiled, giving Luca a silent squeeze of his hand. I walked back to my chair and plopped myself down with an exasperated sigh. Isabelle wasn't going to be pleased, but at that moment, I didn't care.

There was some silence in the room and a few awkward chuckles after Oscar's comment. Finally, another journalist broke the ice, and the questions continued for another seven minutes.

No one dared ask me a question after that outburst. *Good. I was over it.*

Lizzie met me at the front, a deep look of disapproval on her face. I just stormed past her. What could I say to make this better? We entered the Valkyrie garage, and I saw both Fiona and Isabelle waiting in Isabelle's office. Once Isabelle saw me, she called me into her room. Her look told me everything I needed to know.

"What is wrong with you?" Isabelle was staring directly into my eyes, her piercing green eyes once again assessing my every move.

"I don't know," I answered truthfully. Isabelle let out an exasperated groan and sat behind her desk, putting her hands on her head. There was an awkward silence around us, and I could tell she was thinking.

"When are you going to learn to ignore the journalists? They are rubbish. You know this. Why give them what they want?" she asked.

"When are the journalists going to learn to treat me like a human being?" I snapped.

"When you show them you are one." Isabelle picked up her head and shot me a pointed look, and I knew what that look meant. She was a believer that we taught others by example – by being a leader, and as the lead driver, I *was* the team leader.

Isabelle was definitely a believer in '*when they go low, we go high.*' I was starting to be more of a believer in, '*Revenge is a dish best served cold.*' I would beat them at their game one day, but today was not that day.

"I'm sorry," was all I could utter back. I felt defeated. Here I was with a big P2, a leader in the championship, and I felt more dejected than ever. No one said anything for several more minutes before Lizzie took out her phone and checked her messages.

"Matteo just told me that Luca will be waiting for you at his Lamborghini. Do us all a favor and drive it for him; I'm not sure he can drive that car back safely." I took one more look at Isabelle, who still had a blank look on her face, and nodded at Lizzie before exiting the office, picking up my bag in the process.

I could feel the tears forming in my eyes, so I hurried to the parking garage, not wanting anyone to see me cry. I felt bad skipping the fans who had asked me for photos, but I knew a photo of a fan with me crying was only going to show them one thing – my weakness.

Luca was in his car, and he waved at me. He was sitting in the passenger side of the car; clearly, Matteo had told him he was much too drunk to drive. I smiled back weakly and hopped into the driver's seat. I had driven Henri's Lamborghini many times, so it felt natural to me, even if I hated it.

Maybe I should get used to driving a car that isn't a Bugatti; it's unlikely I'll have my seat much longer anyway. I knew thinking like that could be the end of a driver's career, but it was hard to stop myself.

As we pulled out of the parking garage, I could see Luca texting on his phone – likely thanking the hundreds of friends and family that had sent him loving messages, a stark contrast to my phone, which currently had a couple of texts from my bothers and mother, and I knew what Hugo and Henri had to say about this mess, so I had left those texts unread.

Some ten minutes went by, and Luca began idly chatting with me about his plans for the evening. Lizzie had already told me there was a big VIP party, and all the drivers would be attending, regardless of who would be the race winner. I had secretly hoped that I could get out of it, but with Luca P1 and me P2, there was 0% chance of that happening. Luca kept chatting about his day, although I could see his demeanor shift a bit when he finally took a moment to look at me.

Luca

Tears had begun to fall down Georgia's face, and although she was deathly quiet, I could tell something was wrong with her. The press conference had not gone as planned. That asshole had it out for Georgia, and it was infuriating. As if instinctually, I grabbed her hand on the steering wheel. I wasn't sure if that was the right decision because she began crying even harder.

"Pull over, Georgia," I demanded softly. She nodded her head no.

Insufferable woman, I thought to myself – half joking.

"I mean it, pull over." The second time I asked, she complied, pulling over to the side of the road in front of a little café. Her hands were still gripping the steering wheel, and she was staring out of the windscreen, refusing to look at me.

I grabbed her hand and pulled it into mine. Her breathing had started to become heavy, and her tears were falling harder. I unbuckled her seat belt, pulling her out of the driver's seat and into my lap, letting my hand rub circles up and down her back. Georgia was crying harder now, and her face was deep into my neck as tears continued to pour down her face and onto my shirt.

"It'll be okay, Georgie," I whispered into her ear. "It'll be okay." I didn't know what else to say other than that, so I continued to soothe her as she sobbed into my shirt. Everything within me told me this was more than the journalists' remarks. There was still the rest of the season to drive for, and coming in second place was hardly a crying matter.

"No, it won't. I'm going to lose my seat," she whimpered back, trying to get ahold of her breathing.

"Isabelle fire a world champion? I doubt it." I tried to lift my voice, attempting to make light of the situation.

"I won't be a world champion. The press made that clear. Henri and Noah are better drivers, and once the teams fix the reliability of their cars, I won't be on podiums; I won't get to win the World Drivers Championship."

I held onto her tighter as Georgia continued, "If we lose this Maison de Klotho sponsorship because of me, the team won't forgive me. They won't have to because we'll be out of money."

"One outburst isn't going to stop Maison de Klotho from meeting with you Wednesday," I promised, although I didn't truthfully know if that was true. Fashion brands were fickle and moved on quickly; it's part of the reason why most of the Formula 1 teams weren't sponsored by them. "Plus, you and Lily are much too attractive of a team," I added with a wink.

Georgia's tears started to slow down, and she looked at me, a small smile on her lips, "You're a terrible liar, Luca Rossi."

"And you're an ugly crier," I shot back, poking her in the side. She shot me a glare but laughed at my quip. There was an easy silence between us as I continued to stroke her back, letting her wipe away her tears.

As the tears started to slow down, I reached for her cheek and wiped away one of her tears with my finger.

Georgia really was beautiful. Even after all of those tears, she was one of the most beautiful women I had ever seen. She liked to make snide remarks here and there about me dating models, but the truth was, none of them compared to her beauty. She didn't need makeup, false eyelashes, or fake tan. Her natural self was breathtaking. Add that to her hilarious wit and intelligence – Georgia Dubois was a catch.

It's why I had asked her out all those years ago.

It's also why I stood her up on that date all those years ago. She was too good for me. I didn't deserve someone like Georgia Dubois, so five years ago, after I asked her out, I stood her up; too scared to face the rejection I knew she was going to eventually give me. I saw the way she looked at Éliott Simon back then. She would never look at me the same, no matter how badly I wanted her to.

"I should get us back to the hotel," Georgia said finally.

Much to my – *secret* – disappointment, she crawled off of my lap and back into the driver's seat. She put a smile on her face; it seemed forced, but not as forced as earlier. As she rested her hand on top of the clutch, I put my hand on top of hers and let it rest there. We drove the rest of the way back to the hotel in complete silence.

As soon as Georgia and I got back to the hotel, we made quick work of grabbing a bite to eat and throwing on some acceptable party clothes. As soon as 9 p.m. hit, we made our way downstairs, immediately spotting Henri and Lily in front of what was probably the largest limo I had ever seen. If Georgia had told Henri about her outburst earlier, he didn't show it. Instead, he gave her a warm hug, and they sat at the back of the limo together. I knew it was ridiculous to feel jealous of the fact that she had chosen to sit next to Henri instead of me, the race winner. He was her brother, and she had experienced a rough day; it's not like she had chosen to sit next to Éliott over me.

Every part of my brain knew I should probably let that one go. I was a twenty-seven-year-old man holding a grudge against another driver for something I didn't even understand. I wasn't completely sure of what their relationship had been, but Éliott had once let it slip to me a couple of years ago that he and Georgia had briefly dated.

As we arrived at the club, there were photographers and fans everywhere. Henri, Lily, Georgia, and I crawled out of the limo, and I wrapped my arm around Georgia's waist and pulled her close to me, smiling and waving to the fans as we walked into the club. The club coordinator met us at the door and shuffled us into the VIP suite that had been reserved for the drivers, their partners, and a few others who were invited. I saw Éliott seated in the back with Noah Hendriks and his girlfriend. As soon as we walked in, Éliott got up and started walking over to Georgia and me.

"Good race over there, Georgie!" Éliott called out, bringing Georgia into his embrace. He then grabbed my hand and shook it, pulling me in for a hug as well.

"Congrats, Luca, winning at home is an absolute dream. Let's hope we get to see it next week with one of our favorite twins," he added cheekily.

Georgia just slapped his shoulder playfully, batting her eyelashes at him a bit too much for my liking.

"It's not an *if* Éliott. I *am* winning next week's race, and I don't care if it means my brother will never talk to me again." She stuck her tongue out at Henri, who returned the gesture.

I leaned over to Georgia to let her know that I would grab us some drinks, then made my way down towards the bar. I knew Georgia liked champagne with Chambord, so I ordered her one of those and me a glass of champagne. When I came back up the stairs, Georgia and Éliott were sitting together, chatting about something. They looked slightly deep in thought together – Georgia's eyebrows were furrowed as if she was explaining something intense to Éliott.

An immediate pang of hurt hit me, one that I knew was unjust. Every part of me wished that Georgia trusted me like that, but I knew why she didn't. I wouldn't trust playboy Luca Rossi, either. It was petty of me to go over to where the two of them sat. I knew I shouldn't barge into their private conversation, but I was the race winner. For once, I had achieved my dream, and if I wanted to spend it with my girlfriend, I was going to – even if the relationship was fake. *But God, part of me wished it wasn't.*

"Your drink, Georgie," I said with a big smile, making eye contact with Éliott as I sat down next to Georgia. There was a slightly uncomfortable silence, but she turned and gave me a smile and a nod.

"Thanks, Flash." At hearing the nickname, I immediately perked up a bit. Her dress had a fairly high neck, but as I looked down to her chest, I saw the small gleam of the necklace I had given her on Friday. Before I could stop myself, I grabbed the necklace softly from inside her dress and pulled it out, putting it on display.

She quirked an eyebrow at me, clearly not amused with my action.

"Don't want anyone to get any ideas," I grinned. Georgia just rolled her eyes and turned back to Éliott, asking him about his race, making a clear effort to ignore me.

Fine, two can play at that game.

I got up as Éliott began to answer and sauntered over to Oliver and his girlfriend, Lisa. More of the drivers began to arrive, and as the clock reached 10:30, the dance floor opened up with a new D.J.

I was back at the bar, getting another drink, when I saw Éliott and Georgia move to the dance floor. The dancing looked innocent enough, but still, anyone could misinterpret their innocent dancing for something more. I felt anger start to rise inside of me. For someone so worried about losing her seat, Georgia had no problem putting the entire plan at risk by dancing with a driver that the press was convinced was an ex-boyfriend. I couldn't tear my eyes off the two of them, and as I saw Éliott get a little closer to her, I felt a tap on my shoulder. I took my eyes off Georgia and Éliott for just a moment, only to see a beautiful woman standing next to me, a large grin on her face.

"Buy me a drink?" Her voice was silky and smooth, and if she had approached me a month ago, I would have undoubtedly gone home with her.

"Sure," I said with a smirk and called over the bartender, ordering me another beer and her a martini. As soon as our drinks arrived, I felt her hand on my arm, squeezing my muscles underneath my shirt as she tried to flirt with me. I immediately pulled my arm back, slightly annoyed by the presumption that she could touch me. As soon as I pulled back, I saw Georgia's stare meet mine, and I knew she had seen it; something like jealousy passed on her face, quickly disappearing as she turned back to her conversation. A small grip of pleasure washed over me, and I leaned in slightly closer to the woman, returning my gaze to hers.

Fortunately for me, before I could do something stupid like ask the woman to dance, Henri approached the two of us. Unsurprisingly, Hermes' golden boy had an incredibly disapproving look on his face.

"Do you mind if I get a word in with my teammate?" The woman looked at me for approval, as if silently begging for me to tell Henri to piss off – *which part of me wanted to* – but I didn't. Instead, I let her walk away in a huff as I steadied myself. I knew I should thank Henri for saving me from that reckless move I was about to make. It didn't matter how jealous I was of Georgia and Éliott – dancing with a random woman who had made it into the VIP section was a much worse decision than Georgia dancing with a childhood friend.

"Thought you were supposed to be dating my sister?" Henri hissed; his eyes were laced with anger.

"I thought the same thing, but Georgia and Éliott don't seem to remember that," I snarked back at him.

In Henri's eyes, his friend Éliott could do no wrong. *Neither could Georgia.* Henri just rolled his eyes at my comment with a look that said I was the stupidest person in the room.

"Nothing is going on between Georgia and Éliott, you know that. They're just friends, *always have been*." I gave Henri a look that said, *'How stupid are you?'* before scoffing in disbelief.

"Friends that fuck more like it." I hated myself the moment the words left my mouth. Henri's eyes went wide, and for a moment, I could see the wheels turning in his head, as if he was replaying hundreds of conversations that he had witnessed between his sister and best friend. Henri turned back to Georgia and Éliott, who were now chatting away back at their original booth, and it's like a light-bulb went off in his head.

Well, now, at least I'm not the only miserable one here, I thought to myself. It was an atrocious move on my part, but I was drunk, frustrated, and *jealous.*

Henri stormed over to where Georgia was sitting and plopped down, looking her straight in the eyes. I'm not sure what he said to her because I was out of earshot, but I could see Éliott's face go pale, and he looked at me, anger laced in his expression. Georgia exchanged a few more words with Henri and then got up, storming her way over to me.

"We're leaving," she demanded. Georgia grabbed my hand, and we rushed towards the club entrance, not giving me a chance to say goodbye to the group. Edward and Oliver whistled and cheered on our way out, no doubt hoping our rushed exit was because I was getting laid.

I knew I had something much worse in my future.

Georgia

I rushed Luca into the cab. How dare Henri come up to me and demand to know if I had dated Éliott? Where did he even get that idea from? He had some nerve to pretend to be all hurt. It was six years ago. I was barely eighteen, and we dated for all of six weeks. Not everything was my twins' business.

Across from me was a very drunk Luca, which was not incredibly exciting for me. He was sitting there rather awkwardly. I supposed I didn't have to drag him home when it was me who was angry, but when Henri told me Luca was incredibly drunk at the bar, I knew I had to take him home.

I had seen him flirting with that woman, and truthfully, I was feeling a little jealous. I didn't own Luca; we weren't even *actually* dating, so I knew I didn't have a right to be jealous. It's not like he grabbed her onto the dance floor because then I would have been furious. The hypocritical nature of my comment was not lost on me since I had spent the night dancing with Éliott, but it's not like anyone knew we had dated. We were friends, and I had a right to be able to dance with my friends; plus, Edward and Lauren had joined us.

Luca started to look more visibly relaxed in the cab, and by the time we got to the hotel, he had scooted a little closer to me in his seat. As soon as we got to our hotel room door, I realized that the alcohol had now clearly caught up with Luca, and he went and laid down on the couch, kicking his shoes off and flopping them across the room – without a care in the world. I couldn't help but laugh at his drunken state.

"Cara," he called out, "it's nice to see you laugh again." He stuck out both his hands as if he was inviting me into a hug. I moved closer to him but sat on the couch next to his feet, not taking his invite for a hug.

"Oh?" I said casually, pretending not to know what he was talking about.

"You were so sad earlier... it made me feel sad." He said simply, putting a big, stupid grin on his face. "I thought maybe you were regretting our kiss," he mumbled out. His eyes were closing shut and then quickly opening again, like a kid who was too tired to stay at Disney World but refused to let his parents see his sleepiness.

Ahh, so he had thought about the kiss. I smiled softly and looked at him. Luca looked adorable this drunk.

"Had to show all those pretty women who Luca Rossi was going home with at the end of the evening," I said with a wink.

Come on, Georgia, you can flirt better than that, I reprimanded myself.

As Luca began to sit up, he leaned in towards me. His eyes looked directly into mine, and he let out a deep breath. He reached his hand up to my chin, his mouth just inches from mine.

"You're the only person I wanted to go home with tonight," he whispered.

My heart stopped for a moment. I needed to remember that Luca was drunk – very drunk. And yet, in his eyes, something seemed genuine. It was what I had wanted him to say all those years ago when I had originally agreed to go on a date with him. I had the biggest crush on him, and when I came back from Indy Car for winter break, Luca had asked me on a date. I was ecstatic. Luca was kind and funny, and Edward spoke so highly of him.

So when he didn't show up for our date, when he left me in that Monaco restaurant all alone, I was embarrassed. I went back home and cried. He hadn't even sent a text to say why he had stood me up. Instead, all I saw was a social media story of him out at a club with Edward and Noah. He never reached out to me to explain, but I knew why.

I was boring – that much had been made clear by several of the men I had tried to date. I was the boring Dubois twin who competed in a man's sport. *What was sexy about that?*

And yet here I was, all those butterflies that I had experienced at the podcast show returning in full force. He leaned in slowly; his lips were barely touching mine. It's as if Luca was waiting for permission to kiss me, waiting for me to meet him 10% of the way since he had put in the 90%.

I leaned in a little and softly kissed his lips. They tasted of whiskey and champagne. His hands stayed on my chin gently, and he guided the kiss a little deeper. I smiled, kissing him back just a little bit more before he pulled away and looked at me.

"When I saw Éliott with you, I was so jealous, so angry. It shouldn't bother me that you have history, but it does." I pulled back a bit, looking right into Luca's eyes.

"What did you say?" Before he could say anything, I stood up and backed away from the couch. It all made sense now. That's how Henri had known that Éliott and I had dated – *Luca had told him.*

I was speechless – and angry. Luca looked confused as I backed away. He opened his mouth to say something, but I put my hand up to stop him.

"Did you tell Henri?" I asked.

"Wha-"

"No, tell me the truth," I demanded. Luca didn't say anything, but I knew the truth. I could see the guilt in his eyes.

"It wasn't your place to tell him!" I screamed back.

"I didn't realize when Éliott told me that it was a secret," he huffed back at me, wobbling as he stood up. He reached out to me, but I just backed away more. I was livid. I turned on my heels and headed towards my room.

But before I slammed the door in his face, I yelled back, "And to think all those years ago, I was actually sad you stood me up. Looks like I should be thanking you. Really spared me from a whole lot of heartbreak. "

Chapter Eleven

CAN I OFFER YOU A HAMSTER?

Georgia

When I woke up Monday morning after the Monza race, I was still livid at Luca. I quickly packed my bags and met Edward, Henri, and Noah at the airport, not saying a word to Luca as I left our shared hotel room. Noah had hired us all a private jet back to Monaco since the three of us all lived there. Henri was still not speaking to me, which was fine because I had absolutely no interest in speaking to him.

Edward noticed the tension between us and tried to lift our spirits but to no avail. Truthfully, I was too focused on my anger at Luca to really delve into the Henri situation. The week had started off incredible, with Luca and I finally starting to connect. When I had that panic attack in the car, he comforted me with the kindness that I knew he had buried inside him somewhere. That kiss we shared at the race was phenomenal, and I felt like I was starting to get past the resentment I held for him. It felt like there was a possibility we could be something other than enemies.

As the plane landed at the airport, Henri and I hopped into a shared car we had hired to take us home. When I found out I had received a spot on the Valkyrie F1 Team, I immediately purchased a condo in Henri's building. His next-door neighbor was selling, and it just made sense to move close to Henri since we would be traveling so much of the globe together. Plus, it was fun to live so close to all my brothers again, but at this very moment, I was regretting that decision. The tension in the car was palpable. Clearly, neither of us knew what to say. As we unloaded our bags at the complex, Henri let us in, and we both proceeded straight into our apartments, not uttering a word to one another.

Did I deserve the silent treatment? Maybe. I knew I should have told him about my relationship with Éliott, but it had been six years. Seemed a little too late and irrelevant to bring it up now. Not to mention, I didn't owe him, or any other man, anything.

The next morning, I woke up to a knock on my door. Luca wasn't coming into town until after the Maison de Klotho meeting on Wednesday, so I knew it couldn't be him. Fortunately, Lizzie had alerted me that it was still on. It felt like a huge weight had been lifted. I could breathe again.

As I opened the door, I came face to face with Henri, baked goods in one hand and two lattes in the other.

"Can I come in?" he asked, nodding for me to take the coffee.

I nodded and took the bag of baked goods, setting them on the coffee table as I sat down on my sofa next to him. Henri unpacked the baked goods from the container and set them on a plate next to us.

We let another few moments of silence engulf the room as the two of us silently sipped our lattes.

"I'm sorry," Henri finally admitted, a sad look on his face. "I'm sorry for what I said to you. You're right. You don't owe me an explanation. And while I am upset that you didn't tell me, I never asked you if you had feelings for Éliott. It's not like you lied to me." I nodded in agreement, taking another sip of my coffee as I contemplated my next words.

"I am sorry I didn't say anything. I can understand how you would feel blind-sighted by this. Truthfully, it only lasted six weeks; there didn't seem like much to say. We were young and eighteen. We were a terrible fit, so we went back to being close friends. If it had progressed, we obviously would have told you. Although Éliott was too nervous to tell you," I added with a chuckle, and Henri grinned.

"As he should be. I guess I was more upset that Luca knew. You didn't even tell your own brother, but he knew? But when I mentioned it to Éliott last night, he said a couple of years ago, he had told Luca at a party accidentally." I wasn't entirely sure that I believed Éliott had told Luca *accidentally*. Éliott knew that Luca had stood me up because he was the one I called that night. I suspected he had purposefully let it slip, but I would discuss that with Éliott later.

A few more moments of silence went by before Henri added, "Don't be so mad at Luca. I was mad at him for talking to that woman at the bar, and when he mentioned you and Éliott dancing as a defense, I yelled at him that you guys were never a couple and implied that what he was doing was worse. I was kind of an ass to him," he admitted. I could see Henri, all high and mighty, Hermes' golden boy, arguing with Luca, thinking he had the upper hand.

"And then when he scoffed at me, I pressed him further, telling him he was stupid for thinking that you guys were ever an item and that Éliott was simply a friend and you were allowed to dance with a friend." Things were starting to make sense. I had been so angry at Luca, thinking that he had just gone and just told Henri unprovoked because he wanted to get under my brother's skin. But what I had really done was thought the worst of Luca. I had expected him to be a dick, but in truth, he was just defending himself – and drunkenly, nonetheless. I knew as much as anyone that alcohol caused loose lips.

"Thank you for telling me that. I guess I was blaming Luca for just telling you out of the blue, but honestly, I can't really think why he would do that. Luca had no reason to think that you didn't know... I didn't know that Éliott had told Luca. Éliott and I didn't want to make anything weird between the group, so we just didn't say anything."

As we continued to talk, I was starting to feel better; another weight lifted off of my shoulders, but I also felt guilty for yelling at Luca. I was so disappointed in him that night. He had texted me yesterday, asking if he should just get a hotel instead of staying at mine.

Luca had won the Monza that day, and I made him feel like shit, but I would make amends. I didn't know how, but I knew I had to apologize before Monaco. I picked up the phone and texted Luca that, of course, he should stay at mine. I debated on whether I should text him an apology but decided it would be better to do it in person.

I arrived at the Maison de Klotho offices in Monaco shortly after 10 a.m. Isabelle, Lizzie, and Lily were already outside, waiting for me to arrive. We walked into the beautiful conference room together and sat down. While there was still an awkwardness between Isabelle and me, we had both decided to just ignore it. Today had to go perfectly.

Within a few minutes of us sitting down, the Maison de Klotho executive, Sara, walked into the room, all smiles. "Good morning, ladies. Thank you so much for meeting with us before a race weekend. We are so excited to have Formula 1's newest female drivers here!" She squealed. I was a little taken aback. I wasn't sure what I was expecting, but it wasn't a fangirling executive. Before I could respond to her earlier statement, I was dragged into a hug by Sara, and a beautiful Maison de Klotho purse was placed in front of me and then in front of Lily.

"Just a little something from us as a thank you for the meeting." Sitting in front of me was a beautiful shoulder bag colored with our team colors. Lily clapped her hands in excitement, a huge smile on her face.

"Thank you so much, it's beautiful," I said with a genuine smile.

"Lovely! Glad you like it. We're just so excited here at Maison de Klotho. And when we heard that your precious boyfriend Luca

Rossi was interested in doing some modeling with you?" she turned and pointed to me, "We were just thrilled! Luca sent us the *sweetest* note on Monday, and when we noticed that beautiful Aphrodite's Jewelry necklace he had designed for you, we figured it would be some great cross-brand promotion with one of our subsidiaries.

"Honestly, I have never in my years at Maison de Klotho seen a note that cute and adorable as the one Luca sent to us about you." There was a shocked silence in the room, with none of the Valkyrie women knowing what to say to that.

"You're a lucky woman, Georgia; that man clearly loves you. Who knows, maybe we'll get a little engagement ring promotion between the two of you," Sara added with a giggle as she wiggled her shoulders like a mom who had consumed one too many mimosas.

I tried not to choke on my coffee. Even if this relationship wasn't fake, I wasn't going to marry Luca Rossi after only dating for a month. Had it even been a month?

I'm not sure if my face showed it, but I was completely stunned. Luca had reached out to Maison de Klotho. I turned to Isabelle, but she looked as shocked as I did. It's not often that I saw Isabelle have a look of surprise on her face, and honestly, it was a little refreshing. She was shocked and possibly – *no, definitely* – relieved. I felt like I was drowning in questions.

Luca: 1 Isabelle: 0

Sara didn't even register our shocked expressions as she continued, clearly lost in her sales pitch. "We have a lovely new men's and women's collection we would love for you and Luca to try on. Luca told me you would be in Majorca after the Monaco race. We have an office in Madrid, thought you both might like to stop by before you head on your little trip."

So, Luca had planned a little vacation for me? News to me, I thought to myself, a little annoyed, but I knew I should have expected it. Had the asshole assumed that he would get back in my good graces because he had reached out to Maison de Klotho?

Cocky bastard. Although, he wasn't entirely wrong on that front. I smiled and nodded at Sara, trying to regain my composure.

"That sounds lovely!" I managed to squeak out, not sure what to think about all of this. My mind was running a million miles a minute. Sara smiled at me, a nice, warm smile. She truly seemed thrilled that Luca and I would be representing the brand together.

"And Lily, we have some lovely purses that we would love for you and Georgia to represent. I was thinking Silverstone would be a great time to launch the line since that is Lily's home race, I hear." Lily smiled in response, clearly excited about the idea of launching something at her home race. Edward and Eric always came out with collections.

The meeting continued for another hour. Sara showed us various products and sketches of some shoots she wanted us to attend over the next few races. If Maison de Klotho was concerned about my outburst on Sunday, they didn't show it.

Once the meeting was over, I bid goodbye to the team and headed back to my apartment. Luca was going to arrive in the next few hours, and I had barely gotten the place ready for a guest. By the time 3 p.m. rolled around, I heard a knock on my door. I opened it to see Luca dressed in a beautiful purple shirt with a pair of jeans that made his ass look incredible, not that I would let him in on that secret.

"Georgi-"

"Luc-" We said at the same time, both of us chuckling. He motioned for me to go first.

"I spoke to Henri... I'm so sorry, Luca. What I said was really rude and uncalled for. You had just won Monza, and I should have been there for you at the club."

"No, it's me who should apologize. I am sorry I told Henri. When he insisted that you and Éliott had never dated, I felt frustrated with him. I let my jealousy get in the way."

I let my jealousy get in the way.

You're the only person I wanted to go home with tonight.

Those words echoed through my mind. Was Luca *actually* jealous of Éliott?

"I'd like to start over if we can," Luca admitted. "I've been a dick to you, I know that, but I'd like to be friends if you think you can forgive me."

"Well, I have to say, you have a heck of a way of apologizing. Reaching out to Maison de Klotho, not a bad move." I could see Luca's expression lighten, happy to hear that his move had won him some favor.

"And don't try and deny it; they outed you at the meeting today. Along with our vacation plans next week," I added with a raised eyebrow.

"I figured if you were going to be mad at me, we might as well be angry in Majorca during our break," he said with a chuckle.

Luca and I spent the next hour chatting. It felt nice to be less angry at him. Shortly after, Henri popped over and apologized to Luca. Henri and I had the F1 Podcast about home races that evening. I warned Henri not to go too crazy at the podcast. Truthfully, I was really worried about what he would say but decided not to let it get to me. Today, I had won the Maison de Klotho sponsorship, but I knew the battle was just beginning.

Henri and I arrived at the podcast fairly early, around 6 p.m. We had discussed some of the questions they would ask us, and while they didn't mention my relationship with Luca, I knew that was definitely going to be on the table.

As Henri and I walked onto the stage, I could see Luca, Noah, Edward, and Oliver sitting in the front row, a huge grin on Edward's face. I smiled and waved back at them, prompting Edward to blow me a kiss and nudge Luca next to him. Luca just rolled his eyes, clearly not ready to put up with Edward's antics. The more I stared at them, the more I began to see their dynamic – why their friendship was so revered among fans. I smiled at that thought. I loved Edward like a brother, and the more I thought about it, if Edward liked Luca so much, there had to be a reason.

"So Georgia, we've been very impressed with your rookie season.

We're several races in, and you're leading the championship, just incredible." I smiled at the podcaster's kind words, a little surprised at the compliments. Maybe Josh didn't want me to yell at him in front of a live audience on his podcast. *Good.*

"Why do you think you have what it takes to win in your rookie season?"

"Dedication. I know I have what it takes to win. I've never had a training regime this intense before, and I feel like this is the fittest I have ever been in my life. I have an incredible team around me. I am so incredibly fortunate to have a world-class strategy team at my finger trips. And I've got the fastest car on the track," I added slyly, winking at Henri, who just flicked me off across the table.

Josh laughed at that and nodded, turning to Henri. "Henri, how is it battling it out with your sister on the track?"

"It's been a dream come true. I always knew I was the better Dubois sibling at driving, and now I get to show it to everyone on an even playing field," he joked.

"But in all seriousness, it's been incredible to have Peaches with me on this journey. When I made it to Formula 1, and she didn't all those years ago, I felt like a fraud. Like I had also taken her dream. Now, we both get to live it – *together*." The audience awwed at Henri's statement, and I gave a little pretend gag, earning me a shove from Henri.

Oh Henri, Hermes don't even know how lucky they are to have you, I thought to myself – half sarcastically. He truly was the driver every team wished for. He was kind, intelligent, could work a crowd, and *actually* knew how to drive a car.

"So tell me, what would it mean to win Monaco? Georgia, you can go first."

"I've wanted to be a Formula 1 champion since I was a young girl. I want to show young girls all around the world that they can compete in Formula 1, and there is no better place to do it than to win one of the crown jewels of motorsport. If I win this tournament, I will be the second driver to win the Triple Crown of Motorsport. I won the Indianapolis 500 last year and somehow scraped out a win at the 24 of Le Mans the year before. It would mean the world to me to win this honor in front of my home crowd." Henri smiled at me and grabbed my shoulder for a moment, giving it a big squeeze. We both wanted this win desperately, and I knew that meant tensions would be high on Saturday and Sunday, but today we were two siblings with a shared dream, and it was a nice feeling.

"Yeah, I second that feeling," added Henri. "Winning at home... it would be a dream come true. I want the championship, but I really want this win in Monaco."

"Well, it's going to be an interesting race, I dare say! So Georgia, not to change topics here, but rumor has it all the women in this room hate you, you know," the presenter crooned, a cheeky smile on his face.

"Really? I didn't realize you had packed the room full of journalists?" I quipped back, earning a laugh from the audience. The laugh told me one thing – *even they knew I was being bullied by journalists.* Josh laughed too, albeit a tad awkwardly, a small reminder that he was still a journalist himself.

"I kid, I kid. I couldn't possibly think why," I added, letting my voice go just a bit higher, playing the dumb female racer all of the sponsors wanted me to be.

"Oh, come on now, we all saw that kiss you and Luca shared on Sunday. I have a lot of friends, but I don't think I've ever kissed any of them like *that*." Josh had me there.

"So tell us, Georgia, how did Luca Rossi manage to snag everyone's new favorite driver?" I had to stop myself from snorting at that. New favorite driver? Whose new favorite driver? I was struggling to get sponsorships over here from the F1 Old Boys network. I doubted if I was *anyone's* favorite racer – even my own mother had to split her affections.

"Luca insisted we ask you last weekend when we chatted to him."

"Well, you know, Josh, Luca can be pretty convincing when he wants to be," I said with a wink, much to the audience's amusement. "But in all seriousness, it was just sort of sprung on me."

Not a total lie.

"Luca and I have been friends for a while, and then one day, I looked into his beautiful eyes, and I realized I wanted more than a friendship. Plus, the man asked me out like a *hundred* times. Finally decided to throw him a bone. His persistence really paid off on this one." I had intended to make Luca look a bit like a soft idiot, but that comment clearly backfired because as soon as I said the words, every single woman in the room sighed with absolute love in their eyes, clearly cheering for Luca. These women really had it bad for him, and judging by his face, Luca was loving this a little too much.

"Well, we really are happy for you both, but more importantly, the question we all want to actually talk about. It's no secret you've had a bit of a tough time with the media and fans. Your team is new, and as a community, we can be a bit tough on newbies."

Sure, that's it, Josh. They're mean to me because I'm... new. I couldn't help but let a smile form at his comment.

"But I think you've been painted a bit unfairly. In fact, I was hoping your brother could help spill the beans on some of these pranks you've apparently been pulling across the paddock. I've heard rumors that they are brilliant!"

I turned to Henri and quirked an eyebrow at him, very curious about what he was going to say. Henri just kept looking at Josh, laughing away at the podcaster.

"Oh, Josh, if only you knew the half of it. Peaches has actually been banned from the Wilmington garage."

"Oh, do tell." Josh leaned in as if he and Henri were two school-girls gossiping at the lunch table.

"I don't think this is a story anyone wants to hear," I butt in, a little embarrassed, already knowing where Henri was going with this one.

"Nonsense!" Josh just put his hands up as the audience booed at me.

"Well, you see, Josh, Edward is terrified of rodents – mice, rats, hamsters, gerbils, it doesn't matter."

"I'm not terrified, mate!" I heard Edward yell from the front row. We both stopped and gave him a look that said, *"Don't even bother Edward – we all know the truth."*

"So Georgia thought it would be hilarious if she brought a hamster to Edward's driver's room a couple of years back. We bought it a nice cage and set it up in the room, with a note about it being a gift from Wilmington's Team Principal, Arthur. The only problem? Georgia apparently didn't close the door to the cage, and about an hour later, Arthur opened his bag to find a hamster burrowed in his expensive Armani briefcase. Needless to say, he called Edward into his office, demanding to learn more about the hamster – only to be yelled at by Edward, who was angry at Arthur for giving him the hamster in the first place."

Edward...such a good sport, I chuckled to myself.

"Fortunately, Luca was there, and he was able to catch the hamster. It now lives proudly at the Wilmington offices, from what I understand. Although, it did earn Georgia a ban on visiting the Wilmington garage the rest of the year." I knew my face was probably bright red at this moment, and I thanked the Gods above that this was not a video podcast.

"Well, well, well, who knew the Dubois family had such a prankster! And did Edward manage to get his revenge?" Josh asked.

"Ooooh, yes!" Edward announced proudly from the front row, standing up and waving at the audience.

"Delightful! I'll have to ask you at Silverstone how that ended. The saga continues, ladies and gentlemen!"

Once the crowd's laughter had calmed down, Josh asked us a few more questions before ending the podcast.

"Well, this has been a lovely podcast. You have both been an absolute delight to have on here. We look forward to seeing you both on the podium this weekend!"

After the event, the drivers had been asked to come to the podcast's after-party. Since the podcast was on Wednesday, I wasn't able to get out of it, no matter how much I begged Lizzie. Fortunately, Lily was able to join us at the after-party. She had a sponsorship deal with some British investors earlier in the day, so she had to miss the podcast, much to her chagrin.

Lily and I stood at a table some ways from the bar. In the distance, I could see Henri and Noah chatting with a couple of fans, taking photos, and enjoying a few drinks.

"So... you and Luca made up, yet?" Lily asked, giving me a little side eye in the process, but she kept her eye on Henri and Noah in the distance.

I quirked an eyebrow at her. I hadn't told her that Luca and I were fighting, although I suppose she had figured it out, or maybe Chris, my trainer, had told her.

"Yes, we're fine," I grinned. "All sorted out now."

"Have anything to do with Luca helping to secure the Maison de Klotho deal?" she asked. We both knew his letter had helped. Clothing companies rarely got huge deals with male F1 drivers, so having one agree to do some modeling for them was a huge offer, especially for a driver from a team with such a huge fan following. Hermes F1 was one of the oldest teams in the sport, and they didn't need Maison de Klotho, but Maison de Klotho would certainly take Hermes.

"That, and some other stuff," I responded honestly. I didn't want to overshare with Lily yet. We were friends, but I felt like I had talked about all of this so much recently. I just didn't have it in me to go around again.

"So... that kiss at Monza. You can't tell me that kiss wasn't at least somewhat real," she prodded. I wanted to shrug her off, but when I turned to look at her, she had the world's biggest grin on her face, one that could only possibly match Edward's grin in terms of size. It was hard to be annoyed with Lily when she had a face that looked like a million suns beaming at me.

"Like I said, a polite woman never tells," I responded cheekily. I knew I was winding her up, so I took another swig of my champagne and looked over in Luca's direction. He, Edward, and Oliver were deep in some conversation the three of them clearly found quite funny. Lily just chuckled at that and grabbed my hand, pulling me towards Edward and Luca. As we walked on over, I felt Luca put his hand on my waist, giving it a tight squeeze.

"Nice little interview you gave there," he said with a smirk. He looked a little too pleased with what I had said, and I rolled my eyes, giving him a small shove.

"Don't let it go to that big head of yours," I quipped back.

"You know what I think this calls for – shots!" Oliver called out, coming back from the bar with enough shots to feed a small army.

"Absolutely not," I insisted. I had already broken my alcohol rule at practically every race this season, but I was not about to start doing shots, even if we didn't get into our cars until Friday.

Before I could offer another rebuttal to what Oliver was clearly going to say, Noah blurted out, "Geez, no wonder they call you the boring twin." The group started to 'ooooh' as if Noah was about to get in trouble. The fact that Noah *fucking* Hendriks had called me boring was the pot calling the kettle black. That man's life consisted of video games and racing – nothing else. I wanted to retort something rude, but I knew that would only spur them on more. So instead, I did the unthinkable – I grabbed one of Oliver's shots and downed it – *like the fucking champion I knew I was.*

The crowd erupted into applause. I tried to hide my gagging as soon as the tequila hit the back of my throat; tequila was not my favorite thing to drink, but the look on Oliver's face was worth it. He clearly was not expecting me to do that. I winked at him as I put the shot glass back on the table. The rest of the group took their shots, still clearly in amusement over my antics.

As the night progressed, I was starting to feel more comfortable. Another round of shots – this time vodka – was consumed, and then a few more glasses of champagne. I was starting to feel good, perhaps a little too good. After coming back from the bathroom, I tripped over and landed on Henri, who just laughed as he caught me.

"I think Peaches probably had enough for this evening, huh?" he asked me in a soft voice, although it was loud enough for

Oliver and Luca to hear. I just giggled at him, wiggling my finger in his face.

"Nopppppppe," I said, popping the P at the end. Henri chuckled, but before he could help me walk further, Luca came up to me, a huge, cheesy grin on his face.

"Come on, Amore," he whispered in my ear. I scoffed at the silly nickname, even though I was starting to get those butterflies again. It's as if Luca could tell that I was about to push away from him, demanding to be allowed to stay at the bar, because he followed it up with, "If you come back with me now, I promise I'll let you drive to the track on Thursday and Friday?"

It's as if my drunk brain couldn't handle the excitement. I nodded a little too excitedly and grumbled, "Fine, Mr. Rossi, you got yourself a deal." I grabbed his hand and shook it, making Lily, Oliver, and Henri laugh in the process. We said our goodbyes, and I wobbled my way out of the bar. Fortunately, Luca was able to call us a cab, and we made it back to my apartment fairly quickly.

"You know, I'm not even that tired," I slurred out, pointing my fingers at Luca. "I'm going to watch a movie when I get back." Luca just chuckled, nodding at my insistence.

"Only if I get to pick it," he insisted.

"Fine, but don't pick something boring," I argued.

Luca

As soon as we walked into Georgia's apartment, she plopped herself down on the couch and kicked off her heels. I followed her, bringing with me a glass of water, a hydration packet, and some liver supplements. At first, she stuck her tongue out at me, insisting she couldn't possibly be hungover in the morning. I did my best not to scoff at that. Georgia didn't strike me as someone who got drunk often; she was definitely going to be hungover in the morning. Her tolerance was shit, as evidenced by the fact she was very drunk after two shots and a couple of glasses of champagne.

But I knew if I didn't convince her to take the items, she would regret it tomorrow. Plus, I don't think Isabelle would be pleased with me if I showed up at the paddock tomorrow with a completely hungover Georgia – something told me I would be blamed for that one.

So, again, I made her a deal – take the items, and I would let her pick the movie. I didn't want to watch a film, and I knew she was just being difficult, but I figured she was drunk enough to fall asleep in all of five minutes.

Plus, it was pretty adorable seeing her this drunk. She was much touchier than usual, grabbing onto my arm as she got into the cab. At one point, she had almost fallen asleep, and her head had just barely drifted onto my shoulder before she woke up. I knew it was pathetic that I was so excited about her just barely touching me. I was like a high-school teenager whose crush had shown him some minor attention.

Georgia drank the hydration packet and then scooted closer to me on the couch, grabbing a blanket from behind her. As if it was completely normal, she put the blanket over us both and mumbled something that sounded like, "Wouldn't want you to be cold." I tried not to laugh at that as she snuggled closer into the blanket.

She had selected Atonement, which shouldn't have surprised me. After a few minutes into the movie, I looked down at her, expecting her to be asleep. But she wasn't. In fact, she didn't even look like she was watching the movie at all. I had seen that look before, and something told me her brain was a million lightyears away.

As she began to sink a little more into herself, I took my arm and wrapped it around her shoulder, pulling her closer to my chest. I half expected her to pull away, but she didn't. Instead, Georgia leaned in and put her head on my chest, snuggling up closer into my warmth. I tried not to let a smile creep onto my lips, but it was impossible. Here I was with the most beautiful girl in the paddock, wrapped up in my arms.

I was worried after last Sunday that she would never speak to me again, that the progress we had made would be ruined. It's why Maison de Klotho was the first call I made on Monday. Well, one of the reasons why. Besides the fact that I did want to do something to make Georgia forgive me, the idea that she could possibly lose her seat was disastrous to me because it meant that I wouldn't see her at every race weekend.

And that had begun to become an unbearable thought.

Even if this was fake, even if she wasn't mine, I had become attached to her in such a short amount of time. I meant what I said in the podcast. Ever since that first meal in Miami, Georgia was making me a better person.

I suddenly heard something come from her lips. I leaned down and looked at her face. Her eyes were closed. *Had she said something?* She opened her eyes and looked up at me.

"When you're being like this, all comfortable and nice, it's really hard to dislike you, Rossi," she whispered again. This time, a hiccup followed the end of her sentence. "And it's really fucking annoying," she added.

Georgia put her head back down on my chest and then closed her eyes again. I'm glad she couldn't see me because there was no way I was hiding the huge smile on my face. I picked her up and moved her to her bedroom, placing her under the covers. She was already fast asleep.

"You too, Dubois, you too."

Chapter Twelve

THREE'S A CROWN

Georgia

Thursday morning, I was woken up by Luca standing over me, a cup of coffee in one hand, a paracetamol in the other – and a huge fucking grin on his face. I groaned, turning over in bed as I dragged the covers above my head. I didn't care if Luca and I had agreed to be friends; I was not in the mood for his antics this morning.

"Good morning, Cara," he whistled out, walking over to my curtains and opening them all the way, letting the blistering sunshine into my room.

"Fuck, Luca, why are you in my room? Ever heard of knocking?" I yelled at him, taking one of my pillows and chucking it at him.

"I did, Principessa, but judging by the look on your face, you were much too asleep to hear my knocking."

"Well, maybe you should have knocked harder," I quipped back, attempting to grab the paracetamol from his hands.

He smirked at that, raising the two pills higher above my head. "This is only for *hungover girlfriends.*" I didn't really appreciate his emphasis on girlfriend, or hungover, but I let it slide. My head was pounding, and he had lifesaving pain medicine as far as I was concerned.

"Who said I was hungover?" I muttered grumpily. A headache, nausea, and undying thirst after a night of drinking didn't *necessarily mean* I was hungover.

Unfortunately for me, I 100% *was* hungover, no doubt about that, but I wasn't about to let Luca know that.

Luca laughed at me and set the two pills down next to my bottle of water from last night. Truthfully, I wasn't sure how I even got into bed last night. Had Luca taken me to bed? Last I remembered was attempting to watch a movie. I swallowed down the pills and took the coffee from his hands, downing the mug in two sips.

"Well, good, if you aren't hungover, then we can start our day today," he trilled, pulling the blankets back entirely. I got up quickly for a moment, horrified that I had no pants on. I usually slept in an oversized shirt, no pants required. Although to be fair, the results of what Luca and I saw when he pulled back the covers were much worse – I was still in last night's clothes.

How drunk had I gotten?

It's as if Luca could read my mind because he declared, "Much too drunk considering how *little* you drank." The smug look on his face said everything I needed to know. I got up and pushed him aside, grabbing my towel from the banister.

"Why don't you do us both a favor and get lost, huh?" I barked at him, closing the bathroom door with a bang. I knew I was being a bitch. I mean, he had brought me coffee – black with no cream or sugar, just how I liked it, plus some paracetamol. Still, he had done it with the intent to tease me, which I was not in the mood for. Today was day one of the Monaco Grand Prix. I had to survive what felt like eight hours of journalists, press, and fans before getting into a car tomorrow to drive a race that was probably the most important of my career to date.

And I had to do the first half of that while hungover. *What an idiot.*

As I finished in the shower, I grabbed my phone to check Instagram. I'm never sure why I felt the need to check Instagram before a race. It never made me feel better, but I guess as a woman in her twenties, *it was in my nature.*

 LightsOutPodcast

Liked by Valkyrie F1 Team and 30k others

LightsOutPodcast This week we checked in with Henri and Georgia Dubois and learned about their racing passions – both on and off the track. Most importantly, we finally got down to the elusive hamster story. Click the link in bio to learn more! #HenriDubois #GeorgiaDubois

I scrolled through various posts before finally arriving at the one about the podcast. To my relief, the reviews were pretty positive. There were calls that there wasn't enough Henri content, but that was to be expected. Hermes' golden boy could have had his own podcast, and the women of the world would still be demanding more content of *just* Henri.

Still, the fans loved the prankster side of me, which I found to be quite shocking. I had spent so much time hiding this part of me from the world – I didn't expect for that to be the one thing the fans held onto. It was as if it was the one thing that made me human... that made me relatable.

Maybe I should pull a prank on the journalists; then they might also see me as human, I chuckled to myself.

As I sat there trying to weigh out how likely I was to lose my seat if I pranked the F1 media community, Luca walked into the room with bacon, toast, and a second cup of coffee. As he turned and saw me in just a towel, he stuttered for a moment and then gave me a quick once over before backing away, but not before I could pick up my pillow from the bed and throw it at him.

Unfortunately for me, that made my entire towel drop to the ground, and I pulled my covers off of my bed to cover myself, screaming at Luca, "Come into my room one more time, Luca, and I will personally make sure you can never have children with whatever pathetic woman decides to marry you! Understood?" I could hear laughter from behind the door as Luca closed it. Insufferable man.

I quickly got dressed and threw some makeup on, putting my hair up in a braid. I scarfed down my toast and bacon as quickly as I could, then headed to the kitchen, where Henri and Luca were both sitting, enjoying a cup of my coffee.

"Thanks for breakfast," I mumbled to Luca, not looking in his direction. Truthfully, I was too embarrassed to look him in the face.

"Don't worry, Cara, now we've both seen each other naked. You know, me just now and you in your dreams," he said with a wink. I froze for a moment and then turned to Henri, who had just spit out his coffee onto my nice Persian rug. Henri turned to me and quirked an eyebrow up, although I could see his expression was asking me if this was actually true.

Before I could stop myself, I blurted out, "Umm... you weren't naked!" I said it with way too much sass for someone who had experienced a sex dream about their fake boyfriend. Luca just smirked, but his interest was definitely piqued.

Fuck, why had I just said that? It was clear that Luca knew, that I knew, that he knew – *unfortunately* – that he had starred in my

167

recent sex dream, but now I had basically just confirmed it in my pit of anger. I turned my back and internally cringed, pretending to busy myself with the empty coffee maker.

"Better hope you haven't seen my sister naked," I heard Henri mutter to Luca. He clearly wasn't amused at the joke, although arguably for very different reasons. I knew my face had gone a new shade of red, so I continued to play with my coffee maker, my back to the two of them.

"Wouldn't *dream* of it," Luca quipped back. I truly could have died in that moment.

Fortunately, before the awkward silence could continue, Henri's cell phone rang. It was their team principal, and he was requesting him in the paddock a little early to do a couple of extra social media stints for his home race. Henri came over and gave me a big hug, waving at Luca on his way out – albeit a little coldly.

Luca and I finished our coffees in silence – *a smug silence for him and a mortified silence for me* – and then we headed towards my parking garage. As we arrived at my Volkswagen Beatle, Luca turned to me, a horrified look on his face.

"What the fuck is this?" He asked with some amusement – but mostly horror – in his voice.

"This is a car," I deadpanned back, getting into the driver's seat. Luca just stood by the passenger door; he couldn't quite shake the look of disbelief from his face. I think in that moment, I had actually stunned Luca Rossi into silence, and I felt quite victorious.

Georgia: 2 Luca: 1

As we arrived at the Monaco paddock, the place was buzzing with people, more so than I expected for a Thursday. I parked the car in the assigned parking garage, and then, hand in hand with Luca, walked through the VIP areas and into the main area with the garages. We took some selfies with fans and waved to the cameras as we were instructed.

Luca walked me to the Valkyrie garage, and just as he was about to leave, Isabelle called us both over with just a wave of her hand. Luca turned to look at me, and I could see he was a little nervous.

Isabelle had quite the reputation in the paddock, and even though she was Francesco's wife, I always felt like Luca was still terrified of her. Francesco was a piece of cake compared to Isabelle. I took a small amount of pleasure in seeing Luca squirm as we walked towards her office.

Before we walked in, I took a big breath and put on the biggest *'I'm not hungover, don't be silly Isabelle'* face I could muster. Isabelle looked up at us as we walked in and scrunched her nose, clearly assessing the two of us, and I immediately knew I had been caught.

"Had too much to drink last night, Georgia?" she asked – a clear tone of disapproval in her voice. I could hear Luca let out a small chuckle before Isabelle turned to him and chastised, "Don't look so smug, Luca. Takes one to know one." And with that, we both sat down quietly, like two toddlers who had been scolded by their mother.

Isabelle: 1 Luca: 1

After a few more awkward moments of silence, Lizzie, Hugo, and Lily filtered into the office, followed by Francesco and Matteo.

What is this, a party at the Valkyrie paddock? I grumbled.

"So, I have called you all here because the BBC has asked to do a segment on Luca and Georgia. Apparently, F1's newest couple will be good for ratings," Isabelle announced. "As much as I would like to push back on this, I think it would be a bad look for the team. The BBC is very good at getting their story out regardless of participation, and if we don't agree, then we won't be able to control the narrative. They are going to add this into the next season regardless; might as well be a part of that."

I cringed a bit. I had never dreamed of being on TV. Hell, I think the idea of being on the next season of Full Throttle just as a driver was infuriating, never mind as someone's girlfriend. While I hated media events, the BBC documentary felt worse because I knew this would be readily available to millions of people across the globe. People who didn't even watch Formula 1 would watch this.

I felt Luca shift a bit in his seat next to me. I had expected him to be pleased about this, but his face told a different story, which intrigued me. Was it because he knew we were going to break up at the end of the season, and he didn't want the embarrassment? *Probably*.

There was a silence in the air as if no one knew what to say. Putting a fake relationship on in the paddock was one thing; presenting it to the world on a huge national TV show was another. After a few more minutes, Isabelle dismissed both Luca and me, neither of us truly knowing what to say.

Will deal with that after Monaco, I decided.

When I woke up Saturday morning, I heard the pitter-patter of rain on my window.

Well, shit. Not exactly the weather I was hoping for. Rainy days were good for the teams that were in slower cars, but I planned to be in pole position after today, and the Valkyrie car wasn't the best in the rain. Or, to be more precise, I wasn't the best in the rain.

Still, I'd never backed down from a challenge before.

Luca and I got ready quickly on Saturday and headed to the track in his Lamborghini. The rain continued to pour down, and as we got to the paddock, Mel, my race engineer, informed me that FP3 had been delayed by thirty minutes in the hopes that the rain would cease. Based on the weather forecast, that felt very unrealistic, but I knew the FIA was willing to send us out in pretty terrible, blistering conditions.

Sure enough, as thirty minutes passed, I was loaded into my car and sent off to the third free practice of the weekend, only to be recalled back into the pits twenty minutes later, after another driver had crashed into the wall. They were fortunately fine, but the FIA decided that FP3 was too dangerous to continue, so everyone else was called back in to see if the rain would calm down.

As I hopped out of the car, Lizzie motioned for me to come over.

"This might be a while. Why don't you go pop round the Hermes garage, hmm?" I gave her a pleading look; it was cold and wet, and I did not feel like dealing with either Luca or my brother, but I saw Isabelle behind her give me a nod, and that was that.

I grabbed Lily, and we padded on over to the Hermes garage, where we saw Luca and Henri sitting in the garage, playing chess. We walked into the garage, waving at Francesco on the way in as we made our way over to the boys, who looked up as we approached.

"To what do I owe the pleasure, Principessa," Luca said with a slight shiver in his voice. I looked down, and he was wearing his Hermes F1 jacket, but still, he looked quite cold.

"Figured you boys would need some company," I said sweetly, sitting next to Luca on the bench. As soon as I sat down, Luca scooted a little closer to me, linking his arm to mine and putting his head on my shoulder. I looked at Henri and Lily, a look of shock on my face, which I quickly changed to a look of love. There was never a moment in public when we weren't being watched.

Even though Luca and I weren't actually dating, it had become clear to me that his love language was touch. Luca was the most touchy-feely person I had ever met. Henri and Lily just smiled at me, clearly noticing my discomfort.

"Awww," Lily said, "aren't these two just the cutest." Henri nodded, his eyes turning to meet mine. Behind his eyes, I could see his mind assessing the situation. It was as if he had another thought behind the joyful face he was giving me, like he was evaluating the two of us, trying to piece together what he was actually witnessing in front of him.

I did my best to ignore Henri as I looked down at Luca and I's hands, which were now intertwined. Luca was still staring at the chess board, clearly oblivious to the three of us around him. I looked around to see if a Hermes F1 social coordinator was watching, but the garage was surprisingly quiet. For a moment, those pesky butterflies returned as I tried to wrap my head around the fact that Luca was holding my hand and snuggling with me without any prompt from Matteo and without any media around us.

It's as if he was enjoying my company. I tried to shake that thought from my head. Now was not the time to be getting sentimental with anyone, especially not the enemy.

As the rain began to clear up, I heard Lizzie call for us to return to the Valkyrie garage. Qualifying would begin soon, and the rest of free practice had been canceled. We quickly said our goodbyes, and I gave my brother one last hug, wishing him luck – well, good luck on getting P2, of course.

Luca

The rain had briefly slowed down to just a drizzle, and I had been asked to hop into the car since Q1 was beginning in five minutes. As I slowly went out on track for my out lap, I could feel how slippery the roads were – even with my wet tires. The Monaco streets were old, and they didn't drain well.

I didn't do as well as I had hoped in Q1, only coming in P5. Henri had managed P1, and Georgia P2, only a hundredth of a second between them. As Q2 began, the rain had picked up a bit, but we were still instructed to continue, the FIA insisting that the track was dry enough. Within one minute of starting, one of the Stella Luminosa team cars had spun out and crashed, causing a yellow flag to appear. The small wreck was quickly cleared, but it meant the teams had less time to get their flying laps in – and on a track like Monaco, that was a major problem.

Still, I was able to squeeze out P4, which would send me into Q3 of qualifying – where the actual pressure was on. Monaco surprisingly had a low pole-to-win ratio, and yet, every driver that took pole was the expected winner of the race. The track was nearly impossible to pass, and with the right defense, you could hold on even if you went under your top speed. As we put in our flying laps, I could feel the rain start to get harder – the track was getting more dangerous.

"We continuing?" I asked my race engineer, who responded in the affirmative.

I asked about the lap times, and he informed me that Henri was still P1, with Georgia a very close P2 behind him. Still, she had time for another flying lap – and then one after that. As I expected, after the next round of laps, Georgia was P1, and Henri was now P3 since Noah Hendriks had put in a solid lap, although after that lap his front wing had taken minor damage, and he was asked to come into the pits.

We were all instructed to do one last lap, and I was the third car to cross over the racing line before time ran out. It was Georgia, then Henri, then me over the line – with Oscar Parker of Rennen and Edward Davis of Wilmington right behind me, also on flying laps.

Last lap, Luca, let's make it count, I encouraged myself. I could see Henri in front of me. His precision and movements looked incredible, and I started to believe that he just had to take the pole after this. It seemed like the lap of his life. I felt a little pang in my heart for Georgia. She was the presumed pole sitter, and while I obviously wanted to take pole position, a small part of me desperately wanted to see her up there.

But then, as I turned the corner, I saw a nightmare unfold in front of me. In Henri's aggression to get P1, he had hit Georgia's car, and it was tumbling into the corner before the Monaco tunnel. Her car spun twice before hitting the barrier, but fortunately, Henri's car had stopped right before it could crash into Georgia. As I watched the wreck in front of me, I felt a huge pang of fear in the pit of my stomach; even though the safety in Formula 1 was top-tier, there was always a risk when we raced.

I immediately slammed on the brakes, got out of the car, and ran towards Georgia's car, ignoring Henri as he climbed out of his car, hot on my trail. Georgia wasn't getting out of the car, and that had me worried; that kind of force against a barrier would leave a driver stunned. I approached the cockpit of the car, but Georgia still wasn't making a move to get out. As I started to pull her out, she began to move a bit more. I wasn't sure if she was injured, or just in shock, but I wanted to get her out of this car before any potential engine fire could happen.

I could feel Henri come up behind me, attempting to push me out of the way so he could get to his sister. I stood my ground, turning my back to him so I could get a better grip on Georgia's shoulders as I pulled her free from the racing seat. She held onto me, still not saying a word, as I felt her wobble a bit, using my body for balance. I put my arms around her and pulled her into me.

At that moment, it felt like time had stopped – for just that moment, I felt like Georgia and I were the only people in Monaco.

She then looked up at me, and I could see her eyes lock onto mine. I couldn't see her whole face, but I knew that she had a look of utter despair. My heart felt like it was breaking into a million pieces as I looked around and saw debris from her car all around her. Still, I let out a sigh of relief because while her car was damaged, she was alright.

I stumbled back a bit as I felt Henri grab his sister, turning her to him. He had taken off his helmet, and he was pulling hers off, demanding to know if she was alright – although the look on his face was anything but concerned. Georgia took a step back as her helmet came flying off, taking a deep breath before picking up her pointer finger and poking Henri in the chest. At that moment, I wasn't sure which Dubois twin had the scarier look on their face. They looked as though they were about to enter a boxing ring.

"You *fucking* idiot!" Georgia spat out at Henri – there was nothing but rage in her eyes, just rage and fury. Edward stepped forward, putting his hand on Georgia's chest as if to signal she should take a moment to breathe.

"Me? Why were you driving like an absolute moron, blocking my flying lap?" He demanded, squaring up to his sister. "Scared I was going to beat you?" he added, his voice laced with venom.

"Whoa, mate, let's calm down a bit, eh," I heard Oscar say to Henri. "Your sister just had quite an accident; let's get her to the medical tent." Oscar went to put his hand out to Georgia, but she just ignored him, still staring down her brother. We must have looked quite the site to fans, the five of us drivers now all standing in the middle of the wreckage, our helmets off, arguing away.

I heard the ambulance sirens behind us, and as the safety car arrived with the ambulance, we were instructed to hop into the SUV. Both Georgia and Henri were to head straight to the medical tent. As we sat in the safety car, no one said a word as we approached the makeshift paddock. Georgia stormed out of the safety car and into the medical tent situated within the paddock. After a few minutes, I entered the tent, and I saw both Isabelle and Fiona hovering over Georgia, who was getting tests done.

"Do you think the car can be fixed?" Georgia asked in such a small voice I had barely heard her. There was sadness in her voice, and if I looked closely enough, I could see tears forming in her eyes.

"We're assessing the damage now. We'll stay all night if we have to," Fiona confirmed. Georgia just nodded to her, her eyes catching mine. I approached the medical bed and smiled at her.

"You ok?" I asked, nodding to the bruise on her arm.

"I'll live," she replied simply. She turned to Isabelle and opened her mouth, but it was as if Isabelle knew exactly what she was going to ask.

"Yes, you are going to do press. You are on pole, and you are racing tomorrow as far as Valkyrie is concerned. Now, let's get you out of this racing suit and into your jeans and a team polo. You're expected at the conference in fifteen. Once that conference is done, I want Luca to take you home, and you are to go straight to sleep. I need you at your very best tomorrow."

Georgia nodded and stood up from the bed, stumbling a bit before catching herself. I grabbed her helmet for her, and she gave me a small smile. I motioned for her to go before me, and as we began to leave the tent, Fiona approached us.

"Georgie, I know you are upset with your brother," Fiona said, taking a moment to pause before she continued with her thought, "and you have every right to be. I saw the recording. Henri was driving too aggressively, and you never left the racing line. His race engineer did not give him enough space to complete the lap at the pace he needed to get pole, and that is on Hermes.

However, the press are going to desperately want to see you both fighting. They're going to want to turn you guys against each other because that will sell their papers. Don't give in to that. As mad as you are, don't give the media what they want. When you win tomorrow, you'll get the justice you deserve. I promise."

Georgia stilled for a moment, and I heard her release a huge sigh next to me. I'm not sure what compelled me to do this, maybe it was the look of devastation on her face, but I reached my hand down to hers and laced our fingers together, giving her hand a tight squeeze. Surprisingly, she squeezed back.

I leaned down and whispered, "She's right, you know. Don't feed the bears – they'll only come begging for more."

Georgia

As Luca took my hand and squeezed it, I looked at him. For the first time, I could see that his face was laced with concern. Was he concerned I was going to beat up my brother? *Maybe.*

I hated to admit it to myself, but Luca staying with me and holding my hand made me feel immensely better. As I looked up into his beautiful brown eyes, my anger started to dissipate.

Henri was having a tough season with Hermes, and I didn't doubt that they had screwed up his qualifying strategy. Still, it was no reason to ruin my race. Henri was known for his competitiveness and impulsive behaviors, and now I was on the receiving end of those. I decided to listen to Fiona and kept my thoughts to myself. No matter how much the journalist community tried to poke and prod at my anger towards Henri, I sat there and smiled – a nice, big Cheshire cat smile.

Wonder who I learned that from?

The next morning I woke up at six a.m. to a text from Isabelle and Fiona saying that the car had been repaired. The team had spent the entire night rebuilding the car and scrounging parts, and they had been successful. I had asked – *no, begged* – to be allowed to stay up with the team and help, but no one would hear of it. Apparently, I needed all the sleep I could get after that impact. To be fair, they weren't wrong; I had gotten twelve hours of sleep, and I felt almost 100%.

I asked Luca if he would be okay getting to the paddock early. My race nerves were on edge, and I felt like I just needed to be there with my team. I had training with Chris in the morning. My reactions needed to be perfect in Monaco. Mistakes were easy – and common.

Unlike most mornings, Luca was quiet. I suspected he knew that I was not in the mood for chit-chat, and while he usually ignored my pleading requests, this time I knew he understood. As a race champion of his home race, he understood what I was going through. For the first time in a long time, Luca and I truly had something in common, and it made our silence refreshing and almost comforting.

My arrival at the paddock was truly madness. I thought it would be empty at 8 a.m., but I couldn't have been more wrong. There were fans everywhere – waving the Monaco flag and the Valkyrie and Hermes team flags. I was shocked at the number of Valkyrie flags waving in the wind. No words could describe how I felt about the turnout from my country.

The next several hours were probably the slowest of my life. The rain had been off and on all morning, but it looked like we were going to have 'cloudy' sunshine for the actual race. I still hadn't spoken to Henri, and while I was still incredibly mad at him, something in my heart told me I needed to wish my brother luck. We had never gone into a race angry with one another. It was a rule we had. Formula 1 was dangerous; too dangerous to go into a race angry at someone you loved so dearly. Henri truly was my best friend, my twin. I pulled out my phone and sent him a text.

> Georgia: Car was repaired. Just wanted to wish you luck. Whoever wins, I'm proud of you.

> Henri: Francesco told me. Relieved to hear. Love ya, sis, may the best Dubois win.

I smiled at his response. I meant what I said – if Henri came out on top, I would be happy for him. The only thing more important than winning the World Driver's Championship was my family. That wouldn't change today.

As 2:50 p.m. rolled around, we were shuffled into our cars. The rain had cleared, and it looked like we would race with cloudy but rain-free skies. As the formulation lap finished, I heard Mel come on the radio.

"Good luck, GG. Let's bring the bitch home." I smirked at that one; the F1 commentators always groaned when we cursed on our radios. Sometimes I did it just to piss them off, much to Isabelle's annoyance.

As soon as the five lights went out, I launched into the start of the race. Being pole in Monaco meant one thing – the race was yours to fuck up, and it was somehow easy to do. Hermes F1 had managed to screw it up several times for my brother. But this year I had something Henri didn't have – an all-female team with an undying desire to take home the race trophy all of the constructors wanted the most. This race wasn't just about me showing off my driving talent. Truthfully, Monaco was a boring track compared to other races in the season. I didn't need to be the best driver on the grid with the best car to win – many drivers had won with luck alone. The race wasn't won simply on the driver's ability to mind the narrow streets – in Monaco, the pit stop strategy mattered.

Something which became very evident by lap forty-five. More than halfway through the race, and I was still leading after a pitstop. My tires were feeling good, although I could feel they were wearing.

As I came into the pits for a second set of tires, the front wing became stuck, causing an extra two seconds to be added to my pit stop time.

"Fuck. What happened?" I demanded into the mic.

"Wing failure. Just keep driving. We'll make up the time," Mel responded.

"We'll need a fucking miracle," I deadpanned back. Mel proceeded to respond to me, but I ignored her. I could see Henri in front, and at this point, I knew it was Hermes' race to lose. Still, I pressed on. Every lap of this race meant Hermes had an opportunity to screw up, and I was on fresher tires, gaining speed on the back of Henri. Fortunately, Noah in P3 was too far behind, so I was able to nurse my tires. Another twenty laps went by, and it was now lap sixty-five, just thirteen laps to go.

And then, like lightning in a thunderstorm, luck struck.

As Henri went into the pits to get his softs, his left tire malfunctioned, causing him to come out behind me in P2 once all the other pit stops had been completed by the other drivers. I was in front again with eight laps to go.

"GG, defend like the lioness I know you to be," was all Mel said on my radio.

And defend I did. I went through the next eight laps with more precision than I have ever had in my life. I drove within millimeters of the barriers and set my eyes in front of me, not even worrying about Henri behind me. This was my race to lose – and no man was going to take it from me.

As I started the last lap, I began to hear a little whistle in my car.

Fuck, fuck, fuck, I thought to myself. *This can't happen now. I will push this car to the finish line before I DNF out of this race.*

"Mel. Noise. Why?" I panicked, barely able to get out the words and definitely not able to get out a full sentence.

"Debris stuck in the floor."

"Fuck. What do I do?"

"Remember when we went to that stupid fair in Paris?"

"How is this fucking relevant?" I bit back.

"We went on that silly go-kart track, and you were so mad you qualified behind me, so you just blocked the way for everyone like an absolute menace."

"Yes..."

"Now's your time, GG. Be that menace."

And what a menace I became. I could feel the debris in the floor, so I slowed the car down and then did the unthinkable – I started to drive closer to the middle of the road, not caring about the racing line. I didn't need to be faster than Henri this lap; I just needed to keep him behind me. I could see his car swerving, trying to find an opportunity to pass.

But this was Monaco. I grew up on these streets. The only person who knew these narrow streets as well as I did was behind me. As soon as the checkered flag came into view, I launched my car with all the might and power I knew the Valkyrie car had. I saw Henri right behind me, making one last attempt to get past me.

But it was too late for Henri – *I had crossed the line first.*

I had won the Monaco Grand Prix, with Henri a 1000th of a second behind me.

The emotions in that moment were inexplicable. It was like every emotion I had felt in the last year, since taking the seat at Valkyrie F1, had finally bubbled up to the surface. Tears started to spill from my eyes as I made my way into the pits; the floor was absolutely damaged, and that was going to cost the team, but at that moment, I didn't care. This race win was going to bring us the sponsorships we needed – the sponsorship the team *deserved.*

I heard the radio turn on, "Georgie, this is Isabelle. No, this is the entire Valkyrie team speaking... well done, love, well done. Also, that's P3 for Lily. Double podium today."

"Wahoo!" I screamed into the radio. "This one's for you all. For every single one of you that stayed up all night working on this car. This trophy belongs to you. You believed in me when no one else did." I took a moment before adding, "This win is for every little girl who is told she can't compete with the boys. Let this be a lesson to those who want to keep women out of motorsports. We're here to stay."

As soon as I parked in the P1 spot, I jumped out of my car, hands in the air, classic window washing dance as I stood on top of my car. Soon after, Henri parked in the P2 spot, and Lily parked in the P3 spot – her first-ever podium. Apparently, Blaue Flügel had made an error on the tires, and Lily was able to sneak past Noah Hendriks with a better change of tires.

I ran towards the Valkyrie paddock and jumped into the arms of Mel, my race engineer, tears on both of our faces. Fiona ran over, grabbing my shoulders and pulling me into a deaf-defying hug. As I walked back towards the cars and presenter, Hugo grabbed me and gave me a huge hug – followed by Henri. My twin brother came up to me, grabbed my helmet, and pulled me in for what can only be described as an absolute chokehold of a hug.

"I'm so proud, Peaches," I heard him say over the commotion. "So proud."

I took off my helmet and fireproof cap and ran over to Lily, who was also celebrating with the Valkyrie F1 mechanics. Surprisingly, she jumped up into my arms, wrapped her legs around my waist, and gave me a huge hug and kiss on my forehead. I chuckled and spun her around. At that moment, I wasn't sure what I was happier about – me winning, or Lily finally getting that podium she deserved, and in Monaco, no less.

A double podium for Valkyrie; there was absolutely nothing that could spoil today.

As other racers started to come up to me, I looked for Luca in the crowd. Finally, I saw him coming up the paddock walkway, a huge grin on his face. As he reached me, he pulled me into a huge hug. All of a sudden, I felt myself being leaned backward. I looked up at Luca's face, and he had the world's biggest grin on his face, like he had a plan in motion that he couldn't wait to see hatch. Before I knew it, Luca's lips were on mine, and I was leaning back, being kissed as if I was Cinderella and Luca was my Prince Charming.

After a few seconds, Luca slowly lifted me back up and pulled my face to his. "Go and celebrate, Principessa. I'll give you your real prize later," he said in a voice much too sultry for my liking – well, maybe to my liking.

He picked up his helmet and began walking towards the Hermes garage, a huge grin on his face. Before I could process what had just happened, I was being pulled towards the presenter and then the cool-down room.

After the trophy ceremony was complete, I made my way back to the garage to get ready for the media circus. For the first time in the history of my Formula 1 career, I wasn't the least bit nervous for the press debrief. Hell, they could have told me that my car had caught on fire, and I wouldn't be able to compete for the next five races, and I wouldn't have cared. *Nothing could ruin the magic of winning Monaco.*

As I was changing my clothes, Isabelle knocked on the door.

"Come in!" I was surprised to see Isabelle at my door. Typically, she was pulled into a constructors meeting after the race.

"I have something for you," she said in her thick Italian accent. She handed me a small bag with blue tissue paper. I opened up the bag and pulled out a team polo. I gave Isabelle a confused look, and she just chuckled at me – actually chuckled.

"Turn it over."

As I turned the polo over, there it was. The words I had wanted to say since the beginning of my F1 career. Isabelle had taken my team polo and had the words "Triple Crown of Motorsport: 2022" stitched onto it. The words were sewn in beautiful lettering, clearly hand-stitched by someone with incredible detail and care. I looked up at her, my mouth wide open, unsure of what to say. This shirt would have taken weeks to make. The fact that Isabelle had so much belief that I was going to win, going to accomplish my dream, left me speechless.

"Tha- thank you," I stuttered out.

Isabelle smiled a lovely, pearly white smile. I had never seen her smile that wide before. She had a beautiful smile with just one dimple on her left cheek.

"Wear it to the press conference," she said simply. With that, she got up and headed towards the exit, but not before adding, "Wear it, and remind the vultures that a lioness has arrived at the paddock, and she has a bone to pick with them."

The press conference had been an interesting one, one of the few press conferences that I would be willing to relive. It was as if the press had no idea what to say to me, and that was fine by me. They asked the usual boring questions – about the strategy and tires, but for the first time in my career, not a single person uttered even a slightly personal or offensive question to me.

Good, I thought to myself. *Let them stew on that for a while.*

The celebrations that evening had been some of my best. Unlike Wednesday, I had elected to drink less. I wanted to remember this day. I wanted to remember everything about it. Luca had also decided to drink less for some inexplicable reason. He had been a bit odd when we got back to my apartment after the race. He was kind, courteous, but, most of all – he was quiet. Even at the bar, he was attentive when I asked him questions but kept to himself more than expected – as if he was trying to give me some space.

Truth be told, I was kind of annoyed. I had won the Monaco Grand Prix, my home race, and for some reason, Luca had decided *this* was the time he was going to give me the space I had been craving. I had spent the last several races demanding it, and now, for some blasted reason, I was angry and jealous. Jealous that he had spent a good portion of the evening celebrating with Lily. Jealous that he seemed to talk to every single damn person in this club except his girlfriend.

Fake girlfriend, I corrected myself, but Luca's words rang in my ear, '*Go and celebrate, Principessa. I'll give you your real prize later.*' At around midnight, I said goodbye to my friends and grabbed Luca's hand.

"We're leaving," I demanded. He quirked up an eyebrow but let me drag him into the cab I hailed outside of the club. The ride to my apartment was silent. Truthfully, I didn't know what to say.

As soon as the car arrived, we quickly shuffled into my living room. I was starting to feel more and more annoyed with Luca. He padded over to my fridge, grabbed a bottle of water, and turned back to me, smiling slightly, "Well, what a good day. Night, Georgie."

And with that, he waltzed into his room.

I. Was. Fuming. *Why was I fuming?* Not for any decent reason I cared to admit.

Before I could stop myself, I marched on over to his room and flung open the door. Inside the room, I saw a startled Luca, who was of course shirtless, just staring back at me. His eyes conveyed a look of shock, but the ever-so-slight curl of his lip told me otherwise.

I decided to ignore that – for now.

"What was that all about?" I demanded.

"Hmm?" he asked casually, setting his water down at his bedside table.

"You!" I yelled back, starting to raise my voice. "You spent the whole night ignoring me... by, like, not ignoring me." I knew I sounded like an idiot. I knew I should probably stop myself, but I couldn't.

"I thought you'd want your space," he responded easily, too easily in my opinion.

"Why would you think I'd want space from my boyfriend," I gritted back.

"*Fake* boyfriend," he added quickly. I could tell he noticed that my cheeks had gone a bit red. I had let that slip, and I was definitely a little embarrassed. I stuttered a bit, not quite sure how to respond to that. I had been caught. *Caught doing what?* I wasn't completely sure.

"What is it you wanted me to do, Georgie?" he asked. Luca stood up from the bed he was sitting on and started to slowly move towards me. As he got closer, I could see his lips start to form into a sly grin.

"Hmmm?" he asked again as if he expected a response.

I took a little step back, still a bit unsure of what to say. *What had I wanted Luca to do?* Luca kept moving closer. After a few more steps, my back was against the wall, and Luca's face was mere inches from mine. I could feel his breath close to my lips, and his left hand came up and cradled my face ever so gently with just his fingertips. I saw his eyes flicker down to my lips and then back up to my eyes, his brown orbs staring intently into mine.

I bit my bottom lip as I watched him, letting it slowly leave my mouth. God, at this moment, Luca looked so sexy – so kissable. His lips were mere inches from mine, and without a shirt on, he truly was the most handsome man on the grid. His shoulders were on full display, and he was towering over me. I tried to keep my eyes focused on his, but it was next to impossible, not as he snaked his right hand around my waist and pulled my entire body flush with his.

I wanted to say something sassy back. Hell, I wanted to say *something* back. But I was frozen. What did I want from Luca? Truth was, I hadn't had sex in a very long time, and with Luca being my fake boyfriend, there wasn't exactly an opportunity to have sex with other men. *Why shouldn't I try it with Luca?*

I mean, he had been good in my dream. I knew he had to be even better in real life. Luca just chuckled as I stared at him, his smirk growing larger on his face.

He leaned into my ear and whispered, "Oh, Amore, I'll let you get away with not answering me this time as a reward for winning today, but next time I ask you a question, I will expect an answer. Only good girls get rewards." As soon as his breath hit my neck, I felt goosebumps go up my body. His words should not have turned me on as much as they did. I suddenly had images in my mind of

Luca issuing me a punishment for not answering him, and all of the options seemed better than the next.

Luca turned his head back to my face and pressed his lips against mine. I took my hand and placed it on his back, pulling him closer to me, not that there was any need. Luca had my body pushed up against the wall, our lips still connecting in a feat of passion. He put his hands around my thighs and tapped them, a silent ask for me to jump up and wrap my legs around his waist, which I happily obliged.

Luca turned around, opened the door, and headed straight to my bedroom. Soon, I felt my back hit my fluffy king-size bed, and Luca climbed on top of me, his arms on both sides, caging me in as he kissed me deeply.

I was a panting mess, and Luca took advantage of this as he pulled off my top. He looked up at me, asking silent permission to pull off my skirt, earning him a frantic nod of agreement, even though the back of my mind told me this was a bad idea. I silently shoved my concern deep down, choosing instead to ignore the nagging in the back of my mind. This was my race win, and I was going to enjoy my spoils.

Luca smirked and hooked his fingers around my skirt band, pulling it down rapidly. Before I could protest the sudden movement, he started to kiss his way up my leg slowly, paying attention to every mole, scar, and scratch he saw – kissing each one individually.

I felt his mouth get to my thong, and he pulled it aside, placing gentle kitten licks around my core – placing them everywhere except where I desperately needed him most. Luca slipped a finger inside my thong and tugged it down, pulling it off me and then flinging it across the room like a sling slot.

I rolled my eyes at him in annoyance, which was quickly replaced with pleasure as he went back down on me, pulling my legs over his shoulders as he worked his way back up to my core, his lips once again kissing slowly up my leg, my whimpers getting louder as he got closer to my core.

"Luca... stop teasing," I demanded. All I heard was a chuckle from the Italian, but to my surprise, he gave in. His tongue slid up my entrance to my clit, and I sucked in a breath. I started to squirm from the pleasure, and I felt Luca's hand press down on my hips, keeping them in place as he stopped my movements. Unconsciously, I had begun to move myself on his tongue, hoping to get some additional friction, but to no avail. Luca had me locked down, and damn if it wasn't making me even more turned on.

Luca began to pick up the pace, working me like he was a starved man who had just been presented with a feast. His tongue was fast and furious and then light and soft. He would do this up and down, driving me absolutely mad with pleasure. His rhythm was incredible, and when he sunk a finger inside of me, I was a goner. I was a moaning and panting mess, and I knew the bastard was enjoying every sound that left my mouth, but at that moment, I couldn't find it within myself to care.

His mouth kept working me until my toes began to curl, and I could feel that electrifying feeling all the way down my body. I let out the most animalistic sound I think I have ever made as Luca sunk a second and then a third finger into me, sliding them in and out of me, hitting that sweet spot each time, all while sucking and licking on my clit. With a few more thrusts, I was cumming hard and fast. Shockwaves of pleasure were coursing through my body. Luca helped me ride out my waves of pleasure as he licked up everything I had to offer.

As soon as I came down from my high, I started to catch my breath and come to. I opened my eyes, and I saw Luca right above me, a huge *fucking* grin on his face. He pecked my lips and then stood up, backing away from the bed slowly.

I could see the huge bulge in his pants, and just as I was about to propose that I could help him with that, he uttered, "Now we're even, Principessa," with so much cockiness in his voice, he might as well have been the one who won the race tonight.

And now, for the second time in our fake relationship, I was left speechless. Luca put on that classic Cheshire cat grin, turned around, and left my bedroom.

Had the bastard planned this revenge from the beginning? Of course, he fucking had. I wasn't sure if I was impressed that he had known his ignoring me would get under my skin enough for me to cave – or annoyed that I had fallen for it like a complete buffoon.

Both. It was definitely both.

Georgia: 2 Luca: 2

Chapter Thirteen

IF LOOKS COULD KILL

Luca

I woke up the next morning to my phone buzzing on the bedside table. As I leaned over, I saw a text from Henri pop up on the screen. Apparently, he, Éliott, Oliver, and Hugo were all coming over for a surprise brunch, and they wanted to know if Georgia was awake. Considering it was 8:30 a.m., I was surprised they were awake. *Who wakes up that early after a race weekend?*

Truth was, I barely got any sleep after last night. After I walked out of Georgia's room, I hopped straight into the shower and finished myself off. It was nothing like Georgia's mouth had been a few weeks ago, but it would have to do. It took all of my energy and self-perseverance to leave her room last night. When I saw her reach out to me, I wanted nothing more than to stay. I wanted to rip that bra off of her and make her see stars all night as a reward for winning. But in that moment, I let my pride get the better of me. I stood up and walked out, letting her know that we were even.

But we weren't even. Georgia was all over my mind. I couldn't stop thinking about her, her touch, her lips. Even after last night, it felt like she was winning this game of cat and mouse.

It's fine, I thought to myself, *I have Majorca to regain control.*

Nothing but sand, sea, and Georgia in a bikini on my family yacht. I grinned to myself at that thought. She truly was beautiful, and I had most definitely selected Majorca so I could see her out in the sun, her beautiful skin on display. Before that, however, I had to survive the Maison de Klotho photoshoot, which had somehow turned into a GQ photoshoot, with Maison de Klotho sponsoring the clothes. The photos would be used in both the magazine and for the new clothing campaign. I had done several shoots like this for Hermes before, but this felt different. I would have to be constantly aware throughout this photoshoot, always checking over my shoulder to see who was watching me and Georgia interact. For the first time, we would have to be a couple for several hours in public.

In the paddock, we had to pretend to be a real couple, but most of the time, we were working or hanging out with friends or other drivers. It felt like we were rarely alone without strangers.

Still, a secret part of me deep down was pleased. For the first time, I would get an entire day with Georgia where she would have to act like my girlfriend. I had missed the opportunity all those years ago to make it real, so now I would have to settle for the *fake* thing.

Another half hour passed before I saw a text from Henri alerting me that he and Éliott would be there in thirty minutes to get the brunch set up. Henri had told Georgia to be ready for a coffee date with himself, but instead he intended to surprise her by bringing in several *uninvited* people into her home.

I laughed at that – sometimes, I felt like Henri didn't know his own twin. While Georgia was social with her friends, she also valued her privacy, and she never struck me as a surprise party kind of person, even if it was with close friends and family. Yesterday was exhausting, and if it were me, the idea of having several people sprung on me all of a sudden would be horrendous. Still, I wasn't going to tell Henri that. If there's one thing Henri liked to make clear, it's that he knew *his* Peaches the best, and everyone else was literal dirt compared to him when it came to her.

Sometimes, I wondered if that's why I wanted her to like me so much. I loved how much the idea of me dating her got under Henri's skin. He hated the idea from the start. It's why I loved to drop hints that maybe we were more. Henri was many things – a friend, included – but his propensity to always need to be first, his competitiveness, was also his greatest weakness.

After I hopped in the shower and got ready, I ventured out of my room. There was Georgia, sitting on the couch with a cup of coffee, reading the latest issue of GQ magazine. So, her team had finally told her that we would be featured in the next issue. Georgia looked ready to go out, and I felt some pity for her. Little did she know in all of two minutes, Henri and Éliott were going to come bursting through her door, followed by several other people, invading her home.

I cleared my throat, and she looked up, a small smile forming on her lips.

"Morning," she said cheerily, taking another sip of her coffee. I could tell she was trying to act as normal as possible, considering what we had done last night.

So we are going to ignore last night. That's fine, I thought to myself.

"Morning. Sleep well?" I asked, sitting down on the couch across from her. She ignored my question and continued to read her magazine.

Another second went by, and then we both heard a knock at the door. Georgia yelled for Henri to come in and went back to reading. I kept my eyes on her the whole time, not wanting to miss her priceless expression when she saw a group of hooligans walk into the apartment.

And boy, oh boy, she did not disappoint.

As Henri opened the door, in walked Henri, Éliott, and Oliver with what looked like twenty balloons and six bags of food from Georgia's favorite restaurant and bakery.

If looks could kill, hers would have slaughtered the entire paddock. But just as quickly as she could, her face turned to the biggest, lightest, most cheerful composure I think I had ever seen.

Oh, come on, Georgia, now they're going to know that smile is fake, I chuckled to myself. But they didn't. Henri marched up to his sister and gave her a massive hug, eating up her grin and fake excitement as if that was the best breakfast in the world.

"Surprise!" Oliver yelled, picking Georgia up and swinging her around the living room like a rag doll.

"Wow, I didn't expect this," she said cheerfully, but her eyes told a different story. Her eyes shifted to mine as if to accuse me of knowing.

I gave her the biggest smile I could plaster onto my face and replied, "What a lovely surprise your brother planned. *All by himself.*" Henri beamed when I said that, and I gave him a pat on the back. I knew Georgia would get the hint. A few moments later, Hugo and Lily walked into the flat with more balloons and flowers. It was starting to look like a circus in here, and Georgia was the main act.

Before Éliott could take a seat next to Georgia at the table, I took the spot to her right, forcing Éliott to sit across from her. I could see from a quick glance that he was annoyed, but I didn't care. I was petty and proud. Something about the two of them irked me to no end. I knew they had a history, but after the skirmish with Henri, I felt like Éliott had not-so-innocent intentions for telling me about him and Georgia. Had he known I had asked Georgia out all those years ago? Was he marking his territory? I couldn't blame him if he was; Georgia was undoubtedly one of the most beautiful women I had seen.

Still, they weren't together, and I had to remember that. It wasn't Éliott that made her see stars last night – it was me.

As the brunch started to come to an end, I felt a tap on my shoulder. Henri was behind me.

"Hey, you got a minute?" he asked casually, although he looked nervous. I nodded and stepped away from the table, following him to Georgia's balcony.

"What's up?" I asked, leaning on the balcony railing, my eyes drifting off to the view of the water down below.

"So, I... uhh... just wanted to see what was going on between you and my sister?" I sucked in a deep breath and then turned to face him directly, making eye contact with his hazel eyes.

"What do you mean *what is going on with your sister?*" I was a little taken aback by his questions, although I guess after my comment over the weekend about seeing his sister naked, I should have expected it.

"I see the way you look at her. Back on Saturday before qualifying..." Henri paused for a moment as if he was contemplating what to say before continuing on, "...the way you and Georgia were all snuggled up together... it made me concerned."

"Concerned?" I asked lowly. Truthfully, I wanted to say more than that, but I was really curious where Henri was going with this, but he just sighed in response, and I could tell he was getting frustrated that I wasn't catching on.

"Look, Luca, I'll just spit it out. Me and you, we've always been honest with one another, so here's the truth. I can see my sister starting to fall for you."

I scoffed a bit at his comment and turned my eyes towards Georgia, who was now sitting beside Lily on the couch, laughing away. I could feel my heart leap as Henri said the words, but I stuffed it back down. Henri had already proven today he didn't know his sister as well as he thought. There was no way Georgia was falling for me – not after I broke her trust all of those years ago. I could tell she could barely stand to be in a room with me.

Before I could get a word in, Henri continued on, "She falls hard and fast for people. And after that asshole she dated back in America, I don't want to see her hurt again. This might be a fake relationship for you, but I'm worried the lines between fake and real will begin to blur for Georgia."

I wanted to stop myself, because I knew this was going to sound pathetic, but at that moment, I couldn't help myself. "And dating me would be so bad?"

"Luca... come on, mate, you've never been a serious dater. You said yourself at the beginning of the season that you didn't want anything serious for another few years. Georgia, she isn't like that..."

she doesn't do *casual*." I could tell Henri was trying to be nice about it, but the tone of his voice was almost pleading.

My blood began to boil. How dare he assume what I wanted with his sister. How dare he assume what Georgia wanted.

"I just don't want you to lead her on, is all. Georgia wants something real, something long-term. Plus, my teammate *actually* dating my sister... I mean, would you like me if I dated *your* sister?" The truth was, I didn't like Henri at all right now – and the thought of him dating anyone I knew made me want to punch him.

I eyed him wearily, not really knowing how to respond to this attack. Based on Henri's tone, he clearly didn't know I had asked Georgia out all those years ago, or this conversation would have been a lot worse.

As far as I saw it, I had two options. I could escalate this argument, but if what Henri said was true and Georgia was actually starting to fall for me, I knew I would lose any chance I could possibly have with her.

Or, I could grin it and bare it for now – and make Henri squirm later.

It took every piece of me not to escalate the conversation, but I knew the latter option would be more satisfying in the end. Henri couldn't control how we acted in public. Regardless of what he wanted, Georgia and I were still dating each other, with no plans to end this fake relationship in sight.

"The only thing going on is that Hermes has insisted I date your sister. If you don't like that, I suggest you take it up with our team principal, Francesco," I retorted, probably with a little bit more malice than intended, but no one accused me of being perfect. Before Henri could respond to that, I plastered a big smile on my face and slapped Henri on the back, grabbing his shoulder and pulling him closer to me.

"But don't worry, *mate*, I'll be sure to keep my irresistible charm and good looks in check next week in Majorca. I mean, your sister is much too intelligent to fall for a man just because he has a yacht off the coast of Spain, right? " I added with a grin and a wink.

As soon as the words were uttered from my mouth, I walked away, knowing full well that Henri was now contemplating how he could get himself invited to our mini vacation next weekend. The image of his sister in a bathing suit on my yacht was clearly etched into his mind.

Good.

Georgia

Luca and I were instructed to meet in Madrid on Tuesday. After the surprise brunch on Monday, I felt like I needed a day to myself, but unfortunately, Lizzie insisted we had to be there as soon as possible. Maison de Klotho were eager to get their photos taken, and the partnership with GQ was too good to pass up.

Truth was, I was slightly annoyed after the brunch on Monday. I knew Henri had meant well, but the race was enough socialization for a lifetime. I didn't need a bunch of people being dragged to my safe haven; it was bad enough that Luca was there all the time. Although, truthfully, Luca was the least annoying part of that brunch. Unlike everyone else, he gave me the space I was craving on Monday. On the plane ride to Madrid, we barely said two words to each other, and I was relieved.

After the photoshoot, Luca and I were to spend the evening in Madrid at his apartment. Since the technology center for Hermes F1 was based outside of Madrid, Luca kept a small condo in the city for easy access to the offices. I assumed that Luca had booked us a fancy dinner somewhere, although I wanted nothing more than to crash that evening in his guest room. Still, Lizzie was clear: we needed to make this part of our relationship look real, and what was more real than a big fancy date with F1's most eligible bachelor? After that, we would head to Majorca with his family on Wednesday, and Henri, Hugo, and Lily would meet us on Thursday. I wasn't sure why Henri was so insistent on coming on this vacation, but I was happy to be able to spend time with my brothers. Éliott, Oliver, and Edward were on Edward's yacht as well, and Luca said we would probably meet up with them over the weekend.

As much as I wanted some time alone – *time to myself* – I was excited to have a mini break on the yacht. Luca's family was incredibly sweet and charming, and it would be nice to spend some time away from the F1 world and prying eyes of fans. Lizzie had asked that we take several photos and post them on our social media pages since we would be so far away from journalists and photographers. She didn't want our relationship to 'get lost in the shuffle' – whatever that meant.

Once we touched down in Madrid, we hopped into the private limousine that Maison de Klotho had sent to pick us up. Inside the car was a small bottle of champagne, which Luca quickly poured for us. I thanked him quietly, trying – and failing – to put a small smile on my face.

I had never done a photoshoot like this before, and as we started to get closer to the offices, I could feel myself getting even more nervous. I hoped that I was hiding it well, but considering Luca kept shifting his eyes onto me, I could tell that I wasn't.

Great, just another reason why Luca thinks I'm an idiot, I thought to myself, a little embarrassed. I was a Formula 1 driver who raced some of the fastest cars on earth, and here I was, scared of a photoshoot.

As the driver pulled up to the front of the beautiful Madrid office, a coordinator from both Maison de Klotho and GQ was waiting for us at the front. Luca got out of the car first and then held his hand out for me, helping me out of the car. I tried not to roll my eyes too much. I could get out of a car by myself – my incompetence was around journalists, not cars. Still, this was Madrid, a city that felt more old-school and traditional, so I accepted his hand.

"Good morning!" The voice came from the Maison de Klotho coordinator, whose name was Lilah. Apparently, she was to be our escort for the day.

More like a prison warden, I mused to myself. Luca and I both exchanged good mornings and after a round of chit-chat with Lilah, we made our way inside.

The offices were absolutely incredible on the inside. As you walked in, there was a huge marble staircase that led you up to some of the executive offices. They had various outfits throughout the years that they had designed for movie sets and royalty alike in glass enclosures. I stopped in front of one. It was a dress they had made for Grace Kelly, the American actress who later became the Princess of Monaco.

"It must be so neat to work here," I mused out loud.

"Oh yes, it truly is a dream come true," Lilah agreed, a huge smile on her face. As we continued the tour, we were shuffled into a room that looked like a break room. It had sodas, snacks, and coffee laid out on a small table surrounded by some nicely decorated couches and furniture. After a cup of coffee and a breakfast bar, Luca and I were introduced to the photographer, writer, and stylist that we would be working with throughout the day.

After introductions, Luca and I were shuffled into different rooms to try on various pieces of clothing. GQ had sent a writer to hang out with us during the shoot, so as we got ready and went between rounds of photos, Mark, our assigned writer, would sit and chat with us – "get to know who we are as people, not just world-class racers." He felt as though he could see the 'real us' – *his words* – when we were interacting with each other on set.

That, of course, was my fear. Nothing about the Georgia Dubois being photographed on set really said, '*Hey, this young lady is doing well mentally.*' Not exactly the Georgia that Valkyrie F1 was looking to feature in the magazine.

When I came out of the dressing room in my first outfit, I saw Luca already in the studio, chatting away with the journalist and photographer, charming them, no doubt. As I walked in, I heard a wolf whistle come out of Luca's mouth. I let out a small smile and rolled my eyes, feeling a little bit of heat rush to my cheeks. Luca was in a beautifully tailored suit. His hair was nicely combed and slicked back, but the fluffiness was still on full display. He reached out his hand, and I took it.

Luca let his gaze go slowly up and down my body, probably a little too obviously, but I knew he wanted the journalist and photographer to catch that.

"Beautiful," he whispered loudly enough for the entire room to hear, and I couldn't help but blush.

"You don't look too bad yourself, Rossi. Much better than those Hermes suits Francesco always put you in," I joked. I then turned back to the photographer, my eyes shifting to the ground. I could feel my hands begin to sweat, and I decided that looking at the ground was much easier, lest I say something stupid.

Suddenly I felt a hand interlock with mine, and I looked up, turning slightly towards Luca. He was still chatting away with the photographer, but he squeezed my hand just a little bit tighter. I hated to admit it, but I felt a rush of relief go through me. I began to relax my shoulders and then looked up at the photographer and smiled, trying to at least pretend to be involved in the conversation, even if I hadn't said a word.

We chatted a bit more about the poses they wanted us to do; some of the photos would be of both of us, and some of them would be individual shots. Fortunately, Lilah was there to help the photographer and explain more of what he wanted.

As Luca was taking his individual shots, Mark approached me, a huge grin on his face, and I knew he wanted something. That pang of anxiety that had started to leave my body quickly returned, and I could feel my back stiffen up.

"So Georgia, that win in Monaco, quite spectacular, if I do say so myself." And he did – *clearly*. "For Luca to win his home race, and then you to win yours... you really are quite the Formula 1 power couple right now." I wasn't sure if there was a question hidden in there somewhere, so I just nodded, trying to keep my eyes on Luca's photoshoot, silently begging for it to be over soon so he could relieve me from this nightmare.

"It's been an exciting couple of weeks," I responded, trying to find my voice. Mark was so intently looking at me, like he was observing every move I was making through a microscope. I felt as though his eyes were piercing my soul, trying to read all of my deepest and most private thoughts.

"Tell me, the world sees you and Luca at these races; you both walk around hand in hand, but you spend most of the time in your own garages and prepping for the races or meeting with sponsors who have flown in. What does Georgia and Luca look like off the track? What does a boring Wednesday look like in your lives?"

Ahh, the question I knew was coming eventually. I let my eyes glance one more time at Luca, who was still going through the photoshoot stills, likely trying to decide which one made his beautiful brown eyes pop more. I took a deep breath and closed my eyes for just a second, letting myself think for a moment. I could answer this alone. *I didn't need a man to help me.*

"We're like any other couple," I said simply.

"Oh, come on, I don't believe that. What do you do for fun? How do you guys relax?" The more I thought about those questions, the more I realized I didn't actually know. What did Luca do for fun? I thought back to all of our conversations in the paddock and at the hotels. We hadn't discussed much else besides racing.

"We like to play chess," I responded finally. "Luca is an amazing player; we often try to sneak away and play in the garages when we have time. As for at home, we really do live simply when we're together. We like to go on walks or make dinner together. Luca loves mac and cheese – it's his favorite food, so we'll often go to a local grocery and get the ingredients and just open a delightful bottle of red and make pasta together."

I thought that answer was quite good, but Mark just continued to write in his stupid notebook, not even looking up at me. I guess, to be fair, what twenty-seven-year-old man liked to make mac and cheese for dinner? *Who was going to believe that nonsense?* Before Mark could respond to the comment, Luca had returned, and he could see I was in distress.

"Cara, are you telling the world about my embarrassing love for mac and cheese?" he scolded gently. I giggled in response, lifting my cheek up for a kiss, which he aptly provided.

"Your girlfriend was just telling us about how you guys make pasta together in your free time," Mark added, no doubt looking for Luca's reaction to see if he would be surprised at that comment. But Luca, ever the charming Cheshire cat, could not be fooled.

"Did she tell you that she prefers her brother's pasta bolognese to my mac and cheese?" he quipped to Mark, winking at the journalist. "I try not to take offense. I mean, Henri does make a delightful spagbol, but I would argue it's not as good as my fresh mac and cheese."

Luca looked quite proud of himself at that statement, and I couldn't help but wonder if he actually made a good mac and cheese. Something that I realized I probably would never find out, and for some reason, my heart ached at that thought, but I decided to push that feeling deep down. Instead, I smirked at Luca, grabbing his arm as I leaned in just a bit closer.

"Love it. A couple who cooks together, stays together, my mum used to say," Mark chimed in. "So, how has it been with your brother, Georgia? I know last weekend was probably a little tough for you."

"You know, it was tough because we both love that circuit so much, and we both wanted to win. But being able to share the podium with my brother was amazing, something I'll remember for a lifetime."

"Sure," he said, clearly not that interested in my diplomatic answer. "So Luca, how is it dating your teammate's sister? Any arguments yet?" I looked over at Luca, and there was a slight twitch in his mouth, which he quickly replaced with a smile and a nod.

"Honestly, no," he said with a chuckle. "I'm almost surprised at how supportive he is of our relationship. Sometimes it seems suspicious," he added with a sly grin.

"Oh?" Mark asked, his interest clearly piqued by Luca's last statement.

"He's just always asking about what dates we'll go on next and telling me about all the cute things Georgia sends him about me," he added with a smug grin. I felt myself dying a bit inside, but I batted my eyelashes at him playfully, keeping the bit alive.

"I once joked that he was making me nervous to date his sister. I mean, I think she's beautiful and amazing. That's easy to see, so why is Henri pushing her so much? Makes me wonder if she has any skeletons in her closet." Both Mark and Luca laughed at that while I sat there, trying not to be awkward. Luca stuck out his tongue, and I gave him a little shove in return.

"Henri didn't find it quite as funny," Luca added.

"Oh please, Rossi, if anyone has skeletons in their closet, it's you. Don't even get me started about how you once scolded a goose on the golf course and had to run away because it started to chase you," I teased. "Someone's a little afraid of birds," I whispered to Mark, winking at Luca.

Mark laughed along with us as we told more stories. I started to feel more at ease, which was nice. Shortly after, Luca and I were ushered back into our changing rooms, and we went through another three rounds of clothing before being told that this would be the last photo grouping of the day. The designer had dressed me in a tiny, black evening dress that featured a low back while Luca was once again in a suit, although this time, his shirt was buttoned halfway down his chest, exposing a good amount of his broad chest.

"Lovely, lovely," Lilah called out, "but let's try something a little different. Have a little fun. Georgia, face towards Luca, and show us your back. Luca, rest your hand on Georgia's lower back. Now look at each other and stare deeply into each other's eyes."

As we followed the instructions, I felt Luca grip my lower back tightly and look down at me with those gorgeous brown eyes. He pulled me closer to him, my body now flush with his front, my hands on his chest. Suddenly this photoshoot felt a lot more romantic than I had anticipated. Luca's face was soft, and he let out a little encouraging smile when he looked down at me.

It's as if Luca could tell I was still feeling uncomfortable from the forced movements because when he leaned down, he got closer to my ear and whispered, "Why so shy, Principessa? You weren't this shy Sunday evening." As soon as he said the words, I looked up and saw a little smirk form. Luca was now turned to the photographer, a smug grin dancing on his lips.

I went to say something back to him, but in the distance, I heard the photographer call out, "Lovely Georgia – much better, you look so relaxed."

Did I? In my frustration towards Luca's cheekiness, I had forgotten about the photographer and writer, and Luca knew that I would drop my guard as soon as he whispered that comment. He always knew how to get a rile out of me, just like I had done at Monza when he was nervous about the speech. Apparently, this was becoming our thing. I shifted a bit and looked back at Luca, who was still staring at the photographer. The smirk on his face seemed even bigger than before.

I'm not sure what came over me, but all I wanted was to wipe that smirk off his face, and there was only one way I could think of doing that. Before I could stop myself – *and truly see reason* – I hopped up on my tippy toes and pressed my lips to Luca's, putting my hands on his face, pulling him into a kiss. He looked a little shocked at first but then he started to deepen the kiss, letting his hands graze the top of my ass. As we kept on kissing, I heard more cheers and celebratory laughs from the growing crowd.

Luca parted our lips for a moment and then picked me up in his arms, bridal style. I let out a screech as I tried to make sure my ass wasn't on display. Our lips connected again, and this time, I found myself deepening the kiss. It's as if everyone else in the room started to disappear, and it was just me and Luca in the room.

"Alright, you two love birds!" Lilah called out. "That's a wrap!" I quickly parted from Luca, and he put me back down on my legs. I toppled over a bit, steadying myself in the process. My cheeks were undoubtedly flushed from the long make-out session with Luca. As I looked around the room, I felt horrified for a moment.

Had I just made out with Luca in front of all these people? In the moment, it didn't seem so terrible, but now, I felt mortified at the thought. Luca looked down at me and smiled, grabbing my hands and pulling them up to his chest.

"Sorry, Lilah, just can't help myself sometimes – as Georgia likes to say, *it's in my nature*," he grinned, pulling my hand to his lips and giving it a kiss.

"You two are too much!" Lilah exclaimed, clapping her hands together. "I cannot wait to see how these photos look." Mark, still sitting next to the photographer, stood up and grinned, his notebook in his hands.

"You know, I came in, trying to see if the chemistry was there between the two of you – you seem like such an odd pairing, but after today, I can really see that it is. Good luck, you two. I'll be sure to have several copies sent to your offices."

And with that, the photo shoot was over.

Chapter Fourteen

GIRLS JUST WANNA HAVE FUN

Luca

The photoshoot had gone much better than I expected. I could tell Georgia was nervous through most of it, so I did my best to help relieve that anxiety and stress. I couldn't help myself when I whispered that little comment about Sunday into her ear. Watching her squirm like that, knowing only she could hear me, it riled some primal part of me. I knew she had enjoyed last Sunday evening. I had immensely enjoyed it, being able to get my mouth on her.

When we got back to my apartment after the photoshoot, Georgia muttered something about getting into the shower and getting ready for tonight. I was a little confused, not sure why she needed to get ready for a night in, but I nodded and said I would do the same. After I finished my shower, I slipped into my favorite set of sweatpants and a V-neck. I headed towards the kitchen, pulling out the ingredients to make none other than my famous mac and cheese.

Georgia might have joked to the journalist about my love for mac and cheese, but I meant what I said. Plus, I figured if she couldn't love me, she was at least going to love my cooking. As soon as I started grating the cheese, I saw Georgia come out of her room, wearing a beautiful black dress. Her makeup was done, and she had heels on, clearly ready to take on the night.

Had she thought we were going to go out? Had I misread the situation?

I looked up and gave her a small smirk, "Well, I know my cooking is pretty good, Tesoro, but I think you might be a little too dressed up for mac and cheese. Although I am honored that you would dress up for my cooking, it is pretty good if I say so myself."

The look on her face was priceless – a general mix of shock, and then relief, and then happiness. That made my heart swell, not that I could let her see that. I figured after the last two weeks, Georgia wouldn't want to go out to eat. I knew I certainly didn't want to go out after all of the commotion from the last two races. These last two weeks had been nothing but racing, partying, and putting on a dog and pony show for the sponsors. I was exhausted, and I knew Georgia had to be too.

"Are... are we not going out?" She asked, her voice a little too small for my liking. So she had expected that we would go out. I shook my head and went back to grating the cheese.

"Oh," she said simply, heading back into her room. Not even a minute later, she came out, wearing a pair of black leggings under her dress.

"So, I, uh," she began, shifting her eyes uncomfortably, "I sort of forgot a comfortable shirt. I only packed workout clothes and beach items. Do you, um, mind if I borrow one?"

"Of course," I said, perhaps a little too excitedly.

Did I mind if one of the most beautiful girls in the paddock wore my shirt?

Is the Pope a catholic?

I felt like a high-school boy whose crush had just asked to borrow his letterman jacket. I ran into my room and opened my drawer, pulling out the deepest purple Hermes shirt I could find, and walked back into the living room, handing it to her. Her face pinched up as she observed the shirt – clearly, she wasn't thrilled about wearing a Hermes shirt, but I didn't care – the idea of seeing her in my shirt stirred something within me.

"Really?" she deadpanned, holding up the shirt in question. "This is the only shirt you could find." I nodded innocently and winked at her, heading back towards the kitchen.

"I mean, if you don't want to wear a shirt, I am definitely fine with that too," I added cheekily, causing her to give out an exasperated sigh as she trotted back into my guest room to change. As she came out, I gave her a little wolf whistle, and she stuck her middle finger at me, and I couldn't help but chuckle at that. It felt nice and relaxing to be in my home with her, especially with her wearing my shirt.

"Thanks for not making us go out," she said finally.

"After the two weeks we've had, I figured neither of us actually wanted to go out to eat," I responded, still grating the cheese. She nodded in appreciation, and I could see a look of relief spread across her face.

"Want to open a bottle of wine?" I asked, nodding my head towards the wine cabinet.

Georgia walked on over to the cabinet, looking through the bottles I had collected throughout the years. She selected a lovely Spanish Tempranillo from the cabinet and brought it over, opening the wine and pouring out two glasses. I nodded my thanks and took a sip from the glass she had handed me. A perfectly blended Spanish wine, one of my favorites from the Basque county.

"So, I'm finally going to get to eat this famous mac and cheese," she said with a smirk as she eyed the cheese I was grating.

"And what an honor that is," I responded proudly. She snorted at that, grabbing her glass of wine as she headed towards my open-plan living room, admiring the many photos that I had scattered across the walls. I had various family photos – photos of me karting, photos of friends, photos of my family. Georgia stopped by one of my dad and me next to a rally car. Post-retirement from Formula 1, my dad had taken up rally car, a scary, albeit exciting new world for him.

"I've always wanted to try Rally car," she said suddenly, staring at the photo.

"Oh?"

"It looks so freeing, so refreshing. The teams, they always seem so bold and brave." I nodded in agreement at her words. I understood what she meant. Formula 1 might have the fastest race cars on earth, and that was scary in itself, but racing Rally took a different type of bravery – bravery that I wasn't sure I truly possessed. Georgia definitely did – her fearlessness was remarkable.

Georgia nodded, as if she was contemplating something, but couldn't find the right words. It was weird seeing her like this, walking around my apartment wearing *my* shirt, drinking a glass of *my* wine. It felt domestic, and I liked it.

Truth is, I liked it a lot.

"I heard you got to have quite a bit of fun in America," I said, thinking back to some of the clips I had watched of Georgia driving monster cars and other off-roading trucks. "Those monster trucks looked pretty scary. Henri told me you once won one of the races, much to the chagrin of the other drivers." Georgia smiled that beautiful big smile, clearly thinking back to her time in America.

"Sometimes I miss it, you know, the comfort of knowing what to expect. The comfort of knowing the team, the car, the crowd... the journalists. There were no surprises in Indy Car." Georgia said the last part quietly as she stared off into the distance; for a moment, she looked as if she had forgotten where she was. "In Indy Car, I was just a champion. I wasn't a meal to be sold."

"I get that," I replied, walking over with the bottle of wine, refilling her glass, and nodding for her to take a seat on the sofa. The mac and cheese was in the oven, and we had some time before it was finished.

"But you've done incredible in Formula 1. You look so comfortable in the car, and if I didn't know any better, I'd say it was easily your third year in the sport. A real natural."

She smiled an appreciative smile at me and then joked, "Say that to all the girls, Rossi?"

"Just the pretty ones," I said with a wink.

After a few more moments, I pulled out the piece of paper that

Matteo had given to me all those weeks ago – the one full of 'getting to know you' questions. I waved the piece of paper a little and then opened it, clearing my throat slightly.

"Matteo said we'll be interviewed by BBC next week, figured we should get a few more questions in?"

Georgia's body posture tightened up a bit when she heard the word BBC, but she nodded in response. We needed to be on point when it came to the interview, needed to be ready for all of the crazy questions they were going to throw our way. The film crew had told the teams they intended to do a more in-depth episode about dating while being on the grid. They had several drivers and their girlfriends or wives lined up, but Georgia and I were top of their list for the episode. We were pigs perfectly wrapped up for the slaughter with nowhere to go as far as I was concerned.

"What is your favorite book?"

Georgia scrunched her eyebrows for a minute, clearly pondering her answer. I'd heard from Henri that Georgia was an avid reader – reading no less than 2-3 books a month, which I thought was fairly impressive.

"I read 'Fish That Ate the Whale' back when I lived in the U.S. It was a phenomenal biography about an American immigrant; his perseverance was remarkable."

"Maybe I should read it."

She smiled at that but didn't respond. I wasn't sure if I should be slightly insulted. It was no secret that I didn't read much. I had basically told the press as much through an F1 article I did years ago, back in 2018, before I knew better than to tell everyone all of the stupid thoughts that crossed my mind. Reading had sort of seemed stupid back then. I was more of a music person, but now, as I had gotten older, I had begun to read more during our travels. It was usually engineering books or race strategy these days. The more I knew about the car, the better chance I had to beat Henri.

Georgia signaled for me to hand her the piece of paper, which I did.

"What kind of music do you listen to?" she asked. "I notice you have a lot of records in your spare bedroom."

"I like a good mix of things," I said honestly. "I don't really have a favorite band, but recently, I've enjoyed the American group Bon Iver after seeing them in London. Beach House is pretty good, too; saw them at a festival back in France." She quirked her eyebrows at me, clearly a bit surprised at my answer. I motioned for her to answer the question.

"Didn't expect party boy Luca Rossi to have a secret love of indie music," she laughed.

"There's a lot of things you don't know about me," I quipped back, a smile on my face. I loved the surprise in her voice. She always had this stuck-up air about her – it's like she felt as though she already knew me, so it was nice to surprise her.

"A man of mystery, apparently…" she joked. "I've been loving the Lumineers recently, but my true love will always be with Mika. His music in both French and English is incredible. Happy Ending has to be one of the most beautiful songs ever written." We sat in silence for a bit, me not wanting to disturb her thinking and her deeply lost in thought.

"Well," I started, breaking the silence, "there is something I wanted to ask you. Something the press might ask…"

"Go on." I chuckled nervously.

"So I know you and Éliott dated for a few weeks, but nothing public." She nodded, clearly not sure where I was going with this. "Has there been anyone else? Anyone in America? Figured they might ask…" I added the last part rather pathetically. The BBC probably wasn't rude enough to ask us about our past dating history, but still, I had to try and save face.

Georgia shifted a bit uncomfortably in her seat before taking another big sip of wine – likely contemplating what she was going to say, or at least what lie she was going to craft. Henri had mentioned another boyfriend, and I couldn't help but let my curiosity get the better of me. Curiosity might have killed the cat, but this cat had nine lives, and I was willing to take the risk.

"There was a guy in America – Anthony. Race car driver for NASCAR." She took a pause, and I expected her to say something else, but she didn't, instead electing to take another sip – *gulp* – of her wine. I wanted to press her for more but stopped myself, remembering something my mother used to tell me. 'Sometimes, it's easier to get answers by answering something yourself.'

"Has anyone managed to actually woo F1's most eligible bachelor?" she asked with a grin.

If only she knew the truth.

"There was one girl, yeah," I said honestly, taking another sip of my wine. The bottle was almost finished, and I was starting to feel it. "But we didn't work out. Dating while on the grid is tough. It's difficult to get to know someone intimately when you're traveling half the year. Sometimes I feel like I am getting there with someone, but then it becomes clear that she only wants me for the fun and money that comes with being a Formula 1 driver."

I could see Georgia was thinking about my answer, weighing what she should say next. "And this girl... she was different?" Georgia asked, scrunching up her nose as she finished her glass of wine. If you looked closely enough, it looked like there was a hint of disappointment on her face. Clearly, I had piqued her interest. Her question had me internally smiling.

Watching Georgia be jealous of *herself*, now that was entertainment. Much like Henri, Georgia was terrible at hiding her feelings. The Monegasque drivers were nothing if not terrible liars. Playing Henri at poker was one of the easiest ways to make a quick buck.

"No," I said simply, trying to play it off as being no big deal.

"Why didn't you work out?" she blurted out. I raised an eyebrow at her, and she followed it up by mumbling an apology.

"Sorry... sorry, none of my business."

"No, it's alright. I pulled a Luca and screwed it up. I was scared of what committing to her would mean. My parents have been married for decades. While it's an honor to watch their relationship, it's also terrifying. Finding something like that – it feels like one in a million."

"Never took Luca Rossi for being a coward." The words sounded harsh, but she said it with a large grin on her face, letting her adorable dimples go on display.

"Like you said... man of mystery." We both laughed at that, toasting our glasses as we both finished off the last bit of wine.

"What about you and Anthony?" I asked, wanting to not sound too interested but suspecting that I had probably failed.

"Anthony and I had a slight disagreement about our relationship. He thought he could put his dick in any and every vagina that he saw, and I thought the ring on my finger meant I had the miserable pleasure of being the only one to see his dick." Georgia said the words as if they were a joke, clearly one that she had told a few times, but I could see the sadness behind her eyes. Henri hadn't mentioned they were engaged? Must have been quick. Georgia wasn't in America very long. I wanted to ask more, but I could see from her expression that she felt like she had overshared. The wine was likely hitting her, too.

"Well, what did you expect," I said with a grin, "the guy drove NASCAR. If they didn't make the track a perfect oval, the drivers would be too stupid to stay on the track." At that moment, Georgia threw her head back, letting out one of the loudest laughs I think I had ever heard.

"He wasn't known for his brains, I'll tell you that much," she conceded with a smile. I chuckled a bit and grabbed another bottle from the wine rack, opening it and pouring us both another glass. I was enjoying this Georgia; her cheeks were flushed, and she was more relaxed from the wine. I felt like I was seeing a glimpse of the real her, the one that Henri and Hugo talked about all the time.

"I'm a little nervous for this vacation," she admitted.

"Well, who's the coward now, Dubois," I retorted cheekily. She took the couch cushion and threw it at me, rolling her eyes playfully.

"Do your parents not think it's weird that I'm intruding on this vacation and then bringing my family with me?"

"Honestly? Not really. My mom's a huge fan of yours if you

couldn't tell by the Valkyrie shirt she wore on Sunday." Georgia smiled at that. I knew she was pleased with my mom's choice of shirt. "And my dad? Pretty sure if my dad got to pick my *actual* girlfriend, you'd be top of the list."

"Oh?" she questioned, intrigued by that answer.

"A talented race car driver who doesn't break the rules, get wasted at parties, or steal yachts – pretty sure my dad would happily swap the two of us." I said it as a joke – or at least, I had originally meant it as a joke – but in the end, I knew it had come out rather pathetic.

But truthfully, I felt pathetic.

"You make me sound so boring, Rossi," Georgia smiled, refilling the glass of wine I had in my hand. While I was thinking about my last comment, she shuffled closer to me on the couch. I smiled weakly at her, silently thanking her for cutting the tension of my terrible joke.

"I don't think boring people put hamsters in team principal's bags."

"Well," she said, filling up her goblet with another round of wine, "then here's a toast to being the most real, non-boring, fake couple on the grid." I raised my glass and clinked it with hers, chuckling in response.

Henri was right about one thing – one of us *was* starting to catch feelings.

Georgia

The dinner at Luca's had gone much better than I had anticipated. I had expected us to have a fancy dinner at some restaurant in Madrid and was pleasantly surprised that Luca had read the situation well enough to realize that a dinner after that photoshoot would have been my personal hell. And to be fair to Luca, that mac and cheese was one of the best pasta dishes I had ever experienced. I had, of course, told him it was one of my Top 10 favorites, but truthfully, it was probably #2, behind Henri's bolognese – and if I was even more truthful, *it was #1*. Not that I'd ever tell Luca that – didn't need his ego getting any bigger.

I was a bit embarrassed that I had opened up about Anthony, but in that moment when Luca was being so vulnerable, I felt like I owed him the truth.

We spent Wednesday traveling to Majorca and ended the day with his family at their house close to the beach. The one thing I loved about Luca's family was their overwhelming welcomeness. As much as I wanted to dislike them because no one could be that nice without having an agenda, I couldn't find a single reason to pass judgment on either of Luca's parents – they only seemed to have one agenda, and it was to make everyone part of their family. Which is why when Henri had mentioned to Luca's mother that he was jealous he wouldn't be able to spend time with me this weekend, they had, of course, invited him and Hugo along.

I could sense that Luca was annoyed that Henri had bagged himself an invitation, and I couldn't blame him. I was thrilled to see Henri, but I also didn't have to spend every waking moment of my race weekends with him, only to have to spend the entire following week with him at the factory. This was Luca's opportunity to relax before we continued into the next stage of the season, which involved several doubleheaders. Henri's competitiveness was overwhelming at times, and I had no doubt that he intended to bring that with him on this vacation.

Luca had decided to invite Edward and his girlfriend Lauren early, which, truth be told, I was thrilled about. The friendship between Luca and Edward was a unique one. They had several years of difference in age, and yet they had the reputation of being two of the closest drivers on the grid.

I woke up that morning and threw on a new royal blue bathing suit set that Lauren had gifted me when she and Edward came aboard. I threw on a white sun dress over it and made my way towards the kitchen area, where breakfast was being served. Seated at the table were Luca, Henri, and Edward – already digging into their breakfast, all while they planned the day's activities. As I walked in, Henri patted the seat next to him as he handed me a mimosa.

"So, Peaches, we were thinking today would be a lovely day to race jet skis," Henri announced. Out of the corner of my eye, I saw Luca roll his eyes, but I kept my laughter to myself. Hermes' golden boy never stopped racing.

"Henri, have you ever contemplated that not everything in life is a race?" I asked, already knowing the answer I was going to receive from my brother, but I couldn't help myself. I heard Edward and Luca snicker a bit to my left.

"If it has an engine, we race it," Henri replied as he narrowed his gaze towards me. "Unless, of course, you're scared I'm going to beat you." Oh Henri, he always knew what to say to get a rile out of me. My mother said she knew we were going to be athletes because we had been competing since the day we were born.

"Oh, don't worry, Henri, I'm happy to show that I'm the better Dubois both on the track and *on the water*," I grinned, much to the amusement of Luca and Edward, who were now openly chuckling away at our antics.

After a few more bites of breakfast, Luca's father entered the kitchen area and announced that the jet skis were fueled and ready to go. By now, Lauren had woken up and had joined us on the back deck, where Edward was attempting to get her onto the back of his jet ski, albeit with some protests from Lauren, who insisted Edward was going to go much too fast for her.

"How about this," Edward proposed, "A little race between the couples – see who is actually the best couple on the grid." Luca let out a huge grin, and before I could protest, I was being lifted by huge hands onto the jet ski that Luca had claimed for himself.

"Umm, excuse me," I protested, quickly shifting to the front of the jet ski, putting my hands on the steering bars. I turned back to Luca, who was still standing on the dock.

"Who said you get to pilot? Maybe we should let the Formula 1 leader take this one." I stuck my tongue out at Luca, who just flicked me off, but he hopped onto the back of the jet ski, wrapping his arms around my waist.

"Fine by me, Principessa," he whispered in my ear, "Who am I to complain about having to snuggle up to a beautiful woman in a bikini?" With that, he shifted forward a bit, wrapping his arms even tighter around my waist. I could feel his breath close to my neck, and I immediately felt something stir inside of me, my mind flashing back to Sunday night where Luca's mouth was somewhere else entirely. I was glad that I was facing forward because I knew my cheeks had gone completely red.

"You guys ready... or are you going to keep flirting over there!" I heard Edward yell out, pointing to where we were meant to start the race. I turned back to the boat, where I could see Henri and Hugo waving at me. Hugo had a smile on his face, but Henri had an expression that I couldn't quite recognize.

As Luca and I arrived at the starting line, I heard Hugo blow a whistle from the boat, and we were off into the sun, racing our hearts out on the jet skis. We had agreed not to go too fast so Lauren could cope with the jet ski speed, but clearly our definition of 'not too fast' was different than hers. As we arrived at the finish line, I could see Edward and Lauren some ways behind us, and I laughed as they approached the finish line. Lauren had a look of terror – *and anger* – on her face. As Edward turned around and gave her a kiss, I saw her features relax, and she playfully shoved him a bit.

"This is the last time I agree to race with any Formula 1 driver," Lauren chuckled.

"Promise I was going slow!" Edward raised his hands, signifying that his promise was told with a scout's honor. Lauren just responded by pushing him into the water.

As we arrived back at the yacht, I heard Hugo and Luca's parents clapping for us. I stood up on the jet ski and took a bow, only to find myself in the water two seconds later, having been pushed in by Edward. I bobbed my head up out of the water and started kicking my legs at him, splashing him in the process.

"Asshole!"

Hugo reached his hand out, and I took it, pulling myself up out of the water. I took off my life jacket and rinsed off in the shower on the deck. When finished drying off, Hugo handed me a margarita.

"So, Georgie, how did the photoshoot go?"

"Better than expected. I'm a little nervous about the GQ writer; this was all so different. Instead of an interview, he just observed me and Luca throughout the day, occasionally asking us questions between shoots. It was all a bit strange," I responded honestly.

"I'm sure it went fine," my brother assured me. "Lizzie told me it should be out right before the race next week, so hopefully, it brings some good press with us to Baku." I hoped Hugo was right, for both Luca and my sake. This article was huge for us and our teams, and we had to nail it perfectly.

As I finished my margarita, I heard Henri call me over, "Hey, let's get that race in before you get too drunk on Margaritas!" I raised my glass in the air, and then downed the rest of the drink. If I was going to race on vacation, I was going to do it with margaritas and mimosas.

As the four of us drivers hopped onto the jet skis, we discussed the course and agreed on a start and end point. We lined up at the starting line and waited for Hugo to blow the whistle. Luca's father had somehow managed to find a megaphone on the yacht, and he handed it to Hugo, who was more than happy to become our announcer for the day.

As soon as the whistle blew, the four of us were off on the jet skis. We probably looked ridiculous to the other boats in the area, but we didn't care. Nothing was more important to a Formula 1 driver than winning, and as soon as I heard the whistle, all thoughts and cares about just letting Henri win so he would stop bothering us to race were gone – the competitiveness was definitely hereditary, and I had never been one to back down from a challenge.

As I started the last lap, I saw Henri in front of me. Luca was right behind me, and I knew by the look on his face that he was smack-talking me. Just as I was about to turn the jet ski, something suddenly jumped out of the water, causing me to lose control as I tried to avoid the jumping fish that had popped out of the water.

For a moment, everything went black.

I knew I had been thrown from the jet ski. I landed on the water face first with an impact that felt like I had hit a ton of bricks. There was an intense ringing in my ears, and I could feel myself in the semi-cold water. After a few seconds, I felt my head pop above the water, my life jacket bringing me to the surface. I wanted to open my eyes and call for help, but I couldn't – my entire body felt frozen, and there was water in my nose and airways, causing me to cough uncontrollably.

After only a few more moments, I felt someone next to me, grabbing me from behind and pulling me closer towards them and onto my back. As I finished coughing up the final bits of water from my lungs, I opened my eyes to see Luca staring at me, a look of absolute panic in his eyes. I wanted to say something, but I couldn't seem to catch my breath.

"It's ok, I got you..." Luca soothed, rubbing his hands up and down the back of my life jacket. "Just keep breathing. You're okay," he said over and over again, his hold on me tightening. Behind me I heard a noise and turned to see Hugo and Luca Sr. in the mini speedboat with Hugo's hand outstretched towards me. Luca helped lift me up onto the boat, before taking his dad's hand. I coughed a bit more, and my breathing started to steady. My body felt like I had just done an all-day, full-body workout.

Back at the yacht, I saw Henri, Edward, and Lauren waiting for us, a look of panic on their faces.

"Is she alright?" Henri jumped onto the smaller boat and grabbed my hand, helping me up. Luca's hand was still on my waist, steadying me as I took Henri's outstretched hand. I still hadn't said anything, but I could slowly feel my body come to as I nodded in response, taking a step back and letting out another cough. I could feel Luca still standing behind me, his hand on my waist as I leaned onto his chest, catching my breath.

"I...I'm okay," I said finally to the expectant group. Henri nodded and then grabbed me away from Luca, leading me toward the kitchen.

"Let's get you some water."

After another hour of assuring everyone I was alright, Edward had made Lauren and I a comfy spot at the front of the boat for the two of us in the shade of an umbrella. Once Henri and Hugo had stopped fawning over me, I had convinced the boys to go snorkeling, promising that Lauren and I would be okay sitting on the boat drinking smoothies – which she had conveniently spiked with some rum when no one was looking.

As we sat on the back deck and chatted away, Lauren finally asked the question I could tell she had been dying to ask all day.

"So, you and Luca seem much closer than I expected," she gushed, a look of mischief in her eyes. "You know Edward..."

Before she could finish her sentence, I chuckled and cut her off, "Edward is betting on us actually getting together. Yes, I know."

"Well..."

I wanted to tell her about Sunday. Hell, I wanted to scream it from the rooftops, but I knew better than that. If I told Lauren, Edward would know by sunset, and then he would be congratulating Luca – and I couldn't be having that.

"There's nothing to tell. We agreed to be friends, and here we are on vacation."

"Oh, bullshit," she blurted out. My eyes went a bit wide at that. Lauren had always been so quiet and reserved, and her outburst was unexpected. "Sorry, I just see the way Luca looks at you. Edward sees the way he looks at you. It's not like he looks at other people. I mean, your brother *clearly* sees something."

"Henri?" I asked incredulously. "Henri is the most oblivious person on the planet."

"Oliver sort of overheard Henri telling Luca off at Monday's brunch."

I gave Lauren a questioning look, and I could see the hesitation in her eyes, but finally, she relented. "Apparently, he's a bit concerned about Luca's intentions."

"Little late now," I scoffed. "If Henri had a problem with this, he probably should have said something back in Spain when I was being bombarded with this ridiculous idea." Lauren judged me silently and then nodded, not quite sure what to say.

So that's the reason Henri had been so adamant about joining our trip. And here I thought my brother had actually wanted to spend time with me – not take up a gig as a bodyguard.

"Look, I'm not sure what everyone thinks is going on here, but Luca is clearly not interested in me that way. As long as I've known him, I've only ever seen him date models. He's incredibly attractive and wealthy. I'm sure he's got plenty of women. He doesn't need the added stress of a professional race car driver as a girlfriend." Lauren gave me an annoyed look.

"If you wanted to be a model, Georgia, I could call any agency, and they would happily take you," Lauren announced. I rolled my eyes at that and playfully swatted at her shoulder. Lauren – not a mean word could come out of her mouth. "Look, all I'm saying is, I see how Luca looks at you. It's different." I sighed as I took a sip of my rum smoothie.

"How much has Edward bet on this? Must be a lot if he's got you over here hawking Luca at me."

"Fine, fine, believe what you want. At least tell me you're getting some on the side." Lauren wiggled her eyebrows at me as she shimmied her shoulders. "That man is just too fine for you not to be getting some."

Oh, little did she know.

"A polite woman never tells." *Why had this become my go-to answer?* Lauren just gave me a knowing look, which I ignored.

"Fine, fine, keep your secrets."

Luca

By the time we boys had arrived back at the yacht, it was dinner time. Henri was, of course, burnt to a crisp, and I watched Georgia scold him for being irresponsible, which I knew he would ignore. My parents and sister had decided to head to the shore for dinner, so it was just us drivers plus Lauren and Hugo for dinner on the yacht tonight. We had decided to dress comfortably and have dinner while watching the sunset at the front of the boat.

The wind had picked up more than I had expected considering how warm the day was, and it had begun to feel fairly chilly on the top deck of the yacht, although I was appreciating the coolness on my face since I had picked up a little bit of sun today. Georgia sat to my right, which I knew was due to some sort of engineering between Edward and Lauren because Henri had desperately tried to get her to sit next to him. When Edward plopped down next to Henri's open seat, I could see the annoyance on his face, but he said nothing.

As Georgia sat next to me, I could see her quietly shivering. Now that the sun had officially set, the temperatures had dropped. I picked up my jacket, which was sitting behind me, and placed it over her. She gave me a small smile and offered her thanks, putting her arms into the holes of the Hermes jacket.

"The color purple looks good on you," Edward teased as she huddled into the jacket further for warmth. The jacket was quite big on her, and she looked adorable, snuggling deeper into her LR52 jacket.

"Well, the color red doesn't look quite as good on you, Edward, so maybe use some more sunscreen next time." Edward gave Georgia the middle finger as she stuck her tongue out at him.

As Henri came back from the bathroom, I saw his eyes land on Georgia wearing my jacket before quickly moving them to meet my gaze. He had a stern look on his face, indecipherable to anyone who wasn't in the know, but I knew he was pissed. He had told me to stay away from Georgia, but that had only fueled my desire to be with her more. Watching her in my jacket as her brother looked on in frustration, it riled something up in me.

The only thing worse than seeing your sister in another driver's team jacket was seeing her in your teammate's jacket.

Well, if he didn't want to see it, he shouldn't have gotten himself invited, I thought to myself.

I had been well and truly annoyed with that, but my parents were too kind to say no. They had at least asked me, knowing that I needed this break too – but how could I say no? Depriving Georgia of seeing her family seemed too cruel, even if I wanted her all to myself. At first, I thought having the other drivers on board would ruin my plans, but as she sat here next to me in my jacket, chatting away with Lauren and Edward, I actually felt relieved to have them there. It's why I had invited Edward, to help alleviate some of the tension with Henri.

"Hey Hugo, mind if I take your spot for a bit?" Henri asked Hugo as the two of them swapped seats. Henri plopped down next to me and smiled, but I could see the strain in his eyes as he looked at Georgia and then back to me.

"So, Luca," he whispered, "thought any more about what I said on Monday?" I let my eyes drift to Henri before nodding.

"Definitely did." I grinned at him and put my arm around Georgia's waist, pulling her closer to me. If she noticed my movement, she didn't say anything, still laughing with Edward, Lauren, and Hugo. Truthfully, I was now just doing it to annoy Henri, although I wasn't sure that he noticed that.

"Right, well, just remember what I said, hmm?"

"Sure thing, Henri, sure thing."

Henri and I sat in silence for a bit longer, both of us sizing the other one up. I knew angering my teammate wasn't a brilliant idea, but the more I thought about his warning, the angrier I got. Still, I had to remember, I was playing the long game. Watching Henri squirm would be worth it.

Finally, Georgia got up, giving her legs a good stretch. "Well, I think it's time for me to get some sleep. I desperately need a shower and a good night's sleep after today."

"Yeah, why don't we keep the drowning to a minimum tomorrow," Hugo laughed, standing up and giving his sister a hug.

"You know, I'm going to crash too," I agreed, patting Henri on the back as I stood up. "Sun really takes it out of you. I'm going to head to bed."

As Georgia and I started to walk towards the bedrooms, I turned around one last time and saw Henri watching us, a dark look of frustration in his eyes.

Don't worry, Henri, I thought to myself, *I'll be sure to take good care of your Peaches.*

I walked Georgia to her room and said goodnight. My room was in between hers and Henri's, which was definitely on purpose. The three of us had the middle deck, while the rest of the rooms were on the lowest deck. I took off my shirt and threw it in the laundry basket, heading to the shower to get the water started since it took a little while to warm up. Suddenly, I heard a knock at my door. When I opened it, I saw Georgia standing there, my jacket in one hand and a towel in the other.

"Hey, um, just dropping off your jacket." As I took the jacket from her, I noticed she was also holding a towel. I tossed her an inquiring look before she continued, clearly a little unsure of herself. "So, the hot water in my shower isn't working great. I was wondering if I could use yours?"

"Ah, Cara, came here to steal all of my hot water, I see," I teased, moving out of her way so she could come in.

"Promise I'll be quick." She said indignantly, rolling her eyes in a slight bit of annoyance, which was intriguing since she was here to use *my* shower.

"Not sure I trust you to be quick. I've seen how long your showers are. I think you practically took an hour-long shower after Monza!"

"I did not." I could see the impatience on her face as she tapped her foot.

"Well, you're welcome to *share* my hot water *with* me unless, of course, you want to go ask your brothers to use theirs. I'm sure Henri will find a way to make it a competition," I grinned, knowing full well that she also needed a break from her brothers.

I could tell she was contemplating her options for a moment. The only other option was Edward and Lauren's shower, and I figured that option was probably worse than her brothers. One could only imagine what they got up to in that shower.

"Just keep your hands to yourself, Rossi."

"I'll be a perfect gentleman."

"Doubt it," she quipped back, taking off her sundress.

Georgia

I put my towel on the towel rack next to Luca's towel and then slipped into the hot shower with my bikini still on, giving it a rinse. Luca quickly followed me into the shower and rinsed off his swimming trunks before taking them off and hanging them over the shower curtain. It took everything within me not to turn around and stare at him. I'd seen him almost naked before, back at Monza when I gave him that treat, but this felt different. Now, we were on a level playing field.

Truthfully, I wasn't sure why I had come to Luca's room. Everything in me said to go to Henri and Hugo's room and ask to use their shower, but to Luca's point, I knew it would somehow turn into a competition or talk about racing, and I just wanted a break.

Plus, after Luca had helped me out of the water, I was feeling incredibly hot and bothered around him. I was embarrassed that his rescuing me had turned me on so much, but I was only human. He had been so caring, so calm, and patient with me. And then, when he gave me his jacket tonight, all I could think about was coming back to his room and straddling his incredibly thick thighs.

After I had gotten a taste of Luca in Monaco, I wanted more.

But I knew his ego, and I knew I had to be coy about this, or I would never hear the end of it from him. Still, I knew how to get him interested. After rinsing my bathing suit, I took off my top and bottoms and put them on the shower curtain hook. I heard a small noise behind me which sounded like a groan, and I smirked to myself. I took the soap from the dispenser and started to lather up my body.

"You know, if you needed help with your back, I'd be happy to be of assistance," I heard a cocky voice say behind me. My first reaction was to tell him to piss off, but then I remembered I was here to get some action, and what better way to get Luca interested than to let him massage my back in a steaming hot shower.

"So much for hands to yourself."

He chuckled and pumped the soap into his hands as I backed up into him, letting him lather up my back. Pretty soon, he was traveling down to my ass and then to the backs of my legs and feet. As Luca started to move back up, I felt a hand on my waist and another on the back of my thigh.

"So beautiful," I heard him whisper as he started kissing up my thighs. When he stood up, he turned me around to face him. His cheeks were flushed, and he was looking directly into my eyes. I felt my back hit the shower wall, and Luca's body was pressed up against my front. I could feel his hardening cock press into me, and I gulped. His beautifully plump lips were now inches from mine. I felt a hand come up and caress my cheek ever so gently.

"You are one of the most beautiful people I have ever met."

His voice was silky smooth, and I wrapped my arms around his chest and pulled him a bit closer. Luca was still looking at me with a face I had rarely seen before. In that moment, I felt like the most beautiful girl on the planet. As if on cue, those pesky butterflies arrived again.

Had Luca actually meant that? Or was he just trying to get me to kiss him?

Truthfully, the reason didn't matter – his plan had worked. I leaned up and kissed his lips gently, something which Luca took advantage of as he deepened the kiss, becoming more forceful with his tongue. The kiss was passionate, raw, and breathtaking. His strong arms wrapped around me, and he hoisted me up in the air, signaling for me to wrap my legs around his waist. As Luca broke free from the kiss, I was looking down at him. His pupils were blown, and he licked his lips like he was a cat about to play with its prey.

"As much as I want you in the shower, Amore, I want to worship this body with the respect that it deserves."

Luca took us both out of the shower, and he placed me gently down on the bed, crawling on top of me. I should have felt bad that I was getting his bed all wet, but I didn't care. The only thing I could look at was Luca and his beautiful eyes as they stared back at me. He began to pepper light kisses against my neck, and I let out a soft moan. I slid out from under him, and he groaned in annoyance as I flipped us both over, straddling his thighs. I began to kiss down his chest towards his aching cock, leaving small and delicate kisses along the way.

"Stop being a tease," he demanded, grabbing my hair just a little.

I ignored him and kept up my slow pace, slowly making my way down. As soon as I had arrived, I put some soft kisses on his cock which caused him to buck his hips up in the air.

"So greedy," I murmured as I looked up at him. His dark eyes gave me a look that told me if I kept teasing, I was going to regret it later. I let my mouth sink down onto his cock, and Luca let out a loud moan in appreciation. I slowly began to bob up and down his length, hallowing out my mouth just at the right moment. Just as I had done at Monza, I let his cock slide to the back of my throat, and I took as much of him as I could, putting my hands around the part of his length that I couldn't fit inside my mouth. I let my hands wander down to his balls and gave them a gentle squeeze, which earned me another moan from Luca.

I continued to pick up the pace, and suddenly, I felt a hand on my head, stopping me. Once again, I was on my back, and Luca was now above me, giving me another deep kiss.

"As much as I enjoy your mouth, this time, I am cumming inside of you."

I bit my bottom lip and nodded, knowing how much it killed him when I did that. He growled a bit and then began to work his way down to my core, much to my delight.

"Oh, Principessa, are you this wet from sucking my cock?" he asked. I didn't appreciate the cocky way he said that, but as he sunk a finger into me, all I could do was nod as I let out a gasp. Luca began to pump his finger in and out of me, just like he had done on Sunday. It's like he knew the exact spot to hit because as he entered his third finger into me, I was beginning to feel entirely too close to my orgasm.

Luca suddenly took his fingers away from me, causing me to look up as I attempted to catch my breath, a questioning look now dancing on my face.

"Sorry, I just couldn't help myself. Needed a taste," he said with a wink. I could have died in that moment, watching Luca suck my juices off of his fingers.

I felt the bed sink a bit more, and Luca was climbing up the bed, kissing my stomach and then my breasts, making sure to pay attention to each one as his tongue swirled around each peak. Finally, he made his way up to my mouth and gave me a deep kiss, letting his tongue dance with mine.

He leaned over to the bedside table, and I saw him take out a condom, which he slid onto himself. I licked my lips again, and Luca chuckled, clearly enjoying me staring at his huge cock. As he reached my entrance, I felt his tip start to slowly slide into me. Luca was huge, and while he had worked me open with his fingers, it didn't feel like any amount of foreplay could possibly make me ready for the size of his length.

Still, he went slow, whispering into my ear about *'what a good girl I was'* and *'how proud of me he was for taking him.'* His words made me melt inside. I definitely had a praise kink, and Luca had picked up on that with no issue. The more he said those things to me, the more of a good girl I wanted to be for him.

Finally, after what felt like several lifetimes, Luca was completely inside of me. He felt incredible, and after a few moments, he leaned down and asked if I was okay.

"God, Luca, please move," I begged, wrapping my legs around his waist. He chuckled a bit but obliged my request, slowly beginning to move in and out of me. After several more thrusts, his slowness was beginning to become excruciating. I needed more of him, and I needed it now.

"Luca... faster... please..." I panted into his ears.

"Ask politely." Cocky bastard. Did he expect me to beg for this? As I contemplated how to respond, Luca continued to move in and out of me at a slow pace.

"Pl-please."

"Please, what?"

"Please, Luca, fuck me harder." I wanted the words to come out as a demand, but when the words fell from my lips, they definitely sounded like a pitiful beg, something I am sure Luca enjoyed.

"Good girl." Luca rewarded me by picking up the pace, slamming into me, causing my body to move up the bed. It felt incredible, and soon, I could feel myself building toward my orgasm, that familiar feeling building up inside of me. I could tell Luca was starting to get closer as well, his thrusts getting sloppier. His hand reached down to my clit, and he began to massage it, causing my toes to curl in absolute pleasure. He continued to hit that incredible spot inside me while his fingers worked me with delicate strokes.

After a few more moments, I felt that familiar coil snap, and I let out a loud moan as I screamed his name, probably a little too loud since my brothers were sleeping next door. I put my hand over my mouth and tried to muffle my sounds, but Luca ripped it from me.

"I want this whole fucking boat to know that you're mine," he grumbled as he reached his end, spilling himself inside of me.

We both lay there for a moment, panting away and catching our breaths. Luca leaned onto his forearms and gave my forehead a kiss before standing up and heading toward the bathroom. He threw the condom away and came back with a hot towel, cleaning me up.

I went to get up, but Luca laid back down next to me and pulled me onto his chest, surprising me. There was still silence between us, and truthfully, I had no idea what to say.

"I...I can go, let you get some sleep."

"Oh no, Cara, if you come in here, pretending to need a hot shower so you can have sex with me, then you have to pay the price." I wanted to be snarky at that, wanted to insist that I hadn't actually come in to seduce him, but we both knew that was a lie, so I decided to keep my mouth shut. I quirked my eyebrow at him in question.

"Oh? And what is this fee?" I joked.

He pulled me closer and wrapped his arms around me. I laid my head on his chest, and I could feel his heartbeat start to slow as he began to relax.

"Cuddles, of course."

I huffed out a laugh. "Didn't think F1's most notorious party boy and model seducer was such a cuddler."

"Well, I didn't think F1's goodie two shoes *'I've never broken a rule in my life'* Dubois was such a bad liar. But I guess we both learned something new about the other."

Chapter Fifteen

TO BE OR NOT TO BE

Georgia

I woke up Friday morning to the usual sound behind me. Still groggy from sleep, I blinked my eyes open and looked around the room, but nothing looked familiar. I wasn't in my room. And then it hit me – I was still in Luca's room – and in his bed. As if on cue, I felt a slight movement behind me. Luca's body was pressed up against my back; his arm was wrapped around my torso, pulling me slightly closer to him. I could feel his hard-on behind me, pressing into me, and it made me chuckle a bit.

Last night had been amazing. It wasn't hard to convince him that I was interested in having sex, and he definitely rewarded me for my boldness. I figured if we were going to be saddled together for the long haul, I might as well get something out of it. Plus, my feelings for Luca were starting to evolve. He no longer irked me the way he used to. His cockiness and overinflated ego started to bother me less – they almost seemed cute.

'I want this whole fucking boat to know that you're mine.'

'You are one of the most beautiful people I have ever met.'

I knew that Luca had likely only said those things in the heat of the moment, and for some reason, that made my heart ache. Did I want what he said to be true? I mean, he had asked for cuddles after, which I tried to play off as silly, but truthfully, it felt amazing to be held like that. I hadn't been that close to someone since Anthony, and for some reason, it felt different with Luca even though we weren't actually together – it felt better. I hadn't slept that peacefully in a long time.

I looked at the clock next to me. The time read 5:30 a.m., which meant the sun was just about to rise. I figured since I was up, it would be nice to go out and enjoy the sunrise. I should also probably sneak back into my room before my brothers noticed I was gone. I hoped to God that they hadn't heard Luca and me last night – the mere thought was mortifying. But as I moved to get out of bed, the arm around me pressed me back down, and I heard a chuckle from behind me.

"Leaving without a good morning kiss?" the voice mumbled groggily behind me. I let out a small groan but turned around to look at Luca. As much as I hated to admit it, Luca looked incredibly handsome in the morning, with his messy hair and soft lips. He opened his eyes and let out a sly smile, looking directly into my own eyes.

"Cuddles not enough for you, I see?" I quipped back. Luca just answered by pulling me closer to him, his lips resting inches from my face.

"Not when I have a woman this beautiful in my bed."

A part in the back of my mind couldn't help but wonder, '*Did he really mean what he was saying? Or was he just trying to get in my pants?*'

"I'm sure you say that to every lady that enters your bed." Much to my surprise, Luca let out a loud laugh.

"Oh, Amore, I probably have said that before. You have me there," he said truthfully. "But that doesn't change the fact that I currently have a beautiful, completely naked woman in my bed who I would love a kiss from."

I wanted to be mad at him for admitting his pick-up line to me, but his honesty was refreshing and had annoying won my body over. Luca let his arm drape over me, and he pulled me flush against him, pecking my lips and giving me his infamous Cheshire cat grin.

"Trying to flatter me so you get laid this morning, Rossi."

Luca let his hand slip down to my core, his fingers dancing around my upper thighs where he could definitely feel the wetness starting to build.

"I'd say I don't need to flatter you to get what I want." I rolled my eyes at his cockiness and turned around, giving him my back, making sure not to move too far away. As I laid back down, I could feel his cock starting to get even harder against my back. Luca was undeterred, that much was clear. He moved closer to me, letting his chest become flush with my back as his hands went up to grope my breasts, paying attention to each one as he spooned me.

I let out a soft moan as his other hand snuck underneath me and started to play with my folds and then my clit. Luca took the hand massaging my breasts and lifted my leg up, guiding it over his hip, exposing my entire front. My new position gave him better access to my core, which he continued to massage and play with.

"I mean, if you aren't interested, Principessa, just say the word, and I'll stop."

He said the words with such a sultry voice, and I knew he was teasing me. I didn't want him to stop, that much was clear. I pushed his hand further down, giving him the consent he wanted, and I heard a chuckle from behind me, but he obliged my request and let his hand slide further down as he sunk two fingers inside me. He pulled me closer and leaned a bit more on his back, pulling me with him so that my chest was now angled towards the ceiling, giving him even greater access to my body. My back was up against his chest, and I felt him place gentle kisses along my neck as his fingers worked their magic, stroking that intensely pleasurable spot inside of me.

"Such a good girl for me," he whispered into my ears. "Have to get you ready so you can take me."

As Luca continued to whisper praises into my ear, I could feel myself getting closer and closer to my orgasm, my body squeezing his fingers more and more. He picked up his pace, letting his thumb work my clit as his now four fingers went in and out of me at impressive speed. My moans started to get louder, and I knew I should keep my voice down lest I wake up the entire boat. But it felt too good, and my cries started to get louder, which I knew was only spurring Luca on. He'd made it clear, he didn't care if everyone heard us having sex. After a few more moments, I reached my climax, and my body started to shake in absolute pleasure.

"Fuck Luca, Luca, Luca." I chanted his name over and over as he worked me through my high, fingers finally slowing down as my breathing started to slow. No one had ever fingered me like that before. Even with just his fingers, Luca managed to give me one of the most mind-numbing orgasms I'd ever had.

"So fucking hot," Luca whispered into my ear. His breath was warm, and goosebumps went down my body as it tickled my neck. He leaned over to his bedside table and pulled out a condom, putting it on himself. I felt him shimmy down a bit and line his cock up with my entrance.

"Think you have another one in you, Cara?" I nodded, still out of breath from the last orgasm.

"Such a good girl. I know you can give me another one."

I was feeling a little sore after yesterday, but he had done an excellent job getting me prepared. Luca slid his tip into my core and then started to work the rest of his length in slowly. As he bottomed out, I heard a groan from behind, and it sounded like absolute heaven, knowing that I was the one making him feel this way. As Luca slid in and out of me, I could feel my walls start to clench around him, a second high starting to approach.

"You feel fucking incredible." Again, with the praise that had me wrapped around his little finger. His pace began to pick up, and his hand snaked around to my clit, where he started to gently rub. I was still very sensitive, but as he continued to slowly move in and out of me, I could feel that sensation start to build again in my core. After a few more moments, the pleasure that had been building finally burst, and Luca gave me my second mind-numbing orgasm of the day.

"Fuck, I've wanted this for so long. You're so perfect."

All I could do was moan in response. My body felt completely spent. I could tell Luca was chasing his climax; his thrusts were becoming erratic. Finally, after a few more pumps, he let out a loud moan and spilled himself inside of me.

As both of our breaths began to settle, Luca turned me back toward him. He was staring intently into my eyes, but his look was different than usual. It was as if I could look into his soul and see that he wanted to say something but just couldn't find the words.

Finally, after a few more breaths, Luca whispered, "I meant what I said, Georgie. You are one of the most beautiful women I have ever seen. Even if you hadn't slept with me sex, it wouldn't change the fact that I find you breathtakingly beautiful ... *albeit incredibly annoying at times.*" He added that last sentence with a hint of mischief and a chuckle.

My heart started to flutter at his words. I wanted to respond with something sassy, but I had nothing to say. If Luca wanted me to believe his words, he was doing a very good job at convincing me. We both lay there for some time, enjoying the company of one another for a little while longer, his arms wrapped around me as I laid my head on his chest.

Finally, I looked at the time and realized that the sunrise would be almost complete, so I began to shift in bed.

"No...just a little while longer," he whined, trying to pull me back into his bed. Luca – truly a cuddler.

"Since *you* initiated the sex, I'd say I don't owe you the fee," I said jokingly. "I want to go watch the sunset. You can, of course, join me if you can bear to get out of bed before 7 a.m." I heard Luca groan next to me, a confirmation that he was not a morning person – unless sex was involved. I got up as Luca huffed in response, annoyed that I had left the warm and inviting bed.

"Tis so cold without you," he hummed, although I could see him close his eyes, already giving into his post-sex haze.

"Such a baby." I grabbed my bathing suit and dress from yesterday, throwing them on quickly. As I stepped outside of Luca's door, I looked to see if anyone was in the hallway. Once I saw that the coast was clear, I hopped into my room which was conveniently next door. I slipped into a pair of leggings and grabbed a comfy shirt out of my suitcase.

I headed out to the front of the boat, and as I got closer, I saw a figure standing at the very front, looking out into the sunrise. As I walked closer, I saw it was none other than Henri, who conveniently had not one, but two, cups of coffee next to him.

"Hey!" I called out behind him. "You hogging all the coffee on this boat?" I joked as I approached my brother. I heard a small chuckle from Henri, and he turned around, handing me a cup of coffee. But as he turned, his face dropped, and he looked directly at the shirt I was wearing.

Shit. It was Luca's Hermes shirt that he had let me borrow back in Madrid. In my rush to get out to see the sunrise, I had thrown on the first shirt that I could find.

"Wearing his shirt now, too, I see." Henri sat down on the couch and took a sip of coffee, motioning for me to take a seat next to him. His voice had a hint of disdain, and I could tell he was displeased.

"Luca, let me borrow it when I forgot to pack a comfortable shirt." Henri just nodded at my guilty words, but his silence said everything I needed to know. He was clearly upset about something. After a few more moments, I heard Henri take a deep breath, but I kept looking at the sunrise, not wanting to look at my brother's unsettled face.

"Heard you come out of Luca's room this morning. I figured you would come watch the sunrise." As he said the words, I felt myself cringe – so he had heard us. *Fuck.*

"I'm sorry..." but before I could finish, Henri cut me off.

"I just don't want you to get hurt, Peaches." Henri shrugged his shoulders and looked away from me. His face looked deflated, and he was staring at the ground, clearly not entirely sure what to say next. It's as if he was weighing his options, trying to decide what to tell me.

"I know what I'm doing."

"Do you?" he responded dryly. "This is Luca Rossi, F1's biggest playboy. A new girl in his bed each race. And here you are, being one of *those* girls." I stilled for a moment, leaning back, a look of disgust on my face.

"Excuse me, I am not one of *those* girls – whatever that means."

Henri sighed, rubbing his hands over his face. "I didn't mean it like that... I'm just worried he's using you to get back at me."

Henri definitely meant what he said about me being 'one of those girls,' but I decided to let it slide, curious as to why Luca would be trying to get revenge back on Henri. Henri was a bit of a drama queen, but his face told me he felt very serious about this accusation.

"Back in Monaco, I asked him to stop leading you on. And before you say anything," he added quickly, clearly anticipating my response, "I see the way you look at him, Peaches, don't deny it. You've never been good at hiding your feelings, and you've never been someone to have casual sex. I just... I asked him not to hurt you.

But, of course, Luca was pissed at me, I could tell, and I'm worried he's doing these things to show me he can do what he wants when it comes to you. He's never been a serious dater. He's said multiple times he doesn't want to settle down until he's almost retired from F1. I just don't want to see you hurt."

I took a deep breath and looked out towards the sunrise, which had almost completely risen by this point. The sky was a deep pink and blue and yellow, utterly beautiful. I felt like the opposite of the sunrise, dark and dreary. What if what Henri had said was true? Was Luca just having fun and trying to score points over Henri because Henri had told him to back off?

'*You're the only person I wanted to go home with tonight.*' He'd said those words when we were back at Monza. It was hard to reconcile what Henri was saying to me with the words that Luca kept whispering in my ears.

"Look, Henri, I'm just having some fun, okay? I'm fine." I wanted the words to sound more confident, but they didn't. I knew they fell flat, much like my heart, which now felt deflated. The more I thought about it, the more disappointment started to creep in, and I hated myself for it. This was Luca Rossi; of course, he just wanted casual sex, and if it got back at Henri, that was probably an added bonus for Luca. But also, it was hard to be mad at Luca because we weren't *actually* together. I was the one who initiated the sex last night, and I didn't have a right to be angry at him.

Why would he say no to me coming into his shower?

And yet, I was feeling angry and stupid. I was feeling disappointed if I was being more truthful, and that disappointment was leading to anger. I'd said it over and over again – I wasn't his type. What did I expect to happen? Henri was right; part of me was starting to fall for Luca, and that had to stop now.

After a few more moments of awkward silence, our quiet time was interrupted by laughter coming back from the hallway. Edward and Lauren appeared, and as Edward came up the stairs to the front deck, he walked over and gave me the biggest high-five, clearly unaware of the tense conversation that my brother and I had just exchanged. Lauren just gave him a shove and told him to knock it off, but based on the mischief in Edward's eyes, I could see that he had no plans to stop his antics anytime soon.

"Want to go grab some more coffee?" Lauren asked, pointing in the direction of the kitchen. I nodded in response, and we both got up, leaving the boys to sit and chat a bit longer. However, I could tell from Henri's conversation that he had no tolerance for Edward or his jokes today.

"So, have a good night last night?" Lauren asked, wiggling her eyebrows at me with anticipation of the juicy gossip. I chuckled slightly and started up the coffee maker.

"So, did the entire boat hear?"

Lauren chuckled darkly and took the cup of coffee from my

outstretched hands, motioning for us to sit down at the breakfast table.

"I'm just glad you took what I said to heart. Maybe we can go on a double date when we get back to Monaco!"

"Whoa, getting ahead of yourself there. It was just sex, nothing more."

"Oh, come on, Georgie, there's no way it was just sex. The way you two loo-"

"Lauren, good grief, there's nothing between me and Luca. We're barely friends. We had sex because it was convenient, that's it," I lied. Lauren looked a little taken aback by my words, which came out much more forcefully than I wanted, but I was frustrated – *and angry*. Angry that she and Edward kept feeding me these lies about Luca when it was clear he just wanted an easy fuck, and he couldn't get it anywhere else.

We were both silent for a moment, but she nodded in response. "Well, I hope it was at least fun," she said, trying to lighten the mood. I chuckled and nodded in agreement, giving her a knowing, sly smile. We continued to chat a bit more, changing the subject to the Maison de Klotho clothing spread I had been emailed yesterday.

Luca

After Georgia and I had slept together in Majorca, I felt like I was on cloud nine. The sex had been incredible, and I had even convinced her to stay the night and cuddle. Typically, the girls left after thirty minutes or so, but when Georgia fell asleep in my arms, I was stoked. I did everything in my power to stay still, too afraid I would wake her up, and then she would leave and head back to her room.

I felt a little guilty that her brothers had probably heard us. Edward informed me – *fairly quickly* – that he and Lauren had heard some noises coming from our room. That morning, after I finished getting ready, I made my way to the breakfast room only to hear her and Lauren chatting. I knew I shouldn't listen in, but my ego got the best of me. I *wanted* to hear her bragging about the amazing sex we had.

What I heard couldn't have been more different. Instead, I heard Georgia say that the sex had meant nothing, that we were barely friends. I felt my heart drop in my stomach after that. It had meant something to me, but clearly, I was alone with those feelings. For some reason, I felt used, which I knew was ridiculous.

How many times had I had meaningless sex with women? More than was good for me.

Georgia and I had agreed to be friends, but we weren't close friends; I knew that was true. I kept telling myself that I shouldn't be offended by her comment, that her body didn't lie to me, but still, my heart felt disappointed.

I spent the rest of the trip trying to keep a bit of a distance from her. If she noticed this, she didn't say anything. She never came back to my room.

And now we were both in Baku, preparing for the Azerbaijan Grand Prix on the day the GQ article was meant to be released. Georgia and I had barely said a word to one another since that morning in Majorca. She was incredibly busy both Wednesday and Thursday evening in Baku, so we'd only seen each other in passing at the hotel, but I could feel the awkward air between us, the unsaid words that we would have to discuss eventually.

Free Practice 1 this morning had gone better than expected. Georgia was, of course, P1, with Henri P2. I had settled into P5 in both free practice sessions. For some reason, in Baku, I couldn't get the car underneath me to be any faster. It felt terrible – probably because I felt terrible. My mind was elsewhere, and Matteo could tell. As I returned back to the pits from FP2, I saw Matteo waving at me to get out of the car and come find him. He was in the Hermes conference room with the GQ article up on his laptop screen.

"They loved you!" he shouted in excitement as he bounced up and down, frantically pointing at his laptop. I had never seen him this excited before, not even when I took P1 at my first race win. I chuckled a bit, trying to let some of the tension leave my body before I read the article – but dread had already started to fill my body.

That day at the photoshoot had been fun and relaxing, and it was a fond memory. A memory that I felt would turn sour as soon as I started to read the article because of where Georgia and I currently stood.

Matteo sat me down in front of the screen, and I started to go through the article, paragraph by paragraph. The GQ article was incredibly well written, and much to my surprise, the article was full of gushing compliments towards us, intertwined with interesting tidbits about our lives and driving. A particular section caught my eye.

'The couple have a natural air about them. While you would think F1's hottest couple would be egocentric and opinionated, this couldn't be further from the truth. Georgia is surprisingly shy for someone who spends her time battling journalists with the ferocity of a lion, and Luca has a sweeter edge than I expected, always checking in on Georgia and making sure that she is comfortable. The subtle exchanges between the two – the gentle hand-holding, soft whispers – is a real contrast to how most of us see them on race weekends.

When I asked Georgia what they were like as a couple, she said domestic and normal – boring even. I told her that was a cop-out answer, but as we went through the photo shoot, I began to see what she meant. They spend their days homemaking pasta and watching classic movies. They laugh at the silliest things and spent no less than half the photoshoot taking the piss out of each other. It was fun to watch and an honor to be a part of those moments with them.

As I finished the article, I looked up at Matteo, who was still beaming with pride at me, but his expression quickly changed when he saw the tears starting to fall from my eyes. I tried to wipe them away quickly, but I had failed to do so before he managed to catch me.

"Luca, what is it? This article, it's amazing. Helios Sunglass Company has already reached out to the team – along with a couple of other big sponsors." His voice was full of urgency, but I just nodded and instead elected to look out of the small window.

"I fucked up, Matteo."

"Did you not hear what I just said-"

"No," I put up my hand, halting his reassurances. "I fucked up with Georgia." Matteo eyed me cautiously, not entirely sure what to say to that. "I slept with her in Majorca, and after we were done, I heard her tell Lauren that it meant nothing. Henri told me to stay away from his sister, to keep things professional, and I didn't, and now I'm paying the price. I'm sure he warned her to stay away from me, that I was only after her for sex. She will barely look at me now."

All of this kept spilling out of me, more tears falling down my face. Matteo was quick to shut the conference room door, and he took a seat next to me, patting me on the back.

"I had no idea you felt this way. I thought you considered her to be an annoying, stuck-up brat. At least that's what you told me when I first suggested this entire thing to you." I let out a forced laugh and shook my head.

"The truth is I asked her out several years ago when she came to visit Henri and Edward, but I stood her up on that date. I was scared and pathetic and convinced she wouldn't want me. I've hated myself ever since. I proved to her that I wasn't to be trusted."

"Oh, Luca, is that what you think?" he said in a soothing voice, leaning a little closer and giving me a brotherly hug. "You *are* worthy of love. If Georgia can't see that because of your *past* actions, then it's your job to show her with your *current* actions. Your heart has no boundaries." I smiled at him, appreciating his pep talk, even if I was still struggling to believe it.

"How about this, I'll text Lizzie and say you guys need to have dinner after that article. You can use that opportunity to do something special for her. Show her who you are as a person. Show her that you can be the Luca from *this* article."

I looked up and into Matteo's eyes. They were soft but pleading, and I nodded in agreement. He was right – I had to show Georgia who I really was.

Georgia

I arrived back in the garage from FP2, having gotten P1 in both free practices, and I was feeling over the moon. I hopped out of the car and turned to my left, only to see Lizzie, Lily, and Fiona waving at me ecstatically, each of them looking like they had won the lottery.

"I mean, P1 is pretty good guys, but I think this might be a bit much for a Free Practice," I chuckled, knowing that there was no way they were celebrating the car and the good practice sessions. Even Lily had managed to get P3 and P4 in both sessions, and the team was overjoyed. That thought in itself made me chuckle. Here I was, having the drive of my life, and these fools were celebrating something else entirely.

"The article is out, and it's amazing!" Lily gushed, holding up her phone and shoving it in my face. Before I could take a look at it, Lizzie ushered us into the conference room. The article was already up on her laptop, and she sat me down in front of it, clearly eager to get my opinion. As I read through the article, I stopped at one of the blurbs and re-read it.

'It's not hard to see that Georgia was extremely nervous during the photo shoot, which I found to be interesting for someone who had such a public life in America, but it allowed me to see how someone like Luca compliments her. His charming personality and attentiveness to her is endearing, and we can see why she fell so hard for someone who was considered to be F1's biggest playboy. During the last photo session, when I could tell Georgia was feeling nervous, I heard Luca whisper a dirty joke in her ear, which caused her to laugh and relax, much to everyone's amusement.'

Good grief, so everyone had heard that comment. My cheeks

went a little red, and Lily leaned over my shoulder and chuckled, clearly waiting for me to get to that part of the article.

"You know, for a couple that's meant to be fake dating, you sure do look hot together," Lily teased as I continued to scroll through the article. I wanted to retort back something rude and tell her to piss off, but I couldn't. All I could focus on was my heart and how it ached reading this article. Luca and I were nothing like this article had written, and as the week in Baku had gone by, the more I realized that I wanted something more. I wanted this article to be true. I felt like in Majorca, I had to keep reminding myself that this relationship was fake, but articles like this made it hard to remember that fact.

"The fans have just been loving this article. I heard Isabelle on the phone earlier with a few of our sponsors, and they are interested in having you and Lily feature their products. Such great news!" Lizzie was doing a little dance in the middle of the conference room, jiving to the invisible music in her head. I let out a small huff and a chuckle at her antics. I'm glad she was pleased. Truthfully, I was glad that this gave the team the extra funding that we needed. If we truly had secured these extra deals, we were going to be set for development on next year's car. We had another year to prove ourselves.

I had another year to fight for the championship. I went to say as much to Lizzie, but before I could get the words out, I heard Lizzie's phone ding with a text.

"Oh, Georgie, Matteo just texted me. He thinks after this article, we should get some press on you and Luca, keep the momentum going. They want you guys to do a dinner tonight. I have an address for you."

"Lizzie, tonight is my only night to myself," I pleaded, but the look on her face told me it was a dead cause. I knew she was right. We had all of this interest, and if continuing on this charade meant I could get these deals confirmed with the other sponsors, then I would put up with it. I'd done an excellent job avoiding Luca over the last week, but I knew it had to end eventually.

"Fine, I'll be there, but I'm not dressing up, so it better not be fancy."

"I'll be sure to let them know," she hummed in response, already texting Matteo.

I went through the article again and then went through some of the comments online. Lizzie was right; the comments were overwhelmingly positive – it was almost shocking. While I was dreading this dinner with Luca, part of me was starting to feel more relaxed. This was working, and I should celebrate that fact.

Luca, for some reason, had to return back to the hotel earlier, so Lily and I drove back to the hotel together, which was nice. I felt like we hadn't caught up in a while. Lily was buzzing about her Free Practice sessions. We were both hopeful for a good qualifying session tomorrow. When I arrived back at the hotel, Luca was nowhere to be found. I had a text from Matteo letting me know that a car would be picking me up at 7 p.m. I took a quick shower and changed into something comfortable – some jeans and a nice sweater – before making my way downstairs.

As I arrived at the elevator, I pressed the button and said my usual silent prayer to the universe – begging for it to be empty, but as per usual, the elevator gave me the middle finger. As I walked into the elevator, I saw several Sponsors and VIPs that had been at the Valkyrie F1 hospitality all day, all clearly making their way out to the team principal dinner that the FIA had set up. Isabelle was frustrated that she and Francesco had to attend, but even Isabelle couldn't scare the FIA enough to have them change it.

"Oh, look who it is!" One of them called out to the group. As I turned to the left, I saw none other than Lilah, our Maison de Klotho coordinator, along with Sara, the executive we had met back in Monaco. I gave them a warm smile and nod.

"Heading out somewhere?" Lilah asked.

"Yes, dinner plans with Luca tonight," I hummed in response.

"How did you like the article, Georgia?" Sara asked, a grin on her face so large I was worried it might split her in half.

"Just lovely, thank you. My mother is already begging me to get some of the prints so she can hang them around the house."

"Of course! We'll be sure to get some your way, along with the clothes from the shoot, so we can have you and Luca start wearing them to races." I nodded my appreciation and huffed out a light thanks.

"You have a good one, that Luca. We were worried that his playboy image would put a damper on the brand, but we've had several of our designers request him after that article. He's lucky to have you. You really straightened that one out." I felt a pang of guilt when she said it. Truth was, I hadn't done much. Luca had been instructed to play a role, and he was clearly playing it well. Still, I gave them the huge smile they wanted because I also had a role to play.

"Well, let's just hope that doesn't carry over into his racing. Still have a championship to bring home," I said with a sly smile, much to the amusement of the elevator. As soon as the door opened on the ground floor, I waved to the group and took off, wishing them a lovely weekend at the hospitality suite.

As promised by Matteo, the car was waiting outside for me promptly at seven. I hopped in, and the driver took off. As I sat in the car, I saw a text on my phone from Lauren.

Lauren: Hope you have a good time tonight.

Georgia: Does Luca tell Edward everything?

Lauren: Just the important stuff ;)

I rolled my eyes and continued to watch as we headed closer and closer to the water. "Where are we going?" I asked the driver casually, but he only laughed and said he was instructed not to tell me, which piqued my interest even more.

As I arrived at the docks, I hopped out of the car at the driver's instruction and looked around, trying to see if I spotted Luca anywhere. Out on the dock, I saw someone waving at me, and I headed down to the dock only to see Luca standing in front of me with a picnic basket, a bottle of champagne, and a huge grin on his face.

"Nice of you not to be late this time."

"Well, you know me, never one to be late to surprises."

Luca reached out for my hand and helped me onto the small boat. He led us to the back, where a table had been set up for us with a lovely white tablecloth and two champagne glasses.

"Mr. Rossi, Ms. Dubois, I will be your server this evening," a man said from behind me. His name tag said Yusif, and I thanked him, taking a seat at one of the places set at the table. Luca took the spot next to me, so we both faced out towards the ocean. The boat captain also came down and said hello before I heard the all-too-familiar sound of the boat setting off. Yusif poured us a glass of wine each and then disappeared with the picnic basket.

"So, you are taking me out to sea before you kill me." Luca smiled at the joke and picked up his glass, signaling for me to do the same.

"I know this last week – *no, these last several years* – have been weird between us, and I'm sorry for that. I was an idiot all those years ago when I stood you up on that date. I can't take it back, but I am hoping you'll let me give you the date you deserve."

I looked at Luca – absolutely stunned. I wasn't sure if Luca ever thought back to that date that never happened. I had imagined him not caring enough to remember, even if it still haunted the back of my mind. Luca smiled a smile so warm and inviting that it was hard to stay mad at him. I clinked my glass with his, continuing to eye him a little suspiciously. *Who was this Luca?*

He took a sip of the champagne and went back to looking at the sunset. I felt his hand move towards mine, and he interlocked our fingers together, all while I continued to stare at him. Luca was incredibly handsome in the setting sun, his beautiful Mediterranean tan on display. The light made his warm features look calm and relaxed.

It was as if he knew I wouldn't have anything to say yet, and he was okay with that, so we just sat there for some time – Luca watching the sunset and me watching Luca. Finally, the words I wanted to say came to the front of my mind, and I found my voice again.

"You did all this for me?"

"Yes." He said it so simply, as if I was an idiot for thinking anything else. I saw a small smile form on his lips, and he looked over to me, as if he was trying to read my emotions – trying to read my soul.

"Henri was right. I haven't been someone worth dating."

"Luca–" I began.

"No, Amore, it's true. Your brother was right to warn me away from you. I know he told you that he told me to stay away. His cold shoulder in the paddock all weekend basically confirmed it. But then I read that article, and I realized that I wanted to be like the Luca from the GQ photoshoot. That Luca is worth dating." His brutal truth and honesty took me aback for a moment as I stared into his beautiful brown eyes.

"I don't know what to say."

"You don't have to say anything, and I don't expect anything from this date. I just wanted you to have that date you deserved all those years ago. I wanted you to know I was sorry."

I took the hand that wasn't interlaced with his and reached out for his cheek, stroking it gently. His face was a little scruffy because he hadn't shaved in a while, and I could see the stubble growing in. After a few more moments, I leaned in a little closer and pressed my lips against his. Luca released my other hand and placed his hands on the back of my neck and my lower back, pushing us closer together as he deepened the kiss. We both heard a clearing of the throat from the hallway, Yusif standing there, trying not to interrupt our moment.

"Sorry to interrupt, but the appetizer is ready." In his hand was a delightful cheeseboard filled up with all my favorite cheeses and meats.

Lauren must have helped with this, I thought to myself. The server set the cheeseboard down and then refilled our glasses, quickly disappearing down the hallway of the boat.

"Surprised this cheese isn't in mac and cheese form."

"Lauren insisted that no first date should involve mac and cheese." I felt more butterflies returning to my stomach as I contemplated how this *actually* was our first date.

"Who says this is a first date?" I quipped at him, smiling with a mouthful of cheese.

"Do you kiss your friends like that," he teased back.

"Only if they're incredibly sexy," I said with what I hoped was a sultry voice, at least as sultry as I could get with a mouth full of cheese and crackers.

"Ooh, Cara, come on, you can do better than that pickup line." At that, we both laughed. Maybe Lizzie was right, my flirting probably did need work.

"Well, if you want better pickup lines, you're just going to have to earn them." Luca chuckled as he picked up his glass.

"Challenge accepted."

Chapter Sixteen

COME HELL OR HIGH WATER

Luca

The date Friday evening with Georgia had been undecidedly one of the best moments of my dating life. It could not have gone more perfect in my head, and it almost scared me how good it felt. After the kiss, we spent the rest of the date chatting away about anything and everything – movies, books she loved, her relationship with her brothers. It's as if I was finally getting Georgia to open up about herself, and when she did, I began to see the part of her that everyone adored. She put her rocky exterior away, and her personality started to shine through.

I was a man trapped and suffocating, and she was the breath of fresh air I needed.

When we got back to the hotel, we immediately went into our separate bedrooms. While the date had been amazing, I meant what I said. I didn't expect anything from her. I needed to show her that I was different. Even though I wanted to do nothing more than pull her into my bed and make her moan my name all night, I had made significant progress, and I felt like that would take us a step back. When I said goodnight to her from my own suite door, I noticed a slight look of disappointment on her face, which secretly brought me joy, although I tried not to show it.

As I opened my eyes the next morning, I looked at the clock; it was 7 a.m., and I knew what that meant – the social media posts officially announcing our relationship had dropped.

While the entire world already knew that we were dating, we had never announced it on social media, something Lizzie and Matteo insisted was incredibly important. I had no idea why; I barely used any of my social channels, but the social media coordinators decided that it was an important tool for our relationship.

Georgia had tried to push back and insist that if this relationship was *actually* real, we wouldn't be posting on Instagram or Twitter because we would want our privacy, but that argument fell on deaf ears. Lizzie wanted to keep the momentum going, so after careful consideration between her and Matteo, the two posts were chosen.

GeorgiaDubois38

Liked by Valkyrie F1 Team and 30k others

GeorgiaDubois38 Canoe think of a more perfect day? Neither can I.
@LucaRossi52

As I looked at Georgia's Instagram post, I let out a laugh.

Classic Georgia – always cracking a joke. Looks like she won the battle with Lizzie – somewhat, at least. She'd told Lizzie if she was to make a post, she controlled the caption. The caption was undoubtedly the most real part of the Instagram post.

 **LucaRossi52**

Liked by HenriDubois67 and 150k others

LucaRossi52 Sunsets are better with you.
@GeorgiaDubois38

As I scrolled to my own post, I took a good look at the photo. I had told Matteo to just pick one from the vacation in a huff of annoyance, but I was surprised he picked this one. It was one of my favorites of the two of us from Majorca. Georgia looked so incredibly relaxed. This was taken the day before Henri, Edward, and Lauren had arrived. Georgia and I had joined a day early with my family, and we had spent some time on the beach relaxing before jumping back onto the yacht. She had barely worn any makeup that day, and instead, we opted for a quiet walk along the beach.

Between the constant pinging of Instagram and text messages from friends congratulating me on the announcement, I saw a text from my team principal, who was insisting I get to the paddock by 8 a.m. It was as if Georgia had gotten the same text because as I walked into the shared living room of the hotel suite, Georgia was already sitting on the couch, reading a book, sipping on a cup of coffee – already ready for the day. I looked down at the coffee table, and there was a second cup of coffee, black with no sugar or cream.

As I reached down to grab the cup of coffee, Georgia slapped my hand away, a cheeky smile on her face.

"Whoa, Rossi, you think one boat ride means you can steal my backup cup of coffee?" I stepped back, chuckling, nodding to her as she laughed in response. "I kid, I kid, it's for you. Just don't need you getting all presumptuous over there," she said with a wink.

"How you tease me," I quipped, quickly picking up the coffee and taking a sip. I plopped down next to Georgia and looked at her book, eyeing her as she read the pages between her hands. She looked up from her book and quirked an eyebrow, now watching me watch her. We stared at each other for a few more moments, and then she went back to reading.

I kept sipping my coffee, enjoying the silence and just being in her presence. I assumed that she had seen the social media posts but was not interested in talking about them. Part of me wanted to ask her if she loved that photo as much as I did, but the cowardly part of me won out.

After another ten minutes went by, it was 7:30, and we were to be at the paddock by 8 a.m. We made our way to the elevator and down to her car, which was conveniently already waiting for us. Lizzie knew we would be late, so she had called ahead every morning to get our car brought forward so we could leave immediately from the hotel.

As we got into the car and started driving, Georgia finally spoke up. "That was a nice photo you chose." So she did like it. I tried to hide the huge grin on my face, knowing it would make me look like a lovesick fool, but I couldn't help it.

"Yours was... very you." She chuckled at that and gave me a light shove.

We arrived at the paddock shortly before 8 a.m. and walked through the security gates hand in hand, although this time it felt less forced than previously. I dropped her off at her hospitality suite and then continued on to the Hermes garage, which was closer to the front. As I passed Wilmington, my old team, Edward came running out of the doors, clearly trying to wave me down.

"Luca! Luca!" I turned and faced Edward, who was now slightly red in the face as he stood in front of me, panting away.

"I knew you were my biggest fan, but no need to run," I teased.

Instead of answering, Edward grabbed my arm and began to drag me inside the Wilmington hospitality suite. As we entered, I tried to avoid the weird looks from various Willmington employees, and fortunately no one said anything. Edward and I had been so close for so long that it wasn't a major surprise that I occasionally dropped by to say hello to my old team and teammate. When we got to the VIP area, Edward pushed us behind a wall, as if he was trying to hide the two of us.

"Edward, I'm going to be late. What is so important?"

"He's here," he said in the loudest whisper I had ever heard.

"Who?" Edward just pointed towards a man who was standing at the back of the room, chatting to Arthur, the Wilmington team principal, and a few other VIPs.

"You don't know who he is?" Edward questioned, still in a hushed voice. We must have looked ridiculous to anyone who passed by at that moment, the two of us huddled in a corner, clearly having a secret conversation.

"No, Edward, I don't know who the random person talking to Arthur is." I was starting to get very annoyed with Edward at this moment. I glanced down at my watch, and it was almost 8 a.m. At this point, I wouldn't have time to get a second cup of coffee before my team meeting. Although, being late to a team meeting with Henri didn't sound so bad.

"That's Anthony," Edward hissed, still pointing towards the driver. "Georgia's old dick of a fiancé."

Now, that caught my interest, and I looked up again at the man standing at the back of the room. He had slicked-back brown hair and, if I was being honest, a grin much too smug considering he was a guest.

"Why is he here?"

"I've been told he's the new Indy Car driver. They also paid for him to do some Formula 1 testing. Rumor is after Oliver's contract is up, he might take his seat. They're putting him in Indy Car to see how he does in America. God, I hope he fails. What a miserable teammate he would be."

"I didn't realize you'd met him."

"Oh yeah, met him a few times. Georgia once brought him over to London when I still lived there. Absolute moron and so rude – incredibly American." The way Edward said American had me grinning. One of his favorite places to visit was America, and he absolutely loved the Miami race, spending half the time telling me how he was going to move there. Still, there was no love loss between us European Formula 1 drivers and the American NASCAR drivers, even if so many of us went to drive for NASCAR after we left Formula 1.

"I've been trying to ignore him all morning, but I know I won't be able to forever. Arthur has given him all access to the garage, and he'll be here all weekend," Edward groaned, rubbing his eyes in frustration.

"I want to meet him," I said suddenly. Edward looked a little shocked, wondering why on earth I'd want to meet the asshole who broke Georgia's heart.

"Gross. Why?"

"Because I want to thank him for being stupid enough to end his relationship with Georgia. I want to thank him for letting me show Georgia what it's like to be with a boyfriend who values her. I want to rub my relationship in his stupid fucking face." That last part came out in a whisper, but I knew Edward heard it.

"Luca Rossi, such a softy," Edward teased. "Something tells me he probably won't care since, I mean, he was the one who cheated on Georgia." *Did everyone know this story except me?*

"Oh, he'll care." *I was sure of it.* "Georgia isn't someone you just *get over.*" I knew this from first-hand experience, and I had no doubt in my mind that even though Anthony had been the one to cheat, he was missing her all the same. She was beautiful, smart, funny. It would be impossible not to miss her.

Edward looked incredulously at me but chuckled, glancing back at Anthony.

"I've got to head to the Hermes garage, but I'll see you after qualifying."

He nodded in agreement, and I left the hospitality suite as discretely as I could, heading towards the Hermes garage. It was only a few minutes past 8 a.m. when I got to my garage, and I took my seat inside the conference room. Fortunately, Francesco was also running late from an engineering meeting. *Unfortunately*, that meant it was just Henri, Hugo, and me sitting awkwardly together in the Hermes conference room.

"I saw the photos from the boat ride last night," Hugo said, finally breaking the deafening silence in the room. "Georgia sent me a couple of photos."

"It was good fun." I let my eyes glance at Henri, who still hadn't said anything. He didn't look too shocked, which told me that he knew about the date but had decided not to say anything.

"So, Henri, you read the GQ article?" I asked casually, knowing full well that he would have been instructed to read it. Hell, Francesco wouldn't even have needed to tell him to read it. Henri's jealousy would get the better of him, and he would *want* to read it. I knew he wanted it to be him and Georgia – a fun brother/sister spread in the magazine talking about their life together. He had mentioned it before, and the duo had done a few articles for Monegasque and French magazines, but nothing of this size.

Part of me felt pleased that he was jealous, and I knew it was petty. Everyone under the sun knew that Henri was the number one driver. He was the driver that Hermes had put all of their hopes and dreams on. By all means, this should have been *his* article. He should have been the one to get the big spread, but instead it was me, Hermes driver number two – the irresponsible 'playboy' who had put several sponsorship contracts at risk.

And fuck it, I was pleased. Not a lot of things had gone my way this season, and I was going to revel in the few things that did. Henri looked at me, clearly pondering how to respond to that. He knew I was baiting him in front of his brother, but his pause told me that he was debating on whether he should take the bait.

"Peaches looked beautiful." Henri's eyes narrowed, looking directly into mine.

"Well, Georgia doesn't need a professional photographer or fancy clothes to do that," I responded back, letting a sly grin form on my lips. *Should I be pissing off my teammate before a qualifying where I needed a tow? Probably not.* But no one had accused me of being level-headed, and this was far too fun.

I could see Henri's jaw twitch a bit, but he remained mute and instead turned back to his phone, continuing to scroll through whatever he was reading. Part of me felt a little bad; in truth, I understood where he was coming from on a deeper level. He was a protective older brother whose sister had been hurt before. I would be acting like him if it was my sister, and I knew it.

As I considered this, I thought back to Anthony who was hanging out in the Wilmington garage. I wondered if Henri knew that Anthony was here. I expected that he didn't; even Edward seemed shocked to see the American NASCAR driver this morning. I pondered for a few moments if I should tell Henri and Hugo and decided that it was the right thing to do. If it was my sister, I would want to know that her asshole of an ex-fiance was here.

"So, I, uh, saw Anthony at the Wilmington garage this morning." Immediately, Henri and Hugo looked up, their attention fully fixated on me.

"What do you mean he's here?" A look of concern spread across Hugo's face. "Does Georgie know?"

"Edward pulled me into the Wilmington garage this morning. Anthony was in the VIP suite. Apparently, he's had some Formula 1 testing at Wilmington, and he has been given an Indy Car seat. He's here all weekend, moseying his way around the paddock as he gets further acquainted with the Wilmington team."

"Why would the Wilmington F1 Team, or any team, want that asshole?" Henri loudly scoffed, slamming his hands on the table. I jumped back, a little shocked by my teammates' outburst. Henri ruffled his hands through his hair as he muttered a frustrated sigh. Hugo put both his hands on his hips and began to pace the room, and I could see the wheels turning in his head.

"We need to keep her away from Anthony," Hugo said finally, stopping mid-pace as he sifted his hand through his hair.

"With all due respect, Georgia is a big girl. She can handle herself." I didn't like to pick fights with Hugo, but I couldn't help myself. I understood that her brothers were concerned, but I also felt like Georgia wasn't a child.

Hugo let out an irritated chuckle but nodded in agreement. "You're right. She can handle herself, but this is a huge weekend for her, and Anthony is very good at getting under people's skin. They ended very badly, and I have no doubt that he'll do everything in his power to get into her head. She doesn't deserve that, not after everything he did."

"Well, we're having a quick lunch together after FP3. I figured we'd stick around the Valkyrie hospitality area, probably the safest place to be."

"I will come and have lunch with you," Henri piped up. I tried to hide my displeasure as I nodded at my teammate. It would be best to have a small group. I'd ask Edward to come too – might as well add company to misery.

Free Practice 3 had been excruciating. I hated these city tracks, favoring the more traditional racing tracks like Spa and Silverstone.

Still, Georgia and Henri had done their usual – P1 and P2 as normal, with Noah in P3. They were separated between something incredibly miniscule, like a thousandth of a second.

I knew my P6 result was pathetic for the car, but I was not fairing well on the track. I felt uncomfortable and displeased with the car's setup, but we were stuck with what we had this week. As I hopped out of the car, I saw Henri wave me over. He had his suit wrapped around his waist, clearly ready to head to lunch so he could brag to Georgia that he had beaten her into the P1 slot at FP3.

We arrived at the Valkyrie hospitality suite and took a seat outside. It was somewhat visible to guests who walked by, but they wouldn't be allowed in unless they had a VIP pass. Georgia had insisted on sitting outside, even though Henri tried to convince her otherwise. Unfortunately for Henri, the weather was too nice for Georgia to possibly believe that we stay inside, just in case it rained.

Edward had arrived shortly after we sat down, a knowing look on his face. Henri gave him a small shake of his head, letting him know that we hadn't told Georgia. I had been team *'Georgia deserves to know,'* but I was overruled by her brothers, who said absolutely not, or at least not until qualifying was over. We all knew we couldn't hide her all of Sunday, so we struck a deal – let's get through qualifying.

But, as I suspected, the universe had other plans.

Georgia insisted on having a short walk to get her legs going before qualifying. I offered for Edward and Henri to head back to their garages, but they both insisted on staying. About halfway through our walk, I saw Edward's face go wide, telling me what I needed to know – Anthony had spotted us, and he was heading over to our group. *Fuck.*

"Well, well, well, Edward, I had wondered where you had gone off to!" I heard a voice call out. Edward ducked behind me as if that was going to hide him from Anthony. Georgia immediately looked up at the person standing in front of her, a look of dread – *and then anger* – on her face as she turned to see Anthony standing there with a female redhead, their hands intertwined.

Edward said nothing, his eyes shifting to Georgia, who was already giving Edward a pointed glare with a questioning look on her face, clearly expecting an answer out of the Brit.

"Just having lunch with friends," Edward replied with a dry smile.

"What the fuck are you doing here?" Henri gritted out, standing slightly in front of Georgia – Georgia's knight in shining armor as always.

"Oh, Henri, how I've missed you," Anthony drawled out in his ridiculous Southern accent. "Been a while. You remember my girl-friend, Anna."

Henri ignored Anthony's introduction, once again demanding to know why Anthony was at the grand prix. I turned to look at Georgia, who was still a little wide-eyed. She was staring at Edward, and they were clearly having a secret conversation with their eyes and body language.

"I'm a personal guest of the Wilmington F1 Team this week. Just signed a contract to be their Indy Car driver," he gloated, as if the four F1 drivers in front of him would be impressed by that. Georgia being the first woman to win Indy Car was impressive, but she was now a Formula 1 driver, something that Anthony would never achieve. It was likely Wilmington had only asked him onto the team because his dad was one of the richest oil barons in Texas. *Money talked in racing.*

I could tell that Edward wanted to say something, but he held his tongue. There was no need to make his time in the Wilmington garage even more miserable. The war between Wilmington drivers wasn't worth it, and the press would crucify the team if they caught wind of drivers not getting along.

Before anyone could respond to that, I slipped my arm around Georgia and put on my classic Luca smile, the one I always wore when I met annoying little shits like Anthony. The smile that said go fuck yourself, while still looking pleasant to the outside world. As I leaned into Georgia, I wrapped my arms around her shoulders and pulled her closer to me. Georgia looked up, confusion in her eyes, not entirely sure what I was trying to do.

"Indy Car... wow... so impressive," I said half – *no, mostly* – sarcastically. "I stopped watching after someone kept winning all the races. Got a little boring," I said, looking down at Georgia and giving her a wink and a sly grin. I was pleasantly surprised when Georgia leaned a bit more into me, grinning at my comment.

"Can't help that none of the other teams put up decent drivers or competition," she quipped. It was at that moment I realized she was wearing her Triple Crown polo that Isabelle had gotten her. The entire garage had swapped their shirts, and now everyone had the triple crown logo on their backs, a reminder to all the teams that a lion was among us.

Anthony scoffed as he dragged his girlfriend Anna closer to him, clearly sizing me up. I had no doubt that he had heard Georgia and I were dating, and judging by his body language, he was trying to judge us as a couple.

"Hard to compete with someone who can sleep her way to the championship," Anthony bit out. I felt Georgia immediately go stiff in my grasp, could feel her anger start to bubble, but before she could get something out, I moved forward and stood close to Anthony, my face mere inches from his.

"From what I heard, Anthony, it sounded like the only person trying to sleep their way to the top was you, but you were so lousy in bed even that didn't work, so Daddy had to *buy* you a spot at Wilmington." I said it low enough voice so that only the six of us around could hear, recognizing that a small crowd had started to form around us.

I knew Georgia could defend herself, but I also knew Georgia, and I knew that look on her face. She was boiling with anger – at us for not telling her, but also at Anthony, and she would say something she regretted. The media's opinion of her was turning the tide, and I didn't want something to get out into the press. The group of us together was starting to gain attention, and I knew this interaction needed to end – and quickly.

I heard both Henri and Edward snicker behind me. I didn't even look at Georgia, but out of the corner of my eye I saw the smug look on her face, clearly pleased with Anthony's reaction. I grabbed Georgia's hand and turned around, dragging us both toward the Valkyrie garage. As soon as we got to the garage, Georgia let go of my hand and turned to face Henri, wagging a finger in his face.

"I'm going to take a wild guess here and say that you three knew about Anthony's presence this weekend," Georgia accused.

"Look, Peach–" Henri started.

"Don't 'look, Peaches', me. What the fuck is going on with you, Henri? I get you're trying to do the whole protective brother thing, but knock it off. I already have one protective brother. I don't need another one. I thought you were on my side, but recently, it feels like you're always hiding something from me."

"And you," she pointed to Edward, who looked a little worse for wear. "You couldn't drop me a text? Oh hey, Georgia, that asshole I told you to break up with during your trip to London a few years ago is here. Like nothing from you? Really?"

Both Henri and Edward just stared at her with blank expressions, neither of them really knowing what to say. I braced myself for my turn, but nothing came. Either Georgia had run out of steam, or I had been spared because of my comment to Anthony. Regardless of the reason, I'd take it. It was nice to not be on the receiving end of Georgia's frustrations for once, and if I was being honest, a little fun to watch Henri stand there uncomfortably. Both Henri and Edward mumbled fairly pathetic apologies, but Georgia just rolled her eyes.

"I have to go get ready for qualifying. I don't have time for this." And with that, she pranced into the Valkyrie garage. I wanted to utter an *I-Told-You-So* , but that seemed in poor taste, even for me, so I just shrugged my shoulders and started to walk back to the Hermes garage with Henri following me in total silence.

Georgia

I didn't have time to really process what had gone down with Anthony before qualifying. I was annoyed with Henri and Edward, but I understood why they didn't want to tell me before qualifying. I texted Hugo about my frustration, but he only backed them up, insisting that nothing good would have come of it – insinuating that they were going to tell me this evening, although I wasn't sure if I believed that.

I insisted that finding out an hour before qualifying by running into my ex was worse, to which he agreed and apologized, asking me not to be so hard on Henri. This was a classic Hugo move. He knew I couldn't stay mad at him long, so he took the blame so Henri could get some relief from being the center of my anger. He had that same sweet personality that our mother had, and he was always willing to protect his siblings.

Truthfully, I was more annoyed because Henri was supposed to be my partner in crime, not my bodyguard, but recently Henri had shifted from best friend to protective older brother, and it annoyed me. I wanted my best friend and confidant back.

Still, I put all of that aside and did what I came to do in Baku – come in first, which is exactly what I had done in qualifying. I was buzzing, as Oscar Parker would say. As I jumped out of the car, I went and stood with Noah and Eric, who had qualified P2 and P3 alongside me. We took our photos and chatted with the event VIPs for a bit before being ushered back to our garages so we could get prepped for the post-qualifying press conference. I made my way back to the Valkyrie garage, a huge smile on my face. Not even the appearance of Anthony could ruin this for me.

As I stood in the conference room with Lily, waiting for Lizzie and Fiona to give me a rundown of what to say at the post-qualifying press conference, I had a thought. In the corner of the office was a beautiful leather binder with Fiona Schmidt's name engraved on it. The binder was full of important papers, and Fiona carried it all over the paddock. I walked over and emptied the binder of its contents, putting them neatly to the side. I picked up some empty pieces of Valkyrie header paper and stuffed it inside. Lily eyed me warily, an unsure look on her face.

"You know, Georgie, your career as a racing driver is okay. You don't need to join the strategy team," she joked. I smiled at her, letting a mischievous grin fill my face.

"I'm going to prank the journalists – and Fiona Schmidt."

Lily's face widened, and she began to laugh – a little too loudly. I quickly shushed her and set the binder next to my spot at the conference table. I knew Lizzie and Fiona would not appreciate my joke on the journalists, so I motioned for Lily to keep quiet.

"You're also going to give Fiona a heart attack," she cautioned, although I could see the incredibly excited look on Lily's face.

After about ten minutes of prep and discussion, Lizzie signaled that it was time to head to the qualifying conference. Lily gave me a knowing look and winked as I passed by, binder in hand.

"What you got in there?" Lizzie asked casually, eyeing the binder.

"Just some papers that Fiona asked me to review about next week's upgrades in Canada, plus some reports from today. Didn't want to forget about it." I knew if Lizzie was thinking straight, she would have said absolutely not, put that binder from Fiona down, but there was so much commotion about me taking pole.

I walked into the press conference with the binder, and sat for a bit at the back as I waited for Noah and Eric to arrive. Noah was notoriously late, so I knew I had a few moments to set my plan in motion. As I sat there reviewing the empty pages, I saw Michael Clifton, the lead F1 presenter, come up to me and congratulate me on pole. I quickly shut the binder quickly, knowing it would pique his interest.

"Thanks, Michael, just another day at Valkyrie F1. The work never ends, you know," I said cheekily, motioning towards Fiona's binder. "You'd think coming pole meant I had to read fewer reports. Pretty sure it just means more." At this point, a couple of other journalists had moved closer to listen into the conversation.

"Anything good in there?" one of the other presenters asked, nodding towards the binder with a cheeky smile on his face.

"You'll have to see tomorrow!" I kept a casual smile on my face, and as they walked away, I opened up the binder again, pretending to read the blank pieces of paper.

As soon as Noah and Eric walked in, I made my way to the top of the press room and took my seat in the middle, placing the binder under the seat.

"You going to take notes, Georgie," Eric teased, motioning to the binder.

"Oh, you know Fiona, always giving me reports to read. Can't catch a break," I quipped. Eric just nodded; he and Fiona had been friends for a while, and to be fair, it was much like Fiona to be constantly reviewing data and reports.

The press conference went on for about an hour. The journalists decided to ask their safe, boring questions, which was a nice change of pace. As I had begun to find my footing in Formula 1, I felt like they were beginning to accept my presence on the grid. After the GQ article this week, it seemed like none of them felt like being on the wrong side of Valkyrie or Hermes. The article was all over social media, and asking the female racer on pole sexist questions after a GQ writer had called them all out on it wasn't exactly the move to make.

As the press conference began to wrap up, I could see Lizzie eying the binder that I was holding, a concerned look on her face. As she looked down at her phone, I knew Fiona had probably sent her a text wondering why I had her binder. I knew I only had a few more moments before Lizzie pulled the binder out of my hands, so I got up and moved toward Michael to thank him for the press conference. The moment I reached out for Michael's hand, I dropped the binder, letting the contents all spill out on the floor. I heard a shocked gasp from Michael, who quickly moved towards me to help me pick up the pieces of paper. I could tell he was not entirely sure if he should be looking at the documents, but I knew he wouldn't be able to help himself.

Michael let out a sly smile as he saw that I had dropped several blank pieces of paper, not strategy documents as he was expecting, and he looked up at me, a large grin on his face.

"Well played, Georgia, well played." Michael stood up and handed me the binder and empty pieces of paper, still chuckling to himself. The Sports Broadcasting presenters behind him let out a laugh at my prank, and I could see from the twinkle in their eyes that they were somewhat impressed.

"Fiona is going to have your head for that prank!" Eric slapped me on the shoulder on his way out of the press conference, snickering to himself.

Lizzie approached me with an unamused look, but her chuckle told me she had definitely enjoyed my prank. We made our way back to the garage, and I was stopped by a few fans who asked for selfies as they laughed about the press conference prank.

Well, at least the fans had enjoyed it.

"By God, Georgia Dubois, if you pull that prank again, I will have you off this team!" I heard Fiona announce as she snatched the binder from my grip. As I looked at her, I saw her anger turn into something that looked like amusement, and I knew she would thoroughly get me back for this prank.

"You are the worst." And with that, Fiona stalked off to the conference room to refill her binder with her actual strategy reports. Lily gave me a thumbs up and waved her phone at me, indicating that she had gotten a photo of Fiona. I walked over to her and took a look at the phone. The picture was actually priceless.

I said goodbye to the rest of the Valkyrie crew and made my way outside to the parking spots, where Luca was waiting for me, a huge grin on his face.

"Oh, Cara, you really do know how to stir the pot," he laughed as he got into my Bugatti passenger seat. "Francesco got a text from Isabelle during the conference, and he said she made the entire Valkyrie garage look for the documents in that binder to make sure that you hadn't actually brought them to the press conference. She was apparently ready to march down there and grab it from you herself if you had." I couldn't help but snort at that. Isabelle knew me well, and she knew that I would never jeopardize the team that way.

"Felt like things were getting boring, Rossi, had to mix it up a bit."

That evening I attended a small dinner with my family. Henri and I kept it cordial, opting to focus on Hugo and our parents. I knew he was annoyed at coming P4 in qualifying, and I was truthfully still mad at him from earlier this morning, but neither of us wanted to stir the pot. My parents had arrived for this race, and we were having a nice dinner with the five of us.

Sunday morning, I woke up around 8 a.m. and went to check social media, only to see the Valkyrie page's post pop up first.

Valkyrie F1 Team

Liked by LucaRossi52 and 30k others

ValkyrieF1Team The look on Fiona's face when Georgia brought the binder to the press conference.
@GeorgiaDubois38

I couldn't help but laugh at the post. I hadn't played a prank on the team in a while, and it was nice to feel myself again. When I left my Indy Car team, the team principal there told me she would be devastated to see me go, but very happy never to see one of my pranks again. I took that as a compliment.

As I continued to scroll through my feed, I saw a text from Henri pop up asking if he could come over. I didn't particularly want to see him, but I knew it was best if we talked before the race. I never raced well when I was at odds with my family, so I told him to come over in thirty for a cup of coffee.

I took a quick shower and got ready for the day, putting on my polo with the triple crown logo on the back. This had easily become my favorite piece of clothing to wear, and I wore it everywhere. Right on time, I heard a knock on the hotel room door, and I walked over to the door and opened it, only to see Henri standing there, dressed in his Hermes team garb.

I guess he is expecting to stay for a while, I grumbled.

"Morning!" Henri said in a voice much too chipper for 8 a.m. He walked straight into the living room and plopped himself down on the couch, looking as if he owned the place. Henri put down the coffee holder he was holding, which had three cups of coffee in it, and signaled for me to take one.

So he brought a cup of coffee for Luca, too. Guess he is in an apologizing mood.

"Someone is in a good mood," I said plainly, taking a sip of my coffee as I watched Henri eat his pastry. Henri looked around, and I could tell he was trying to spot Luca.

"He usually journals this early in the morning," I informed my brother.

"Ahh... yes," Henri acknowledged, taking another sip of coffee as he took in a deep breath. I knew he was preparing for a speech, so I braced myself.

"So I – uh – wanted to come and apologize, Peaches. I know the last several weeks I have probably been a lousy brother... and a lousy teammate to Luca, too."

"Probably?" I quipped. Henri shifted his eyes uncomfortably, but I nodded for him to continue, a small smirk forming on my face.

"It was different when you were in America. Now that you're here and we see each other so often, I started to get protective. I just want everything to be perfect so that you will continue to want to stay here, in Europe, with us. I shouldn't have said anything to Luca, just after everything that happened with Anthony, I didn't want you to go through another situation like that. Still, I didn't have any faith in Luca, and it's becoming clear that maybe he wants to change."

I felt for Henri in that moment. I knew me going to America was hard on the family, because it meant we saw each other so little. When I had called in absolute tears over Anthony, I could tell they were worried for me – worried and thousands of miles away, across an ocean.

"You're an amazing brother, Henri, and I am so lucky to have you – even luckier because I get to share our dream together, but I need my friend back. I miss my best friend." Henri leaned in for a hug, wrapping his arms around me. I returned the hug, leaning deeply into my brother. Henri had always been a wonderful hugger, and I felt incredibly comforted in his arms – relaxed even.

"Come hell or high water, Peaches, you know I will always be here for you. Always be your best friend," Henri whispered as he broke away from the hug. I smiled at him and leaned back against the couch, taking another sip of coffee as I contemplated my brother's words. We sat in the living room for another ten minutes, chatting about the track and weather for today.

Luca came out of his room and eyed the two of us warily; I could tell Luca was suspicious as to why Henri was here. Henri immediately got up and handed Luca a cup of coffee, which Luca took cautiously. No words were exchanged between the two of them, but after a few sips, I saw Luca give my brother a warm smile as he plopped beside me on the couch. I knew this was Henri's way of apologizing to Luca.

"So..." Luca said, finally breaking the silence, "which one of you is going to be on my left and which will be on my right when I stand on the Podium today." Luca winked at the two of us and downed his coffee at an impressive speed.

"In your dreams, Rossi," I retorted back, finishing my last few sips of coffee. "If you're ready, I'm good to head to the paddock early." Both of the boys nodded, and we made our way downstairs. Henri gave me one last hug before venturing off to his car, and Luca and I hopped into his car and, once again, made our way to the paddock, hand in hand. Luca dropped me off at the Valkyrie garage, which was at the beginning of the walkway, wishing me luck.

"Keep your luck to yourself, Rossi. You're the one that is going to need it." Luca stuck his tongue out at me in response, and I smiled at him cheekily, blowing him a kiss before heading back inside the garage.

"And there we have it! Georgia Dubois has crossed the checkered line in the first place!"

"Fuck yes! That's how we do it!" I screamed back into my radio. Baku had been exhilarating, one of my best races to date. Lily had just missed out on a podium, which was disappointing, but it was nice to have Noah and Eric up there with me. Henri and Lily had come P4 and P5, respectively, while poor Luca dropped out of the race due to mechanical issues. I truly felt for Luca; I knew how badly he wanted a podium today, but the car just wasn't performing up to standard, and he was going to need to take a new engine in Canada which would place him at the back of the grid with a penalty.

"So proud of you, Georgia. You've made up for your horrendous prank yesterday," I heard Fiona yell into the microphone.

"I don't know, Fiona. I'd say pranks might be our winning strategy."

"They aren't," she responded dryly, and I heard the radio click off.

I pulled into the assigned P1 spot for the winning car and hopped out, immediately launching into my signature window-washing dance to the sound of the team's cheers. As I looked down, Eric was standing there with his hand out, which I took happily. He then pulled me into a big hug, congratulating me on my race win.

As I rushed towards the team to give them a hug, I saw Luca standing to the side with Henri, a big smile on both their faces. I made my way to them and gave Henri a hug first, congratulating him on P4. As I went to give Luca a hug, he pulled me into a kiss.

"If I didn't know better, Tesoro," he whispered into my ear, "I'd say you won just because you hoped you might get a little reward from me later." I looked back up at him, a slight blush on my cheeks.

"Don't be silly, Flash. I *know* I'll get a reward from you later," I whispered back. I saw amusement on Luca's face. Henri gave me a questioning look after the exchange, but I just shrugged, deciding it probably wasn't best to share that tidbit of information with my brother – he and Luca had only *just* made up.

The rest of the day was consumed with photos with VIPs and press meetings. After the podium celebration and winners press conference, I was shuffled back to the Valkyrie conference room because Isabelle had asked the team to gather before we all made our way back to the hotels. Since Baku was such a long flight, almost everyone was leaving tomorrow, which meant a party tonight for all of the teams.

By the time 1 had arrived at Luca's car, I was already fairly drunk. When I saw him in the lot, I beelined it to the black car, hopping into his arms so I could give him a huge hug.

"I WOOOONNN!" I yelled, bouncing up and down as he set me down. Luca snickered at my antics as he caught me.

"Yes, Cara, I saw that. Let's get you back to the hotel, hmm?" I let out a little pout at Luca's request but obliged him and hopped into the car, trophy in tow. The drive back to the hotel was fortunately short for Luca, who had the task of getting me out of the car and into the hotel without me running into too many things – or fans who wanted photos. After a few – *well, several* – more fan photos and another glass of champagne with Oliver, who had caught us at the hotel bar, Luca shuffled us back upstairs.

It had been my intention to grab Luca and drag him to my bed for my celebratory reward that I suspected I was *easily* going get out of him, but when my head hit the pillow, I fell asleep almost immediately. Luca let me sleep for a couple of hours before waking me up, insisting that it was time to get ready for the party, which started at 9 p.m. My head was a little dizzy, but I was glad Luca had let me nap before the party, lest I face another hangover.

After another glass of champagne, Luca and I were squeezed into a taxi with Lily, Henri, and Oliver, who had opted to come with us instead of Edward due to Anthony being part of the Wilmington party. When we arrived at the club, we were shuffled up to the top floor, where Éliott met us with Eric. I ran over to Éliott and Eric, giving them a joint hug. I could see Éliott give Luca a look out of the corner of his eye, and I heard Luca laugh behind me, likely confirming that, yes, I was still a little drunk from this afternoon.

But I didn't care. I was a race winner again. I was top of the championship, and nothing could ruin my moment, not even Anthony.

As if on cue, I saw Anthony begin to walk towards us, hand in hand with his girlfriend Anna, followed by Edward and Lauren. I remembered Anna from the many races that she had attended back in America. Anthony had insisted that she was only a friend, but it was clear that my gut was correct.

I felt Luca lean in closer as he grabbed my hand, giving it a gentle squeeze. When Lauren and I made eye contact, she ran over to me and gave me a huge squeeze.

"So glad I made it today!" Lauren squealed. "You were on fire!"

"Thanks, Lauren. It was an absolute dream of a race. The car felt incredible underneath me."

As soon as Anthony had moved out of earshot, Lauren leaned in. "We had to have dinner with Anthony this evening. What an actual bore. How did you manage to date that guy?" I gave her a chuckle as I shifted my weight back and forth at the uncomfortable question.

"What can I say? I was young and stupid."

"And his girlfriend Anna? She acts like he's already an F1 driver, walking around with the most pompous attitude. I'm not sure who's more boring, him or her. If I hear one more comment about her social media, I am going to lose my mind." Lauren kept droning on and on about them. Her loyalty made me feel warm inside, but I put my hand up, motioning for her to stop.

"I appreciate the camaraderie, but let's not let them ruin our incredibly fun night, hmm?" Luca and Edward had come back from the bar with several glasses of champagne.

"Absolutely!" Lauren said, clinking her glass with mine.

As the night carried on and drinks continued to flow, I excused myself and made my way to the bathroom. As I came out of the restroom, I ran into a stiff body. Jumping back, I went to mumble an apology, only to see Anthony standing in front of me.

"Well, well, well, no bodyguard here to protect you?" Anthony asked, hinting at the fact that Henri, Luca, and Oliver had spent the entire night with me, not letting Anthony get close.

"Don't be silly, Anthony. I'm the one guarding them."

"Whatever, Georgia. You think I can't see through your sham of a relationship with that Italian. Please, we dated for eighteen months, and you never once posted about our relationship on your social media pages. I know you're just using Luca for his fame and money." I was a little taken aback by Anthony's accusation. I had told Lizzie that posting on social media would cause alarm from people who knew me or people who had followed me for a long time, but I was quickly shut down.

And yet, here was Anthony, literally calling it as he saw it.

I tried to hide the shock on my face – probably not very well – as I attempted to move around Anthony, ignoring his last comment. Anthony shuffled in front of me, blocking the path back to the dance floor.

"Maybe I never posted about our relationship on social media because it wasn't worth posting about," I shot back, attempting to move around him, but Anthony just kept moving in front of me. "What the fuck is wrong with you?"

"Oh yeah, what does Luca have that I don't?" he demanded.

"Loyalty," I shot back.

Before Anthony could continue on, I felt a hand reach out to me. Luca was now standing in front of me, pushing Anthony to the side.

"Amore, I've been looking for you. Edward is demanding a group photo, you know what he's like. Oh, Anthony, maybe you could take it for us?" Luca's tone was condescending, and I knew he was hinting at the fact that the photo was only for F1 drivers. Anthony backed up a bit, sizing up the two of us before walking back to the table, completely ignoring Luca's request.

"You okay?" Luca asked, concern laced in his eyes.

"Fine, fine. Anthony just accused us of being fake, so I feel a bit shaken." Luca nodded warily, pulling me closer into a hug. I hated to admit it, but the smell of him and his warmth made me feel more relaxed. Apparently, being in Luca's arms had that effect on me these days.

"Well, then, let's go show him how wrong he is." Luca grabbed my hand and pulled me onto the dance floor next to Éliott, who was dancing with Lily. Edward and Lauren joined us as soon as we entered the dance floor. Luca pulled me in close, letting our bodies sway to the beat of the music. I wrapped my arms around his neck, letting the front of my body rest against his. The more we danced, the more I could feel the front of his pants getting harder, and I grinned as Luca brought our faces closer for a kiss.

Luca spun us around, and my eyes caught Anthony's. He was standing at the edge of the dance floor with Anna, who was scrolling through her phone, no doubt picking a photo to put on social media. I let a smirk cross my lips as our eyes met and winked at Anthony before turning back to Luca and giving his plump lips a deep kiss. Luca reciprocated the kiss and pulled me even closer to him, still swaying to the beat of the music. I could feel Anthony's eyes burning into the back of my head.

Good, let him see what he is missing.

"Get a room, you guys!" I heard Edward call out as Éliott and Lily whistled at us.

Luca leaned down and whispered into my ear, "Anthony might have missed out on being with you, but tonight, I fully intend to make sure I don't."

Chapter Seventeen

YOU KNOW WHAT HAPPENS WHEN YOU ASSUME

Georgia

Baku had been an incredible race. While Anthony had done everything in his power to make this as miserable as possible for me, he couldn't take away how amazing I felt with my race win. The more I thought about it, the less I cared about him being in Formula 1. It just meant I could beat him again and again on the track.

I was worried about Anthony's exposing the relationship, but Luca was right – what could Anthony possibly say? Who would believe him? Still, a part of me couldn't shake the horrible feeling. It just took one wrong step, and Anthony would weasel his way in, ruining everything Luca and I had established.

Plus – *and I would never admit it out loud* – but I loved seeing Luca jealous. As soon as we stepped back onto the dance floor, Luca hand's were all over me, and it felt amazing. It's as if he was a man starved, and I was the only food he had seen in weeks.

When we had gotten back to the hotel, Luca had kept his promise – he'd given me quite the reward.

After another hour of dancing at the club in Baku, Luca grabbed my purse from the VIP table we had been seated at.

"Go say goodbye to your friends, Cara. Time to go home."

As I looked up at him, I knew that this wasn't up for debate. Luca had that stern look in his eyes, the one that said he wanted something, and he would stop at nothing to get it. I walked over to Henri, Lily, and Oliver and said my goodbyes before slipping out of the club with Luca. Luca quickly got us a taxi, and we made our way back to the hotel.

The moment we made our way into the room, Luca dragged me over to the bed and threw me back against the comforter. I expected Luca to join me on top of the bed, but instead, I saw him just stand and stare at me for a bit, a sly expression forming on his face as he watched me.

I propped myself up on my elbows, giving him a once over as he began to undo his button-down.

"Am I getting a little strip tease as my reward for winning today? Now, this I could get used to."

"Don't get too used to it, Principessa," he said with a smirk, continuing to unbutton his shirt. Once his buttons were undone, he slid the button down off and then continued with his belt and pants, leaving him in just his boxes. As his pants fell to the ground, I let out a whistle, wiggling my eyebrows at him seductively – well, as seductively as one could after an entire bottle of champagne.

Once Luca was left in only his boxers, he hopped on top of me and whipped my dress over my head, leaving me in just my bra and underwear – a beautiful purple lacy set I had bought because I liked the color purple, not because it was his team color, I insisted. I saw a grin form on Luca's face as he saw the lingerie, but he let it go as he began kissing down my body, paying attention to my breasts, giving each one their own time and attention.

"So beautiful," he murmured as he continued down my stomach, eventually getting to where I really wanted him and his mouth. I found the more I had sex with Luca, the more my body began to crave his touch. He was phenomenal in bed, and for these few months we were meant to be dating, he was all mine, and I secretly reveled in that fact.

As Luca reached my core, he moved my panties to the side, placing gentle kitten licks all around, making me moan loudly with each one. Soon, I felt the lacy underwear slide down my legs, the scrap piece of fabric now thrown to the side. Luca returned his mouth to me, pulling my legs over his shoulders as he once again resumed kissing where I wanted him most. As I pushed myself down, I heard him cluck his tongue, quietly scolding me.

"Oh, Principessa, you know better than that."

"I thought this was my reward."

"Oh, you'll get your reward, but you still have to behave." And with that, Luca returned to his mission, still slowly licking up and down my slit. Eventually, he started to push his tongue inside of me. It felt like absolute heaven after all of the teasing. I wanted to push myself down again but stopped myself. I knew Luca meant what he said, and I couldn't stand the thought of him continuing to tease me.

Luca inserted a finger and then a second as he started to work them in and out, letting his mouth suck on my clit. The pleasure was starting to build quickly, and soon I was a writhing mess on the bed, incredibly glad the walls of the hotel were thick as I started to chant out his name like he was some kind of God.

Luca began to pick up the pace, and I felt myself hurdle towards my high. As my first orgasm of the night tore through me, I let out a loud scream, grabbing anything and everything close to me as Luca and his tongue worked me through my orgasm. After a few more moments, Luca stopped, letting me come down from my pleasure as my body became too sensitive to his touch. Luca began to climb up my body, slowly kissing his way up.

"You were so good, Principessa, so good for me," he hummed as I felt my cheeks blush. Luca's praise made me preen every time, and I loved it.

Once Luca made his way up to my face, he gave me a sloppy kiss, and I felt my strength start to return. I pushed myself up, flipping our positions so that I was on top, straddling him. Luca looked up at me, and he arched an eyebrow in question, curious as to what I had planned. I reached out to his bedside table and grabbed a condom, quickly opening it and sliding it onto him.

"This is my race win, and I want my reward how I want it," I challenged, knowing full well that Luca liked to be in charge. Still, I could tell he was curious. I leaned down for a kiss, tasting myself on his lips.

"And what does my principessa want with me?"

I smirked at him as I raised my hips, lining myself up with his cock. I let myself slowly sink down onto him. Luca put his hands on my hips as I adjusted to his size.

"Fuck..." I let out, stilling myself as I put both my hands on his chest. If I wasn't too blissed out in pleasure, I would have been annoyed by the cocky look on his face.

After a few more moments, I began to move my hips, picking up the place as Luca lay there, watching me with his large, brown eyes – enjoying the show. It didn't take long before I could see Luca starting to move closer to his orgasm. His hips started to buck up into me, and each thrust was becoming more erratic. Luca moved his fingers to my clit, massing it gently, making my second orgasm continue to grow inside of me.

Before I knew it, I felt my body start to tremble as pleasure started to hit me in waves.

Once again, I started chanting Luca's name, enjoying his now brutal pace. After a few more thrusts, Luca let out a final grunt, calling out my name as I felt him finally reach his high. I collapsed on top of his chest, panting away as I attempted to catch my breath. I felt Luca's hand come to my back, and he started to gently rub up and down.

"That's decided. I should win races more often."

After the Azerbaijan Grand Prix in Baku, Luca and I traveled to Montreal, Canada, where I managed to score another podium, although this one was behind my brother. Still, the car continued to feel incredible, and I knew that the upgrades in Silverstone next week were going to make me even faster. I was slightly disappointed at coming P2 in Montreal, but as Fiona reminded me, Hermes had more grid penalties coming up while we still were quite a ways off from taking one.

In between the race weeks of Baku and Canada, and then Canada and Great Britain, I spent quite a bit of time with Luca in Monaco. After we slept together in Baku, I told myself that I would take it slower with him, but that lasted no longer than a day. Before

I knew it, I found myself spending my evenings either with Luca on my couch, chatting away about life, movies, books – *anything* – or texting Luca from my bed when I had to be at the factory.

I hated to admit it, but Luca was starting to become a good friend. His advice on the Valkyrie F1 car was interesting, and I was beginning to learn that there was more to him than met the eye. When Oliver had come to visit Monaco for a couple of days, Luca had decided to stay an extra day, and the three of us had a fun, civil dinner. *Maybe hell really was freezing over.*

And now the week Lily and Edward had been waiting for had finally arrived – the British Grand Prix, held at the prestigious Silverstone racetrack. In truth, all of the drivers loved this old, classic track. It was one of the oldest in Formula 1 and definitely one of the most revered. Winning Silverstone felt like winning the World Drivers Championship for whoever won it – especially if that driver was British. The crowds were loud, and the seating was jam-packed with people, everything you needed for a successful Grand Prix.

This year, there were four British drivers on the track, the most F1 had seen in a long while, and Lily was one of them. As promised, Maison de Klotho released a Silverstone special edition purse, and the advertisements were plastered all over posters and various social media channels. It was impossible to get to the track without seeing Lily and I pawning their purses on a billboard.

Still, it was the funding the team needed, and we had finally secured an official 3-year sponsorship deal. Isabelle had informed the team last week at the office, and I felt like the Atlas, except the weight of the world had finally been lifted from my back.

"Hey Georgie, Isabelle wants to see you in her office!" Lily called out to me, pulling me from my haze. I gave her a quick nod of acknowledgment and then proceeded to leave the engineering office for Isabelle's.

As I entered her office, I saw Fiona Schmidt sitting next to Isabelle on the office couch, sipping a cup of coffee. She motioned for me to take a seat across from her, which I did.

"Georgia, thanks for joining us. I know you and Mel are busy discussing some of the new Silverstone car upgrades, so we'll keep this quick. As you know, we have officially secured the Maison de Klotho funding along with several other brands. It seems as though we're finally on the up and up, thanks to some brilliant results from you and Lily." I nodded in response, not entirely sure where Isabelle was going with this.

"So, after some chatting with Francesco, we wanted to discuss ending you and Luca's relationship." I felt frozen in shock; all I could do was just stare back at her blankly. I knew that she expected me to say something, but I couldn't find the words to express how I was feeling a million feelings in that moment – none of them good.

Forget Atlas, I felt like Thanatos, the personification of death.

The moment Isabelle said the words, my heart sank down into the pit of my stomach. This is what I wanted from the beginning, but now that I was faced with it, I could feel my heart start to break. When we started this sham, I demanded that we end it the moment we secured several sponsorship deals, but now, with everything that had happened between Luca and me, I just couldn't help but feel sorrow over a relationship that had never been real.

"Right, well, obviously, it can't be a quick thing. We were thinking we'd spend the next several races reducing the content we put out of the two of you, and then after Summer break, announce the split. Francesco wanted to wait until the end of the season, but I said you had both earned a break from one another." Isabelle said the words as if she was triumphant, like I should be thanking her for this favor she was doing for me.

But I couldn't thank her, I could barely look her in the eyes.

"Is Hermes discussing this with Luca?" I finally found my voice, but it sounded more pathetic than I would have liked.

"Yes, of course. We wanted to get your opinions on the matter and then decide on the best course of action. So, any thoughts on this?" Isabelle looked up from her notes, and I wasn't sure if she registered my hesitation – my uncertainty.

"No!" I blurted out, and I could see Fiona and Isabelle trying to process my outburst. It was clear that they had run this scenario a few times, and that answer hadn't been one of the possible outcomes.

"Did you want it to be sooner?" Fiona asked cautiously, not entirely sure what she was going to get out of me.

"I think this is too soon."

Fiona and Isabelle both hesitated before Isabelle finally said, "Too soon? Georgia, we're giving you a way out of this relationship – something you were demanding a few months ago." Isabelle looked a little frustrated at me. I knew she had not expected me to be so upset at this generous offer.

"Well, you wanted my opinion, and now you have it. Breaking up now would just make this look like it was a farce. It would be embarrassing, especially after the GQ article. You made me do this relationship; don't embarrass me by abruptly ending it." I knew I should be controlling my temper as I spoke to my team principal, but I couldn't help myself. Valkyrie pushed me into this sham. Now, they had to help me keep the charade going.

"Well... ok, sure. I didn't realize you felt so strongly about this. Let me talk to Francesco."

"Good. Am I needed for anything else?" I asked dryly. Fiona and Isabelle both shook their heads, neither of them uttering another word as I left the room. I immediately headed straight for my driver's room, sinking down to the floor with my back to the door.

What a fucking mess. I was still seething with anger as I pulled out my phone to text Lily. Just as I was about to type something, I heard a knock at my door. I begrudgingly got up and opened it, only to see Lily standing there, two cups of espresso in her grasp.

"Thought you might want this after your chat with Isabelle." I nodded and gave her an appreciative smile, motioning for her to come in.

"Thanks."

"Want to talk about it?" Lily asked, taking a seat on my couch as she sipped the coffee in her hands.

"It's just... Isabelle told me that Luca and I could end our relationship sooner than expected, and I told her that was stupid. It would be embarrassing for us to end it now, right? I mean, we just had the article, and we've been photographed hanging out the last two weeks. It would feel ridiculous if we just broke up after summer break!" The words kept tumbling out of me, each word coming out more exasperated than the next.

As I finished my rant, I turned to Lily, who had a small smirk on her lips.

"You have a crush on Luca," she accused, wagging her finger at me.

"Wha- have you not been listening to me?" I protested.

"Oh my god. You have it bad!" As Lily squealed the words, she began to snicker so loud she let out a large snort, forcing her into an even larger fit of laughter. "You don't want to break up because then you'd stop spending all of this alone time with *handsome, sexy* Luca..." She pondered her thoughts a bit more, and I could see the proverbial lightbulb go off in her head.

"I think you like Luca. I think you like him a lot, and I think you're scared that Luca doesn't return those feelings. You're worried that if you end this, he'll revert back to his playboy, womanizing lifestyle... You're scared that if he doesn't *have* to be with you... he won't be." I furrowed my eyebrows as I downed the rest of my coffee, desperately looking for all the reasons that Lily was wrong. I wanted to tell her to fuck right off with her outrageous – *and slightly insulting* – opinion.

But Lily was right, and I fucking knew it.

I knew the real reason I didn't want to end this, and I was too much of a coward to say it. I was scared that if we ended this, then Luca would have free reign to move on – go back to partying. He would forget about all of our fun dates, the intimate conversations swapping stories about our families, the late-night mac and cheese dinners – the sex. He wouldn't be forced to hang out with boring, pedestrian, predictable Georgia "Sassy" Dubois.

Suddenly all of my insecurities came rushing back, and I felt like a volcano about to explode. After a few more moments of silence, I could see Lily eyeing me carefully, like I was a bomb about to go off.

"Wow, you really do like Luca, don't you?" She said finally. "You do realize that you don't actually *have* to break up, right? Like, Isabelle can't stop you two from dating, *for real*, if that's what you both want? Hell, she might even like it. It's been great for the team."

Lily paused again before adding, "It's okay to *want* that, Georgia."

I looked up at her as a small tear fell from my eye. I tried to wipe it away as quickly as I could, but I knew Lily had noticed it. "But what if Luca wants to break up?"

"And what if he doesn't?" Lily countered. "You won't know unless you ask him." I scoffed at that.

Ask Luca what he wanted? Sounded like a good way to be reminded of how fake this relationship was.

"Thanks for listening, Lil, but I gotta get back out there. More scenarios to run with Mel." I left the room, still internally sulking.

Luca

As I entered the Silverstone paddock on that Thursday morning, I felt completely ablaze with joy. The last two weeks hanging out with Georgia, both in Montreal for the Canadian Grand Prix and then in Monaco for a week of rest, had been a blast. We had put aside our differences and decided just to enjoy each other's company. Hell, even my relationship with Henri was starting to heal. Instead of making snide remarks about me and his sister, we opted to play the new FIFA game on his PlayStation or just sit around and drink beer.

I wasn't sure what it was, but just being around Georgia made me a better driver. My drive in Canada had been incredible. From the back of the grid to 5th place, I felt incredibly proud.

"Luca!" I heard Henri call out, pulling me from my thoughts. As

I turned towards my teammate, I saw him motioning towards Francesco's door. "Francesco wants to see you in his office."

I nodded and walked towards my team principal's office, giving it a couple of knocks before entering. Inside was Francesco sitting with my father, chatting away about the good old days of racing.

"Good morning, Francesco." I gave my father a quick hug before sitting down next to him on the purple couch in the corner of the room.

"Luca, as you know, Helios Sunglasses and several other sponsors have come through with some multi-year deals." I nodded in response, unsure as to where Francesceso was going with this. He had already announced the deals back at the factory last week.

"So, you have fulfilled your end of the bargain, and Hermes thanks you for that. As a reward, we're working with Valkyrie to strategically see how we can get a jump start on ending your relationship with Georgia Dubois. I know we had originally said we'd do this all year, but we don't see a need for that now." Francesco said the words with such pride and gusto, as if he was doing me a favor.

"Wha- no!" I blurted out. "It's much too soon. I mean, people will think we only did it as a PR stunt." I felt like in that moment, my heart was beating faster than it did during races and panic started to settle in my chest.

I was finally making progress with Georgia, and this would ruin it all. This would give her the out she needed to leave me. I knew it was petty that I wanted her to keep pretending to date me so that she had to hang out with me, but I was immensely enjoying my time with her, and I didn't care that it wasn't genuine – it was better than nothing.

The more time I spent with Georgia, the more opportunities I had to show her that I was a changed man – *that I wanted to be a changed man for her.*

"Absolutely not," I continued. "It would ruin my image. You want me to be this refined playboy, and I don't see how breaking up with my devoted, loving girlfriend during the summer break is going to help my image. No! I refuse! Everyone will just blame me anyway

– and then I'll be the villain who broke up with Formula 1's sweetheart! If she actually loses the championship, then... they'll blame that on me, too.

And what are we going to do about the BBC interview next week? Think how awkward it'll be for the team when the episode on us airs *after* we've broken up." As the words kept tumbling out of my mouth, I knew I was starting to sound like a love sick fool, but I didn't care if they figured out why I was so upset.

"Whoa, whoa, Flash," my father said, attempting to stop my tirade. "First of all, no one is forcing either of you to leave this relationship. We're just giving you both the choice to end this. I mean, a few months ago, you were both fighting tooth and nail to stop this; we didn't think either of you would care. We still want you to do the BBC interview because it's about dating on the grid. We'll just ask for the questions to be less about you two – and more about dating someone while you're an F1 driver."

That's so stupid, I thought to myself.

"Well, what did Georgia say?"

"Isabelle is talking to her now."

"Well, of course Georgia is going to say yes if you give her the option. Why would anyone want to be trapped in a relationship with me?" My father gave me a sympathetic look. I could see him about to say something in response, but I put my hands in the air, signaling that the conversation was over. Before either of them could say something, I left the room and headed straight for my driver's room. I immediately grabbed my phone my phone to text Edward.

> Luca: You will not believe what Hermes and Valkyrie agreed upon today.

> Edward: Valkyrie trying to recruit you for the 2023 season? ;-) Real power couple they'd have there, and we all know Lily has her sights on Eric's seat over at Rennen when he retires.

Luca: Francesco had the nerve to tell me that Georgia and I can end our relationship after summer break. So fucking stupid, right? Everyone will know it was a PR stunt!

Edward: Probably not an ideal look for you, but I'm sure they'd handle the transition well. It's not like Georgia would badmouth you in the press.

Luca: Here I thought you were my best friend, always willing to support me...

Edward: You want to know what I really think?

Luca: Even if I didn't, I'm sure you'd tell me anyway.

Edward: I wouldn't be British if I didn't give you unsolicited advice ;-) I think you're scared that Georgia will say yes to ending it. You're scared she doesn't return your feelings, which I personally think is ridiculous. But also, you won't know unless you ask her... have you talked to her about it?

Luca: No, I have not spoken to her... of course, she's going to want to end it. I don't need to feel even worse about myself.

Edward: Oh Luca... you know what happens when you assume?

Luca: I hate you and your British phrases.

Edward: You make an ass out of you and me...!

Edward: Just talk to her. You might be surprised.

I sat there for a while, re-reading the texts with Edward before finally getting the courage to text Georgia myself.

Georgia

After a scenario run-through with Mel, I returned to my driver's room to see a text from Luca pop up on my phone.

> Luca: Just spoke to Francesco… look, if you want to end things, I just wanted to say that's ok.

> Georgia: Oh… ok.

My heart sank as I read the words. Did this mean Luca didn't want to continue our relationship? I knew the answer to that immediately. Of course, he didn't, and it made sense. These last few weeks had left me with a false sense of security, and now Luca could go back to his old ways – a different woman on his arm each night as he attempted to "borrow" wealthy people's yachts.

> Luca: I just didn't want you to think that you were still forced to do this. Don't want you to feel stuck in this relationship.

> Georgia: Sure, thanks.

> Luca: I've got a late meeting, but I'll see you at the hotel so we can ride to Edward's podcast together, yeah?

> Georgia: *thumbs up*

As I read through the texts over and over again, I felt a sense of dread. I'm not sure what part of me expected Luca's reaction to go differently, but there was no doubt in my mind that the writing was on the wall for our relationship, and I had to come to terms with that.

Isabelle

Once Georgia left the room, I got up to shut the door to my office. Fiona still had a stunned look on her face.

"That is not quite how I expected the conversation to go," Fiona lamented. I turned from the door and smirked at her, shaking my head with disappointment.

"Oh, Fiona, you've been in love with your husband for so long, you forgot what it looks like to be *young* and in love," I quipped. I emphasized 'young,' earning a scoff from Fiona.

"They don't act in love."

"Oh, but they do, in their own way," I confirmed.

"So why try and end the PR stunt if they aren't miserable?"

"Because I'm tired of paying for it." Fiona let out a chuckle as she shook her head in disbelief. "And I am tired of watching them play the *'will they, won't they game'* as you Brits say. I never told you this, but Éliott's manager was the first to offer this agreement to us, with Georgia and Éliott."

"Oh?" Fiona questioned.

"I turned them down. I suspect there is a history between those two, a history that needed to stay settled in the past. Plus, I felt like there was another driver more suited for her – someone better."

"And Luca was the answer you came up with?" Fiona laughed in disbelief.

"All of these boys, these drivers, they're all suave in their own way. You can't be a Formula 1 driver without some finesse, you'd never get enough money to get through Formula 3 and 2. Any one of them would have helped Georgia during press conferences, but you know why I chose Luca? I knew he'd give her something more. I knew he would challenge Georgia. I knew he wouldn't back down from a fight – or her snarky attitude. Georgia would get as good as she gave with Luca."

The two of them, they remind me of Francesco and me. I hated Francesco when we first met. He was a cocky Italian man who thought he was God's gift to aerodynamics. But as time went on, I saw a different side of him, and I fell in love." As I finished my little speech, I saw Fiona shift in her seat as she contemplated my words.

"You knew full well that Georgia wouldn't agree to end this relationship early?" Fiona was now cackling to herself as the weight of what I had shared with her finally set in.

"I am merely allowing them to confess their feelings, make this real. Georgia was right; it would be terrible for them to break up now, but this weird limbo they're in, it's not healthy."

"Well, let's hope your plan works. What if Luca wants out?" Fiona asked.

"Please, he wants out less than Georgia does. Francesco said he literally stormed out of the conference room, yelling about how stupid this was."

"Isabelle, you are quite possibly sneakier than our little prankster Georgia."

"I suspect by Friday we'll have a list of demands from the two of them." I sat back in my seat, fumbling with my pen.

"Well, for the team's sake, I hope this plays out quickly. A grumpy Georgia is a nightmare."

"All in good time, my friend." And with that, Fiona exited my office, still shaking her head at me.

Chapter Eighteen

THE LADY DOTH PROTEST TOO MUCH

Lily

As soon as Georgia left her driver's room, I pulled out my phone and opened my text thread with Edward. Georgia was out of her mind if she thought that Luca wanted to break up. I had seen Luca and Georgia together countless times; he was clearly in love with her, and I suspected she wasn't too far behind.

> Lily: I'm going to assume that you've heard about the 'breakup?'

> Edward: Luca hasn't stopped whining to me.

> Lily: I wish they saw what everyone else saw. It's quite clear that they're both becoming smitten with one another.

> Lily: Well, Luca was already smitten... but it's safe to say Georgia has joined him. Not an ounce of reasoning to be had with her, she's convinced that Luca will be overjoyed with this decision.

> Edward: Oh yes, Luca keeps going on about how Georgia will of course want to break up with him, because why would someone so perfect want to date him.. blah, blah, blah. Lovesick fool.

> Lily: You know what this means, right?

> Edward: We should respect their boundaries and not interfere with their relationship?

As I read his last text, I couldn't help but laugh. If there was anyone in the paddock less capable of respecting boundaries, it was Edward. Plus, he had bet some money with a few of the other drivers that Luca and Georgia would end up together by the end of the season, and I knew that was a bet he intended to win.

> Lily: Who is this, and what have you done with Edward?

> Edward: Should I be offended that you immediately came to me to help you with scheming?

> Lily: Yes, you should be … now, will you help me or not?

> Edward: You know me too well.

> Edward: What's the plan?

Edward and I texted for another ten minutes, running through the plan that we intended to set in motion at tonight's podcast event. Both Georgia and Luca would be attending – *together* – and I figured this was our best chance to get them to discuss how they felt before the BBC interview. It didn't matter how Isabelle tried to spin that BBC interview. Neither of them were particularly good actors, and if the two of them looked distant and downtrodden, the BBC would twist their words and burn them alive. Tonight was our best chance.

Georgia

When I arrived back at the hotel, there was no sign of Luca. I took a deep breath, letting the relief flow through me. After the events of today, I wasn't in the mood to spend more time with Luca than I had to. I knew the inevitable break-up conversation was coming, and I felt like if I avoided him, I could push this off a little longer, still pretend that everything was normal.

As soon as I turned the water off, I heard shuffling in the living room, and I knew Luca was back. I looked down at the clothes I had intended to change into and had an idea. If Luca wanted out of this relationship, I was going to remind him of what he was missing. It was a bad idea, but I was feeling annoyed enough that I didn't care. I tucked my outfit back into my travel bag, and I walked out into the living room in just my towel. Immediately, Luca looked up at me, his eyes going a bit wide as our eyes met.

"Oh, sorry, Luca... didn't know you were back," I said nonchalantly, trying to keep my cool. The truth was I was fuming inside. I was frustrated at his text, but I said nothing, my face as still as a statue. Luca let a small smirk form on his lips as he nodded at me, his eyes following me across the room.

"No problem, Principessa, nothing I haven't seen before," he quipped, a cheeky smile forming on his lips. I glared at his cool demeanor, even though my insides were burning.

The nerve on that man to flirt with me after telling me he wants to break up.

I wanted to come up with something clever as a response, but the words escaped me as I stood there in my towel, so instead I just huffed it back to my room. As I approached the door, I tripped over the edge of the coffee table. I managed to stop myself from plummeting to the ground, but the towel I had wrapped around my body fell to my feet as I stood up. I went to grab it quickly, but Luca beat me to it. He picked up the towel and handed it to me, that classic Cheshire cat grin on his face.

"Think you dropped this," he said slyly. I knew I had just been caught teasing him, and I could feel my cheeks blush as I quickly grabbed the towel from his grip. Luca made no effort to move out of my way as I pushed past him and into my bedroom, a little mortified at how wrong my stunt had gone.

I stayed in my room until 6 p.m., which was the time we were meant to leave for the Silverstone home race podcast event. I had texted Luca that I would meet him downstairs, and he had readily agreed; I figured he also wanted to avoid the elephant in the room. When I arrived outside of the hotel, Luca had a car already waiting for us. He still had a small grin on his face, which I chose to ignore as we hopped into the taxi.

As soon as we arrived at the podcast event, a coordinator was waiting for the two of us. Luca and I were shuffled into the front row with the other VIPs – Éliott, Henri, and Oliver, who had all opted to come and support the British drivers.

"Welcome everyone to our Home Race F1 Podcast, Silverstone edition. I am joined on stage today by our four beloved British drivers, Lily Wilson, Edward Davis, Oscar Parker, and Eric Spencer." The crowd applauded the drivers as the four waved at the audience from the stage. I gave Lily a thumbs-up, and she blew me a kiss, causing a huge smile to form across my lips. *Ever the saleswoman was Lily.*

"Now, we'll start with Lily. Lily, what would winning Silverstone mean to you."

"Winning Silverstone would feel almost as good as winning the championship. I haven't won a Grand Prix yet, but to take my first Grand Prix at home, that would be something incredibly special." Lily was absolutely beaming up on that stage, a huge smile across her face. She truly was beautiful, and I had no doubt in my mind that when her incredible F1 career was over, she would make a great TV presenter.

"Well, we certainly hope the best for you, and we're glad to hear that Valkyrie announced both you and Georgia will be driving with the team next year!" As Josh, the podcast presenter, said the words, I gave Lily a big thumbs up. I had been so wrapped up in my concern over Luca, I hadn't really been able to congratulate myself on getting my contract renewed. Isabelle had offered me three years, which was typically unheard of for new drivers. The fact that she believed in me that much made me feel warm inside. Isabelle had believed us when no one else had.

"Me too, Josh, me too. It's an honor to be selected to drive for Valkyrie."

"Well, we're excited to see more battles between you and Georgia. You make a great duo. Do you think you are a contender for the Championship next year?" Lily took a pause before she answered, and I could see her debating her answer. This was an awkward question, and the journalists loved asking it. It was no secret that I was the team's primary driver this season, but Lily had managed to hold her own. She was five years younger than me and had considerably less experience, but she had managed to find herself on the podium during her rookie season, a huge success. Most rookie drivers focused on not crashing the car, calling that a win in itself. I knew a race win was in her future. She had incredible talent, but there was a moment when every driver questioned: *Is the team holding me back by prioritizing the other driver?*

"If the car continues to perform like it is today, then absolutely."

"Even with Georgia as your teammate?" Josh asked, annoyed that Lily was avoiding his real question – the question everyone wanted answers to. Journalists, they were all alike.

Everyone wanted the two female drivers to be at each other's throats, but that wasn't our dynamic. *Lily and I were a team, and our mission was unified one – show the world that women deserved to be in the car, sitting on the pit wall, and in the leadership offices.*

Lily let a subtle smile wash over her face; she knew exactly what Josh was playing at. "*Especially* with Georgia as my teammate," Lily finally said. "I'm learning how to be a champion from someone who has dominated F1 in her first season. I can think of no better teacher, can you, Josh?"

Oscar Parker let out a laugh as he playfully shoved Lily. "I don't know, Josh. My teacher has a knighthood, so I think I might have the best," he interjected, winking at Lily. The two of them chuckled as Eric gave an awkward sigh, swatting Oscar on the shoulder. After Eric's fourth win, he had been honored with a well-deserved knighthood by The Crown for his service to motorsport.

"Well, maybe one day we'll see the two of you as teammates, and then we can decide who is the better teacher – Eric or Georgia!"

"Oh, it'll be me," Eric retorted, sticking his tongue out at me from the stage.

"I don't know, Eric," I yelled out from my seat, "you're cracking on a bit there. You sure you're remembering everything?" Eric just showed me his middle finger and turned back to Josh, pretending to ignore my comment.

Josh moved the conversation along, asking the drivers various questions about their lives growing up. I felt a hand reach over to mine and grab it. As I looked down, I saw Luca's hand intertwined with mine. His face was still focused on the stage as he laughed at something Edward said. I slid my hand out of his grasp and moved it to the other side of my lap, and I could feel anger start to boil up inside of me.

Here was Luca, thinking of a ways to end this relationship, and yet he still wanted to hold hands? *Absolutely not.* The nerve of him to think that we could just keep going as normal while we both knew he was going to break my heart all over again. And there it was, the thing I hadn't really wanted to admit to myself all day.

Luca ending this fake relationship would break my heart.

I decided not to look at Luca, hoping that my subtle movement had gone unnoticed. Out of the corner of my eye, I saw Luca turn and look at me, but I refused to turn my head, not wanting to give him the satisfaction. I knew he would be a little confused, and technically, we still were meant to be affectionate in public, but the more I stewed on it, the more annoyed I felt.

I was broken out of my haze when I heard Edward let out a big laugh. I turned my attention back to the stage as I tried to piece together what was going on.

"So, Edward, you promised us a riveting story about how you got Georgia Dubois back for her hamster prank."

"Ahh, did I now," Edward chuckled, a gleam in his eye so bright, you could probably see it from the back row.

I knew Edward had been preparing this story for a while.

I shook my head, letting an annoyed huff escape my lips as Henri leaned over to me, whispering in my ears, "Feeling embarrassed yet?"

I scoffed at him, ignoring his comment as I looked up at Edward, who had spotted the exchange between Henri and me. He was laughing, wagging his finger at the two of us.

"Well, after Georgia released 'Senna The Hamster' into my driver's room, she earned herself a bit of a Wilmington ban from our team principal, who said whenever Georgia came to visit, she would be restricted to the hospitality suite. I knew I had to get her back for that prank, but I also knew that Georgia would be on high alert, waiting for me to seek my revenge, so I lay low for a while until the last race of the season. Georgia decided to join us in Abu Dhabi to watch the final race. Georgia and Henri were having breakfast in Henri's suite, and they had invited me over for a coffee that morning while they got ready for the day. I knew Georgia would still be getting ready because, as Luca has now learned, she is never on time." Edward made a big effort to wink at Luca, earning himself a few chuckles from the audience, but Luca just gave him a slightly strained smile in return.

"As she sat at the vanity, I walked over with a pair of scissors in hand and made a joke about cutting her hair, to which she told me to fuck off. I, however, pretended to ignore her and grabbed the back of her hair, motioning like I was going to cut some off. As she turned around to shove me away, she saw me with a chunk of hair in my hands that matched the color of her hair. Her face went deathly white, but as she grabbed the hair out of my hands in a panic, she immediately noticed that it was actually part of a wig I was holding.

After further investigation, she saw that the scissors I had threatened her with were actually children's scissors I had stolen from my niece. Definitely wouldn't be able to cut a huge clump of hair out of her head. But boy, oh, boy, was she pretty angry for a moment.

Still, after she grabbed the wig from my hand, Georgia was a good sport and congratulated me on a prank well played. Although, she neglected to shake my hand when I offered a truce." The audience was now in hysterics as they started to chant for Edward to take a bow, which he obliged. Even Oscar, Lily, and Eric were all clutching their sides, belly-laughing at Edward's antics.

"Just brilliant, Edward. So you're telling me no truce was called, and we can expect more pranks in the future?"

"Oh yes, Georgia got Edward back for that one by having pretend Krispy Kreme donuts sent to his driver's room, only for them to end up being peaches inside the box. We all watched his live video in the Valkyrie garage, waiting for Edward to share the box of donuts on his live story. His face when he opened the box was hilarious." Edward huffed in irritation at Lily's comment, and I could tell he was still a bit annoyed about the peaches prank, although that one was definitely one of my favorites.

"I was disappointed there were no donuts!" Edward yelled. "Never prank a man with donuts. It's just cruel."

"Well, well, well, there you have it, ladies and gentlemen, the Edward - Georgia prank wars continue on to another season! A big thanks to Edward, Eric, Oscar, and Lily for visiting with us this evening. It's been a pleasure, and we wish the four of you the best of luck this weekend."

Luca

The environment in the hotel room had been fairly tense when I got back from the track. When Georgia came out in her bath towel, I was a little taken aback, although I didn't mind the sight. I wasn't entirely sure what she was playing at, especially since I could see the jeans she planned on wearing tonight sticking out of her bag. Had she purposefully walked out of the bathroom naked? I felt a twinge of sadness when I saw her. For someone who wanted to end our relationship, I was confused as to why she was parading around the hotel room naked – *a reminder of what I wanted but couldn't have.*

When I grabbed her hand during the show, she pulled it away quickly, much to my disappointment. I knew at that moment something was wrong. We were still supposed to be a united front, but with how quickly she pulled her hand from mine, I sensed that she was already keen on the idea of starting to look distant.

As soon as the podcast ended, Georgia moved quickly over to Lily, giving her a big hug, and I did the same to Edward as he came down from the stage. Georgia quickly approached Edward, punching him, *lightly*, in the stomach and then pulling him in for a hug.

"You little shit, telling that story," Georgia lamented. Her words sounded cross, but she had a playful grin on her face.

"Sorry, love, couldn't help myself," Edward joked, shoving her shoulder playfully. "Come, let's go get some drinks, yeah?"

We walked towards the back of the event, where a makeshift bar had been set up. As I ordered my drink at the bar with Edward, I saw Edward's sister waving at him, and he motioned for her to come over.

"Luca, you remember my sister Lucy?"

Before I could say anything, Lucy pulled me into a big hug, which in my opinion, lingered on a little longer than expected. Edward's family was very affectionate, but I was a little taken aback at his sisters' hug and kiss on my cheeks, which I returned so as to not be rude.

"So, Luca, you ready for this weekend? I thought you looked just great in Montreal. Definitely Hermes' most handsome driver, that's for sure." Lucy said the words with a wink, giving my bicep a little squeeze before she went back to her drink.

"Umm, yeah, definitely ready for this weekend." I tried to make eye contact with Edward, throwing him a questioning look, but Edward just kept looking at his sister with an adorable gaze, laughing away at some more jokes as the conversation continued. I was a little shocked at how openly flirty Lucy was during the conversation. I looked around, trying to see if anyone else noticed.

Unfortunately – someone *did* notice.

As I scanned the room, my eyes met with Georgia's. I felt my stomach drop as her gaze met mine, a pointed look of disgust on her face. She turned around, re-engaging herself in a conversation with Éliott. As I watched them interact, I saw his hand slowly come up behind her, rubbing her back ever so slightly as they continued their intimate conversation.

Fuck this, I thought to myself. *Georgia is still my fake girlfriend, and I'm not going to lose her to fucking Éliott Simon.*

I quickly excused myself from the conversation with Lucy and Edward. Edward looked a little annoyed, and he called out after me, but I ignored him as I waltzed over to Georgia, Lily, and Éliott, making a point to grab Georgia's hand and bring her closer to me.

"So, what are we all chatting about over here?" I did my best to keep my cool as I eyed Éliott. If he noticed my annoyance, he certainly wasn't going to show it, and he kept that stupid grin on his face.

"Éliott and Georgia were just sharing some hilarious stories about when they were younger – some of the pranks they did were hilarious!" Lily was still laughing a bit from whatever previous story the two had shared.

"If anything, I'd say you have calmed down in your old age, Georgie," Éliott quipped, earning him a little shove from Georgia. As she leaned over to touch him, I squeezed her hand, keeping her mostly in place next to me. Georgia gave me a look that could have cut glass, but I just kept holding her hand and smiling, taking another sip from my drink.

I knew Lily and Éliott could sense the tension between us, and they both quickly excused themselves, but not before Éliott leaned over and whispered something into Georgia's ear. A subtle smile crossed her face, and she waved him off, giggling at whatever he had said.

Fuck this.

"What the fuck do you think you're doing?" I hissed at Georgia as soon as Éliott and Lily were out of earshot.

"What am I doing?" she said in a huff, pulling her hand out of mine. "What are *you* doing is the real question?"

"Me? You're basically all over Éliott Simon!" Georgia scoffed at that.

"For the 100th time, Éliott and I are just friends. Considering you were all over Lucy Davis, I didn't think you'd care. Already moving on now that you don't have to be saddled with me anymore, I see?"

I grabbed Georgia's hand and pulled us outside on the balcony, which was fortunately empty.

"What do you mean saddled with?" I felt exasperated, and I couldn't hide it anymore. I had no idea what she was referring to.

"You texted me that you wanted to end this!" Georgia declared.

"No, I said I was okay if *you did* because I didn't want you to think I was holding you hostage in this relationship. I wanted to make sure you knew it was okay if you wanted to call it quits, even if I think it's stupid to do so." There was a pause between us, and I could see the wheels in her head turning as she assessed my words.

"You think it's stupid?" Her voice was small and unsure, like she almost didn't believe me.

"Yes, I do," I replied quickly. "I think it's too soon. I appreciate that Hermes and Valkyrie were trying to give us a way out if we wanted it, but I think it would be irresponsible to just come back from summer break broken up. Everyone would think that this was a farce."

"Me too," Georgia said quietly. Another moment of silence went by, and I let out a huge sigh of relief – a huge weight had been lifted from my shoulders.

"So, we're in agreement?" I asked cautiously. My heart started to quicken at the thought that Georgia and I wouldn't be ending our PR stunt.

"Definitely. I guess when you texted me that, I thought it meant that *you* wanted to end this..." Georgia trailed off at the end, a hint of disappointment in her voice which warmed my heart.

"You can't get rid of me that easily, Cara. I mean, I still haven't mastered your coffee skills yet. Not sure how I'd get up in the morning without a cup of coffee brewed by Georgia Dubois herself." Georgia suppressed a laugh as he let her hand intertwine with mine.

"Okay, so then we'll tell our teams tomorrow before the BBC shoot?"

"Agreed."

Georgia flashed me a big smile, and I could see her visibly relax. I had wanted to say more, to tell her how I really felt, but as the words started to form, I stopped myself. This was a big step, and I didn't want to ruin it by scaring her. I felt like I was slowly starting to win her over, but I needed more time to show her that I was willing to be a better man for her.

Georgia

After Luca and I cleared the air between us at the podcast, we returned to our hotel room and watched a movie, which, of course, I fell asleep during. I woke up to Luca carrying me to bed around midnight, mumbling something about needing to be awake for tomorrow since we had a big day. I wanted to protest but stopped myself, knowing that he was right. I was a little disappointed when he left my room, but experience told me if he had joined me in bed, we probably wouldn't have gotten a lot of sleep.

I woke up five minutes before my alarm and immediately checked my phone, seeing a text from Lily on the screen.

Lily: Everything go ok with you and Luca last night?

Georgia: Everything is fine. We decided not to end the relationship... too soon.

Lily: Ahh, good, I'm glad. It's been sort of fun having Luca around, an extra hand to help annoy you.

Georgia: You and Edward wouldn't have anything to do with how flirty Éliott and Lucy were being last night, hmm?

Lily: Are you accusing Edward and I of scheming?! I'm shocked. Shocked and honestly hurt you'd even say such a thing.

Georgia: The lady doth dost protest too much, hmmm?

Lily: ;-)

I threw my phone back on the bed and chuckled to myself. Lily and Edward had become good friends this season, and it was nice to see Lily getting close to the other drivers.

As promised, I made Luca and me a cup of coffee before we headed to the track in Luca's rented Lamborghini. Once we arrived at the Valkyrie garage, we immediately headed to Isabelle's office and knocked on her door.

"Come in!"

Fiona and Lizzie were sat on Isabelle's couch. I noticed a huge grin form on Fiona Schmidt's face as she looked at Luca, who came trotting in behind me, looking a little sheepish.

"Georgia...Luca...good morning. Bringing the enemy into the

home camp, Georgia?" Isabelle joked, although I could see that she was slightly annoyed that I had brought him back to her office without warning.

"We'll be quick. I just wanted to let you know that Luca and I have decided we won't be ending our relationship after the summer break. We both feel as though it is too soon, and it would be embarrassing. We're going to wait until the end of the season and then decide what to do." Isabelle's face was neutral as she assessed the two of us. I had thought she'd be a little more shocked, but she kept a calm composure.

"I see, well, the relationship has been good for PR. If you both feel that way, then I'll speak to Francesco about it. But I don't want to hear any more complaining from either of you about future press stunts. If you want to continue this until the end of the year, then you'll show up to events together without issue."

I felt like I was being scolded by my mother as Isabelle rambled on about our requirements, and yet, her demands didn't seem so bad anymore. *I almost looked forward to them.*

Luca and I both nodded, and Isabelle quickly shooed us out of her office, insisting that Luca go back to the Hermes garage since Lily and I had strategy meetings all morning.

"Well, I'll see you after lunch for the BBC interview."

"Be sure to be on your best behavior, Rossi. I know how you are!" I joked as I walked him out of the Valkyrie garage.

"What? Me? I'm always on my best behavior, Amore." I blushed a little bit at the nickname and shook my head, knowing full well that Luca always had something up his sleeve.

"You wouldn't know how to behave if your life depended on it," I quipped back.

"What can I say? I just can't control myself around beautiful women. What was it you said before? It's in my nature." He pecked a chaste kiss on my lips and slapped my butt gently before walking off, looking incredibly pleased with himself.

Chapter Nineteen

I'D LIKE TO PROPOSE SOMETHING

Luca

I met Georgia for the BBC interview at the F1-sponsored press conference room. Matteo and Lizzie had prepped us all week for the various questions that were going to be asked of us. The majority of the questions were on dating as an F1 driver, and then some on dating *another* F1 driver. Most of them were generic questions, keeping the pressure off of us to answer specific questions about each other, which was important to the teams. Since we had decided to keep the PR stunt going, Georgia and I needed to continue to look like a perfectly in-love, happy couple.

I was informed that morning that the BBC had decided to make this a mid-season special, and it would actually air shortly after summer break. As soon as the journalist said the words, I felt a wash of relief come over me. I was glad Georgia and I had decided to stay together until the end of the season because it would have been even more embarrassing to have it released at the same time we were announcing the breakup. The special would be titled "F1 & Families" and would feature not only romantic relationships but also familial ones. The BBC had also decided to include an interview with Georgia and Henri, the famous brother-sister F1 duo.

"Good afternoon, Luca. So, we're going to start with some questions just for you. While this interview is going on, we're doing the same with Georgia in another room. Afterward, we'll do the interview with both of you in this room. Sound ok?"

"Sounds good."

"Excellent. Right, let's begin. So, you and Georgia have been dating since around the beginning of the season?"

I shifted in my seat, trying to decide if this question was meant to trip me up or if they were just setting the scene of our relationship. We had purposefully kept the start of the relationship vague so we could make it appear even longer than it was. We wanted to make it look natural.

"Sometime around Imola is when I finally got the courage to ask her out," I responded with a wink. "As you can tell, she's very much out of my league, so I was pretty nervous." The interviewer laughed a bit, and I could tell it was mostly to be polite. I supposed I *had* told that one before.

"I know everyone is very curious about what it's like to date your teammates' sister. Any challenges there?"

"There have been some, yes. Henri was unsure about the relationship at first, unsure about how it could change our friendship. You see, in F1, a good working relationship with your teammate is one of the most important ingredients of a successful team. A healthy competitive relationship can make or break a team. Henri and I had a good dynamic going into this season, so with the possibility of that changing, he was rightfully worried – as was I."

"How did you guys work throughout that? Or have you?" The interviewer threw the second part of the question in there slyly. That certainly wasn't on the approved list, but Matteo had told me to expect some extras. The producers were famous for adding a little extra drama if they could.

"In the end, it's all about communication and trust between me and Henri – and between me and Georgia. Our relationship is our own. It's no one's business. Henri understands that, and he knows that I'll treat his sister with respect, which I have tried to do throughout the relationship, and I hope everyone has seen that."

"We definitely have. The two of you have been quite private in your relationship, barely sharing anything on social media. There's been jokes about this being a PR stunt among some fans because you've been so private. Any reason for the privacy?"

"Yes, there is," I answered, perhaps a little too quickly. The journalists' additional comment about the PR stunt took me by surprise, but I did my best to hide the shock on my face.

"Georgia and I value our privacy above all else. I don't need social media to tell everyone about how I feel about her. We're both private people when it comes to relationships, and you can see that in our dating history and lack of social media exposure over the last several years. Truthfully, I am constantly forgetting my Instagram password...my poor media manager!" I hoped that the answer was good enough, although I could still feel sweat start to drip down my hands.

"But if it was a PR stunt," I added jokingly, "then I'm glad they picked the most attractive and intelligent driver on the grid. Would have been miserable pretending to date the *other Dubois*." That comment earned me what I thought was a genuine laugh from the interviewer and other BBC staff, although I could see Matteo was giving me a warning look in the background.

As the laughter settled down, the journalist returned to his list of questions. "We've often seen you as a defender of Georgia during various media events. Any chance this led to your bubbling romance?" I let out a small laugh at that question – if only he knew.

"If there's someone on the grid that doesn't need help defending herself, it's Georgia Dubois. I do, however, feel as though the press have been unfair to her this season, and it's hard to watch someone you lo-," I carefully stopped myself as the word 'love' started to come out of my mouth, trying to decide what word to choose instead, "-care deeply about get hammered by the press. But make no mistake, Georgia Dubois is a lion, and she doesn't need me defending her."

The journalist smiled at my answer, clearly impressed by it, which filled me with joy. Matteo gave me a thumbs up, which caused a flood of relief to go through my body. As the interview came to an end, the BBC coordinator came round with some water and a banana.

Luca: 1: BBC 0

After a few more moments, Georgia entered the room after her interview. Judging by the smile on Lizzie's face, it had seemingly gone well. I saw Lizzie step over to Matteo, who whispered something in her ear. Lizzie turned to me, giving me a stern look. I knew Lizzie wouldn't be too impressed with that PR stunt comment. Behind Georgia were her brothers Hugo and Henri, who had an interview scheduled right after ours.

"Did it go ok, Cara?" I asked Georgia as she sat down on the chair that was pulled up next to me. I made sure to say the words a little too loudly, hoping the journalist and other BBC staff would hear our conversation.

"Yes, yes, just talking about how good it feels to not only beat your brother but also your boyfriend," she quipped.

"How you wound me," I joked back, pulling her in for a quick kiss before the journalist sat down in front of us.

"Georgia, Luca, you ready to begin?" We both nodded as the camera began to roll.

"I'm sitting here with Georgia and Luca, two drivers not only competing for the championship this season... but for each other's hearts." As the journalist said the words, I turned to Georgia, who was trying – and failing – to not let a smile form on her lips at the journalist's cheesy words. "Sorry – too cheesy for the both of you?" the journalist laughed.

"No, no, just laughing at the insinuation that *I* was competing for Luca's heart. Pretty sure that was my easiest win this season," Georgia chuckled.

Who was this Georgia flirting with me on national TV – and could she stay?

"Amore, how you embarrass me on national TV! I thought we

agreed we'd at least lie a little bit," I joked with a wink at her, knowing Georgia would get the private joke. I decided not to look at Matteo and Lizzie, knowing full well how they would feel about this exchange, but I didn't care.

I loved a feisty, flirty Georgia.

"So, Luca, we can obviously see why you fell for Georgia, but Georgia, did Luca have to work hard to win your heart?"

"Absolutely," she said, perhaps a little too quickly for my liking, although her sultry voice definitely made up for it. "Although I think he had to work a little harder to win my brothers' approval."

"Oh yes, we asked Luca about that earlier. And what about you? Did it take long to fall for Luca?" The interviewer was pressing on this, wanting Georgia to give an answer. Georgia turned to me, a smirk on her face.

"Probably didn't take as long as it *should have*, but what can I say? I'm a sucker for a guy in purple." I could feel my cheeks heat up a bit, not expecting that answer from Georgia. The first part of her sentence gave me pause, and suddenly my mind was racing a million miles a minute.

Had she meant that, or was it just fodder for the cameras?

"You and half the women in the F1 paddock," the journalist laughed. Georgia kept a tight smile on her face, and I could tell he was less than impressed at that comment.

"So tell me, on the weekends you have off, how do you manage your time together? I know a lot of time is spent at the factories for the both of you."

"It's tough, for sure. As you'll hear through several interviews, being away from your loved ones for so many weeks is tough. Most spouses and girlfriends can't go to every race. For us, it's almost the opposite because we see each other more on race weekends than off weeks, but we do our best to make time for each other even if we aren't at a race," I answered, the answer feeling completely genuine. It was tough to be away from family, and I was fortunate that my father and mother could travel to most of the races.

"I agree. I think it's also easier because we're both in Formula 1.

We're both drivers who are dedicated to winning the championship, but it also means we understand the hardships that come with being a driver. When I have a bad day, Luca understands what I am going through. He gets the emotional rollercoaster because we're on the same ride. There are such extreme highs and lows, and it's meaningful to have someone who is also in your shoes. There's only twenty-two of us, so to date someone who gets what you're going through, it's been special."

I couldn't help but turn to Georgia and smile at her. Even if we weren't actually dating, being able to talk to Georgia about my relationship with the car and Hermes' bad strategy calls over the last several weeks was a relief.

"That's an interesting perspective, thank you. Now, Georgia, if you don't mind me asking, how do you get along with the other F1 girlfriends or wives? So far, none of the other partners of the current drivers work in Formula 1, but I know you all often hang out after the races."

"I get along fine with many of them. Lauren, Edward's girlfriend, and I are good friends, which has been lovely. I've been sneaking her Valkyrie shirts, much to Edward's dismay. I might be a fellow driver, but all of the partners treat me as *me*, and it's nice. We often just sit around, drink wine, and talk about how silly our boys can be. Really, it's a lot more mundane than you think it to be. We're no different than other women in our twenties."

I took a moment to reflect on Georgia's answer. I hadn't considered if it would be different hanging out with the other wives and girlfriends because she was a driver, but I was glad to hear that, in fact, it was easy. It made sense; we'd all gone karting together, we'd all grown up together, so we were friends, and our significant others were just a natural extension of our friend group.

"Well, this has been truly great. You two are a ball of fun. Anything else you'd like to add?"

"Yes, actually, since I have you all here with a camera crew and photographers, I was hoping I could borrow the spotlight for a moment?"

The journalist looked perplexed at my question but motioned for me to go on. I could see both Lizzie and Matteo looking nervous in the back, Matteo slightly shaking his head, telling me to abandon whatever plan I had. But I ignored their silent pleas. I turned to Georgia and grabbed both of her hands in mine. She gave me a questioning look, clearly trying to guess what was about to happen.

"Georgia Dubois," I began, "getting to know you over the last several years, it's been a dream come true. You are truly my better half. There's no doubt about that. So, for the final question of this interview, I have only one thing to ask." I paused for a moment and got down on one knee.

I could already see panic starting to spread on Georgia's face. I pulled out a small velvet box and pointed the opening to her. I could see her eyes saying, 'Get the fuck up, Luca,' but I continued. She shifted nervously in her seat, the wheels in her head turning, trying to determine what kind of answer she was going to say to the question she assumed I was going to ask.

"Will you make us another round of coffee this afternoon?" I said with a cheesy grin, opening the ring box to display coffee grinds that were now pouring out of the velvet box and onto the floor.

At first, the room was quiet, still processing what had just unfolded in front of them, although after another second, I saw a huge smile spread across Georgia's face, and she erupted into laughter.

"Luca *fucking* Rossi, if you think I'm going to make coffee with poorly ground coffee like this, you're out of your mind!" The group burst into laughter. I turned to face Henri, who had a look of death in his eyes, even though he was laughing with the rest. I gave Georgia a cheeky smile and got up off of the floor, dusting some of the coffee beans off my lap. Georgia gave me a playful punch in the stomach as she also stood up.

"You see what I have to put up with?" she quipped to the BBC presenter. Still smiling, we both shook the interviewer's hand before walking over to Lizzie, Matteo, and her brothers, who were waiting for us at the entrance.

"Pull something like that again, Rossi, and I'll murder you myself," was all Lizzie retorted as she let out a big huff. Georgia turned to me and winked, giving me a peck on the lips before following Lizzie out of the room.

Before Georgia exited, she turned back around and called out, "I will get you back for that one, Rossi!"

I had no doubt that she would, and I very much looked forward to it.

Georgia

The BBC interview had gone much better expected. After our talk with Isabelle on Thursday, Friday and Saturday had been incredibly easy for me and Luca. Something felt different between us, like the lines between *fake* dating and *actually* dating were starting blur. When we were at the track and had free time, we were in each other's garages, laughing away. When we were back at the hotel, we sat in the living room, aimlessly going through notes from our race engineers or chatting about the cars.

I continued to tell myself that in order to really sell this, it made sense that I was spending more nights in Luca's bed rather than my own. And it *definitely* made sense that we spent every dinner together laughing and chatting away with my brothers, right? A small part of me felt alarmed that I was starting to feel this comfortable with Luca, but I told that part of me to piss off.

I was enjoying myself, and I deserved to be happy.

As Sunday rolled around, Luca and I walked hand in hand into the paddock. I was sporting my special edition Silverstone polo. Maison de Klotho had made the entire team new polos for the Grand Prix. Lily and I had been gifted adorable athletic skirts to match. We looked a bit like tennis stars, in my opinion, but our representative at Maison de Klotho claimed it was all the rage these days.

As we reached the Valkyrie garage, Luca gave me a kiss on the lips and said his goodbyes, waving to Lily on his way out. We had barely had any time to discuss my BBC interview, and I knew Lily was dying to hear about how it went. I motioned for her to follow me into my driver's room, and she promptly sat on my couch, making herself quite at home.

"So... how did it go!? I can't believe they wouldn't let me attend, so annoying!" Lily sounded like a little child who had been told they had to go to bed early.

"It went well. They asked some good questions and some probing questions."

"Lizzie told me at the end Luca pulled a big prank on you. Sounded hilarious. I would have killed to have seen Henri's face."

"Henri was definitely pissed off, but I thought it was quite funny. I was surprised Luca had the guts to do it."

"Did you really think for a moment he was actually going to propose?"

"Truthfully, I have no idea what I was thinking at that moment. I was too frozen with fear. I guess I was trying to think about what on earth I was going to say."

"Well, with a face that handsome – you'd obviously *have* to say yes," she said mischievously.

"You're starting to sound like you're on board with this relationship a little too much... how much have you been talking to Edward?" I teased back.

"You can pretend all you want, Georgie, but you can't fool me!" I just rolled my eyes in response to Lily, deciding not to give that comment a response.

"You going to join me on the podium today?" I asked Lily, decidedly changing the topic of conversation.

"Of course... I'll be the one on the top step," she quipped back.

"We'll see about that, Lil!" I shouted back to her as she left my room, flicking me off just before she shut the door. I couldn't help but smile at her determination. I was in pole position today, and I had no plans to give that up, but something told me Lily had a lot of fight in her today.

"Alright, Georgia, that's lap forty-two complete. You're fifteen seconds clear of Henri in P2, so keep your head down."

"Awfully boring out here, guys," I quipped back to my race engineer. I heard a soft laugh from Mel on the radio before she cut out.

On the straights, I could see Henri behind me, but only faintly. Silverstone had huge TVs around the track, and while we were told never to watch the big screens, sometimes it was hard not to. But as I saw the crowd going wild all around me, I dared to look up at the screen, only to see Lily passing Henri.

I knew I shouldn't have been so happy to see someone passing my brother, but my heart soared for Lily. If Valkyrie could get a 1-2 finish at Silverstone, it would be the cherry on top of the ice cream sundae. I couldn't think of a better ending to the weekend.

"Did Lily pass?" I asked into the team radio.

"Focus on your race, Georgia, there's only eight laps to go. Lily won't catch up to you, so nurse the tires and drive sensibly."

And focus I did. The next eight laps felt like some of the greatest, if not the most boring, laps I had ever done. The car was flying, and I had already lapped two other drivers who had been instructed to get out of my way.

"Do we have enough time to pit for fastest lap?"

"No. We're not risking this for a point. Let Lily have it."

I sighed, a little annoyed that fastest lap would probably go to Lily but still, I was glad it wasn't Noah or Henri who were second and third in the championship. Mel was right. There was no reason to pit for one point. The risk of something going on in the garage was too big. No one wanted to compromise the 1-2 finish.

As I saw the checkered flag waving, I took a big sigh of relief.

I was going to win Silverstone, and I felt unstoppable.

As I crossed the line, I heard Fiona Schmidt cut into my ear through the radio. "That's P2 Georgie, P2. Great race!"

I felt sudden horror fill me. P2? No, that couldn't be right. Had I gotten a time penalty?

"What do you mean *fucking* P2?" I split out, but not even a second later, I heard laughter from both Fiona and Mel in the background.

"Hahaha, I kid, I kid. That's P1, Love, but you can consider us even after that prank in Baku!" I heard Fiona joke on my radio.

"Looks like everyone wants to start a prank war with Georgia Dubois these days!" I chuckled back into the radio.

Georgia: 1 Fiona: 1

"In all seriousness, an amazing race from you and Lily. P1 and P2, we couldn't have hoped for better!" Isabelle chimed in.

"Congrats to the team and to Lily. The car felt amazing this week. Really good job from everyone."

I was the last car to pull into the assigned podium parking spaces. I hopped out of my car, did my classic window-washing dance, and then ran over to Lily, forcing her into a huge embrace. She hugged me back – *tightly* – and we started to jump up and down together. I'm sure to everyone we looked like giddy school girls, but I didn't care. Valkyrie F1 had gotten a 1-2 finish. If I wanted to jump up and down like a schoolgirl, then I deserved to.

The podium celebration had to be my second favorite of the season so far. Nothing could beat winning Monaco, but standing up there next to Lily and my brother was truly breathtaking. When I came down from the celebration, drenched in champagne, I saw Luca standing at the bottom of the steps, likely waiting to give me the obligatory race-win kiss.

But as he picked me up in his arms and kissed me, it didn't feel as obligatory as it normally did. Luca released me from his hold and smiled at me, giving me another quick kiss on the lips.

"So proud of you, Tesoro. So proud." I beamed up at him, handing him the bottle of champagne so he could take a drink from it.

The rest of the day felt like a blur. After the celebration and media duties, Luca and I drove back together to the hotel to get ready for tonight. We had a few hours before we had to be at the Silverstone event that was being put on by the driver's association.

Since everyone stayed in Silverstone on Sunday, the FIA typically put on a driver's gala and invited various VIPs and Sponsors to come and hang out with the drivers and team principals. Isabelle had made it clear that Luca and I were to be on time. Lily was to meet us downstairs promptly at 7 p.m. so we would be there for 7:30.

As soon as we got back to the hotel room, Luca hopped into the shower. I knew I should sober up a bit, but the bottle of champagne that Eric had sent to my room was too tempting. Fortunately, Luca had the foresight to have room service delivered, which I happily dug into as I opened the bottle of champagne, pouring both myself and Luca a glass.

After his shower, Luca walked into the living room with only a towel wrapped around his waist, hanging dangerously low around his hips. I couldn't help but lick my lips at the sight of the Italian standing in front of me, but Luca pointedly ignored my hungry stare.

"Georgia, don't you think you've probably had enough champagne?" he *half* joked, grabbing his glass and taking a sip.

"Nopppeee," I responded, popping the p at the end of the word. "I heard race winners can have all of the champagne that they want." Luca reached over to my glass and took it out of my hand.

"I think you've had enough," he said sternly, although the grin on his face told me that he was enjoying this. He placed the glass just out of reach on the coffee table, and I gave him a large pout.

"Come on, Luca, you're no fun!"

Luca pulled me closer to him, and I put my hands on his bare chest. "Oh, I think you know I can be plenty fun, Principessa." Something about that nickname always set my core aflame, and I tried to internally settle myself. *Now was not the time.*

"Well, you aren't being fun right now." I tried to put on a sultry voice as I pouted, but I suspected that I was failing more than I had hoped, especially after Luca just arched an eyebrow.

"Is that what my Principessa wants right now, hmm? Some fun?"

I slowly bit my bottom lip, knowing how it drove him crazy, before nodding my head yes.

"Answer me," he demanded. Luca was always the one to be in charge when it came to the bedroom, and as much as I hated to admit it, I loved it. But something about tonight made me want to challenge him. Instead of answering him, I shook my head no, walking straight into my bedroom as an act of defiance.

As I hopped onto my bed, taking off my shoes, I saw Luca approach my doorway. He leaned on the doorframe, a look of disappointment on his face, but I knew the game I was playing.

"I expected better from you. You know what happens to bad girls."

"I thought race winners *always* got rewards."

"Only well-behaved ones," Luca retorted.

"Fine, maybe I don't want a reward from you, anyway. I'm sure I can give Élio-" Before I could finish my words, Luca was on top of me, his hands pinning both of mine down as his lips connected with mine in a ferocious kiss. A sly smile formed on his face as he pulled back, leaving me breathless.

"Oh, Principessa, how you lie. Éliott could never make you feel as good as I do."

"Maybe we should call him and find out." I knew my words were just going to piss him off more, but today, I loved this side of Luca.

Luca made quick work of taking off my polo and skirt, leaving me in just my underwear. He slipped my thong off and grabbed both my hands, tying them to the headboard. I wanted to play it off as if I wasn't bothered, like I wasn't interested in him, but we both knew that was a lie. I could feel the wetness grow between my thighs as Luca settled between them.

"Wearing a purple thong under that blue outfit, I see. So, you want to play games? Fine, we can both play games." As soon as he finished the taunt, Luca dove straight into my core with his tongue. I let out a loud gasp, not expecting Luca to be quite so forceful straight away, but it felt amazing. He continued to work me with his kitten licks, bringing me closer and closer to my orgasm. Slowly, he let a finger sink into me.

"Luca... Pl...please.. another," I begged him. The pace he set with his finger was teasingly slow, and I was feeling more and more desperate as Luca brought me to my release. As I could feel myself about to find that release, Luca pulled his finger and mouth away, leaving me completely hanging on the balance of what was about to be a mind-blowing orgasm.

"Wha- what was that for?" I demanded, my face turning red with anger as I tried to pull free from the restraints of my now-ruined thong.

"If you wanted to cum, maybe you should have called Éliott?" Luca said mockingly as he began to crawl back up my body, placing light kisses on my neck and shoulders. I wrapped my legs around him in response and tried to pull him down, but his body was too strong, and he didn't budge.

"Please... Luca..." I begged. At this point, I felt like I was at a loss for words. My body was so worked up from the race, the champagne, and the almost climax.

"I think an apology is in order," Luca demanded. I pulled once again at my restraints as I looked up at them, but Luca turned my head back to face him, a smirk now on his lips.

"Fine... I'm sorry." I knew the apology was pathetic, but I didn't want Luca to win quite so easily.

"For?"

I grumbled but gave in. "For not answering you... I promise I won't do it again," I threw in quickly for good measure, hoping it might convince Luca to let me finish.

"Oh, Principessa, I know that's a lie," Luca taunted, "but I'll accept your apology this time."

I felt Luca start to trail down my body, leaving little love bites and kisses in all the places no one could see but the two of us. As he reached my core again, I let out a loud moan. Luca sunk two fingers in – and then a third. As he gently sucked on my clit, he let his fingers slide in and out at a decent pace, and I felt myself getting closer to my high. Fortunately, this time, Luca worked me through my release as it hit me. I chanted his name over and over, writhing on the bed in pleasure as I fought the bounds at my wrists.

Once I started to calm down, Luca pulled away and traveled back up to my lips, giving me a sloppy kiss that allowed me to taste myself on him. He quickly released the thong from my wrists, and he kissed each one ever so gently. The act almost felt intimate, like this was more than just sex for him.

I put that feeling out of my mind, reminding myself that this was just sex. Still, every time I ended up in Luca's bed, it became harder and harder to believe that.

"Such a good girl for me..." he whispered into my ear. "Now go get showered and dressed. Can't be late for your party tonight."

"But what about you?" I asked as I sat up, looking at the towel around his waist. I knew that he had to be extremely hard after that session.

"Oh, don't worry, Amore, I'm not done with you tonight."

After round two in the shower, Luca and I finally got ready and made our way downstairs by 7:05 p.m., just five minutes late, which I thought was fairly impressive since I was typically ten to fifteen minutes late. The car was already waiting for us, and Lily was sitting inside with Henri, chatting away about the race. I knew Henri was annoyed that Lily had passed him, but it was clean and fair racing. His tires had given out, and Lily had taken advantage of that.

"Finally, you two have arrived." Henri looked a little exasperated. "Would it hurt you to ever be on time?"

"Now, what fun would that be, Henri? A race winner must make an entrance."

My brother scoffed at that but said nothing in return, choosing to pick up his phone and send a text, likely to his girlfriend Christine. Lily just winked at me in the taxi, wiggling her eyebrows very suggestively. I knew I should ignore her, but I couldn't help myself, and I winked back at her, grabbing Luca's arm and snuggling in closer to him. I was definitely still tipsy from the champagne, and Luca's and I's "exercise" back at the hotel hadn't done too much to sober me up, especially since I snuck in another glass while I was putting on my makeup.

When we arrived at the hotel where the event was taking place, there were hoards of fans and photographers surrounding the car. Luca got out of the car first, offering me his hand as I followed him, keeping our hands intertwined as we walked into the massive hotel ballroom. As soon as we entered, Isabelle and Fiona motioned for us to join them.

"Georgie, superb racing today as always," Felix, the Rennen F1 team principal and Fiona's husband, complimented. "Perhaps one day we'll get you in a Rennen car." I knew if my performance kept up, I would eventually have offers from Hermes, Rennen, and Blaue Flügel, but at this moment in time, none of those teams interested me.

None of those teams had dared to give me, a female driver, a chance in F1 – only Valkyrie had offered me my dream. The other teams only wanted me now because they saw they were wrong, saw that, actually, a female driver could win in this sport. I knew it was silly to feel so much loyalty to Isabelle and Valkyrie because the truth was, if I had a bad performance, they would eventually drop me, but I couldn't help it.

"Felix, if you even dare attempt to take Georgia away, I'll make your life a living nightmare," Isabelle quipped. Felix had never struck me as someone who was scared of anything, but Isabelle had a way of putting fear into the fearless. Felix gave her a sheepish, polite smile and grabbed his wife's hand, suggesting they head to the bar for drink refills. Isabelle let out a small chuckle as Felix and Fiona headed to the bar. As I looked over, I saw the couple chatting with Lily, Oscar, and Eric.

"They look good together, Oscar and Lily." I was shocked when I heard the words come out of Isabelle's mouth.

"But Oscar is datin-" I began, but Isabelle cut me off.

"Not like that, you muppet. As a driver combo."

I turned back to the group of them at the bar. Isabelle was right. Lily and Oscar did look good together. I turned back to Isabelle, and there was something in her eye – concern, maybe? It made me feel uneasy as I watched my team principal stare at the group of them before she quickly regained her composure.

"You can't keep her forever," Luca finally said, breaking the silence between the three of us. I turned and gave him a warning look, signaling for him not to be so silly, but Isabelle's face said it all – what Luca said was true, and we all knew it. *Lily had a bright future ahead of her, and it likely wasn't at Valkyrie.*

"Eric Spencer is going to retire one day," Isabelle said simply. "The Rennen F1 Team would be a fool not to offer Lily a seat, and she'd be a fool not to take it. I offered her a three-year contract, but she turned me down, saying they only wanted two and an option for a third year." I was surprised to hear that, surprised to hear that Lily had turned them down for three guaranteed years of racing.

"I was frustrated at first," Isabelle continued, "but now I think it was a wise decision. Lily has great things in store, but I'm not sure it'll be for Valkyrie." The thought of that made me sad. Lily and I were so close, but I knew in my heart Isabelle was right. In F1 teams, there was only room for one champion, and I wasn't going to give up my spot.

After chatting a bit longer, Luca and I excused ourselves from Isabelle and made our way to our table. Joining us was Noah and his girlfriend, Kylie, along with Henri, Oliver, and Éliott. The British drivers had a special table, undoubtedly close to various VIPs who would want to meet and take photos with them.

Lily bemoaned the fact that she couldn't sit at what she deemed was the "party table," but I assured her any table with Eric Spencer, Britian's most successful F1 driver, was a party table. When I was in Indy Car, Eric was one of the few drivers who emailed me on a regular basis, always offering advice. He was one of my staunchest supporters and always spoke loudly in support of having a woman drive in F1. *He also bought the best champagne.*

"Well, well, well... can't believe our race winner got stuck with us. Honored to be in your presence," Noah joked as he sat down next to me. I knew the 2x world champion was annoyed that I was winning this season, but we had managed to keep it civil in the paddock – *mostly*.

I leaned over to Noah, a mischievous smile on my face. "It's even worse... I have to eat the same food as you lot."

That, surprisingly, earned me a huge laugh from Noah. He'd never struck me as someone who was easy to get a chuckle out of, but as we got to know each other more this season, I found he was almost as easy as Edward to make laugh. Noah was just selective on who had the honor to do it.

Luca and I had already eaten at the hotel, mostly to help sober me up, but we picked at the food to be polite. As the dinner service ended, Luca asked if I was interested in heading to the bar, which of course I was. I probably had one more drink before I would be improperly sloshed, not just '*race winner sloshed*' as Oliver put it so politely.

As we passed the Wilmington table, my heart sank. There was Anthony, sat next to the Wilmington F1 leadership team, chatting away about Indy Car and his recent success – well, success was an understatement. He had one win under him, not exactly championship-winning material. When Anthony saw Luca and I walk over to the bar, he got up from the Wilmington table and made his way over to us.

"Good grief," I heard Luca whisper under his breath. "Can this guy not take a hint?" Luca pulled me closer to him as Anthony walked up to the two of us, the smugness on his face was hard to ignore.

"Nice to see the two of you are still throwing this farce around the paddock."

"Oh, shut up, Anthony," I bit back, not caring if anyone heard.

"Sorry, Love, just call 'em like I see 'em," Anthony drawled in his most southern accent. He took a moment to observe us, letting his eyes rake over my body, and I felt sick.

"Might want to keep your eyes to yourself," I heard a familiar voice chime in. I turned to see Oliver approach the bar, empty glass in hand. "Luca once threatened to crash my car if I asked Georgia out on a date. Be a shame to see all that Texan oil money splattered about the track. There's enough oil on it as is." I chuckled at Oliver – always one to get in a cheap joke, and I was here for it.

"Well, when I have your F1 seat at Wilmington, Oliver, Luca will have to be fast enough to catch me." The three of us F1 drivers immediately burst out laughing, and I could see Anthony's face turn red with anger. I knew it was unwise to poke the bear, but the thought of him ever being better than Luca was too hilarious of a joke to pass up.

"The Wilmington F1 Team will give you a seat when hell freezes over," Luca quipped, handing me and Oliver our glasses of champagne. Something about Luca's comment gave me pause.

I'd heard that one before.

When we made it back to the table, Henri moved a seat over, whispering in my ear, "What did he want?"

"Oh, the usual, to be a pain in my ass."

"You know, as far as boyfriends go, I think Luca might be my favorite." I gave Henri a pointed look, questioning if that was *actually* true, and then a look to remind him that this was a fake relationship. Henri just ignored me, turning back to Noah and his girlfriend, rejoining their conversation.

"You ready to go, Cara? It's getting late, and we have a flight back tomorrow." I nodded my head, informing Luca that I just needed to go say goodbye to the British drivers seated at the top, and then I would be ready to head back. I had no doubt that Luca had another round of fun planned for us back at the hotel.

I woke up the next morning to the buzzing of my phone on the bedside table next to me. As the phone kept ringing, I heard a groan from behind me.

"Don't answer it," Luca begged, pulling my back closer to him as he continued to spoon me.

"It's Lizzie... I have to answer it."

"What can she possibly want? Your flight isn't until this after-noon. Tell her to leave us alone."

I chuckled at Luca's insistence and grabbed my phone. As the phone stopped ringing, I saw a smile form on Luca's face, which was immediately dropped as Lizzie started to call again.

"It must be important if she keeps calling." I answered the call before Luca could continue to protest, pulling myself out of his grasp so I could sit up.

"Good morning, Lizzie... do you know that it's 8 a.m. after a race win?" I joked to my media manager as Luca tried to pull me back down into his embrace.

"Georgia, we've just been told that a story is about to break in the Daily Report. Fortunately, I went to university with one of their sports journalists, so she called this morning to give me a quick heads-up. It drops in a few minutes. Can you go get Luca?"

I could feel my heartbeat quickening as I immediately put the phone on speakerphone.

"He... he's here," I said weakly.

"The Daily Report claims they have a source that says your rela-tionship is fake, a PR stunt, and they're printing an article on it."

"That's bullshit!" I yelled into the phone. Luca immediately sat up, his attention now fixated on his phone as I heard it start to ping, likely with texts from Matteo.

"We don't know who the source is yet, but we're working hard to find out. Until then, I need you and Luca to stay out of the spotlight and let the PR crisis manager we've just retained handle this. Is that understood?"

"Ye... yes."

"I'll be in touch with how we'll respond, hopefully by the end of the day. With any luck, it'll be a nonsense story that'll blow over after the race next week." I just nodded at my phone, unable to form words as Lizzie said her goodbyes and hung up. Luca was now furiously texting with Matteo. As he looked up at me, his eyes immediately went wide with sorrow, and Luca pulled me into him as tears started to flood my face.

"My F1 career is going to be ruined," I sobbed, my voice cracking with every word.

"No, it won't, Cara. I'm here for as long as you want to keep doing this. I promise you that. Whatever is going to be said about us, we can fight, prove them wrong."

"Even if we break up at the end of the season, everyone is going to accuse us of this being a PR stunt! I can't force you to date me forever." I continued to cry into Luca as he kept rubbing my back, trying to soothe my tears.

"Georgia Dubois, I promise you, I don't care how long this takes - I'll make sure everyone sees just *how much I love you.*"

Chapter Twenty

CURIOSITY KILLED THE CAT

Georgia

The flight back home was miserable. As soon as the call with Lizzie ended, Luca and I both moved our flights up. We had been instructed to head to our factories on Tuesday for a debrief on the situation; an early morning call with the crisis team that had been scheduled. Isabelle spoke to me a bit Monday afternoon, assuring me that her friend in London was the best at what she did. As of right now, the only people who knew about the hiring of the crisis firm were a select handful of people with direct knowledge of Luca and I's relationship.

That Monday morning, I cried into Luca's chest, lamenting about how my career was over. It wasn't until later in the day, as I sat on my plane to Monaco, that I realized what he had said.

'Georgia Dubois, I promise you, I don't care how long this takes - I'll make sure everyone sees just how much I love you.'

How much I love you.

Those words echoed in my brain over and over again. Luca had obviously meant that he was going to show the world that our relationship was genuine, that we were in love, even if we knew it was all pretend.

Right?

I knew that had to be the case, but still, his choice of words had me at a loss. What if he did mean them as something more? Why did I *want* him to mean them as something more? Why did I want Luca "Playboy" Rossi, a man I despised mere months ago, to be something more? That question had been circling around my head all day, and I knew the answer.

Because *I* was falling in love with *him*.

For now, I had to push that thought down because if we didn't clear this up, it didn't matter how I felt about Luca. I'd lose him forever and possibly my F1 seat when all of the sponsors pulled out.

Lily and I were already planning to be at the factory on Tuesday. We had three more races before summer break, and the team had upgrades they wanted to get tested before we went into the break. I knew my first meeting of the morning was going to be about the situation and how it was unfolding.

As promised, the Daily Report released the article that Monday afternoon. Lizzie had instructed neither of us to read it, which I had listened to, although not because she had instructed me to do so, because I was too terrified that if I read it, then this nightmare would actually be real. In my mind, there was still a silent hope that if I didn't read it, the words would never enter the world – never haunt my dreams.

As I sat down in the conference room with my cup of black coffee, I knew that wasn't the case. Elizabeth, the crisis manager, was already in the conference room chatting with Isabelle and Lizzie, who had arrived at the factory much earlier in the morning. I could see Lizzie furiously taking notes as Elizabeth spoke to the two of them. As I entered the room, the three of them stopped their private conversation, waving for me to come in.

"Ahh, Georgia, good morning. This is Elizabeth. She's been retained to help us." Elizabeth shook my hand as Isabelle introduced us. I just nodded and sat down, taking a look at my phone. I had a text from Luca.

Luca: Good morning – how are you this morning?

Georgia: Well, I woke up still a Silverstone winner, so... I guess it's not all doom and gloom.

Luca: That's my girl.

I smiled at his texts and set my phone down as Luca, Francesco, and Matteo's faces appeared on the conference room screen. Lily entered the conference room a moment later, apologizing for being late.

"Thank you for joining us. I know you are preparing for Austria's Grand Prix this weekend, so I will keep this concise and to the point. Fortunately, it wasn't hard to find the Daily Report source. Our private investigator has identified it as the Silverstone event bartender. Apparently, there was a conversation he overheard at the Silverstone Sunday driver's dinner. Seems as though Georgia's ex-fiance has a loud mouth, and he spent a good amount of time chatting to the barman, who thought it was a good idea to pass this information along to the Daily Report."

As Elizabeth announced this to the room, my body froze. Anthony was too smart to go to the Daily Report himself – the gossipy newspaper would likely just write him off as a lover scorned, but having a bartender chat about what *he* had heard? Now, that was right up Anthony's sleeve.

"Absolute wanker," Lily blurted out, causing everyone to look over at her. Lily's eyes went wide as she noticed that everyone was staring at her, clearly not expecting her outburst to be quite so loud.

"Couldn't have said it better myself," Lizzie chuckled.

"Right, well, to cut to the chase, there is good news, and there is bad news. The good news is that without prompting, several drivers have come to Georgia and Luca's defense on social media. Edward even gave them a shout-out yesterday during his podcast."

I looked up at the screen as Elizabeth circled through various social media posts from the other drivers, all standing up for me and Luca. My heart warmed as I went through them on the screen.

Several of the other drivers, such as Oliver, Edward, and Éliott, had reached out to me, asking if I was okay, but none of them had told me about their posts. I had made it clear to Lizzie that I wouldn't ask them to post on my behalf, but I was so incredibly touched that they had done it on their own.

"Oliver and Edward's are especially hilarious," Elizabeth added with a warm smile. "Now, Georgia and Luca, we'll have you post yours this evening. The teams will work with you on what photos are best to share with the caption. I've sent them some ideas.

Lily and Henri, it's best that you only comment on these social media posts. Posts from your teammates and brother might look like we're being too defensive, so we'll take that day by day. Henri and Lily will drop some comments into their conversations with fans because you will be asked about it this week, but otherwise, let's not make a big deal about it.

Georgia and Luca, I've emailed you some comment ideas to post on the various posts if you so wish. Don't need to comment on all of them, but definitely do comment on some. It was very kind of the other drivers to do this. You have some good friends."

I nodded and smiled at that. *Indeed I did.*

"Our strategy boils down to the following: we're going to make the Daily Report feel so stupid, they'll never dare pull another stunt like this again. Now, any questions?" I had to chuckle at that, to be fair to the Daily Report – they had written a somewhat truthful story, and yet somehow, as I sat there, staring at Luca's face on the screen, the story didn't feel truthful anymore.

Before I could speak up, I heard Luca's voice come over the speaker. "Yes.. um... you mentioned bad news?"

"Oh, right, yes. Obviously, you'll need to extend this relationship timeline. Isabelle said there was chatter about a break up after summer break, and then it was moved to December... let's make sure it's pushed out to the start of next season, hmm?"

"Oh noooo," Luca interjected sarcastically, pretending to be upset, "another couple of months dating the most *beauuttiiiffullll* woman in the paddock, what a bummer for me." My cheeks began to heat up as they turned a bright shade of red. I couldn't help but notice a sly look between Isabelle and Fiona, although neither of them said anything. Lily, on the other hand, burst out laughing.

"Don't be silly, Luca, *we* aren't dating," Lily laughed into the camera. I shook my head, chuckling at Lily's antics. Luca and Matteo were laughing on the other end now. "Well, I think this sounds great," Lily concluded, "any chance to make a journalist look like an idiot is a fun day for me."

Elizabeth nodded at Lily's comment and turned back to me. "Any questions, Georgia?"

"What about the sponsors?"

"Ahh, good question. We emailed them all last night," Isabelle responded. "You'll be pleased to know Maison de Klotho got back to me this morning with the following response." Isabelle took a pause, putting on her reading glasses before pulling up the email on her phone.

"Dear Isabelle, thanks for the heads up. We aren't concerned. After spending the day with Luca and Georgia, I think it's pretty easy to see the genuine connection those two have. I'd be happy to set up another photoshoot to help squash this nonsense." I let out a sigh of relief. This had been my biggest concern, but with the sponsors still in play, we had a chance to survive this storm.

"I, of course, let her know that we'll happily set up a photo shoot during summer break for the two of you." Lizzie looked pleased with this arrangement. She had been dying to do another shoot, and this time she was set on coming with me.

"Okay, well, if that is all, I'll let you get back to your day."

After the meeting, Lizzie approached me and told me that we would get together at lunch to go through my posts and Instagram comments. The team would get them all up for me over the next twenty-four hours. I asked Lizzie if I could read the article, but she insisted on giving it a little more time, begging me not to read it yet. I appreciated that she had my feelings in the forefront of her mind, but the more the lady protested, the more I wanted to read the article. Still, I agreed to at least wait until Wednesday. Tuesday was about learning the upgrades.

It certainly wasn't about Luca's blatant eagerness to keep this going – now that I didn't have time to delve into it.

Fortunately, the Valkyrie F1 factory was close to Monaco, so I was able to wake up in my bed Wednesday morning before we took off for Austria. Lily had decided to stay at mine since her home base was in London. I woke up Wednesday morning to the sound of pings out in my living room, likely from Lily's phone. As I walked out into the hallway, I saw Lily and Henri chatting away, casually drinking *my* coffee from *my* mugs.

"I see you've both decided to make yourselves quite at home." They both flashed me a teasing smile before going back to whatever they were doing.

As Lily sat on my couch, scrolling through her phone, I noticed Henri watching her. He was pretending to read a book, but I could see his eyes glance up at her every so often, as if his thoughts were a million miles away.

They'd make a good-looking couple, I mused to myself as I began to make my coffee. I was quickly brought out of my thoughts and back to reality when I heard a screech from Lily.

"They've posted! They've posted!"

I immediately knew she meant the Instagram posts. I saw Henri pick up his phone, likely adding in his comment as he was instructed to. Lily turned on my TV and immediately began casting her Instagram on the screen.

"Look how cute!"

And there I saw it: up on the screen was my Instagram post that Lizzie and I had written yesterday.

 **GeorgiaDubois38**

Liked by Valkyrie F1 Team and 200k others

GeorgiaDubois38 Henri when he found out me dating his teammate might actually be an elaborate prank vs. Henri accidentally walking in on Luca and I's movie night...
@HenriDubois67

Lily continued to scroll down, showing Luca's social media post. I had seen the photo he was going to use, and I was a tad annoyed that Edward had even taken that photo, but Lizzie was right – it was a good, natural photo. The fans would love it, even if I hated it.

LucaRossi52

Liked by HenriDubois67 and 250k others

LucaRossi52 Since we're fake dating, I can post photos like this now, right? Asking on behalf of a very confused boyfriend.
@GeorgiaDubois38

Lily then pulled up the social posts from the other drivers. Since several of them had posted on Monday and Tuesday, the comment sections had exploded with fans laughing and making fun of me and Luca. The comments were overwhelmingly positive, with other drivers chiming in on the funny photos, much to fans' delight. As I went through the other drivers' responses, I couldn't help but laugh. I felt relieved – honored even.

 **EdwardDavis23**

Liked by Valkyrie F1 Team and 200k others

EdwardDavis23 If these two are fake dating, then they deserve an Oscar.
@GeorgiaDubois38 @LucaRossi52

 OliverWilliams41

Liked by LilyWilson and 150k others

OliverWilliams41 A picture speaks 1000 words... except for this one, this one doesn't properly show Georgia threatening to knock Luca off the tree if he doesn't stop teasing her for crying at the sunset...
@GeorgiaDubois38 @LucaRossi52

 **EricSpencer78**

Liked by LilyWilson and 400k others

EricSpencer78 True love is letting your boyfriend have a fry when he asks.
But that is not what is pictured here... pictured here is Georgia telling Luca she will cut off his fingers if he eats one of her fries on cheat day. Love a woman who knows what she wants!
@GeorgiaDubois38 @LucaRossi52

 NoahHendriks24

Liked by HenriDubois67 and 100k others

NoahHendriks24 Not photographed is how my girlfriend and @GeorgiaDubois38 teamed up against me and @LucaRosi52, creating a roadblock so we couldn't pass... least favorite couple to double date with. Relationship might be fake, but her competitive spirit certainly isn't!

ÉliottSimon45

For them to do this for a relationship they all knew was fake was touching in an inexplicable way. The posts seemed so genuine. It was almost as if everyone, for a moment, had forgotten that Luca and I weren't actually dating. But I had to admit, on camera, we looked so real – the *relationship* looked so real.

Maybe I did deserve an Oscar.

Or maybe there hadn't been as much faking as I had previously thought.

"Well, I can't wait until you and Luca finally admit your feelings to one another, so we can be done with all this fake dating crap." I turned to Lily, slightly shocked at the comment that had come out of her mouth. I had never considered myself an open book, but time and time again, I felt as though Lily knew my thoughts and feelings better than I knew them myself.

"Keep your hopes and dreams to yourself, please," Henri teased, rolling his eyes at my teammate.

"Come on.... Have you met your sister? She's no actress!" Lily yelled at Henri. She paused for a moment before turning to me, a sheepish look on her face. "No offense, of course."

"Offense taken. Now, finish up your coffee. We only have a couple of hours before we have to go, and I know how long it takes you to pack."

"Ugh, whatever, Mum," Lily mumbled, getting up from the couch and heading to my guest room. I had no doubt that in thirty-six hours Lily had completely unpacked her entire suitcase, and it would take her an hour just to repack it.

I took my own advice and headed to my room to pack for Austria. Once packed, I pulled out my phone, shooting off a text to Edward and Oliver.

> Georgia: Sorry this is so late... I have been a bit overwhelmed, as you can imagine, but I wanted to say thank you – sincerely from the bottom of my heart. You didn't have to post those photos or messages on social media. Words can't express how thankful I am.

> Edward: No need to thank us, Love. I meant every word. ;-)

> Oliver: Second that. We're here for you, Georgie.

I smiled as I read the texts, and I sent the same thank you to Eric, Noah, Éliott, and Oscar – all of whom had posted hilarious Instagram photos of me and Luca together. The fact that they had rallied together around us made my heart swell more than words could describe.

I was utterly speechless to the point of tears. Not too long after sending the text to Eric, I saw a response from him sitting in my inbox.

> Eric: Of course, Georgie. What they wrote was unfair. Your relationship with Luca is no one's business.

> Eric: But do you mind if I offer you some unsolicited advice?

> Georgia: Always welcome from you <3

> Eric: Don't be afraid to let yourself be happy. Not even Oscar winners can fake the way Luca looks at you. The change I've seen in Luca over the first half of the season has been tremendous. You did that – don't let another woman reap those rewards.

I read Eric's text over and over again, contemplating what to say in response. In my heart, I knew Eric was right, but my head told me to avoid and deflect.

> Georgia: Not you, too, Eric. It seems as if everyone is team Luca and Georgia these days.

> Eric: With each passing day, it becomes an easier team to support. ;-)

Once Lily, Henri, Noah, and I had boarded the airplane in Monaco, I sent Luca a text confirming the hotel and his check-in time.

> Luca: See you tonight – don't eat all of the free hotel snacks like last time.

> Georgia: Surely you've learned that telling me what to do... makes me want to do the opposite.

> Luca: Unless we're in the bedroom, of course

I could feel my cheeks flush as I read Luca's message, a flash-back to our night after my Silverstone win crossing my mind. I was slightly embarrassed that it had only been a few days, and already I was craving Luca's touch.

"Something got you all hot and bothered over there?" Noah asked, a knowing look in his eyes.

"Don't be nosy, Noah."

"I've been accused of many things, Sassy Dubois, but never nosy."

I rolled my eyes and turned away, trying to hide my smile. The more I got to know Noah, the more I realized he and Oliver were the nosiest duo in the paddock, made only worse by Noah's budding friendship with Edward, someone equally as nosy as Oliver. That trio was a menace to society as far as I was concerned, but I loved them dearly.

Our flight began to descend, and I put away everything but my phone, preparing for landing. As I aimlessly scrolled through my social media page, I came across the Daily Report link. Everything within me told me not to open it, to listen to Lizzie's advice.

Lizzie's words echoed in the back of my mind. *'Remember Georgie, curiosity killed the cat.'*

But I wasn't a house cat. I was a lioness.

The Daily Report

Are Georgia Dubois and Luca Rossi actually dating... or is this a scam cooked up by their PR teams?

The Daily Report can exclusively report that the relationship between Luca and Georgia is, in fact, fake – a PR stunt set up to help boost their driver's ratings with fans. According to the insider, Georgia is using Luca's fame and money to get recognition inside the F1 community.

Luca, on the other hand, is trying to downplay that playboy image he's cultivated so well, but our insider has knowledge that Luca has been seeing multiple women on the side. According to our source, Georgia did the same thing during her Indy Car days when she dated NASCAR star Anthony Smith, but this time, Valkyrie F1 hasn't been able to cover up her blatant use of men to push herself to the top.

"It's really a shame because the F1 community believed that they were finally getting a female driver that deserved to be in this sport, not one that slept their way into it," the insider told us.

As part of the agreement, Luca has allegedly been letting Georgia easily pass on the race track so she can secure as many wins as possible.

"We all want a female driver, but not if it's done by cheating."

What will the FIA do about this incident? Check back for more updates.

By the time I finished the article, I was gripping my phone so tightly that Henri and Lily had an alarmed look on their faces.

"Peaches, everything alright?" Henri asked, reaching out to grab my hands.

"These journalists... I'm done with them. *All of them.* They're going to rue the day they decided to mess with Georgia Dubois."

Chapter Twenty-One

CAT GOT YOUR TONGUE?

Georgia

As soon as the plane touched down, I made a beeline for the entrance. I felt filthy after reading that article, and I needed to get off the plane and into the fresh air. Fortunately, our VIP car was already waiting for us, and the luggage was loaded quickly into the SUV.

"You shouldn't have read the article, Peaches," Henri said softly, his face laced with concern.

"Geez... Georgia, why?" Noah just sighed in frustration, shaking his head in disappointment. "They don't deserve your time."

"Have you read it?" I shot back. Obviously, they both had. Hell, I knew they *all* had. I was the only one sitting in the dark about the horrific things the journalists were saying about me, both in this article and on social media. And the comments on the article? Full of sexist pigs agreeing with the journalist. Noah said nothing in return, averting his eyes to the window, a look of uneasiness on his face.

"Why did no one tell me it was *that bad*?"

"It's not *that bad*," Henri interjected.

"They fucking accused me of sleeping my way into Formula 1.

What could be worse than that? And the part about Luca letting me pass? I mean, come on, Luca has only qualified ahead of me twice this season, and I passed him on skill alone. I won my races fair and square." Henri went to interject, but I stopped him, putting my hand up to signal that I wasn't finished.

"And for them to bring in Indy Car. It's fucking ridiculous. I earned that spot. No one let me pass! And the comment about me dating Anthony for his fame? Get real, that man was a loser.

I'm going to be this year's Formula 1 Champion, and no one, not even a journalist, can take that away from me." I knew at this point I was ranting, but I couldn't stop myself. The three of them just sat there, letting me go on my schtick, knowing full well there was no point in stopping me. I felt the tears I had been holding back for the last several days finally stream down my face, like a river whose dam had just been opened.

Henri grabbed my hand and gave me a sympathetic look. "Feel better?"

"No..." I said meekly. "Well... a little."

"When we get back to the hotel, why don't we go up to your room and have a cup of coffee, hmm?" I nodded at my brother; I was truly thankful for his company. I knew I often took it for granted that my family was able to travel around with me so easily. With Henri being a fellow driver, we were able to spend most weekends together.

The car soon arrived at the hotel, and Noah gave me a hug and said his goodbyes. Lizzie, my media manager, met Lily and me downstairs. As I approached her, Lizzie gave me a sympathetic hug and handed me my key. She had the foresight to check me in so I wouldn't have to survive the check-in desk, which was surrounded by fans at this point. Lily's room was right next door to mine this time, so the four of us made our way to the tenth floor.

When I got to my room, I opened the door and let out a loud gasp, causing both Lizzie and Lily to turn around and rush into my room. The sight in front of me could only be described as a botanical garden. The room was covered in flowers – lilies, daisies, roses – all of my favorite flowers were scattered around the room.

"Oh. My. God." Lily gasped, running into the room and spinning around in constant circles so she could observe all of the flowers. They were everywhere – on the desk, the bed, the bedside tables, in the bathroom. Not a counter was left untouched by flowers. As I turned to look at the coffee table, I saw a gift basket that had been wrapped up in cellophane with a blue bow at the top. A note was attached to the basket with my name on it.

"OPEN IT! OPEN IT! OPEN IT!" Lily and Lizzie chanted together, both of them jumping up and down like a child on Christmas Day. Even Henri had a huge smile on his face. I took the beautiful card out of the envelope, reading the note aloud.

> "My Dearest Georgia –
> Sorry I can't be here to meet you. I was pulled into a quick Helios Sunglasses photoshoot. I'll be back later for our dinner with Henri, Oliver, and Edward. I hope the items in this basket help focus you on the race this weekend.
>
> Also, yes, the bow is blue because I know blue is actually your favorite color – you just didn't want to say it on that first date in Miami because it's the same color as your car. Nothing gets past Luca Rossi ;-)
>
> P.S. I will be expecting coffee from these beans tomorrow morning.
>
> P.S.S. Please wear the items in the gold tissue paper on Sunday to celebrate my race win. Under your racing suit is preferable. ;-)
> Your Luca, xoxo"

I read the words aloud to the girls, blushing at his last sentence. *What had Luca gotten me?*

"Why am I going to cry? That is so sweet!" I heard Lily wail. Both Lily and Lizzie scooted over as I began to open the gift basket.

"Did you tell Luca my *actual* favorite color was blue?" I accused Henri. He just shrugged, but the grin on his face told me he had spilled the beans.

"I didn't realize you were so petty you decided to lie about your favorite color on your first date," Henri quipped in response. I scoffed at that – my brother knew exactly how petty I was.

The first item I pulled out was a bag of coffee beans from my favorite coffee shop in Denver, the one Eric and Oliver always took me to when I visited them in America. How Luca had managed to get these over in time, I would never know. Henri immediately took the bag of beans and walked over to the coffee maker, as if he had expected the coffee beans to be in the bag, waiting in my room. It confirmed that Henri was in part responsible for this craziness, and my heart warmed.

When had Henri become so sneaky? I thought to myself.

I continued to pull out several other items – bath bombs and bubble bath supplies, a bottle of perfume from my favorite brand, chocolates from a chocolatier in Paris, some nice lotion, and several other snacks that I loved. The second to last item inside was an Aphrodite's box, which I pulled out in awe. Had Luca gotten me more jewelry?

I opened the box to reveal a beautiful silver charm bracelet that had three charms on it – a lightning bolt, a Formula 1 car with a blue diamond, and a small crown with three spires on top. I was in shock, completely speechless, as I pulled out the bracelet, as were Lily and Lizzie, who just stared at it in my hands.

"Oh my god, he's *definitely* in love with you. Edward was right," Lily gasped, finally breaking the silence in the room.

"Lily!" I scolded, putting the bracelet back into the box. "Luca is not in love with me... and Edward is an idiot," I hissed.

"I sort of have to agree with Lil on this one, Georgie. You don't make a uniquely personal charm bracelet for someone you *aren't* in love with." Lizzie was staring at the bracelet intently, eyeing the beautiful charms dangling from the silver clasps.

"Luca just likes to give extravagant gifts, plus I'm sure Aphrodite's Jewelry would like me to wear it for a promotion," I reasoned, although I could see that the two of them were never going to agree with me. "I mean, look at this lightning bolt necklace he gave me weeks ago."

"So, what you're saying is... he's been in love with you for a while then," Lily chuckled.

I heard a scoff from Henri over in the little kitchenette area. He wasn't as amused as Lily and Lizzie were, although his lack of words left me slightly on edge.

"You're both ridiculous," I concluded as I pulled the last gift out of the gift basket, the item Luca had mentioned that was wrapped in gold tissue paper. I opened the wrapping and pulled out a beautiful purple lingerie set. As soon as I took it out, I dropped it on the coffee table in shock, a little embarrassed that I had opened it in front of my media manager and brother. Lizzie's face had also gone bright red, although she was also sporting a huge grin.

"I *knew* you guys were having sex," Lily mused, picking up the lingerie as she wiggled her eyebrows suggestively. I grabbed it out of her hand, quickly wrapping it back up in the tissue paper.

The words *"of course we aren't"* almost left my mouth, but at this point, there was no denying it – it was the paddock's worst-kept secret, well, except for our fake relationship, apparently.

"I'm going to kill that man," I mumbled. "...after my bubble bath."

"Not if I kill him first," Henri said with a glare, awkwardly staring at the lingerie set on the coffee table. I could see from the look in his eye that if Henri was in on this little gift package, he certainly wasn't in on *that* gift.

"I suppose this is the moment I should remind you that you need to wear your fireproof underwear on Sunday." Lizzie said the words with a laugh, although I could tell she was slightly worried I would actually take Luca up on his offer.

Before I could stop myself, I blurted out, "No need to remind me, Lizzie. I won't need to wear it since Luca won't be winning the race, I will."

"So, let me get this straight," Lily began, ignoring the annoyed look I gave her, "He buys you jewelry and lingerie, takes you on vacation, buys you dinner, and watches late-night movies with you... and you're having sex. How is this not *actually* dating?"

"Because dating requires feelings, Lily," I said sarcastically.

"Well then, I guess it's a good thing he's *in love* with you!" she quipped back, and I could sense a hint of frustration in her tone.

"Don't you two have somewhere to be?" Henri snapped, waving his hands at both Lily and Lizzie in annoyance.

"Oh, get off your high horse, Henri," Lily said, a mouth full of chocolate truffles. "You're just mad that your sister is dating your teammate, aka, the most handsome driver on the grid." Lily just smirked at my brother, fully aware that she was getting on Henri's nerves.

Before Henri could squeeze in a snarky comment, I heard the front door of my hotel suite open. In walked Luca and Matteo. The two of them didn't notice us at first, chatting away about the photo shoot, which, by the look on Matteo's face, had gone very well. I cleared my throat, and the two men looked up at me. As soon as Luca saw me, a huge smile grew on his face, and he shuffled over to me, giving me a warm hug.

"I see you opened your gift basket. Did you like it?"

"Oh, she loved it!" Lily yelled out behind Luca, her mouth full of a Lindt chocolate she had stolen from the basket of goodies.

"It was very nice, thank you. You really shouldn't have," I said, walking over to the basket and pulling out the gold tissue paper. I waved it in the air, rolling my eyes at Luca.

"Yeah, Luca, you really shouldn't have," Henri said sternly, looking directly into his teammate's eyes. I could see Luca blush a bit. He definitely had not been expecting Henri to be here when I opened *that* gift.

"I helped pick that one out!" Matteo yelled proudly, not actually looking at what I was holding in the air. Lizzie, Lily, and I looked at Matteo, a shocked look on our faces.

"No, mate, you didn't help pick out *that one*," Luca chuckled; his face looked slightly embarrassed now.

"Is that not the..."

"No." Luca gave Matteo a look that told him to stop speaking. "Trust me, I picked out this one *all* by myself," he added with a wink.

"Well, this has been lovely," Lily finally said, breaking the awkward silence that had fallen between us. "Thanks for the chocolates, Luca. And Georgia, I hope you enjoy *all* of your gifts," she added as she wiggled her shoulders like a mom who had just gotten a saucy piece of gossip. Lizzie said her goodbye as well and left the hotel room with Matteo shortly in tow, running after Lizzie, likely to discuss a few more ideas they had to quell the newest story.

"Your coffee is ready, Peaches," Henri said, handing me the cup of coffee he had brewed with the Denver beans. He poured his coffee into a to go cup and made his way to the door.

"You not going to stay?" I asked. Henri only grinned in response, a devilish gleam in his eyes.

"I can tell when I'm not wanted." He shut the door after that, but I could hear a small laugh from him as he walked down the hallway, very amused with himself. As the group left our room, I turned to Luca, who had just shoved a chocolate as brown as his eyes into his mouth.

"So... *did* you like the item wrapped in the gold tissue paper?" I could see the smirk on his face as my cheeks turned a little red, a blush creeping on my face.

"You'll just have to wait and find out."

"You saying I can't get a sneak preview today?"

"Nope," I said with a slight pop of the "p" at the end. I gave

Luca a pointed Cheshire cat grin, and I grabbed the gold issue paper before heading off into my room.

Oliver and Edward had organized a small dinner for Henri, Luca, Éliott, and me at a local restaurant that they knew wouldn't be too mobbed with tourists – or journalists. I put on a blue summer dress with white sandals. As I looked at my jewelry collection, I pulled out the Aphrodite's bracelet that Luca had given me today. It *was* incredibly beautiful, a very thoughtful gift.

The detail in the charms were incredible. The car was etched to look exactly like the Valkyrie F1 car. I was amazed that Aphrodite's Jewelry had spent the time to craft this for me, especially since they hadn't asked me to wear it to any of this weekend's events yet. Seemed like a lot of work to have no guaranteed reward. Still, it was so beautiful, it wasn't a hard ask to wear it.

As I walked out into the living room, I saw Luca's eyes stare at the bracelet, and he smiled but said nothing, grabbing my hand and motioning for us to head to the elevator on our floor. I closed my eyes as I waited for the elevator to arrive, issuing a silent prayer to whatever God was listening, begging for it to be empty. For some reason, these hotel elevators seemed to get busier and busier as the season went on.

Luca and I stepped inside the elevator and smiled at the guests inside, huddling together in the corner. The elevator stopped on the next floor, and much to my surprise, in walked Sara, the Maison de Klotho executive who we had met all those weeks ago. She smiled at me and Luca.

"Going to smash it this weekend, Georgia?" Sara asked. If she meant 'smash the journalists,' then her answer was yes.

"As if she knows how to do anything else," Luca quipped, earning a laugh from a few different people in the elevator.

"That Aphrodite's bracelet is just lovely, Georgia," Sara said, observing the bracelet around my wrist. "I've never seen charms like that." Sara's comment took me a bit by surprise, but then again, Maison de Klotho merely owned Aphrodite's Jewelry. Sara didn't actually work at Aphrodite's, nor was she the coordinator who likely helped Luca pick out the charms.

"Luca has exquisite taste."

"In both women and jewelry." Sara gave us both a warm smile as the elevator reached the bottom floor. "Looking forward to seeing you both this weekend!"

Luca and I made our exit and headed towards the front of the hotel, where Henri and Éliott were waiting for us. The four of us piled into the car and headed to the restaurant, where Oliver and Edward were already seated and waiting.

"Hey! Look what the cat dragged in!" Oliver called out as he walked over to me, giving me one of his signature hugs. We all took a seat at the table as Oliver poured us some glasses of wine from the bottle he and Edward had already ordered.

"Good to see Luca has convinced you to stop this pre-race, no-drinking tradition," Edward said with a laugh, clinking his glass with mine.

"Well, it seems to be working out for me so far," I teased back. To be fair, the stress of this season had been immense, and a glass of wine had helped me wind down a bit.

"So, Georgia, I see we'll be in the press conference together tomorrow." I turned to Éliott and saw a little hint of mischief in his eyes as he said the words.

"Well, make sure to bring your shield. Georgia is out for blood," Henri quipped.

"Don't be silly, Henri. I'll be as cordial as I always am." Henri actually choked on his wine at my comment, and I gave him an annoyed look.

"You're many things, Peaches.... cordial to journalists? Probably doesn't make the cut."

"Whatever," I mumbled under my breath. They could tease me, but I had a plan. Kill them with kindness, as my mother would say.

As we finished up dessert, Luca excused himself to the

restroom, and Edward took the opportunity to hop into Luca's seat, grabbing my wrist so he could take a better look at the bracelet.

"Wow, Luca did an amazing job with the design."

"Well, I'm sure the Aphrodite's sponsorship team gave him a few pointers," I joked, but Edward just looked up at me with a serious expression, one I wasn't used to seeing from the Brit.

"Luca did this all by himself." I felt a rush of warmth go through me, and butterflies began to fill my stomach. *Had Luca actually designed this all by himself?*

"I mean, I'm sure he helped, but Aphrodite's sponsor both of us-" Edward cut me off before I could finish my sentence.

"Georgia... Luca designed these charms by himself and ordered the bracelet without any knowledge from the sponsorship team." Edward's voice sounded a bit frustrated, and his face was incredibly smug.

I didn't know what to say.

"Wh-Why?" I finally muttered out.

"That's for you to ask him." Edward put my wrist down and hopped back into his chair, rejoining the conversation with the rest of the group. As soon as Luca came back from the restroom, we got up from the table and made our way outside of the restaurant.

"Want to walk back to the hotel?" I asked Luca, who nodded in response. I said goodbye to the rest of the group, and Luca and I set off on the twenty-minute walk back to the hotel.

"So... Edward, let your secret out," I teased.

"Edward lets everyone's secrets out. Which one did he spill this time?"

"He, umm, told me that you made the Aphrodite's Jewelry bracelet yourself."

"Do you like it?" I could see a hint of worry in Luca's eyes; it was clear he was unsure of himself and the gift.

"I love it," I responded honestly, looking up and meeting his gaze.

I stopped the two of us, and I took both of his hands in mine as

I stood up on my tippy toes, giving Luca a gentle kiss on the lips. "It's one of the nicest gifts anyone's given me."

Some more silence passed between us, and I finally gained the courage to ask the question I had been wanting to ask. "Why didn't you tell me?"

"Because I didn't want you to think you had to wear it. I wanted you to wear it because you thought it was beautiful." The look on Luca's face was the most genuine expression I think I had ever seen from the Italian.

"Well, I'll wear it when I'm beating you on Sunday then." The sound of Luca's laughter was like music to my ears. I loved seeing Luca laugh – loved the way he threw his head back, the way his brown eyes sparkled. His body language was soft and genuine. It was a different Luca than the one I was used to seeing in the paddock. With this experience, I truly got to see a different side of the Italian driver.

When we approached the hotel, we could see a crowd of people at the front. Henri and Éliott were standing just inside the lobby, signing autographs. When Henri spotted me at the back, he gave me an apologetic look. The crowd looked behind them and started cheering for Luca and me to come forward, most of them begging for autographs and pictures. As Luca and I pushed into the hotel, we took a few selfies and signed a few hats.

Just as I felt like the coast was clear, I heard someone yell at us, "Feeling guilty yet for taking a spot from a driver who *deserves* to be here?" I froze as I heard the taunting words, knowing that they were for me. I could see Luca and Henri looking around, trying to spot the man who had said them, but Éliott had beat them to it.

"Come over here and say it to her face!" Éliott called out, causing the crowd to go silent as the French driver made eye contact with the guy who had yelled the rude comment. He motioned for the guy to come forward, and I could see everyone take out their cell phones, ready to film the situation unfolding in front of them.

Éliott pulled me forward, but Luca grabbed my hand and pulled me back to him. Éliott didn't let go, and he pulled me towards the man as he stood behind me.

"Go on..." Éliott said to the man who was now standing in front of me. "Say it to her face." The man was frozen in front of me, and I could tell he was not expecting Éliott, a male driver, to call him out like that. I suppose he figured he would be able to yell it from the back of the crowd, going completely unnoticed. After a few moments of the man saying nothing, I finally found my own voice.

"Cat got your tongue?" I mocked, standing a little straighter as I could feel my confidence surge. Out of the corner of my eye, I saw Luca, Henri, and Éliott smirking, the three of them looking very amused.

"I read what I read – why would they lie?" the guy finally spit out.

"Because cash is king, Darling," I said coolly, "and they know they can con people like you into buying their trash." When the guy finally started to back away, muttering to himself, I just shook my head in disbelief, turning back to the group.

"Let this be a lesson to all who dare mess with the lioness," Éliott announced.

The group of fans around us started to dissipate after a few more autographs, and Luca and I started to head to the elevator. When the doors opened, I felt small hands pull at my dress from behind me.

"Excuse me!" A voice yelled, and I turned around to see a little girl waving at me. I knelt down next to her and smiled as she handed over her hat for a signature.

"Georgia is her favorite driver," I heard her mother say to Luca.

"Mine too," Luca whispered as I finished signing the little girl's hat.

Henri had texted me Wednesday morning to let me know that Georgia had read the article while they were on the flight. Truthfully, I was surprised that she had waited that long, but I suspected that she felt like I did – reading the paper would make this seem all too real.

I knew I wanted to do something nice for Georgia, something to make her feel special. I had already purchased the Aphrodite's Jewelry bracelet. It was going to be my gift for her at the end of the season, but seeing how beaten down she looked in that Valkyrie conference room on Tuesday, I just couldn't bring myself to wait, so instead, I purchased some extra items and stuffed them into a gift basket, hoping that it would bring a smile to her face. Seeing Georgia wear the bracelet made my heart melt.

Seeing her happy made me want her even more.

Thursday, Georgia and I arrived on track several hours before our scheduled press conference. We were to meet the FIA and Formula 1 board along with our team principals. We knew the FIA wanted some explanation for the article before we went into the weekend. The consultant Isabelle had hired to help solve this mess had advised us on what to say, although I felt as though there probably wasn't anything we could do to properly prep for this.

Georgia and I arrived at the conference room last, hand in hand, as instructed by Elizabeth. I could see the nerves on Georgia's face, and I wanted nothing more than to soothe her worries and tell her that everything would be okay, but I knew I couldn't do that.

Truth was, I didn't know if everything *would* be okay.

"Good morning, Luca and Georgia. Please, take a seat." Giovanni Bruno was a staunch Italian man with thick-rimmed black glasses. He had a frown on his face, although Isabelle told me he was always like that. At first, I was pleased that Giovanni used to be the Hermes team principal and hoped that his history with Hermes would give us some clout, but from what Henri had told me, due to the team's recent lack of success, Francesco, the current Hermes team principal, and Giovanni were a bit at odds.

Great.

After we took our seats, Giovanni continued, "So, in recent light of this mess from the Daily Report, we wanted to touch base with the teams to make sure we are all on the same page." There was a pause in his voice, but no one said anything. "To be clear, the FIA does not condone faking relationships so you can get more sponsors."

"Good, neither does Hermes." Francesco quipped, a scoff in his voice, which earned him a look of disdain from Isabelle, clearly telling her husband to leave the attitude behind.

"What do you want, Giovanni?" Isabelle finally asked after a brief pause. "The Daily Report is a trash newspaper that wrote a trash story to sell their trash magazines. You know that. We know that. Hell, I think even The Daily Report knows it. Now, you've called us into this office for a *good* reason, I assume?"

"The FIA just wants to make sure that everything between these two teams is above board." It was clear from Giovanni's voice that he didn't want to directly give us a telling off, but his tone was certainly insinuating one.

"The only thing going on here, Giovanni, is the FIA getting in the way of precious time I have with my driver to help her prepare for this upcoming race," Isabelle said dryly, giving Giovanni a stern look that told him she had no intention of backing down.

"Fine. I want to hear it from the drivers, then you can go." Giovanni turned to look at Georgia and me, expecting us to say something. I could hear Georgia's breath quicken, her nerves were starting to get the best of her.

"There's nothing to tell. I'm with Georgia because I want to be, plain and simple. I like spending my days with her, and I want to continue doing so," I said finally, flashing Georgia a warm smile as I silently encouraged her to share her piece.

"I wish I could say this was one of my elaborate pranks, Giovanni," Georgia said finally, "but it's not. We're just a couple of kids in our twenties racing cars and falling in love. People accuse us of using each other for PR, but how is it different than a driver dating a model and doing PR shoots with them? Luca and I like spending time together. If we want to do some photoshoots together, then so be it. Other drivers do photo gigs with their significant others all the time."

I could see Giovanni pondering our words, and he nodded in response to Georgia's comment, standing up from his seat at the conference room table.

"Fine. But please, do us a favor and don't stir the pot with this, hmm?" Giovanni paused for a moment before turning back towards us.

"Oh, and one more thing, that comment the article made on Luca letting Georgia pass – if we ever find that out to be true, I'll have both of you off this grid."

"That would require the rest of the grid to be able to qualify ahead of me," Georgia retorted, earning an approving smirk from Isabelle.

That's the Georgia I know and love.

Giovanni scoffed at that, but I saw his facial features soften ever so slightly. Our point had been made.

Georgia: 1 FIA: 0

I let out a huge sigh of relief as Giovanni left the conference room. Georgia looked a little more lively, although I could see she was still a bit shaken from the conversation. I grabbed her hand and pulled her into me before whispering softly, "It'll be okay."

And this time, when I said it, I knew it would be true.

Chapter Twenty-Two

SUMMER BREAK - 2019: GEORGIA

Georgia: Summer Break 2019

"Hey, Georgie, Henri said you'll be in town for the next three weeks. Can't wait to see you during summer break." I smiled into the phone as I heard Éliott's voice on the other line.

"Yeah, got in yesterday. Can't wait. It'll be so nice to catch up."

"You got any plans tonight?"

"Yeah, dinner with a friend," I lied, a pang of guilt hitting my chest. After Éliott and I tested the waters of a relationship, we decided to remain friends. Truthfully, he had become one of my closest friends and confidants, and for that, I was extremely appreciative, but telling Éliott that I had a date with a certain Italian Wilmington F1 driver felt odd. Luca had gotten himself a bit of a reputation.

"Nice! Enjoy that. Right, well, gotta be off, but see you soon!"

After Éliott and I hung up, I hurriedly finished getting ready before calling a cab to the restaurant Luca and I were meant to meet at. He was coming straight from an afternoon event, so I had agreed to meet him there at 8 p.m. I had arrived a few minutes late, but fortunately, Luca wasn't there yet.

At 8:15, I pulled out my phone to check my messages since Luca was now fifteen minutes late to our date. I shot him a quick text, asking if everything was alright. When 8:30 rolled around, I decided to check his social media to see if I could possibly reach him there.

And that's when I saw it, the pink highlight around his profile photo, signaling that there had been a new live story. As soon as I pressed it, I realized one thing – Luca Rossi had stood me up. My heart dropped when I saw the photo. I tried to stop the small tear from escaping my eye, but it was fruitless. Not even five minutes ago, Luca had posted a photo of him with Edward and Noah hanging out, the three of them at a restaurant drinking cocktails, various women in the background of the photo, likely with their party.

As I went to Edward's Instagram, I saw he had also updated his social media with a photo of him and Noah, but the background showed Luca sitting next to someone absolutely stunning. His hand was on her thigh, and he looked engrossed in their conversation.

The waitress came back to the table, and I quietly excused myself, telling her they could re-seat the table and that my 'friend' had to cancel. I suspected that she knew I had been stood up, but she just nodded gracefully and gave me a soft smile as I exited the restaurant. I pulled out my phone and immediately called Éliott.

"Twice in one day. What did I do to be so lucky?" he joked over the phone, but his laugh was immediately stopped when he heard my sniffles on the other end.

"I lied to you... I had a date tonight."

"Had? What happened?"

"He stood me up."

"Oh, Mon Cherie, that's awful. Who the fuck was this guy?" I knew I had to tell him who it was now, but I also knew that telling him would likely mean ending the friendship between Éliott and Luca.

"Luca..."

"Luc-" Éliott paused, clearly trying to piece together what I was saying. "Luca Rossi?"

"Yes."

"I'll fucking kill him," Éliott said quietly. "Are you sure he stood you up? I know Wilmington had an event today."

"I saw his live story. He's with Edward and Noah getting drinks."

"Absolute prick. Georgie, I didn't know he had asked you out. Does Henri know?"

"No... and you can't tell him," I added quickly. "I feel like such an idiot, Éliott. Why on earth would one of the most handsome guys on the grid want to date me?"

"Hey – I'm *the* most handsome guy on the grid, and I wanted to date you," Éliott said, trying to lighten the mood of the conversation.

"Thanks for reminding me about our failed relationship. Really know how to cheer a girl up," I huffed, earning me an awkward chuckle from the Frenchmen.

"Look, Georgie, I hate to sound cliché here, but it genuinely is his loss. Luca Rossi is a playboy and an obnoxious moron, and until he learns how to grow up, he isn't worth your time."

"I just... I thought he liked me. I feel like an idiot."

"The only idiot here is Luca. You're too good for him, Georgie, and one day he's going to look back and regret his decision. Guarantee it."

"Thanks, Éliott." My sniffling had settled down by the time I reached Henri's flat. "I'm gonna go eat a pint of ice cream and watch Atonement."

"I'll see you soon. We'll drink so much on vacation you won't even remember who Luca Rossi is!"

"Sounds like a plan. Thanks again. Talk later." As soon as I hung up, I fulfilled my promise to Éliott. I got into my pajamas and crawled into bed with a pint of ice cream, doing whatever I could to ignore my aching heart.

Chapter Twenty-Three

FROM GEORGIA, WITH LOVE

Luca

Unfortunately, my parents were not able to make the Austria Grand Prix. My dad was preparing for one of his own races, and my mother had decided to go with him, but we still kept our traditional morning FaceTime call between the three of us. Georgia was down in the lobby having breakfast with Henri, so it was just me chatting with my parents, which was good because I had something I wanted to talk to them about.

As the conversation was starting to come to a close, my mother noticed my hesitancy to hang up.

"Flash, you look like you have something else to discuss?"

"I just..." I paused for a moment, trying to contemplate how to phrase what I wanted to say to my parents. "How did you know Dad was it for you?" My mother chuckled, looking over to my father, who had started to get ready for his day in the background.

"It was a nice day outside, and your father asked if I wanted to go on a walk. When I met him downstairs, I saw that he had two cups of coffee with him. I took a sip of the coffee, and I immediately recognized that the coffee was from my favorite little shop in town. Your father had gone out of his way to get me my favorite cup of coffee for the walk. He even put the right amount of sugar and cream in it, just how I liked it. I didn't think that your father noticed the small stuff like that. It was such a small gesture, but it truly warmed my heart and made me realize how much I loved him... Why do you ask?"

"I have this feeling that I can't shake. When I look at Georgia, I just can't explain it."

"Oh, Luca, I think you know exactly what that feeling is." My mother was right. I knew what the feeling was. It was *love*.

"You need to tell her, Flash. Tell her how you feel because if you don't, it'll eat you up inside. Georgia is a special girl, and someone that special won't wait around forever. But she also needs commitment from you. She needs to know you're serious about her."

"I am serious, mamma." I could see she was pleased with my unspoken decision.

"I see the way you two are when you're together. Even before this relationship, I felt like Georgia was someone special. Go get your girl, Luca."

"I will... I will."

"That's my boy. We'll chat afterward. Good luck!" I hung up the phone with my parents and smiled gratefully. Today was the day I was going to tell Georgia Dubois that I loved her.

Georgia

I knew the press conference was going to be brutal, especially since the video of Éliott forcing that man to talk to me had gone viral. The entire paddock was talking about the interaction, and if you hadn't read the article already, you had now. Lizzie was somewhat furious because it put us back in the forefront of everyone's minds, but I didn't care.

Éliott was right. I loved facing my critics because it felt empowering. I wasn't scared of the fans or the journalists. *I was a lioness.*

The FIA had decided to switch Luca out of my morning press conference, putting him in the session with Edward instead. I suppose the FIA had decided that the press of Luca and I's relationship was dampening the *actual* press of the race, and I was quickly learning that old European men didn't like to be overshadowed, especially not by a female driver.

I was the last to walk into the press room, and I saw Éliott, Eric, Otto, and Oliver all give me a big smile as if on cue. Their coordination was impressive, and I laughed at them, taking the last open seat, which, of course, was in the middle. *Bastards had done that on purpose.*

"Right, we're going to get started with this morning's first press conference. Welcome to all the drivers. We're looking forward to a great race here in Austria."

The beginning of the press conference always consisted of Michael Clifton asking questions to the group of us drivers before he turned it over to the ravenous journalists. As soon it was their turn, I saw a flood of hands in the air, all yelling to get the attention of the mediator.

"Hi, this is Marcus from Sports Broadcasting. Georgia, we heard you and Luca were brought into the FIA offices this morning. Anything to report on that?" I was told that the meeting was private, but I guess I shouldn't have been surprised that the news had spread like wildfire.

"Marcus, I think you know I can't comment on private FIA meetings," I scoffed in disbelief.

"Well, reports say that the FIA is investigating you and Luca for a fake relationship. No truth to that?" I gave him an incredulous look. I expected this from tabloids but not from Sports Broadcasting, a company that had become the crown of British sports reporting.

"If you have reports, then sounds like you don't need my input."

"So, are you denying it?"

"I'm denying that it's any of your business." Lizzie was now waving at me in the background, motioning for me to end the conversation, but I ignored her wild waving.

"In fact, I'm denying the whole *fucking* thing. If you all think you know me so well, well enough to write articles before you even speaking to me, then why do you bother asking me these questions, hmm?" I could tell Marcus was a little deterred, but his next comment let me know he wasn't deterred enough.

"I'm asking because a serious allegation has been brought against you, and you have yet to say anything about it. Instead, all you've done is ask your driver friends to post little photos of the two of you."

"That's enough!" I heard a voice yell beside me. I turned and looked at Eric, who was now standing up with the microphone in his hand. "If you have proof that the FIA have accused Georgia and Luca of something, then bring it up with the FIA. Drivers press conferences are for us *drivers* to answer questions for the fans – you know, the people we race for."

"Don't you think the fans want to know if Georgia Dubois actually deserves to be in Formula 1," Marcus taunted.

"Not as much as the fans want to know why Sports Broadcasting hired such a lunatic to do their press interviews." I knew it was a petty thing to say – and frankly, not the best quip, but I was fuming that Marcus, a supposedly reputable journalist, had dared to bring this up during a drivers press conference.

"How about we table this discussion and resume it after Georgia wins the championship at the end of the year?" I turned to see Otto, who was now also standing next to Erin, mic in hand. "I can tell you this: as a 3x world champion, I think I am a good judge of who deserves to be in F1. And Georgia? She deserves to be here. Hell, between Eric and I, we have 9x world championships – if we can't be trusted on this, who can?"

Otto walked over to the journalist. He wasn't that tall of a man, and with his silly mustache, he looked more like an 80s pornstar, but I could see Marcus sit down. Battling two beloved world champions wasn't going to get the fans on board. I nodded my thanks to both Eric and Otto, who retook their seats on either side of me.

The long silence was deafening.

"So... do any of you have the same questions lined up for Luca, or does just Georgia get this treat...?" I smirked at Oliver as I turned to look at him, a huge grin on his face. I could tell he wasn't done stirring the pot.

"Don't be silly, Oliver, Luca's answers wouldn't be nearly as spicy as his love for jalapeños," I quipped, earning me a laugh from the other drivers. "Papers won't sell themselves, hmm?"

"Guess this is why they say newspaper is dying, not even worth wrapping day-old bread in it." Even Michael Clifton let out a laugh at Éliott's comment.

"Well, I think it's safe to say this press conference is over," Michael announced to the group, standing up and leaving the room, shaking his head in disbelief.

As I walked out of the press conference, I could see Lizzie wasn't pleased with me. She didn't have to say the unspoken words. When I got to the garage, I walked straight to Isabelle's office, knowing that I had been summoned. Once I had taken a seat, Isabelle slammed the door shut, a blank expression on her face, but her eyes were dancing with frustration.

"Damn it, Georgia – *why?*" Isabelle lamented.

"Why do they get to treat me like this?" I demanded back. "Why can't I defend myself?"

"Because we're supposed to be burying this story, not giving them *more* reasons to bring it up!" Isabelle was angry, that much was clear. She sat down in her chair in a huff, letting her head rest in her hands as she rubbed her eyes in frustration. A pang of guilt hit me. I'd never seen Isabelle look so defeated before.

"I just.... I just want this to go away for you, Georgia. I get it. You're young and ambitious, and yes, it's unfair that they treat you this way, but we need to learn to control the narrative, not feed into it."

Isabelle's comment reminded me of a conversation we had

several months ago, back before I had started dating Luca. *'Unfortunately, the F1 journalist community isn't going to change overnight, so it's our job to help guide them to that change.'*

Isabelle's words from my first race win ran through my head. She was right. I was better than yelling at a reporter, and yet, something told me she was also wrong here. I had spent the entire season backing down, letting journalists say whatever they wanted, hiding in the shadows so we could get Sponsors, but the more I thought about it, the more it was becoming clear that Sponsors wanted someone *loved* by fans – and to hell with the press. I couldn't pretend to be someone else forever.

"I don't care if this doesn't go away. I don't care if the press keeps up with this for the next ten years. I'm not backing down, Isabelle. I won't let them treat me this way. I won't show little girls who watch me on TV that it's okay to let male journalists attack female athletes like that," I said finally, finding my own voice.

"It doesn't matter that what they're saying is true. This relationship started as a fake one, but that doesn't give them the right to attack *my* racing or who *I* am as a person.

I'm going to win this championship, Isabelle. I'm going to win Sunday's race, and then Singapore, and then I'm going to keep winning until there's no more races to win. You hired me to win, to fight – and that's what I'm doing. I'm not going to back down, and if I lose my race seat for being me, then so be it.

I'll have done it being myself, *Georgia Dubois*, the first female F1 champion – and that's good enough for me."

I got up from my seat and made my way to Isabelle's office door. As I went to open it, I heard a laugh from behind me. I turned to see something that I had never seen before – Isabelle was sitting there, a look full of pride and adoration on her face, with a smile stretched from ear to ear.

"Well, then, Georgie, sounds like we have some work to do."

Race day had finally arrived in Austria. The remaining press conferences and Sponsorship meetings had gone smoothly. I kept my promise of not backing down, but unlike before, the journalists could see that I was ready for them, ready to take them on. I guess the challenge was proving to be too much for them. Isabelle wasn't too pleased with how Thursday's press conference had gone, but fuck it – I didn't care anymore.

Éliott was right. Those journalists hid behind their laptop screens, writing puff pieces about nonsense while we went out every race Sunday, driving dangerous cars for their enjoyment.

If they had something to say about me, they could say it to my face.

My morning race prep had been fairly easy. I wasn't asked to do any more press conferences, so the only thing we had to do was the drivers' parade before the race. As requested, Luca met me at the Valkyrie garage entrance, and we made our way to the holding room, our hands intertwined. When we walked in, I heard a wolf whistle, which, of course, came from Edward and Oliver, who were cheering us on as we walked over to the group of drivers.

"Nice of you two love birds to finally join us." I scoffed at that, taking my water bottle from Lizzie, who had followed us in. She had been strictly instructed to watch me up until the drivers' parade, not wanting another press conference or hotel incident to happen.

"You gonna crucify the sports journalist on the parade truck?" Oliver had a twinkle of hope in his eye. I knew all the drivers got a kick out of Georgia "Sassy" Dubois.

"No, she most certainly is not." Lizzie gave Oliver a death glare, warning the driver off from any more shenanigans. Oliver just gave her a sheepish look, clearly getting the message.

"I did not *crucify* them." Before I could continue defending myself, the rest of the drivers were laughing a little *too* loudly, as if I had just told the biggest joke.

"They ended the press conference early!" Edward laughed.

We boarded the vehicle that had been converted to a parade truck, all of us wearing our brightly colored team polos. Luca kept my hand in his as we went to the back of the area, both of us leaning against the rails. Edward, Oliver, and Oscar followed us, and by the look on Edward's face, he had something he wanted to discuss.

"Edward, you look like a deer in headlights. What's up?"

"So, umm, I just wanted to let you know Anthony is here again." Edward's face looked worried. I knew Luca had filled him in on where the article's information had *actually* come from.

"Does he not actually race in Indy Car? He always seems to be *here*." Luca took off his hat and pushed his hair back, something I noticed he often did when he was frustrated or nervous.

"Apparently, they have a break, and he's up for Wilmington F1 testing again."

"Well, thanks for letting me know, Edward, but honestly, there isn't a lot Anthony can do to us at this point." I gave him a reassuring smile and then looked at Luca, whose face looked a little less convincing. I gave his hand a squeeze before the presenter walked over to us; she looked a little wary of my presence, but I gave the camera a nice smile and did the interview as requested without confrontation.

Apparently, Valkyrie could only handle one press blowout a weekend, or so I was told by the team.

The drivers' parade ended without any fuss, and we departed the bus, making our way back to our respective garages. As Luca dropped me outside the garage entrance, he pulled me into his chest and gave me a peck on the lips, offering me a warm smile as he looked down into my eyes.

I looked around to see if there was any press, but surprisingly, the entrance was empty. Luca and I had kissed in private before, but almost exclusively during sex. Luca had never before kissed me in the paddock when no one else was present, and that realization made those pesky butterflies return. The moment felt so tender and warm, and I realized deep down that I didn't want him to let go.

Did he feel the same as me?

"Good luck, Cara. See you on the podium, eh?"

"I'll be the one on the top step as usual," I retorted back playfully, earning me another kiss on the lips before Luca padded off to the Hermes garage. I stood there for a moment, watching him go before a clearing of a throat caused me to turn around.

"Anthony, why the fuck are you here?" Anthony ignored my statement, instead stepping closer to me as he grabbed my arm forcefully.

"I see you and Luca even keep up the charade when no one is around. Good for you guys. I guess you don't know when an unsuspecting bystander could walk by."

"Judging by how much I've seen of you recently, I'd say you're more of a stalker than a bystander."

"I have better things to do than follow around a liar and a cheater," Anthony quipped. He was dangerously close to me, and I looked around the paddock, hoping someone I knew would notice the two of us.

"That's rich coming from you."

"You think you're so special, don't you," Anthony bit out, his voice venomous. "We both know you slept your way into this. Although I'm not sure what Luca is getting out of it, you're pretty lousy in bed." Anthony grabbed my arm tighter as he pulled me closer to him. I tried to pull away, but his grip was too strong.

"Let go, asshole!"

"I'm going to get a seat in F1, and then I'm going to crucify you since apparently the press aren't doing a good enough job at it." Before I could respond, I heard a deep voice behind me, the Italian accent undeniable.

"I believe the lady said let go." Luca grabbed Anthony by the collar and pulled him in. Anthony let go of my arm at the contact with Luca. Edward was with Luca, trying to block the sight of Luca holding Anthony's collar from the growing crowd.

"Touch her again, and I'll ruin that ugly face of yours," Luca spit out.

"He's not worth it," I whispered the Luca, encouraging him to set Anthony down. I could see Luca debating what to do, the wheels in his head turning. I knew every ounce of him wanted to punch Anthony, but with the crowd getting bigger, Luca put the Indy Car driver down and backed away.

"Edward, take this piece of trash back to Wilmington, eh?" Edward let out a snicker and motioned for Anthony to follow him, not even looking back.

As Anthony walked by, Luca leaned over and whispered to him, "Women aren't lousy in bed if a man knows how to make them scream, and oh boy, is Georgia a screamer." Luca winked at Anthony and patted him on the back as he watched the Indy Car driver run after Edward like a dog with its tail between its legs.

"You okay, Amore? I should have walked you all the way in. I'm sorry." Luca had the cutest apologetic face. His plump lips were giving me the most adorable pout, and his eyes were soft as he observed my face.

"Better now that you're here," I said with a chuckle. "Thanks for that. I really hope Anthony fails that Wilmington F1 test."

"Well, unfortunately for Anthony, money can't buy him talent." I chuckled at Luca's comment, although I knew in my mind that Anthony had enough money to buy him a seat – regardless of talent.

"Georgia!" I saw Mel running towards me, waving her hands. "You plan on racing today or what?"

"Sorry, Mel!" Luca smiled at me and gave me another hug before I ran off, waving back to him.

"See you on the podium, Mon Amour!" I yelled back at him.

'And it's lights out, and away we go!'

As soon as the five lights lit up, I launched my car forward, immediately passing Oscar Parker, who had qualified ahead of me in P4. I was annoyed that I had gotten P5 yesterday, but sadly the car had an issue in qualifying, so I couldn't finish my last flying lap which I knew would have put me on pole.

I made it around the first corner, and I was starting to feel more secure in my position. Oscar had fallen back, leaving only Henri,

Luca, and Noah in front of me. We stayed in this position for the next thirty laps before I was able to pass Noah after a poor pit stop from his team, a rare sight from his garage but one I planned to take advantage of.

"Good news, GG. Keep up the pace. You probably would have passed him anyway," I heard Mel say into the radio.

"Yup."

"Hermes cars are pushing, very good pace. Luca gained half a second."

I didn't need Mel in my ear to tell me that. Luca was in front, and I could see that his pace was just slightly quicker than mine, although I was only two seconds behind him. We settled into this for another twenty laps, Luca and I keeping an annoying two-second gap between us.

"And the press thinks he just lets me pass," I grumbled to myself.

Quite the opposite, I'll never hear the end of it if I can't pass him on my own.

"Lap fifty, only twenty-one to go." Suddenly I started to smell something burning, and I desperately looked around for the source.

"Mel, something is burning."

"Keep driving, it's not you." Her voice was calm, but there was something in it, a small uptake in her pitch that told me she was hiding something. But as I watched Luca's car slide off into the gravel, I saw what she wasn't telling me. The smoke I was smelling was from Luca's car, and it was on fire. I could see Luca navigate it off the track, and in my rearview mirrors I saw the car start to go downhill, the flames getting bigger and bigger.

"Fuck, Mel. It's fucking Luca!" I screamed into the radio.

"Stay calm and keep driving. Yellow flag." Mel's voice was as calm as a morning ocean, almost too calm, like she knew she had to work a little harder to make this not seem as bad as it was.

"I'm going back." I could feel myself start to panic. Images of Luca's car on fire kept circulating through my brain, and it consumed me like the flames were consuming his car. I looked up at the big screens and saw it focused on his car, with no emergency crews in sight.

"Georgia, *do not* under any circumstances go to that car. The marshals don't need to put out two fires." My head knew that Mel was right, but my heart – my heart couldn't *stand* her words.

"I'm not going to leave the man I love in a car that's fucking burning!" I screamed back into the mic.

"Georgia, this is Isabelle. There is a red flag, now. Come into the pits." I could picture how that went down in the garage pit wall, Isabelle grabbing Mel and switching the radio over to her headset.

"Is he out of the car?" I cried out. I could feel tears streaming down my face, glad that I was wearing a visor so no one could see my eyes,

"Not yet." I let out a small sob at Isabelle's words. "I should have gotten out and helped. What if I lose him," I blurted into the radio, my voice cracking. "What if I don't get to tell him how much I love him?"

The words kept tumbling out of me into the radio. In that moment, I didn't care that the entire world could hear me confess for love for Luca. I didn't care about the press, sponsors, or even what the FIA would think. I only cared about seeing Luca again so I could tell him that I loved him.

"He knows, Georgie." Isabelle's voice was always confident on the radio. I had heard her yell at Marshals, FIA officials, and press officers, but I had never heard this kind of confidence come from her voice. She sounded like a pious follower who had nothing but her convictions to show for her dedication.

Neither of us said anything else into the radio, and I made my way to the garage. I refused to get out of my car, instead opting to watch the TV screens up in the garage from the safety of my seat, hoping that with each glance I would see Luca, but I knew that the film crews didn't show accidents like this until they knew the driver was out and safe.

Finally, the camera panned to Luca, and I saw movement around his car. *He had gotten out.*

The screams from the crowd were deafening, and the film crews switched the big screen to show Luca hopping out of the car, running away from his car as quickly as he could.

"Luca is out, GG," I heard Mel say into my radio. "He's safe."

I let out a huge sigh of relief, letting my tense muscles relax. I tried not to watch the accident on the big screens, not able to look at it anymore – the horror would likely stay with me for months, a constant reminder of how dangerous our sport could be. Fortunately, Luca's car was able to be moved very quickly, and after a few more moments, we restarted the race.

My restart had gone well, and I was back into P2. I was so lost in my thoughts, that I almost missed the radio turn-on, an unfamiliar – *and yet familiar* – voice came onto the radio.

"You didn't have to set my car on fire to get P2, Mia Cara. According to the press, I would have let you pass me anyway." The thick Italian voice let out a sarcastic chuckle, and I instantly knew it was Luca.

"Fuck off!" I grinned in response, shaking my head at Luca's comment. "I'll keep that in mind for the next race." I knew no one could see my sly grin, but I didn't care. Luca would get the joke, even if Isabelle and Lizzie wouldn't be too pleased about it.

"Oh, and Cara... I love you, too." My heart leaped at Luca's words. *Lily and Edward were right – Luca did love me.*

And I loved him.

I heard some clatter in the background, along with a distant Mel yelling at Luca to get away from the Valkyrie pit wall.

"Sorry, intruders in our camp," Mel chuckled. "Let's bring this one home."

We had ten laps to go, and all I had to do was take on Henri. I had gotten another incredible start after the red flag, dropping Noah fairly quickly as I chased Henri down the straight, keeping the distance within one second, waiting for DRS to be enabled.

As I approached lap sixty-eight, I was able to take P1 from Henri, only for him to take it back from me. Both our tires had the same amount of laps, so it was down to driver skill to determine which Dubois would take home the victory. This back-and-forth happened a few more times, and we traded places another three times.

As I reached the last lap, I put everything into the car – and pushed it to the limit. I was only .3 of a second behind Henri, the front of my car so close to his I could see the small sponsor stickers on the back of the wing as the checkered flag came into view.

In that moment, I felt something I hadn't felt in a long time in the car – *pure joy*. I felt like Henri and I were back in Monaco, just a couple of kids karting as our parents watched on. The battles between us were intense. Our mother said she always knew we'd be in Formula 1 together.

I saw the checkered flag approach, and I gave one last push before crossing the finish line. A second went by, and there was nothing in my ear, nothing in my radio. I waved to Henri, who waved back with a thumbs up as the two of us drove on, finishing our cool-down laps.

"Wow, GG. What a race. P2! You were 1000th of a second behind Henri. FIA had to review the footage. Incredible racing from the two of you. You gave the fans an excellent race. We couldn't be prouder of you, a well-deserved podium. Lily got P4, a great result."

"Whooo! That felt amazing, just incredible! Congrats to the team and Lily, solid result."

"Go ahead and park... I suspect there's someone waiting to see you," Mel chuckled into the radio before turning it off.

I parked in the P2 spot, and I saw Henri getting out of his car. I immediately jumped out of mine and ran to my brother, giving him a huge hug. As much as I wanted to be the winner, Henri *deserved* this win. He had driven like a champion, and I couldn't be prouder of my brother. As soon as I was done hugging Henri, I took off my helmet and scanned the crowd, eagerly looking for Luca. It's as if Henri knew what I was doing because he turned me around and pointed to Luca in the crowd, a smug look on Luca's face.

Damn him and his beautiful Cheshire cat grin.

I ran up to Luca and jumped into his embrace. His arms wrapped around me, crushing me ever so lightly, but I didn't care. I looked down at him, and his beautiful brown eyes were staring back at me.

"Don't ever scare me like that again!"

"I don't know... it did get you to confess your love for me, Amore. I might have to try it again." I slapped Luca on top of the head as he laughed, very unimpressed with his joke.

"Just shut up and kiss me." I didn't have to ask him twice. Luca pressed his lips to mine, deepening the kiss as the Hermes team around him started to "ooooh" and "aww" at the two of us. Luca spun us around a couple of times before setting me back down, our foreheads still touching as he pulled me closer to his chest.

"What can I say? My heart burns for you so much my car caught fire." I groaned at his cheesy joke, but I knew my cheeks were blushing. "Go get that trophy, Cara. Tonight, you'll get your *real* prize."

Before I could respond, I felt Lizzie pulling me away from Luca. "You'll see lover boy back at the hotel," she joked as she pulled me towards the cool-down room.

Noah and Henri were already inside the room, both of them staring up at the TV, huge smiles on their faces as the footage showed my radio chatter with Mel during the car fire. Noah turned when he heard me enter the room, a cheesy grin donning his face.

"Lover boy doing okay?" I gave Noah a pointed look, placing my items on the P2 column.

"You know Luca," I sighed, "not even a car on fire can stop him from making the lamest jokes."

"Glad he's okay. That looked scary from my rearview mirror," Henri said with relief.

"Very..." I agreed in a whisper, knowing that F1 TV was filming our private moment. Henri nodded, backing away a bit before taking a sip of water, continuing to watch the race highlights. I knew we all felt it, the sudden awareness that it could have been us and it could have gone differently.

After the podium celebration, I saw Henri motion for me to come over to him. He wrapped his arms around my shoulders, a huge grin on his face.

"So.... you *love* Luca, huh?" I looked over at my brother Henri, who had a smirk on his lips. He was amused by this situation, a staunch change in demeanor from when we started this whole ordeal.

"What if I said I did?"

"Then I would be happy for you, Peaches, very happy." He grinned at the surprise on my face. I wasn't expecting him to be so accepting of this.

"Why the change of opinion?" I asked my brother, shock laced my voice.

"Because he's good for you. And he loves you, very much. I can see it in his eyes, his body language. He's good for you. Plus... he accidentally told me in the paddock the other day," Henri chuckled.

"And you kept it from me?" I exclaimed, poking Henri in his ribcage.

"Peaches, you're the one who was too stupid to see it. Lily literally told you in the hotel room earlier this week, and you sat there going *woe is me, it couldn't possibly be true*." I gave Henri another jab, but I couldn't keep a smile off my face.

"As long as you're happy, Peaches, then I'm happy for you."

"I am happy – for the first time in a long time, I feel very happy."

Chapter Twenty-Four

START OF SOMETHING NEW

Luca

When I looked into my rearview mirror, I could see Georgia directly behind me. Her pace during the Austria Grand Prix pace was impressive, and there was barely a two-second gap between us. I knew she would be relentless the rest of this race – there was no stopping that woman. Valkyrie's speed in a straight line was incredible, and it would take some serious defending to keep her behind me the rest of the race, but I was determined to do so, determined to beat the woman I loved.

And then, when the podium celebration was over, I was going to tell her just how much I loved her – make her my *actual* girlfriend. I was going to tell her how much my heart longed for her, tell her how I wanted to be a better man just for her. *I wanted to tell her that she had made me a better man.*

But as I started to turn into a corner, I began to smell something burning. It smelled like my engine was on fire.

"Luca, pull over now," my race engineer demanded. I immediately did as he said, trying not to let the slight panic in his voice get to me. "Are you ok? Can you get out?"

"It's very hot. I'm a bit stuck," I called back into the radio, but all he kept saying was, '*Luca, can you hear me?*' over and over again. I realized he couldn't hear me, so I stopped pressing the radio button. I looked outside the car, but the emergency crews were nowhere to be found, and the car was getting hotter by the second.

Fuck, fuck, fuck, I kept saying to myself as I tried to loosen the seatbelt, but it didn't budge. I was stuck.

I knew I needed to keep calm while I waited for the emergency crews. They would already be on their way. I just needed to distract myself and think about something – *anything* – to get my mind off of the fire that was rapidly increasing.

My thoughts immediately went to Georgia and our last conversation. She had called me 'mon amour' as I walked away from the Valkyrie garage. My heart had flown in that moment, and I knew I was a goner for her. Just hearing the words roll off of her lips was enough to make me never look at another woman again.

What if I didn't get out? I started to panic. *What if I didn't get the opportunity to tell Georgia how much I loved her?* Would the gifts be enough for her to know that my life has been so irreparably changed for the better since she came into it?

No, Luca, you can't think like this, I chastised myself. *You have to get out of this car, out of this heat, so you can tell Georgia how you feel. She deserves to know.*

I started to pull frantically at the seat belt, which was locking me in, over and over again, until finally, I felt it budge. I immediately launched myself out of the car and onto the ground next to my car, starting to crawl away as I saw the emergency pit crews running towards me. It didn't take them long to put out the fire. The marshals quickly shuffled me away from the wreck and back to my garage.

As soon as I got back into the paddock, I made a beeline for the Valkyrie pit wall, grabbing Mel's headset, much to her surprise. I had to tell Georgia how I felt. Every second we raced was dangerous, and I couldn't go a moment longer without Georgia knowing that I loved her. When I looked up on the screen to press the radio button, I could see the written recording of the radio messages between Mel and Georgia on the replay.

Georgia had said she loved me.

She had also threatened to get out of her car and help me, which was the stupidest thing she had ever said. The actual thought of her being in danger because of my car made my blood boil – made me want to quit Hermes as punishment for them potentially putting *Georgia* in danger. I would be talking to her later about that one.

"You didn't have to set my car on fire to get P2, Mia Cara," I joked into her radio. "According to the press, I would have let you just have it."

"Fuck off!" she quipped back into the radio. I knew from her voice that she had that beautiful, sneaky, sly grin on her face, although Isabelle looked less than impressed next to me. "I'll keep that in mind for the next race," she added, and I chuckled at her retort.

"Oh, and Cara... I love you, too." As soon as I said the words, Mel grabbed the headset from me, pushing me away from the pit wall, yelling about me being an intruder. The medic had arrived, and he was waving for me to head to the medical center. As much as I didn't want to leave the Valkyrie pit wall, I was glad I had the opportunity to finally tell Georgia how I felt about her.

I sat in the medical tent, watching her and Henri battle it out, my eyes glued to the screen. As soon as I was given the all-clear, I ran back to the garage so I could finish watching the race. The last few laps were intense. Henri and Georgia truly were two of the best drivers of our generation. When they both crossed the finish line, I knew it would have to be reviewed. Their cars were side by side as they drove past the checkered flag.

Once the results were announced, I ran towards the podium, trying to get my eyes on Georgia.

I needed more than anything to hold her, congratulate her – *kiss her*. When our eyes locked, I flashed her my biggest smile, which somehow grew even bigger when she ran towards me, jumping into my arms.

I could get used to this. I could definitely get used to this, I thought to myself as Georgia crashed our lips together.

Georgia

As soon as the podium celebration was complete, Henri, Noah, and I were forced into the post-race press conference – also known as my living nightmare. As we all sat down, I took a moment to observe the room. It was, of course, the same group of journalists from Thursday's press conference, which I guess shouldn't have been surprising, but I secretly had some hope that Marcus from Sports Broadcasting had been sent home.

"Good afternoon and welcome," Michael Clifton, the FI presenter, started, introducing the three of us drivers as he congratulated us on our success. Michael's questions were always fair – always genuine. As the main reporter for FI TV, he had a reputation to uphold, something the other journalists definitely weren't kept to. As soon as the questions were turned to the other journalists, I hunkered down in my seat, hoping after Thursday that they would leave me alone.

But as always, the universe had other plans.

"There's been a lot of criticism online of your radio comments to your race engineer when you wanted to get out of the car. People are saying this is why Formula I shouldn't allow women because women are too emotional in a crisis – any thoughts on that?" I knew by now that whenever journalists said 'criticism online,' they meant *'I have a rude question I want to personally ask, but I'll hide behind a fake internet troll.'*

"I have thoughts, yeah," I responded, "but they're probably not appropriate for FI TV." Noah snorted out a laugh next to me. I saw Lizzie shake her head in the background, knowing that this was going to be a lost cause.

Before another journalist could butt in, Michael stood up and looked at the group. "Anyone have questions on the race?" I could tell by the look on his face that he was getting annoyed with the group. Fortunately, a different sports journalist raised her hand, pulling the mic to her face.

"Georgia, how did it feel at the end, racing side by side with your brother? It was exhilarating to watch the two of you in those last few laps." Finally, the moment I *wanted* to talk about. The moment that *deserved* to be talked about.

"Incredible. Absolutely incredible." Henri nodded his agreement and turned to me as I said the words, giving me a high five. "Racing toe to toe with my brother this season has been a dream come true. Henri is an amazing driver, and it was so fun to switch back and forth. Obviously, I am personally disappointed in P2, but I couldn't be prouder of my brother. He deserves this, and I'll definitely be with him tonight, celebrating his win."

"Do you think you'll be able to hold him off next year, too? Won't be able to use dating his teammate as a distraction. Henri will be used to that one," the female journalist joked, although this time, her tone wasn't malicious – much to my surprise, the journalist was actually joking with me.

"Well shoot, you're right... Guess I'll just have to get Henri a girlfriend... or maybe a hamster," I quipped.

Once the press conference was over, I felt an arm wrap itself over my shoulders, pulling me in for a hug. I looked up at Luca, who had a cheesy smile on his face. He looked like he had just won the lottery.

We walked back to my driver's room in comforting silence, hand in hand – although this time, it felt genuine. This time, I knew he wanted to hold my hand. As soon as we got into the room, Luca pushed the door closed and pushed me back against it, bringing our lips together in a searing kiss that made my entire body light up in flames.

"Oh, Amore, how I wanted to hear those three words come out of your mouth for so long," he sighed into the kiss, letting his arms pull me even closer to his chest.

I couldn't help but giggle – it was as if my brain had gone mush, and all I could do was look at Luca like a little schoolgirl hopelessly in love with her crush. Luca sat down on the couch and pulled me into his lap, wrapping his arms around my waist, and I leaned down to give him another kiss.

"So, I have something to talk to you about."

"Mmmhmmm," I mumbled in reply, kissing his neck as he let out a laugh. I knew he was trying to be serious, but all I wanted to do was distract him with my wandering hands and lips. Luca pulled my face towards him, and I gave him a big pout, giving his plump lips one more kiss.

"You are going to be the death of me," he whispered back, his control being tested. "But I am serious."

"Fine..." I huffed in annoyance.

"I've been thinking about this... us... and I can't do this anymore."

Luca's words felt like a punch to the stomach. I immediately sat back, my face filling up with anger. What did he mean he couldn't do this anymore? I'd just told him I loved him in front of millions of people. Luca saw my expression and chuckled to himself, pulling me back down into his lap.

"Calm down, Cara," he soothed. "I can't do this *fake* relationship anymore, Georgia, because it's too much for me. I can't wake up each day, feeling how I feel about you, without being able to actually call you mine. I love you, Georgia Dubois. I want you to be mine, 100%, every day. I want – *no need* – to be able to tell everyone that my heart is yours... that it has been for years."

Luca's words made my heart race. No one had ever said those words to me before, not with that level of conviction, with such emphasis and meaning. Anthony and I had said, 'I Love You,' but he never looked at me the way Luca was looking at me now – like I was the most precious thing in the world, a rare diamond that he would treasure forever.

Luca really was my number one fan.

"Are you, Luca *playboy* Rossi, asking me, Georgia *sassy* Dubois, to be your girlfriend? Have I actually tamed the infamous Formula 1 bachelor?" I teased, running my hands through his soft, black hair.

"Oh, Georgia, you've owned my heart for much longer than you know. When I asked you out all those years ago, my heart was already yours." I leaned down to kiss him, letting my hands wander down his chest and then to the belt of his pants.

Suddenly, I needed Luca. I needed every part of him like I needed air to breathe. I was a drowning woman, and Luca was my life raft. I began to slowly unbuckle his belt, earning me a soft groan from my boyfriend, but before I could continue further, I heard pounding on my door.

"Love birds, we have to go! You can have sex back at the hotel!"

"Eww, gross, no!" I heard Henri yell behind the door, clearly annoyed with Lily's comment. I had forgotten that Lily and I had driven together this morning. There was a mix-up with the rentals, and hers had to go back today, so we decided to ride together. Henri, however, had just bombarded Luca's and I's quiet morning because he felt like being an annoying prick, so I got the job of driving everyone back to the hotel. Georgia's ride-share service was up and running, apparently, and I suspected I wasn't going to get a very good tip out of this lot.

"Gods, these two are the worst," I sighed at Luca, who was trying to adjust his pants so he could hide the large bulge that had formed during our make-out session. I got up from his lap and went over to the door, opening it only to reveal my teammate and brother, each of them holding a bottle of champagne. It was clear from the looks on their faces that they had *definitely* had too much already.

Good thing I'm driving.

"Come along, children," I said, grabbing my bag from Luca, who was now standing, a look of disappointment on his face, "back to the hotel before we get shit-faced tonight!"

The four of us crawled into my car, which was much too small for four people. Bugatti hadn't actually made their sports cars with passengers in mind. Henri and Lily crawled into the back, rambling on about whatever nonsense they felt was appropriate after half a bottle of champagne.

"So...... Lucaaaa....." Henri slurred, reaching over to the front seat and grabbing my boyfriend. "Now that you're in love with my sister, we have some rules to discuss."

"Oh shut up, Henri," Lily protested, pulling him back into his seat. "Leave the happy couple alone!"

"Non!" Henri's French accent always came out thick whenever he was drunk. "I will set some ground rules!"

"I can only imagine what these will be," I chuckled.

I took a peak at Henri in the back seat. He had pulled out his phone, and my heart warmed at the fact that my brother had actually made a list. I wanted to protest, tell Henri to fuck off and put his phone away, but I felt touched that my brother had actually thought about this relationship. His protectiveness was shining through, and this time, it was endearing to see.

"Shhhh...." Henri shushed me, and I knew he was intent on continuing this list of demands. "No making out with my sister in front of me. No sex when you visit my Monaco apartment. No sex on the Hermes plane, even if I'm not there. That's a sacred place. Oh, and definitely no sex when our rooms are next to each other."

"Too late on that last one," I interjected with a laugh, earning me a glare from Henri and a cheer from Lily.

"You break her heart, and I will make sure your car actually burns with you in it. Understood, Luca?" Luca huffed out a laugh and turned around, only to see a very determined Henri with a frown on his face.

"Don't worry, my friend. Your sister's heart is safe with me." Luca turned his head to look at me. His beautiful brown eyes looked radiant with the distant sunset behind us.

As soon as we got to the hotel, Luca and I made a beeline straight to our room, excusing ourselves from Lily and Henri, who wanted to keep drinking in the hotel bar, but I had other plans. The moment we stepped into our hotel room, Luca pushed me up against the door, his arms once again wrapped around me as he pulled me into him, our lips connecting in a passionate, lustful kiss.

"Guess we won't be needing separate bedrooms anymore," I giggled into the kiss, letting Luca drag me to his bedroom in our shared suite.

"Fuck no. I'm never letting you sleep alone again."

"Seems unrealistic for two people who travel for a living." Luca was not impressed with my joke, something he made known when he threw me down onto his – no, *our* – *bed*. Luca quickly pulled his shirt over his head, and I looked up at him, letting my eyes scan his shoulder muscles, then his chest, and then his abs. He smirked as he watched me ogle his upper body. Luca looked like he was built by Apollo himself, and he was all mine.

"Are you going to be a good girl for me and finish what you started back at the paddock?" I eagerly nodded at him, licking my lips as I moved to the edge of the bed, letting my fingers start to slowly unbuckle his belt. I let the tips of my fingers gracefully graze the top of his boxers before hooking my fingers around the elastic band, sliding both them and his pants down his legs, leaving him completely naked in front of me. I grabbed his length and slowly started to stroke it, causing Luca to hiss and put his hand on my shoulder, using me for balance. I loved the way I could make him putty in my hands, loved the way he melted every time I touched him.

I loved him.

Luca tapped my mouth with his thumb, motioning for me to open my mouth for him, which I obliged as I hollowed out my cheeks in the process.

"Fuck, Principessa, I'll never get used to that mouth of yours... how good you feel," Luca hissed. His comment made me smile, and I let him slide out of my mouth, instead opting to use my tongue to lick the base of his cock to his tip, earning me another raspy groan from the Italian.

"Don't be a tease." By the look in Luca's eyes, I could tell it was a demand, although his voice came out more whiny than he had intended, causing me to smirk up at him, batting my eyelashes as I repeated the motion with my tongue a second time.

I went back to his tip, which was now red and leaking pre-cum. It was aching to be touched. I let my lips wrap around him and started to increase my pace, letting him slide in and out of me as the tip of his cock hit the back of my throat each time. I could tell from his thrusts and heavy breathing that he was getting closer, so I moved my free hand to his balls, gently massaging them. As Luca got closer to his end, he pulled out of my mouth, catching his breath in the process.

"As much as I want to finish in your mouth, Tesoro, I want to finish inside of you more." Luca immediately hopped onto the bed, crawling on top of me. He made quick work of taking my top off, sliding the polo over the top of my head, revealing the purple lacy bra that he had placed into my gift basket earlier in the week.

"Fuck, I knew this would look incredible on you." Luca leaned down to kiss each breast, paying special attention to each peak as he massaged the other with his hand. Slowly, he slid the purple lace off of me before moving to my skirt, sliding it down my legs as I laid down on the bed, now completely naked before him. Luca let his hands play with my folds, testing my wetness there, and his smug grin told me that he was pleased with himself.

"I didn't know you enjoyed giving me head that much," Luca darkly chuckled. I wanted to protest, but he was right – I enjoyed giving him pleasure just as much as I knew he enjoyed giving making me scream. As he started to work his way down my body to my core, I shot out a hand, pulling him back up so I could capture his lips in a passionate kiss.

"I need you, now."

"Well, then, Principessa, your wish is my command." Luca moved back up my body and positioned his cock at my entrance before slowly sliding into my folds, causing me to let out a loud moan. It was as if Luca was feeding my soul. I had been so worked up since we had left the paddock, and the feeling of his cock inside me felt like the air I needed to breathe.

He looked down at me, capturing my lips in a sweet kiss before whispering in my ear, asking if I was okay. I nodded my consent, continuing to kiss him fiercely as Luca began to move in and out of me. Each thrust was slow and deep. Sex with Luca had usually been fast and rough, but today was different. Today, every stroke seemed purposeful as Luca kissed up and down my neck, whispering 'I love you' into my ear in between each kiss.

"Such a good girl for me... I love you so much... You feel amazing... You take me so well, Principessa." The praises kept on coming, and I was reveling in them, each one bringing me closer to my high.

Luca leaned back on his heels, pulling my body with him, and I was now straddling him as he held me in place, moving me up and down on his cock. The new position helped Luca get even deeper inside of me, his cock now hitting my g-spot with each thrust.

"Oh Luca, this feels amazing, fuck... don't stop."

"Cum with me." Luca picked up his pace, and each thrust felt even more amazing as he worked me towards my impending release. I could feel him close, and as soon as he reached his hand down to my clit, I felt my body start to immediately spasm around his cock, triggering his own orgasm. Luca kept thrusting into me as my walls squeezed him, both of our moans filling the room.

I felt a wave of exhaustion come over me as Luca carefully placed me back down on the bed. He quickly ran to the bathroom, grabbing a wet towel to clean me. As soon as he was done, Luca crawled back into bed, pulling me closer to his chest. He looked down at me, noticing the tears that had formed.

"Cara, what's wrong?" Luca asked, panic filling his face. "Did I hurt you?" I pulled Luca closer to me, pressing our bodies so close that I could feel his heart beating.

"I just... I'm just so happy right now... but what if something changes? What if you get bored of me?" Luca let out a loud laugh, running his hands along my back in a soothing motion. His other hand grabbed my chin, forcing me to look him in the eyes.

"Georgia Dubois, if you think you are going to get rid of me that easily, you have another thing coming. Plus, I think your brothers might *actually* set my car on fire." Luca gave me a small peck on the lips before wiping away my tears. "Your heart is safe with me, Tesoro." I smiled up at him, letting him kiss me again before resting my head on his chest, letting a comforting silence fill the room.

"I love you, Luca Rossi."

As promised, we met Lily and Henri downstairs at 9 p.m., where the car service was already waiting for us. Edward had booked a VIP suite at the only decent bar close to the track, and as soon as we arrived, we were ushered upstairs to where Oliver, Éliott, Noah, and Edward were already waiting. As soon as the other drivers spotted Luca and me, they all began to whoop and holler at us.

"Well, well, well, looks like I won my little bet," I heard Edward announce as he approached the two of us.

"Who did you bet anyway?" I knew about Edward's annoying bet, but I realized I didn't actually know who had bet for or against us.

"Well, Georgia Dubois, I am glad you asked." Edward held out his hand to Luca, who immediately went into his back pocket and took out his wallet, handing Edward 100 euros as he shook his head.

"You see, Georgie, I bet Luca that you two would fall in love by the end of the season. Luca was so insistent that you'd never look at him again after he *rudely* ditched you all those years ago, but I knew better. I know a jealous woman when I see one." He threw me a wink, and I scoffed in response.

"I was not jealous!" The protest was weak, and I could tell from everyone's faces that no one believed me.

"Oh, please, the way you babbled on about Luca and who he was supposedly dating or what he was doing and 'how annoying' he was – you were jealous. Figured as soon as you got to know the Luca that we knew, the one who didn't ditch beautiful women on dates, you'd fall madly in love with him." Edward looked incredibly impressed with himself as he finished, literally patting himself on the back after putting away his prize money.

"And so, now I am 100 euros richer, and you two will have life-long happiness. A win-win for everyone."

"Edward Davis... you scheming little muppet, you!" I couldn't help but laugh at Edward, leaning a bit more into Luca as he wrapped his arms around my waist.

"I will get you back for this," Luca promised Edward with a chuckle.

"You can try!" Edward yelled back as he headed off to the bar, a look of smug satisfaction plastered all over his face.

Luca and I eventually made our way to the bar. Henri spotted Luca and me and immediately handed us two glasses of champagne before turning back to Lily, the two of them deep in whatever conversation they were heaving. We took our seats across from Lily and Henri in the booth, both of us steadily observing our team-mates across from us. After finishing their glasses, Lily grabbed Henri's hand, dragging him onto the dance floor after a few protests from my brother, leaving Luca and me alone at the table.

"Maybe we should get Lily and Henri together so they stop bothering us," I joked to Luca, watching Lily and Henri dance in the middle of the dance floor. There was something about the two of them together. They really made a beautiful couple.

"Please, it'll be a cold day in hell before Lily and Henri ever get together," Luca quipped, taking another sip of champagne, his arms now around my shoulder.

"You know, Luca, I've heard that one before."

EPILOGUE

Georgia

"Luca, have you seen my pass?" I frantically started emptying my suitcase, desperately looking for my paddock pass.

Good grief, Georgia, you can't lose this pass yet again; you'll never hear the end of it from Edward, I muttered to myself.

"Amore, you'd lose your head if it wasn't screwed on," I heard Luca laugh from behind me, wrapping his arms around me from behind, my paddock pass in his hand.

"Oh, thank god! After I blasted Edward on Twitter in Austin for losing his pass and getting caught trying to break into the paddock, I can't then lose mine this week!"

"Well, to be fair, you probably shouldn't have told security that Edward was an intruder..." I let out a sly snicker, remembering the delicious prank I had pulled on Edward.

Edward and I had been in a prank war for a few years now, and while we'd called a "truce" after Silverstone, we both knew that wasn't going to last long. As soon as I saw Edward trying to break his way into the paddock with no pass around his neck, it was too good not to tell security that some random fan was trying to break in.

The fact that the American security guards didn't recognize him was even more hilarious. Unfortunately for me, Edward returned the favor the following week when he "accidentally" told Henri that Luca and I were secretly engaged and planning to elope over Christmas. I think if Luca hadn't been in a sponsorship meeting, Henri would have actually punched his teammate. But now it was my turn to get one over on the Brit, and I had a beautiful prank in place.

"So, we're still on for today, right?" I asked, wiggling my eyebrows in anticipation. I had finally talked my boyfriend into helping me prank Edward, and I couldn't be more excited.

"I feel like this is too mean, Cara," Luca said with a sigh. Over the last several months, I had learned just how much of a softie Luca was, especially for Edward. "I think if we actually broke up, Edward would be the only person on the planet as devastated as me."

I rolled my eyes at Luca, grabbing my bag from the sofa as we headed downstairs, meeting Lily in the lobby. I had agreed to have a quick breakfast with her before we left for the paddock. For whatever reason, Lily had become a staple to Luca and I's driving to the paddock. For a while, Henri would also join us, but after the summer break, Henri went back to driving himself to the paddock. Something felt off between Lily and Henri. It felt like they were avoiding each other, and by Austin GP, they were actively making excuses to leave the room when the other walked in, a staunch change from the beginning of the season when I would watch them subtly flirt with each other.

Once breakfast was finished, I turned to my teammate, a smile on my lips. "Ready to go?" The Valet pulled up in my Bugatti, and the two of us hopped into the car.

"Luca not joining us?"

"Nah, he's got a different schedule than me," I mused quietly. I felt a little bad not telling Lily about Luca and I's prank on Edward, but I knew she wouldn't be able to keep it a secret from the Wilmington driver.

"So, tell me, what's going on with you and Henri?" I could see

Lily visibly stiffen up at the mention of my brother's name, although she kept a stoic look on her face.

"What do you mean?"

"I mean, nothing really... just felt like the two of you have been avoiding each other."

"Nope, just busy, that's all. Can't just drop everything for Henri Dubois." It's as if Lily knew her words had come out harsher than she expected, so she added with a smile, "Can only put up with one of the Dubois twins this season."

"Fine, keep your secrets, Wilson." I could see from Lily's face that she wanted to say something else but had decided against it, instead opting to scroll through her phone.

"So, the Full Throttle 'F1 & Families' special went over well! Fans are just loving you and Luca," she mused.

"Yeah, I feel like it put the final nail in the coffin of that Daily Report article. We haven't had a single bad article about our relationship written in over a month." The TV special, along with a second magazine article, had been a lifesaver for Luca and I's relationship.

After I admitted I loved him over the radio in Austria, there were some renewed suspicions about us, but fortunately, the FIA investigation was cleared in Austin, and by Singapore, the news was basically dead, with everyone having moved on to the F1 silly season.

"Well, after you win the championship this weekend, there won't be a single bad thing the press can say. They'll have to accept our us with a female World Drivers Champion."

"Cheers to that," I replied, holding up my coffee cup and clinking it with hers.

Luca

I felt a little bad pranking Edward, but after told Henri that Georgia and I were secretly engaged, I let Georgia talk me into this silly prank of hers. Pretty sure I would have been sporting a black eye for a week if Oliver hadn't caught wind of Edward and Henri's conversation. He immediately ran back to the Hermes garage to calm Henri down.

Henri was less than impressed about the prank, although I knew Georgia reveled in the challenge of one-upping Edward. It was one of the many reasons I loved her – she never backed down from a challenge, and Edward had just opened Pandora's box of pranks.

As soon as I walked into the paddock, I saw Edward waiting for me outside of the Hermes F1 hospitality suite. We had agreed to do a track walk together, get some time to catch up just the two of us.

"Morning, Luca!" I smiled at Edward, gladly taking the cup of coffee he held out for me, my second one of the morning. *Best part about dating Georgia Dubois? The incredible coffee.*

"Morning, Edward. How are things?"

"Oh, you know, can't complain. My podcast is really taking off. It's taking a lot of my time, but I don't mind. How are things with you and the misses?" I froze up a bit at his question, trying to think through all of the coaching Georgia had given me. Her dedication to her craft – of being a prankster – was nothing short of impressive. After this weekend, Georgia might be F1's first female World Drivers Champion, but I'm pretty sure Georgia would consider herself the World Champion of Pranks, too – and she might be prouder of that title than the former.

"Yeah... umm, sort of the reason I wanted to ask you to get coffee with me..." I knew that had piqued Edward's interest. He immediately stopped in his tracks, and I could see concern in his eyes.

God, Edward, what a good friend.

"Georgia and I... we decided to take some time apart during the winter break." I knew the words were as fake as Georgia and I's relationship had started, but damn, they hurt me to even say them out loud. I said a silent prayer to the universe, begging her not to let this ever be true.

"What!" Edward screamed, spilling some of his coffee onto his Wilmington team polo. "Absolutely not. I forbid it." Edward's reaction took everything within me not to laugh. He looked as if he would make a deal with the devil on my behalf.

"What did you do?"

"What do you mean '*what did I do*?'" I was slightly offended that Edward had gone straight to accusing me, assuming that I was the one who fucked up. It was logical, but still hurtful from my best friend.

"Look, mate, I'm just trying to get to the bottom of this so we can fix this."

"She just needs a little space. It's been an overwhelming season." As we came to the end of our track walk, Edward walked me back to the Hermes garage.

"Never fear, Luca – I'm going to fix this." His voice was full of conviction, and I let out a small smile.

"Edward, I told you NOT to get involved. Promise me you won't say anything."

"Fine, fine..." Edward put his hands up in the air, admitting defeat, which was good because I didn't need this prank spreading around the paddock. We'd finally gotten out of the dog house with the press, and I didn't need a fake prank circulating around the paddock like wildfire.

Edward

As soon as I watched Luca walk into the Hermes garage, I immediately texted Lily and Oliver, demanding that they both meet me in my driver's room. I couldn't believe what Luca had told me – those two were made for each other, but I knew if anyone would have insight into their relationship, it would be Oliver and Lily.

Edward: Lil, Oliver – meet me in 15, my driver's room, super urgent

Lily: Edward, some of us have actual meetings and strategies to go over...

Edward: No time for that, Lil. Our friends are in trouble

Lily: Fine, be there in 20

Once Lily and Oliver entered my room, I shut the door – motioning for them both to take a seat on my coach.

"Alright, what I am about to tell you cannot leave this room. Luca and Georgia are taking a break." Silence engulfed my driver's room as the two other drivers sat there, contemplating my words.

"Edward, that's a pile of horse shit," Lily finally scoffed. "Is this another one of your pranks again? Cause I'm not falling for it."

"No, I'm serious, Luca told me this morning on our track walk." Oliver shifted in his seat, eyeing me warily.

"Are you sure you understood right? I mean, Georgia and I literally just went apartment shopping for the two of them in Monaco this weekend." I started to feel more frustrated as Oliver's face looked entirely unconvinced.

"And I just had breakfast with them this morning..." Lily added.

I just stared at my teammate and friend for a moment before it dawned on me – *those fuckers were trying to prank me.* This is why Luca didn't want me getting involved. He knew his terrible, poorly thought-out prank would be exposed.

No, I shouldn't blame Luca on this one. *It had Georgia "Sassy" Dubois all over it.*

"Those sneaky little bastards!" Lily and Oliver continued to look confused, and I knew I would have to spell it out for them. "They're trying to prank me!"

"Well, I'd say you have it coming, considering you told Henri that his sister was secretly engaged..." Oliver snickered. It probably wasn't one of my finer pranks, but Georgia's horror when she realized her brother was about to go beat up her boyfriend was hilarious – the look on Henri's face? That was the cherry on top.

"I only did that because Georgia almost had me arrested!"

"Well, have you ever forgotten your paddock pass again?" I rolled my eyes at Lily's snarky comment. I knew she loved that prank a little too much. "Sounds like you learned your lesson."

Lily stuck her tongue out at me, and I flicked her off, not amused with her response. With each race I was beginning to realize that Lily was actually the sassier Valkyrie driver. Her witty British humor had really blossomed over the last several months.

"Well, two can play at this game! They don't know that I know that they're trying to prank me, and you're not going to tell them."

"Edward, do not involve me in your little prank wars with Georgia. I am not about to start WWIII in the Valkyrie garage," Lily demanded, slowly getting up from the couch. Oliver chuckled as he excused himself, insisting that he didn't want to know what we had planned. Something about undeniability being the best course of action for him.

"What? No! Come on... Edward and Lily scheming again – it's what dreams are made of! We're so good at it!"

"What can you even do on such short notice?"

"Oh, Lily, I am so glad you asked."

Georgia

After both free practice sessions, the FIA scheduled an extra press conference for Noah and me. Only a few points separated us in the championship, and I knew the FIA loved the drama, although Noah and I had agreed to keep the drama on the track, neither of us giving in to the demand that we browbeat the other out of existence. I might have been sassy to the reporters, but I would never badmouth another driver at a press conference – *ever*.

As I sat down in the chair next to Noah, he leaned into me. "I hear congratulations are in order," Noah chuckled.

"Congratulating me for winning the championship already? Interesting approach, Hendriks," I snickered, although my laughter was short-lived when I saw the look of confusion on Noah's face.

"Sorry, Georgia, I get that you aren't telling people yet. Edward has such a big mouth, just wanted to say congrats." Before I could follow up, the press conference started, diving straight into questions about the upcoming race.

As soon as the press conference was over, I pulled out my phone, only to see a text from Henri.

> Henri: Care to explain why Luca had a look of panic on his face during the Hermes strategy meeting today?

> Georgia: Scared he's going to see my rear bumper the entire race? ;-)

> Henri: I'm serious, Peaches...

> Georgia: Did he say something to you?

> Henri: No, he was just... not himself. I asked what was wrong, thought you might know. He looked pale...

> Georgia: Thanks for letting me know.

After another round in the media pen, I was finally released back to the hotel so I could get some sleep before qualifying tomorrow. When I walked into our shared room, Luca was nowhere to be found. Instead, there was a note on the living room coffee table explaining that he would be back later and not to wait up for him. There had been some damage to his car after free practice, so I figured he would be at the garage, trying to help with the repairs.

I waited up for him, but after room service, I soon found myself asleep in our bed.

When I awoke the next morning at 7 a.m., I turned over to see Luca's side of the bed empty. I immediately felt some panic setting in me. What if something had happened to him?

When I grabbed my phone, about to text everyone I knew in a panic, I saw a text from his Matteo letting me know that Luca was safe and had fallen asleep on his couch. I smiled at that – classic Luca, he was always falling asleep on couches. Matteo informed me that he would take Luca to the track that morning since he had gone to bed so late.

I was disappointed that I wasn't able to see Luca before qualifying and even more annoyed that he had only texted me good luck. I had the sneaking suspicion that he was avoiding me, but I pushed those thoughts to the back of my mind, remembering our "exercise" that had taken place Thursday night. I knew he was stressed about the last race of the season, and I would see him after qualifying.

"Alright, GG, Q3 is about to begin. Ready to take your final pole of the season?" I chucked at Mel's radio message. I was more than ready. I was the first one out into Q3, which was nice because I was able to get an early flying lap in with my new soft tires. I was able to improve on my Q2 lap time, and as the track evolution began to quicken, I made an improvement on my second lap in Q3.

"Right, GG – this is the last lap for you." I made my way across the line with just 5 seconds to spare before the end of Q3. "Head down, GG." It was as if the universe had decided to offer me a small slice of forgiveness for all of the times it stuck me in an elevator with journalists, sponsors, and other drivers. For once, things were on my side.

"Fuck yes!" I heard Mel scream into my ear. "Georgia Pole Dubois, you did it again! That's you P1, Noah P2. One step closer to the World Driver's Championship."

"Wahooooo!" I screamed back at Mel. "Let's bring it home, ladies!"

As soon as I arrived back at the pit lane, I was greeted by my team, who had all come out to congratulate me. Lily had gotten P4, a solid position for the team, with Henri in P3 and Luca in P5. Noah immediately approached me and shook my hand, congratulating me on pole position as he promised to outrace me tomorrow.

"Guess I better destroy you this season since I won't get the chance next season," Noah laughed. Before I could respond to his strange comment, I saw Luca motioning for me to come over. Once I entered my driver's room, I was immediately brought into a huge hug by my boyfriend.

"Congrats," he said, picking me up gently and kissing me on the lips. "I'm so proud of you."

"Thank you, Mon Amour. I was sad I missed you this morning. Bed felt empty without you." Luca looked a little guilty, and he shifted his weight from side to side for a bit, clearly unsure of what to say. He grabbed my hands and pulled me into his lap on my couch.

"I'm sorry, Amore. I should have been there. I just panicked for a moment, but I'm going to be here for you, for the both of you." Luca rested his hand on my lower stomach, his gaze looking up at me with the most loving stare I think I had ever seen from the man. I paused for a moment, at first reveling in the loving look, before processing what he had actually said.

"Um... what? Both...?"

"For you and... the baby?"

"What baby? Who the fuck is having a baby?" Luca was now the one sporting a confused look.

"Edward said-" Before Luca could finish his sentence, I immediately jumped off his lap and sprinted towards my door, flinging the door open with such ferocity a team photo fell down in the hallway.

"I'm going to kill him!" Fortunately, I didn't have to go too far to find Edward. As I turned the corner, I heard the laughing of Edward in Lily's driver's room. I burst into the room, not even bothering to knock.

"Edward, did you tell people I am pregnant!"

"I don't know. Did you tell Luca to tell me that you both had broken up?" I immediately stopped in my tracks. *Of course, Edward had found out.*

"Next time you might want to sure up your lie a little better..." Lily teased. I could see from the look on her face that she had spilled the beans to Edward. *I knew I should have included her.*

"Et tu, brute?" I said to Lily, letting a small grin creep onto my face. Edward had bested me on this one, and I couldn't even be mad about it. As I turned around to look at Luca, I saw a smile creep onto his face. *So they had all planned this.*

"Well, well, well, it might have been a joke that Luca and I were taking a break... but maybe now it'll be true!" I had wanted the words to come out fierce and determined – *angry* – but I couldn't help but laugh. I was impressed, and I recognized greatness when I saw it.

Takes one to know one.

"Fine, this makes us even, Edward, but you had better watch out next year."

"Wouldn't have it any other way, Dubois!"

I gave Edward and Lily my middle finger and then exited her driver's room, returning back to my own room, still laughing at their prank. It had been a good one, and fortunately, they managed not to include my brother this time, lest we have another Singapore incident.

As Luca entered the room after me, he pulled me in closer, capturing my lips in a kiss. "So, why were you avoiding me on Friday?" I made sure to make my disdain known, hoping Luca got the hint that I was annoyed about him abandoning me Friday evening.

"Oh, Cara, don't be upset with me," Luca chuckled, giving me another kiss on the lips as he pulled me back into his lap. "What Matteo said was true. We were up so late working on the car that I crashed on Friday... I had to stay and help the team rebuild. I didn't want to wake you, so I stayed with him. I know how focused you get before races, and I meant what I said – I'm not going to jeopardize this win for you."

I smiled at Luca's words, knowing a blush was creeping onto my face. We spent the next ten minutes chatting before Lizzie announced that the post-qualifying press conference would begin soon. As I made my way to the door, Luca grabbed my land one last time, pulling me into him.

"I know that was a prank, Amore, but I just wanted to let you know that someday, I can't wait until it's true." Luca's admission made my heart melt. *Had Luca thought about our future together that deeply?*

"Me too, Mon Amour, me too."

Yesterday, after Edward had admitted that he had 'let it slip' that Luca and I were pregnant to the other drivers, I promptly texted them all to let them know what an ass Edward was. No one was surprised. Noah, apparently, was also in on the joke, which made his comments make considerably more sense. The majority of them had found it to be hilarious – although Eric and Otto made it quite known that they were quietly pleased it wasn't true, the two of them implying that it was too early for Luca and me to have babies, especially before I "crushed the other drivers out of existence." Otto definitely had a way with words.

> Eric: Good luck today, Georgie. Whatever happens – I am so proud of you. You deserve this win.

> Georgia: Thanks, Eric. Couldn't have done it without your support!

> Eric: Nah... this one's all you, Georgie. All you.

I smiled at Eric's texts. If things went well today, I would be crowned the first female F1 champion. Isabelle had called the entire team into the paddock early. Nothing was going to be left to chance. There was more than my driver's championship on the line, more than the constructor's championship.

As I piled into the conference room, which was now full of the entire Valkyrie garage staff, Isabelle stood up on the step stool that had been laid out for her.

"Good morning, everyone. I know I have called you all in here early, but I think we can all guess why." Isabelle took a moment to pause as everyone chuckled, most of them turning to me. I had never felt awkward with the team before, but standing here now, I suddenly felt the pressure of the spotlight. The looks in their eyes showed the same desire, the same want that I felt. We were in this together – as a team, and yet, I recognized the huge role I had to play in this today. For fifty-eight laps, I had to drive better than Monaco, better than Silverstone.

I had to drive like I had a point to prove – like a Valkyrie.

"I just wanted to say, before we all disperse for the season, that it has been an honor to have you all on the Valkyrie F1 team. Even if the result isn't what we want it to be, we have had a hell of a season, and regardless of what happens today, I am so incredibly proud of this season. Everyone thought we would be last in the constructor's championship, and here we are, currently sitting in the top spot. We gave them hell, ladies, and for that – we should be proud."

As Isabelle finished the speech, I felt a tear drop down my face. Lily turned to me, and I gave her my middle finger as she laughed and pointed at me, sticking her tongue out in return.

The time between the morning meeting and the race start felt like an eternity, but when Mel told me it was time to get into the car, I felt frozen in place. This was it, the last time this year that I was going to get into that car. My last moment to show everyone who Georgia Dubois really was.

"You got this, GG," Mel called into the radio as I settled into the cockpit. "Let's bring the bitch home."

As the formation lap ended, I looked over to Noah, who was in

P2. I couldn't see his face, but I could picture the determination on it. He wanted the championship as much as I did, and he wasn't going to let me have this win easily.

As soon as the five lights went, I launched the car into the first corner, making sure to defend my position from Noah, who had decided to be aggressive in his overtaking strategy. *So, it's gloves off then is it, Noah?*

"Careful on tires, GG." I knew Mel wanted these to last, but like hell was I going to let Noah Hendriks overtake me at the beginning of this race. As the race trudged onto lap thirty-five, I was still leading the pack. Noah and I had broken away from the group, but he'd managed to stay within four seconds behind me, just waiting for me to mess up – waiting for me to do a little spin or cross a curb too early, anything to get within DRS range.

"Yellow flag, accident close to the pit entrance."

As soon as I saw the symbol on my steering wheel, I slowed down to the appropriate speed, letting the safety car guide me for several laps. Noah and I had both just pitted, and neither of us wanted to lose track position for a second pit – even if it was a "free stop," as Mel always liked to tell me.

"Doesn't feel free if I have to lose P1," I often reminded her.

"Restart will be behind the safety car. Get ready to push. Noah will be right behind you."

Of course, he was. Just my luck to get a safety car. Unfortunately for me, my luck was continuing to get worse. As soon as the green flag came onto my dashboard, I saw Noah Hendriks fly past me, getting much better traction on his tires as his car flew by.

"Fuck!" I screamed into the radio, but Mel said nothing back to me, clearly assessing the situation from the pit wall.

Lap forty-two rolled around, and I was still stuck behind Noah. No doubt I would have nightmares about his rear wing for the next several years. I was within DRS for several laps, but each time I made a move, Noah was able to defend and elude me, using his tires to exhaustion – and I was quickly getting into the same sinking boat.

"Relax on tires, GG. We think Noah's will give out before yours right now. Keep diligent."

As soon as lap fifty-three rolled around, I could feel my heart start to quicken, fear seeping into me. I was running out of time to turn this around – and quickly trying to balance the tires while not staying too far behind Noah. As soon as I began lap fifty-five, I heard Isabelle come onto the radio.

"GG, fuck the tires. Go for it."

I'm sorry, did Isabelle just come onto my radio and curse into my ear? I felt stunned at first, but as her words sank into me, I knew she was right. What was the point of nursing these tires? I wasn't going to get past Noah if I didn't push harder, so we might as well risk the puncture. I didn't want to be on the podium's second step.

I wanted to be on the top one.

Isabelle didn't have to come back onto the radio to tell me twice. As soon as lap fifty-six rolled around, I absolutely floored it down the straight, getting within .2 of a second to Noah, our cars almost touching because of my aggressive launch. As soon as I saw the second DRS zone, I knew I would have him.

And have him I did.

Noah's DRS flap opened, and I cruised by his car, quickly passing him. If there was ever a time to defend, I knew it was now.

Lap fifty-seven flew by, and I was now in first.

"Final lap, GG."

I started lap fifty-eight, hitting the racing line with such ease I almost didn't recognize myself. Noah had fallen back to 1.2 seconds, so I was safe from DRS in the first zone. As I reached the second zone, I knew Noah was within the one-second requirement. I lunged my car in front of his, blocking his attack with such ferocity I barely knew myself. Was it a tad more dangerous than my mother would like to see? Probably.

As I saw the checkered flag in front of me, I did what someone could only describe as 'sending it.' It was as if, in that moment, nothing else mattered. Not Noah, not the journalists, not even the team's expectations of me. Everything was gone, blank in my mind.

The only thing occupying my brain was the checkered flag in front of me.

When I crossed the finish line, I felt it. My tire had gotten a puncture, but for the first time in my racing career, it didn't matter. I had crossed the line first.

I felt as though time had stopped, and it was as if my brain no longer worked as I tried to utter something into my radio. I heard someone yell into the feed, but the words were fuzzy and confusing, not registering in my brain.

Nothing at that moment was registering in my brain.

"Wh...what was th- that?" was all I could utter back as I heard distant screaming and cheering through the radio, the sound of the crowd roaring so overpowering that I couldn't hear Mel's voice.

But my body knew what was happening. It knew what had just happened. Mel's voice came back onto the radio, and I felt a rush of tears run down my face. It felt as though all of the emotions that I had held in for the last year had been released. The sadness, the excitement, the fear, the ferocity that I had bottled up inside me came pouring out.

I was F1's newest World Drivers Champion.

"Congratulationsssssss!" I heard Mel scream into the radio.

"Georgia, congrats. You had a hell of a season, and this is a well-deserved win for both you and the team. Can't wait to do this again next year, Love." I smiled at Isabelle's words – the softness of her voice was refreshing and new, foreign to me, but it was nice to hear. I had a sneaking suspicion she might even be smiling.

"Lily did incredible, too – we had her pit and grab the fastest lap to ensure that Noah didn't get it."

"I am speechless!" I yelled back into my radio. "Thank you to the team. This one is for you ladies... for every last one of you. Thank you! Thank you to Lily for being the best teammate I could have dreamed of, an absolute star.

"You have outdone yourself today, Georgie," I heard Fiona say into the radio. "Today, you have shown every single little girl that they can turn their karting dreams into a dream of being an F1 champion – just like Georgia Dubois."

I pulled into my assigned P1 spot, not caring that the tire was basically dead and flat at this point. I didn't need this car anymore. She had served me well, and she had earned her retirement.

As soon as I parked, I hopped out of the car, kneeling in front of her, hugging the dead tire as I felt Noah come up to me, patting me on the shoulder. I stood up and faced him, and to my surprise, he picked me up and swung me around in what was probably the biggest hug I had ever seen Noah give.

"Congrats, Dubois. A well-deserved win. I'll get you next year." Noah set me down, and I was immediately grabbed by my brother, who had managed to get P3 in the race. Henri pulled off my helmet and threw it on the ground, grabbing me closer and giving me a congratulatory kiss on the cheek.

"I am so proud of you, Peaches, *so fucking proud.*"

I squeezed my brother as he quickly dragged the two of us off to our family, who had made it to the fencing, their arms wide open for the two of us. I immediately jumped into their arms as the five of us hugged, not a single one of us wanting to let go.

I heard the officials calling for Henri and me to head to the cool-down room to get weighed. I searched the crowd for Luca, desperately looking for my boyfriend, who was seemingly nowhere to be found, but just as I was about to walk into the cool-down room, I felt an arm link around my waist, pulling me into him. Luca grabbed my head and crashed our lips together, pulling my body as close to him as he possibly could.

"I'm so proud of you, Cara. So fucking proud of you." As I broke the kiss, I looked up and smiled at him, letting him pull me once more into another kiss as the FIA official started yelling behind us, much to the amusement of Henri and Noah.

I begrudgingly let Luca go, heading back into the cool-down room where water was waiting for me. It was only a few minutes before we were being pulled onto the podium for the celebration. I watched Henri go out first, spying on my mother and brothers as he walked out. Luca had joined them now, his filming the podium celebration as he cheered us on next to my mother. Noah walked out next, waving to the crowd as he took his trophy.

And then it was my turn. The moment I had been waiting for.

I walked out of the room and onto the stage, watching the masses of people who had gathered in Abu Dhabi to watch us race – to watch me win. I waved at them as I walked onto the top step, taking my trophy from the government official before setting it down so I could take my hat off for the Monaco national anthem.

As soon as the anthems finished, I picked up my bottle of champagne to spray Henri and Noah, but it was too late – they had beaten me to it, absolutely drenching me, and then Mel, who was the Valkyrie podium representative, with their two bottles. As soon as the bubbles died down, I took one more look into the crowd, giving them a final wave before stepping off the podium.

The moment my foot hit the ground, Lily was on me – her arms wrapping around me as she picked me up into a hug, screaming the entire time.

"You did it!" Lily chanted over and over again, the two of us now jumping up and down like school girls. Somehow, this had become our signature move.

I walked back to the garage, trophy in one hand and a bottle of champagne in the other. Fiona was the first to pull me into a hug, but it was short-lived as the rest of the garage crew started to filter over, all of them demanding hugs, everyone wanting to see the trophy. I looked around for Isabelle, my eyes scanning the garage.

Fiona saw my confused look because she leaned over and whispered to me, "In the office." I nodded and made my way to Isabelle's office, knocking on the door. As soon as I heard the words 'come in,' I opened it slowly, looking around the dimly lit room for Isabelle.

There in the corner of her office was Isabelle, sat on her couch, a glass of what looked like whisky in her hands. There was once a point in my Valkyrie F1 career that I thought I would never see

Isabelle, but that seemed like a farfetched idea as I observed my team principal in front of me, tears in her ears.

I walked over to her and set the trophy down on the coffee table before grabbing a glass and filling it up with the whisky that was set in front of her, joining her on the couch. The two of us sat in silence for several minutes, both of us sipping on our glasses, neither of us saying anything.

"You know, when I was a young girl, I loved racing. Loved it dearly. I spent every weekend with my parents in Italy karting with my brother. But as I got older, the karting got more expensive, and there was only enough money for one of us to continue. Even though I was more talented than my brother, my parents chose to continue funding his karting. Apparently, there was no hope I would ever be a professional driver. That just wasn't something in the cards for a woman, so my brother, who could barely win races, got to continue living my dream as I was forced to return to normal life." I observed Isabelle as she told the story, setting my glass down on the counter as I poured the both of us another round.

"It was that day I promised myself I was going to start an F1 team. I decided that I was going to win this championship somehow..."

"And now that we have... it almost doesn't seem real, does it?" I finished for her. I understood what Isabelle was feeling. Deep inside my soul, I understood. I had fought so long to be here, fought tooth and nail to stand on that podium and accept the World Driver's Championship trophy, and now that this day had arrived, it felt almost bittersweet. The illustrious dream wasn't so illustrious anymore. Isabelle smiled at me, her tears drying up as she took another sip of whisky.

"And now we've done it. Today, a female-run and operated team did more than just win the WDC. We proved to the world that women should have an equal seat at the table in motorsports – from mechanics to leadership to drivers, we're here to stay."

"That we are, Isabelle, that we are."

"Next year is a new year, Georgia. New car, new challenges. You ready to do it all again?"

"How many championships do I need to win to beat Eric's record of having the most titles? They have six, so I need seven?" I said with a chuckle, earning me a huge grin from Isabelle.

"Hmm... perhaps we should make it eight... just to be safe," Isabelle countered, a refreshing gleam I had come to know so well gathering in her eyes.

"Well, we have one down." I raised my glass as I stood up, clinking it with Isabelle's. "Here's to another seven championships, Isabelle."

DEAR READER

Thank you for taking the time to read A Man's World. This story was born out of a daydream I had, which then turned into weekly chapters I posted online in my spare time. Writing has always been a cathartic, relaxing endeavor for me, and I am so fortunate that I was able to spend the last year putting this story together. It truly has been one of my most fun journeys to date!

With that said, I hope you enjoy reading this book as much as I enjoyed writing it.

Interested in Henri and Lily's story? "Queen of Me" coming in 2024!

THANK YOU

To all my friends who provided me with priceless encouragement: **Thank You.** This book is first and foremost for you.

Iggy and Poppy: My authors in crime; this book literally wouldn't have been written without you. You were my first readers, first editors, and best critics. You provided me with endless ideas and encouragement. Thanks, loves!

Pooja & Erin: You were the first of my friends to read this book, cover to cover! Without your endless encouragement, praise, and critique, I never would have turned my daydream into a published book.

Kylie, Julia & Elyse: Your love of smutty novels truly inspired this book.

To my husband: Thanks for being my Luca.

ABOUT THE AUTHOR

Meet debut author Grace Newman, a passionate romance author who loves nothing more than a spicy romance novel and a good espresso martini. With Grace Newman, readers can expect sassy heroines who shatter glass ceilings in their battles for gender equality and captivating love stories that blur the lines of love and rivalry.

When Grace isn't immersed in the world of romance, you'll often find her on the racquetball court, where her competitive spirit forgets about her lack of hand-eye coordination, or training what-ever newest foster dog has captured her heart. Grace's life is enriched by her two great loves: her devoted husband, who shares her passion for adventure and her love for all things fast (especially Formula 1), and her hilarious dog Daisy, her most loyal companion who listens intently to every plot twist and provides endless inspira-tion with her wagging tail. Whether they're exploring California's beautiful National Parks or sharing quiet moments at home, these two are Grace's biggest supporters.

instagram.com/authorgracenewman